The Unorthodox Corpse

- - - - -

Death on the Downbeat

- - - - -

The Blonde

- - - - -

Three Novels by
Carter Brown

Introduction by Priscilla Yates

Stark House Press • Eureka California

THE UNORTHODOX CORPSE /
DEATH ON THE DOWNBEAT / THE BLONDE

Published by Stark House Press
1315 H Street
Eureka, CA 95501, USA
griffinskye3@sbcglobal.net
www.starkhousepress.com

ISBN-13: 978-1-944520-91-5

Book design by Mark Shepard, shepgraphics.com
Cover art Robert McGinnis from the Dutch edition of *The Hang-Up Kid*
Proofreading by Bill Kelly

First Stark House Press Edition: March 2020

CONTENTS

Carter Brown and America
by Priscilla Yates

AS LEGEND has it, publicity shots of the mystery-crime writer, Carter Brown, taken in the fifties were considered quite scandalous. They showed him poised behind an electric typewriter, obviously preparing to dash off yet another thousand words to meet the daunting Carter Brown quota of two novelettes and one full length work per month.

The novels were set in America but CB's world of' Americana was the creation of a man who had never set foot in the States. This prompted fan letters with such criticisms as "but Hollywood Boulevard doesn't *go* to the beach." Carter Brown then created the fictional Pine City to pre-empt such criticisms.

The New American Library's decision in 1958 to publish one Carter Brown novel each· month ushered in the complete American-isation of the Carter Brown series.

After 1958, when Yates had been feted by the NAL in New York and been taken to real police line-ups and to school lavatories where young boys had been stabbed to death, the CB world became totally American.

The American influence even caused changes in CB's titles, replacing the elaborate Australian efforts (*Shamus, Your Slip is Showing*) with the slicker American versions like *The Body, The Stripper, The Desired, The Bombshell, The Dame*, and, of course, *The Blonde*, which remains the all-time best-selling Carter Brown title.

Wayne Harrison
Sydney Morning Herald, 23 August 1982

Dialogue With Dad

by daughter Priscilla Yates (PY)

All Carter Brown (CB) excerpts are from my father's autobiography
'READY WHEN YOU ARE C.B.!'

CB: We took the family with us on the second trip to America in 1961. We stayed for four wonderful days in Hawaii, then flew on to Los Angeles.

PY: Television started in Australia in 1956. By 1961 I was well prepared for Los Angeles thanks to shows like 'Disneyland' and '77 Sunset Strip'. I suppressed a regret that we were not going to travel 'Route 66'.

We visited Disneyland and my brother Jeremy and I had our first visit to a Nightclub.

CB: I bought a secondhand Buick station wagon; seven seats and everything electrically-operated. We drove the northern route across to New York. From San Francisco to Reno and on to the places with the wonderful names like Cheyenne and Ogalala. Through the Chicago loop and onto the turnpikes and then finally into New York.

PY: We drove through California, Nevada, Utah, Wyoming, Nebraska, Iowa, Illinois, Indiana, Ohio, and Pennsylvania to New York.

We looked forward to the next Howard Johnsons – where Jeremy and I had discovered the hot fudge sundae.

We also ticked off a series of roadside advertising signs –

HENRY THE EIGHTH/

SURE HAD/

TROUBLE/

SHORT TERM WIVES/

LONG TERM STUBBLE/

USE BURMASHAVE

CB: We found an apartment on a short summer rental at the corner of Central Park West and West 86th Street. It was the top floor of a fifteen-storey building and was airconditioned.

PY: Although Central Park West was quite upmarket, we were only blocks away from the setting of West Side Story, the film opened in October 1961.

Also opening in October 1961, another famous New York film 'Breakfast at Tiffany's'.

The Doorman of our building alerted me to the fact the mother of Carol Lynley ("Return to Peyton Place") lived in the building. After ingratiating myself with her mother I scored a signed photo of Carol.

CB: Central Park separates the East Side from the West Side of Manhattan. In those days only the East Side counted socially. But it wasn't enough just to move from West to East because people would remember where you came from originally. The best answer would be to make an extended overseas trip then come back and settle on the East Side. With the proper attitude the only time you ever admitted to seeing the West Side was when you were on your way to catch the 'Queen Mary' to Europe.

We did move straight across the park from our West Side apartment to an apartment on East 72nd Street but, as we were only foreigners, we didn't count.

PY: The Apartment on 72nd and Park still gave us easy access to Central Park. Later I took skating lessons as it seemed so glamourous, I was, however, never any good at it.

CB: About this time I acquired my first literary agent, John Tiffany Elliot. John had been born and bred in Oklahoma and at the age of eighteen had decided to seek fame and fortune in Hollywood. After three years as an extra, and once having actually delivered a single line in a movie, John decided that there was a strong chance he wasn't the next Clark Gable, and moved into the agency side of the business. When we first met him, John was a successful agent and a typical New Yorker. Manhattan, of course is an island. There is the Triborough Bridge which is Manhattan's main connection to the rest of America. One evening John said very seriously he often felt he would like to go back to Oklahoma and see how it was now.

'I've often felt like doing it' he confided, 'but then I think God knows what lies the other side of the Triborough Bridge'.

Priscilla and Jeremy went to the United Nations School which was within easy walking distance.

PY: It turned out U Thant, the Secretary-General of the UN, also livid in our building and I later met his son 'Tinny' Thant.

It was the first year of Kennedy's term and the UN was buzzing.

It was also the year of 'Bay of Pigs'. There were 10 minute civil defense air raid nuclear bomb alerts in New York where everybody had to take cover.

To add to the atmosphere, one of the set texts I read at the UN school was 'On the Beach'. (Nevil Shute's novel is about a mixed group of people in Melbourne as they await the arrival of deadly nuclear radiation spreading towards them from the Northern Hemisphere.)

New York felt like the edgy center of the world..

CB: There was a great television show called 'Pm East, Pm West'. It ran for an hour out of New York, five nights a week, and then a half hour out of Los Angeles. I appeared on one show devoted to mystery writers and compered by Mike Wallace. Rex Stout was one of the writers on the show. He must have been then close to eighty with a wonderful beard like a thin Chinese screen. A great gentleman and a great writer.

The producer of that particular show was Murray Burnett, who had written the play which provided the 'basis for the movie *Casablanca*". He and his wife, Adrienne, also became good friends of ours.

PY: When Time magazine put Freud on its cover in April 1956, the psychoanalytic moment in America had arrived, and for the next several decades psychoanalysts largely dominated the mental health field.

We were surprised with the number of people we knew visiting psychiatrists.

CB: Murray Burnett told a true story about how, when he had been a producer with NBC he had suffered sudden attacks of violent nausea for no apparent reason. A clutch of doctors could find nothing physically wrong with him and one recommended he see a psychiatrist. After a number of sessions, it so happened Murray suffered an attack just before his weekly visit to the couch, and told the psychiatrist what had happened.

'Did you have an argument with someone before the attack?', the psychiatrist asked.

'Yes, as it so happens', Murray admitted.

'And you wanted to kill him?'

'Right', Murray agreed.

'But because you are a very moral man with strict taboos about violence, you suppressed the feeling into your subconscious', the psychiatrist continued. 'And it had to find an outlet so it found a physical one.'

Murray said he realized the psychiatrist was right and asked why he hadn't said what the trouble was in the beginning?

'Because you wouldn't have believed me in the beginning.'

Murray said he had to agree with that, too.

There was a short silence around the dinner table then one of the guests asked if Murray had ever had any further attacks after the psychiatrist had told him the root cause.

'No', Murray said, 'now I get migraines'.

We went by train back to the West Coast, spending New Year's Eve on the 20th Century.

PY: Happily reflecting on our time in America.

The Unorthodox Corpse

- - - - -

by Carter Brown

CHAPTER ONE

Her ample curves were lovingly enfolded in a brown knit dress that was doing a big league job of enfolding, and I would have given anything to understudy them. With the deep tan she'd picked up over the summer, Annabelle Jackson looked as if she had been sculpted from milk chocolate, her blonde hair wrapping her head in gold foil. If you get the impression that she looked good enough to eat, you're pretty close.

"I have to hand it to Sheriff Lavers," I said with a sigh. "He certainly knows what's required in a secretary."

Her limpid blue eyes were cool as she looked up from the filing cabinet. "Sheriff Lavers is a gentleman and I enjoy working for him, Al Wheeler. Except when he finds it necessary to have you around the office, that is."

"You mean I distract you?"

"Distract me?" Annabelle took a deep breath, and the knit dress rose to the occasion magnificently.

I managed to get a word in before the southern tornado gathered full force. "That settles it. It's our duty to Pine City taxpayers to pursue our beautiful relationship strictly outside office hours. Are you doing anything tonight, honey-chile?"

"If I'm not, I'll think of something! Now I'll tell the Sheriff you're here—he wants to see you urgently. Will you walk this way please, Lieutenant." She headed toward Lavers's private office.

I watched the play of the rounded hips against the tight skirt, then sighed again and shook my head. "No can do, Miss Jackson. I just don't have the proper equipment."

She pushed open the door and stood there holding it for me. "Lieutenant Wheeler, Sheriff. Don't think it isn't nice to have you around here, Wheeler," she murmured as I walked past. "Because it isn't."

Even the Sheriff jumped when she slammed the door behind me. He shook his head. "It takes some people longer than others to get unpopular. But one thing I got to say for you: you break the track record every time out." He motioned to a chair. "Sit down."

"Yes, sir," I said and sat down.

"I've got a job for you."

"That's fine. Believe me, Sheriff, that's what I need. A nice, complicated murder is right up my alley at the moment." I looked at him expectantly. "Who's dead?"

"Nobody," he grunted.

"Oh." I thought about it for a moment, then shrugged my shoulders.

"Well, what is it? Armed hold-up? Narcotics? A nice juicy case of blackmail, maybe?"

He finished lighting his pipe, then picked up an envelope and tossed it across to me. "Read it."

I caught the envelope and saw it was addressed to Sheriff Lavers. It was a very expensive envelope made of heavy paper and it smelled vaguely of expensive perfume.

"If it's somebody blackmailing you, sir," I said, "or a threat against your life, don't worry, Wheeler can take care of it."

"Read it," he snarled. "And stop babbling at me."

I gave him my hurt look which normally is reserved exclusively for blondes who say no. It wasn't very effective because I get to use it so seldom. I opened the envelope and took out the folded stationery. The handsomely embossed letterhead read: "Bannister College for Young Ladies', and the elegantly handwritten note was addressed to "My dear Sheriff Lavers'. I read the message quickly:

We are all gratified that you have agreed to give a talk to our students and faculty on Monday evening, April 24th, on the subject of Modern Police Methods. Also on the evening's program will be a display of magic by The Great Mephisto. Altogether it should be an interesting time for all, and I am looking forward with pleasure to meeting you at the College at seven-thirty Monday evening.

The note was signed "Edwina Bannister".

I didn't get it. I looked at Lavers and said, "A cover, huh? It's this Mephisto character? He's a crook?"

"Possibly," Lavers said. "I wouldn't know."

"Then it must be Miss Bannister," I said. "Got it! She's a white slaver! Using this college racket as a cloak for her nefarious activities! How many girls have disappeared since they joined her school?"

"Not one as far as I know," he said. "Wheeler, do you mind if I say just two words to you?"

"Not at all, sir," I said. "You go right ahead."

He took a deep breath and the veins stood out in his forehead. "Shut up!"

"Yes, sir."

He puffed furiously at his pipe for about ten seconds. "You probably don't know it," he said, "but April twenty-fourth happens to be today's date. Bannister College is the most exclusive finishing school in the state. Its pupils are the daughters of some of the most exclusive parents in the state. Parents such as the mayor, a few senators, and such like. To refuse an invitation as guest speaker is to stick one's neck out. So I was hijacked into agreeing to give the pupils a talk. But this morning I realized I had a way out." There was something sinister about the grin he gave me as he said that.

"Way out?" I asked.

"You!" he said.

"Me?"

"No one else. Later today I'm coming down with an acute attack of laryngitis. It'll paralyze my vocal chords. I won't be able to even whisper. But luckily I have an able substitute to send in my place—you."

"Me?" I croaked again.

"It should be an easy chore for you, Wheeler," he said. "With all your experience with women."

"Women," I said. "But not schoolgirls!"

"You won't have to talk for more than half an hour at the most. And I'm sure you'll be thrilled by The Great Mephisto."

"Enchanted."

"Then that's settled," he said. "You will present yourself to Miss Bannister at seven-thirty tonight and make my apologies to her and tell her you will give the talk in my place." He leered at me. "What's the matter, Wheeler? You look pale."

"I can see them now," I said in a hollow voice. "Five hundred fiendish little faces. Five hundred little schoolgirls with their slingshots tucked in their tunics all ready."

Lavers shook his head slowly. "You've got the wrong picture, Wheeler. This Bannister joint is classy. And it's a finishing school—I thought I told you that before. There is a teaching staff of ten—six women and four men. And there are only about fifty students, all between the ages of eighteen and twenty-one."

"Oh," I said, and then, "Oh!"

"I see the light dawns. I would have thought I was placing you in your natural element. Any building that contains fifty young and probably highly attractive females—and only four men—is surely your idea of paradise."

"I agree," I said. "But I never figured on being cast in the role of lecturer on the duties of the guardian angels!"

"You can tell me how it went tomorrow morning," he grunted. "Now get out of here, I'm busy. Oh—and Wheeler, wear a dinner jacket," he added, and buried himself in his deskwork.

A dinner jacket, yet! I spent the next hour or so in the outer office trying to write a speech while I watched Annabelle Jackson at the typewriter. She really threw herself into her work, and it was fascinating—every inch in perpetual motion.

Finally she looked up, annoyed. "Well, what is it, now? You've been staring at me for the past ten minutes."

I shrugged. "I'm fascinated with your typing speed."

"Then your eyes must be out of focus. In case you haven't noticed, I type with my fingers. And that's not what you've been staring at."

"My mind's been occupied with this talk I have to give. At Bannister College, you know? Fifty students—all girls."

"In that case you'd better save your strength, you may need it." She went back to pounding the typewriter and ignored me. After a while I got the idea and sauntered out to find another source of inspiration.

Later, in my apartment, I put the finishing touches on the talk, checked it over, and added a few high spots of humor. Then I dug up a bottle of Scotch in the kitchen and got ready for a long hard evening. It was almost seven when I finally left the apartment and headed for the garage to pick up my Austin Healey.

Bannister College was in the suburbs. I took Route 7 out of town. It was a steep, tortuous climb that hugged the shoreline most of the way. Somewhere beyond the black abyss that yawned to the right there was a rumble of surf, the boiling and hissing sound of water retreating from the beach.

I kept a close look at the speedometer. When I had gone exactly three miles outside of Pine City, I swung off on a macadam road that meandered almost a mile. Suddenly, just ahead and set back from the road I could see the outlines of what was undoubtedly the college.

From the outside it gave no indication of its character; it looked like any other huge estate that had been kept up. Shrubs and lawns all looked to be in good condition and it was only by the bronze plaque my headlights picked up that I knew I had arrived.

I swung the car off the macadam road through two large stone pillars onto a crushed bluestone driveway which wound and curved its way through a row of trees to the building beyond.

It didn't have any ivy growing on the walls. In fact, it looked as much like a college as I look like an undergraduate. It was an immense, one-story building with a flat roof and great areas of glass which were all brilliantly lit from within.

I parked the Healey between a Cadillac and white Imperial. I walked the fifty yards to the front entrance and up the six concrete steps and then I saw the door corpse open and someone was waiting for me.

She was blonde with bright blue eyes and wearing no make-up whatsoever because she didn't need it. She wore a blue blazer with a large B woven in white on the pocket. Underneath the blazer was a white blouse. A neat gray skirt, nylons, and sensible shoes completed the outfit. She smiled warmly at me. "I'm Miss Tomlinson," she said with a British accent. "The Sports Mistress." She said that in capitals. "Welcome to Bannister, Mr. Lavers. I must say I expected a much older man."

"The youngest sheriff ever," I said.

"My heartiest congratulations," she said.

"That is, I would be if I *were* the sheriff. But I'm not. I'm Lieutenant Wheeler."

"Oh?" she said, not so warmly. "We were expecting Sheriff Lavers."

"I'm here in his place," I said. "The Sheriff extends his apologies but he's suffering from an acute attack of laryngitis so …"

"I'm so sorry," she said. "You must come and meet Miss Bannister. She's waiting in the library for you. She thought the Sheriff—that is, she thought you might care for a drink before your talk."

"Drink?" I brightened for a moment, then relaxed. Tea was probably Miss Bannister's idea of an excellent thirst quencher. "Fine," I said.

"I'll lead the way, shall I?" She set off at a pace which would have taken the prize money in Indianapolis.

I managed to catch up with her when she stopped and knocked on a door. She opened it and stepped inside the room. I went in behind her, still trying to get my breath back. The first thing I noticed was a table and a tray on the table and on the tray a couple of glasses, a bowl of ice, and a brand-new bottle of Scotch. I began to brighten up a little.

"Unfortunately, Sheriff Lavers couldn't come, Head," Miss Tomlinson announced. "So he's sent Lieutenant Wheeler in his place." She gestured toward me. "Here he is and I must say I think it's jolly sporting of him to fill in at such short notice. Shows them—" she smiled roguishly "—coppers have an *esprit de corps*, what?"

I lifted my eyes from the level of the Scotch bottle and looked at Miss Bannister. She was somewhere in her mid-thirties and she looked like Ava Gardner with her hair cropped short. She was wearing a short evening gown. It was flame colored, and it sported a neckline that was discreet without being modest. It was doing a half-hearted job of concealing equipment that deserved better than banishment to a school for girls. Her waist was thin; the full skirt hinted at long, shapely legs. I blinked.

"Welcome to Bannister College, Lieutenant." Her voice was throaty and it played a xylophone up and down my spine. With that voice and that figure she would have been a cinch on television. "I'm sorry the Sheriff is indisposed."

"So was I," I said. "But now I'm beginning to change my mind."

"That will be all, thank you, Miss Tomlinson," she said to the sports mistress.

"Oh!" Miss Tomlinson sounded disappointed. "Oh well … if you say so, Head. Of course, I had hoped—" the roguish smile curved her lips again "—to get the low-down on the heist mobs and the torpedoes!" She giggled self-consciously. "That's the lingo the jolly old crooks use, isn't it, Lieutenant?"

I winced. I couldn't help it. "I'm not sure. I've been out of touch since Al Capone died."

"Oh, well—" she sounded disappointed "—I'm sure I'm right. I read all about it in a magazine. Anyway, I must buzz off now. See you later. Bung-ho, Lieutenant!" She strode briskly out of the room, closing the door behind her.

Miss Bannister looked at me and smiled. "If you're wondering if she's real, Lieutenant, I can only say I often wonder, too. But she is a most efficient sports mistress."

"I can see her wielding a hockey stick right now," I said.

"Would you like a drink, Lieutenant?" she said, moving closer to the tray.

"Thank you," I said, "on the rocks."

She leaned over and picked up the bottle. As she did, the sudden droop in the neckline made me catch my breath. She looked up and her full lips parted, revealing the even whiteness of her teeth. "On the rocks?"

I sighed. "Any place." I caught myself, bobbed my head. "On the rocks would be just great."

She peered up at me from under expertly tinted eyelids. "I'm very sorry the Sheriff couldn't come." She straightened, held a glass out to me. "The girls were impressed by his title. Maybe they had some idea he would turn up in spurs and a ten-gallon hat—do you think?" Smiling, she reached down and picked up her glass with an encore of the devastating effect on the neckline. "But I've got an idea you could be interesting, Lieutenant. Really interesting." She held her glass up, then lifted it to her lips. I got the full effect of the slanted eyes across the rim.

"Thanks." I took a deep, hasty gulp of the Scotch. I wasn't sure whether it was because I needed the drink or I wanted her to pour again. "I figured on talking for about a half-hour—is that right?"

"Perfect," she said. "Perhaps I'd better explain, Lieutenant. You probably know this is a finishing school. When a girl comes to us, she has already finished with formal education. We concentrate on teaching her the things she will need to know to be a lady, as well as a woman. Languages, of course. Then such things as fashion sense, deportment, elocution, cosmetic sense, conversation, an appreciation of the arts, sports, and so on. But the school isn't run on formal lines at all."

I finished the Scotch and studied my empty glass hopefully.

"If you would care for another drink, Lieutenant," she said, "you might help yourself. I'm never very good at judging the right amount."

"Thanks," I said, and did. "I was wondering, did anyone ever tell you that you look just like—"

"A headmistress?" she said with a faintly mocking glint in her eyes.

"No, Lieutenant, they didn't, I'm happy to say."

"I just wondered."

"I feel I should explain to you about this evening," she went on calmly. "I have these evenings once a month. I feel it does the girls good. I generally manage to have someone lecture on some aspect of civics—such as yourself tonight, for example. And to coat the pill, the rest of the evening is devoted to some sort of entertainment. Tonight we have a magician."

"That sounds jolly."

Her lips twitched momentarily. "I'm so glad you think so, Lieutenant. The program is that I introduce you to the girls and then you give them your talk. When you've finished I will allow ten minutes for questions and then we will join the audience while The Great Mephisto takes over. Afterward, I hope you will stay for refreshments."

"Thanks," I said, looking hard at the Scotch bottle. "I guess I'll be real thirsty by then."

"Miss Tomlinson supervises the making of some absolutely spiffing cocoa," she said, her face deadpan. "I know you'll enjoy it."

"I can hardly wait," I said.

"There was just one other thing I'd like to warn you about, Lieutenant."

"Warn me?"

"About the questions. All the girls here at the College are quite intelligent and, one might say, well, sophisticated. Please don't be surprised at any of the questions. Just remember they are genuinely seeking knowledge."

"What sort of questions do you think I'm likely to get?"

"I haven't the faintest idea," she said. "Only I suggest, Lieutenant, if you know of some way to kill someone without being detected, it would be just as well not to mention it."

"Maybe I should have worn my bullet-proof vest," I said and hastily poured my third Scotch in hope that it would clear my head.

CHAPTER TWO

"… So you see, police work is most often painstaking and dull work," I concluded, "rarely brilliant deduction." I sank back into my chair and there was a burst of applause from the audience.

Miss Bannister got up from her chair beside me. "I'm sure we all thank Lieutenant Wheeler for his most interesting talk on police methods. And I'm sure he will be pleased to answer any questions you may have."

She sat down again and I stared numbly at the audience. In the front row sat the staff—six females and four males—and behind them sat the students. The only female who appeared to be wearing the school uniform was Miss Tomlinson. All the students wore different clothes. I noted one redhead who wore a formal evening gown that seemed to be made entirely of transparent chiffon, or maybe it was the lighting. I couldn't be sure, but she'd thrown me off my lecture four times.

A languid blonde got to her feet. She was wearing a rhinestone-studded charcoal sweater, green frontier pants, and long pendant earrings. I had the feeling that the diamond pendants were real and worth about five years of my salary.

"Lieutenant," she said, smiling slowly at me, "isn't it true that you yourself use very unorthodox police methods? I've read about you in the papers ... you're always solving murder cases, aren't you? That is, when you're not out with a blonde? That is, blonde, brunette, or redhead ..." She sank slowly into her seat again.

I gulped. "Well, er ... yes," I said. "I mean—no! That is—"

"I thought so." The blonde smiled lazily at me. "Stick around long enough, Lieutenant, and I may arrange a murder for you!"

I looked helplessly at Miss Bannister, who smiled at me. "We believe in freedom of expression here at Bannister," she said. "And quite a number of the girls are high-spirited."

"Full of practical jokes, I'll bet," I said. "Like putting arsenic in the cocoa?"

"Lieutenant?" A brunette whose hair clustered in tight curls around her head was on her feet. "Lieutenant, what's the most effective way to kill a man at close range without leaving any signs of violence?"

I suppose this was the question Miss Bannister had anticipated. I looked at her coldly and said, "Perfume."

Another blonde stood up. I thought if she wasn't cold, she should be. She was wearing a playsuit here and there, and a deep tan. "Lieutenant," she drawled, "do you figure she was just bored or her old man caught her on the porch with the iceman?"

"Who?" I muttered.

"Who? Lizzie Borden," she said. "Who else?"

"I figure she was a female," I said tautly, "and you don't need any more reason than that!"

She took a deep breath; I expected she and the playsuit would part company but they didn't. It was nice contemplating it, though. "I've never met such an understanding man before!"

The redhead who'd put me off my lecture got to her feet and I saw it wasn't the lighting after all.

"Lieutenant," she said and fluttered her long eyelashes for a couple of seconds. "I'd like your advice. I'm just furnishing a new apartment and I wondered—for a girl living on her own—do you consider etchings are the right thing?"

"It's a switch, anyway," I said hoarsely.

"Of course—" she fluttered the eyelashes again "—if you could only take a look at the apartment, Lieutenant, I'd appreciate it a lot. It's on Wilton Avenue, number five-oh—"

"Well, I think that's all the time we have for questions," Miss Bannister said briskly. "So Lieutenant Wheeler and I will step down from the platform and make way for The Great Mephisto. This way, Lieutenant."

I followed her gratefully off the stage and down the side steps out into the body of the auditorium. Two chairs in the front row had been left vacant for us. I settled down beside Miss Bannister. Miss Tomlinson was seated on the other side of me.

"Top-hole!" she said enthusiastically into my ear. "Really fabulous, Lieutenant!"

"Thanks," I said and wondered if I could light a cigarette.

The curtains were closed across the front of the stage and a recording of Sinatra's "Just One of Those Things" was playing.

"If you'd care to smoke, Lieutenant," Miss Bannister said, reading my thoughts, "go right ahead."

"Thanks," I said and offered her a cigarette, which she accepted. I offered one to Miss Tomlinson, who shook her head.

"No thanks, Lieutenant," she said. "Never touch 'em. Bad for the wind. A girl needs to be a good runner, I always say."

"Not too good," I pointed out, "otherwise she might never be caught."

She thought about that for ten seconds, then bit her lower lip between firm, white teeth. "I've never thought of that before," she said in a worried voice. "You're absolutely, jolly well right!"

The Sinatra recording finished. There was about half a minute's silence and then the house lights went out suddenly and the footlights came to life. The curtains parted slowly and there was The Great Mephisto. He wasn't very tall, but he had a stage presence that made him seem like a giant among the pygmies—you could feel it right away, and you would have picked him out even in a DeMille mob. He wore evening dress—white tie and tails. An opera cloak was slung over his shoulders. It had a crimson satin lining, and I wondered if he'd lend it to me sometime to impress Annabelle Jackson. He smiled and bowed to the audience and a collective sigh went up from the students.

"Man!" I heard a voice back of me sigh. "He's with plenty of woodle."

"That's no fable, Mabel!" another voice murmured.

"You can strip my gears and call me shiftless but he's groovy!"

"He curdles me!" a third voice said. "An icky square with a beaver! I'll take the cop—he's real George!"

I figured next time I came to Bannister College I'd bring an interpreter with me. The only magic I go for is the rustle of a skirt in the spring-time—and summer, autumn, and winter, of course. But I had to admit that Mephisto was good, polished. After about fifteen minutes of small stuff he made a switch by pulling a hat out of a white rabbit and I brightened up a little. He came forward to the edge of the stage and signaled with his hand so that the house lights came up a moment later.

"Ladies and gentlemen," he said in a deep and resonant voice, "for my next illusion, I shall need the help of an assistant. Perhaps one of the charming young ladies in the audience would care to assist me?"

There was a shrill moan from the students and the next second the stampede started. The Great Mephisto regarded the first half-dozen up on stage with a benevolent smile, then nodded to the languid blonde in the glitter-sweater and frontier pants. "You will do nicely," he said. "May I ask your name?"

"Caroline," she said breathlessly. "Caroline Partington."

"Then I regret, ladies," Mephisto said, bowing to the others, "that I have an assistant."

The rest moaned their disappointment and went back to their seats in a sad shuffle. Mephisto clapped his hands together and a male assistant clad in black, looking like something out of *The Last Days of Hitler*, appeared, trundling a long wooden box on wheels in front of him.

The box had a macabre resemblance to a coffin. What made it even more macabre were two wooden uprights secured by a crossbeam. A triangular knife fitted into the grooved sides of the uprights and was held against the crossbeam by a rope which was wound around a peg lower down on the outside of one upright. I'll try and make it simple—it was a miniature guillotine.

Mephisto lifted the lid from the box. "Now, Miss Partington," he said in his deep, funereal voice, "would you please lie down in the box?"

"Why, Mr. Mephisto!" The blonde fluttered her eyelids at him and drew a roar from the audience.

For a moment, the bearded man was flustered. "Face down, of course."

The blonde fluttered her eyelids again. "That is a switch," she told him. She stepped into the box and lay down as instructed. Her head protruded from the end under the blade, resting on a blood-red pillow.

Mephisto nodded curtly to his assistant, who replaced the cover on the box so that the only portion of Caroline Partington visible to the audience was her head.

Mephisto signaled again and the house lights went out suddenly. Slowly the footlights changed color until the whole stage was bathed in crimson light. You could hear the silence as Mephisto walked slowly toward the footlights.

"Ladies and gentlemen," he said, his voice somber, "I must ask you to be silent for my next illusion. It requires an immense effort of concentration—I cannot afford to make a mistake. One slip—one error, however slight—could have disastrous results for my assistant. I beg your co-operation."

There was still no sound in the audience.

"As you see," he continued, "Caroline lies in the box, her head directly below the knife of Madame Guillotine. I should explain that the knife is razor-sharp, honed to the finest edge possible. I am going to show you something unique, something that the medical profession has long known but has feared to demonstrate because of the mortal dangers of error."

He gazed sternly down at the audience.

"With such a guillotine," he said softly, "the head is severed from the body in a split second. If it is removed at once and then replaced not more than five seconds later, the subject will live, will not in fact be harmed in any way! And if you think my claim is fantastic … then watch!"

He bowed low, then slowly retraced his steps to the guillotine. Someone in the back of the house giggled hysterically and his head came up like a lion that's just discovered his lioness has left town with another lion. "Please!" he said. "I beg of you! No noise—no sound! If my concentration is distracted I cannot answer for the wellbeing of my assistant!"

The giggling stopped abruptly.

Slowly Mephisto unwound the rope from the peg, pulling down on the rope so that the knife stayed up against the crossbeam.

A slow beat on a drum sounded from the side of the stage and I guessed his male assistant was earning his living. The beat quickened and then rose to a frenzied climax and stopped suddenly.

"Now!" Mephisto shouted and let go of the rope. The knife squeaked faintly in the grooves and thudded home.

"Behold!" Mephisto cried and grabbed Caroline's hair in his grasp. A moment later he held her head high in the air above his head and a split second after that, the lights went out.

Then all hell broke loose. There were fifty students and most of the female teaching staff screaming their heads off in the pitch darkness. In the middle of it, the stage lights suddenly came on again and Mephisto was standing there, smiling at the audience.

"Please be calm," he said. "I told you no harm could be done if my concentration was absolute—and it was."

He walked back and hoisted the knife blade to its original position against the crossbeam. I had to admit I felt happier when I saw the blade was clean. Then he removed the lid of the box.

"Caroline," he said, "I would be glad if you'd get out of the box and prove to your friends in the audience that you have suffered no harm."

There was no movement from the box.

"Caroline," he said in a louder voice, "please! This is no time for jokes—your friends are worried about you."

There was still no movement from the box.

"Caroline!" he shouted. "Enough of this tomfoolery! Sit up!"

I felt a sudden pressure on my arm and turned toward Miss Bannister. "I fear something may be wrong, terribly wrong," she said in a low-pitched voice. "Would you please go up there, Lieutenant, and find out?"

"Sure," I said and got out of my seat and walked quickly to the side of the stage and the steps that led into the wings.

As I hurried onto the stage a new blast of noise behind me hit my ears. It sounded as if the whole student body was screaming at the same time.

Mephisto turned toward me, his face lit only by the crimson footlights. "I don't understand," he said. "Nothing could have happened to her—it's purely an illusion! I told her so before I started. It must be her nerves or ..."

I brushed past him and looked down into the box. The blonde was stretched out limp without moving. I took a closer look—she was still breathing anyway. I started to wonder.

The Great Mephisto had a diamond pin in his starched shirtfront. "Excuse me," I said and yanked it out went back to the box and jabbed a sixteenth of an inch of the sharp end of the pin into the tightest stretch of antler pants.

There was a violent shriek and Caroline Partington hurtled out of the box onto the stage. She got to her feet and looked at me indignantly. "Why, you—you!"

"You were in a state of traumatic shock," I said. "You needed another shock to bring you out of it. But please,"—I held up a protesting hand—"don't thank me."

"Thank you!" she gurgled. "You deliberately stuck that pin in me, you brute!"

"Little girls shouldn't play games and ruin The Great Mephisto's act," I said.

She sighed and started to fall forward. I caught her in my arms and then her arms wound tight around my neck.

"Can you blame a girl, Lieutenant?" she murmured into my ear. "I knew if I pretended to be dead, you'd investigate. Is that a crime—wanting to get to know you better?"

I jerked my head free of her arms and stepped back smartly so that she fell on her face.

"A girlish prank—as Miss Tomlinson would say," I said to The Great

Mephisto. "Why don't you really guillotine her? I'll bear witness it was justifiable homicide."

"She frightened the life out of me," he muttered, dabbing his forehead with a silk handkerchief and not even noticing the two white mice that fell from it to the floor.

The blonde noticed them when they scampered over her ankles. She gave a horrified yell. Then in a blur of speed she got to her feet, jumped the footlights, and dove into the audience while they all applauded.

Then all the lights went out again. And once again the deafening squeals went up from the audience.

"What fool did that?" I yelled to Mephisto over the noise, and got no answer.

I waited impatiently for the lights to go on again and the din inside the auditorium got worse. The darkness seemed to last forever.

Then, when I'd about decided to lie down in the box—if I was going to spend the night at the Bannister College, I thought I might as well be comfortable—the lights went up again—the house lights, the footlights, and the overhead floods on stage. There was a wild burst of applause from the audience and Mephisto started to bow automatically. And then some idiot screamed again.

I glared down at them and saw that no one had kept their seats. They were all bunched together in the aisles—including the teaching staff. The scream again, and I saw it came from Caroline Partington and I thought if ever a girl needed to be bent over her father's knee while he wielded a hairbrush …

Then I saw she was pointing at something as she screamed and everybody else saw it at about the same time—and then they all started screaming again.

When I saw what she was pointing at, I couldn't blame them. I felt like screaming myself. I had been wrong about all of them rushing into the aisles when the lights failed. One of them had kept her seat—the blonde who'd had a feeling of kinship for Lizzie Borden. She was slumped forward, her arms dangling limply over the chair immediately in front of her. There was the hilt of a knife protruding from her shoulder blades. From where I was, she looked to be quite dead.

"A fine thing when a man's off duty!" I said bitterly to Mephisto. I got no answer and I wondered if he had fainted.

A couple of girls close to the blonde had fainted already and it looked as if they were going to be followed any second by the rest of the student body.

I looked around to check on Mephisto and saw the stage was empty. Mephisto had disappeared completely—vanished apparently into thin air.

CHAPTER THREE

The student body stood in a circle around the body, at a respectful distance. That is, what was left of the student body. The faculty was busily engaged in carting off the ones who couldn't stand the sight of blood. I pushed my way through the closely packed femininity. At any other time it would have been a delightful experience that I would have stretched out as long as possible. Right now, was in a hurry to get to the body before anything was touched.

The girl had evidently been leaning forward or getting up when she was stabbed. She had slumped forward and now hung over the seat in front like a rag doll. A spreading dark stain darkened the narrow back of the playsuit's halter, and a dark red stream snaked down her bare back, contrasting with the deep tan. I walked around in front of her and jabbed my finger against the carotid. I knew when I did it I was wasting my time. The open eyes, the teeth pulled back in a grimace of pain, the trickle down the side of her mouth that matched the stain in the back told me the whole story.

But they'd be expecting me to make like a detective, and to tell the truth, I couldn't think of what else to do at the moment. I looked up and spotted Miss Bannister chewing on the knuckle of her index finger. The color had drained from her face, leaving her lipstick and eye shadow as garish stains on the pallor.

"Miss Bannister, please."

She nodded and walked reluctantly toward me. She licked at her lips. "A student. Her name is—was Jean Craig."

I nodded as though that was an important bit of information. "I'll need your help."

She bobbed her head wordlessly, while she lost a battle to keep her eyes off the dead girl.

"I want this area cleared. I don't want a thing touched," I said. She nodded her understanding. "I want the girls and the faculty available for questioning."

I waited while Miss Bannister rounded up what was left of the faculty and passed along the orders. In remarkably little time, the auditorium was cleared. Miss Bannister came back to me. "Anything else?"

I nodded. "Can this place be locked up?"

She stared, nodded. "Of course, but—" Her eyes went to the girl. "What about her?"

I considered, and shrugged. "She won't be going anyplace. And she's not likely to get lonesome."

"I can lock the auditorium if you're sure it's all right."

"Unless you'd prefer to stay with her while I make some calls—"

"No, thank you. We'll lock it."

Back in Miss Bannister's office, I put through a call to headquarters and conveyed the cheery news to Doc Murphy, the medical examiner, that he'd have to forego his regular dose of TV stomach acid tonight while he earned some of the loot the county paid him. He was duly grateful for the interruption.

As soon as the doc hung up, I called Lavers's home. There was no reason why he should be sitting home all nice and comfortable while the rest of us were working. And with no overtime, yet!

The phone jangled three times before he got around to lifting the receiver off the hook. "Yeah?"

"This is Wheeler, Sheriff. Just reporting mission accomplished. I took up the required half-hour and the girls were duly impressed."

I could hear him growl across the wire. "I don't know why you feel you have to disturb me at home. You can make your report in the office in the morning—"

"Oh, I am sorry. I just thought you'd like to know, so when the reporters—" I broke off. "But you're right. I shouldn't bother you at home."

There was a wary note in his voice. "Reporters? What's this about reporters?"

"Well, if you insist ..."

"Damn it all!" I could picture the red flush climbing his neck. "When I ask for a report, I want a full report. What about the reporters?"

"Well, for one thing the lights kept failing during the magician's act."

"Let him take it up with his union. Why should the press be interested in—" He paused. "What happened while the lights were out, Wheeler? If you made a pass at one of those girls—"

I sighed at the unfairness of it. "Nobody made a pass at any of the girls, Sheriff." I could hear him letting out his breath in relief. "Somebody did stab one, though," I added.

"What!"

"In the back," I said. "It was fatal."

There was silence for about five seconds.

"You're drunk!" he said.

"Sober as a sheriff," I said.

"If this is your idea of a joke, then let—"

"No joke!"

"You're serious?"

"Entirely."

"Who did it?"

"The lights were out," I said wearily. "She was sitting in the auditorium along with the rest of the students and all the teaching staff. None of them kept their seats—when the lights came on again they were all standing in the aisles. That gives us roughly sixty suspects who were in the auditorium, not including anyone who could have sneaked in while the lights were out."

"Have you notified Dr. Murphy?" he roared.

"You know me, Sheriff. Everything by the book. The doc didn't like it—"

"Neither did the girl! Get in touch with headquarters and have a couple of boys from Homicide ride out with the doc and his boys. But you'd better handle it—" He broke off for a moment.

"What's the matter, Sheriff? Thinking?"

"No. Praying. I could be putting my whole future on the line by putting you in charge. But I've got no choice. You're already on the scene. So take charge." A wistful note crept into his voice. "And every time you get out of line, try to remember it's going to reflect on me."

"I'll make you proud, Sheriff."

"Don't. Just find out who did it and find out the fastest way possible. Without fireworks. Understand?"

"I understand, sir," I said. "But I don't like it."

He said something that was very rude for a sheriff to say, then hung up. I put the phone back on the cradle and lit myself a cigarette.

Miss Bannister came in. Her face was white and her hands were trembling slightly, but when she spoke, her voice was quite calm.

"I've sent all the girls to their rooms, Lieutenant," she said. "I've told Mr. Pierce and Mr. Dufay to stay near the auditorium door and see that no one comes near until the police arrive. I hope that was the right thing to do."

"That's fine," I said. "Who are Pierce and Dufay?"

"Mr. Pierce is the art master," she said. "Mr. Dufay teaches languages—French and Spanish."

"Okay," I said. "Have you seen anything of The Great Mephisto?"

"No," she said blankly. "You don't think …"

"Not as a general rule," I agreed. "He disappeared when the lights went out."

"He seemed upset when Caroline pulled that terribly unfunny trick on him. Seeing the body must have unnerved him completely." She rubbed the flat of her hands up and down the backs of her arms. "I can't believe it actually happened. It's like a nightmare. I keep thinking I'm going to wake up and that Jean will be mincing down the halls, full of mischief."

I lit a cigarette and took a deep drag. "It happened all right. She's dead. Or else they're going to play her an awful dirty trick when they do the post-mortem." I blew a stream of dirty white smoke at the ceiling. "Do you know of anybody who had a reason to want her dead?”

“Of course not,” she said, then bit her lip. “I’m sorry, Lieutenant. No, I can’t think why anyone should want to kill her.”

“What do you know of her background?”

“She comes from Nevada. Her father is a very wealthy rancher. She’s only been here for about six months.”

“Nothing else?”

“Nothing that I know,” she said. “I realize that’s not very helpful. I’m sorry, Lieutenant.”

“I might find out more about her from someone else here,” I said.

“You mean you’re going to question everyone?”

“She was murdered, Miss Bannister,” I said patiently. “The usual procedure under these circumstances is to make an attempt to find the murderer. That’s known as an investigation. Most people making an investigation ask questions.”

“It was just that I was thinking what this will do to the college!” She shuddered. “I hate even to think about it.”

The door opened violently and Miss Tomlinson bounced into the room.

“What is it?” Miss Bannister asked in a disapproving voice.

“The cops have arrived with the meat wagon!” Miss Tomlinson announced.

Miss Bannister closed her eyes. “Miss Tomlinson, will you please—”

“I’d better go and see them,” I said and walked toward the door.

“It’s terrible about poor Jean,” Miss Tomlinson said, her eyes shining. “But I just can’t help being excited, you know? A real murder happening under our very noses. Well, it beats badminton hands down, doesn’t it?”

Out in the corridor I was greeted by the sound of lumbering feet.

“Hell, Lieutenant!” the human elephant panted, “I was just telling my old lady how you’d slay all these young dames with this talk of yours, but I didn’t …”

“Sergeant Polnik,” I interrupted, “flattery will get you nowhere.”

He looked puzzled. “I’ve got Detective Slade and Burns, the photographer, in the car outside. Doc Murphy’s gone on with the ambulance guys—maybe one of them is this Flattery you’re talking about?”

“Skip it,” I said. “Tell Slade to take the photographer in—the body’s in the auditorium at the end of this one. There was a magician on the stage when it happened. Calls himself The Great Mephisto. Small guy with a beard and a big personality—he’d stand out anywhere, even in an espresso joint bristling with beards. He vanished when the lights came on and the corpse was found. Look around and see if you can find him. If you do, bring him into the auditorium.”

"Sure, Lieutenant," he said.

I walked to the main hall. Doc Murphy was trying the door to the auditorium, swearing softly when he found it locked.

"Just a minute, doc, I'll open it for you," I offered. He stepped aside, grunting while I inserted the key and opened the door.

"I heard a rumor that Lavers had gone soft in the head and let you loose in a girls" school, Wheeler. What could he expect but trouble?"

"I like you, too, doc. Killed any good patients lately?"

He followed me down the aisle to where Jean Craig's body was still draped over the seat in front of her. The handle of the knife and a few gleaming inches of steel protruded grotesquely from the middle of her back.

"I don't have to kill any patients. Somebody keeps doing it for me." He leaned over and studied the wound with a squint. "I suppose you'll want the cause of death."

"It's a real tough one to figure out," I said.

He straightened up. "I'll let you know as soon as we do the PM." He turned and signaled to two men in white, who wheeled in a stretcher. "Shouldn't be much before tomorrow."

"You're kidding. That knife blade between her shoulders isn't part of her outfit. I know the cause of death and I know the time. I was there, remember?"

The photographer from Homicide walked up, then started snapping pictures from all angles. When he was finished, the two ambulance men rolled up the stretcher.

"Want to have a look at the weapon, doc?" one called over.

Doc Murphy nodded. His assistant removed the knife carefully so as not to smear any possible prints, placed it in a plastic bag, and brought it over.

"Pretty fancy," the doc grunted.

He held it up for me to see. It was a fine piece of steel, triangularly shaped. The handle was carefully chased with strands of gold. Whoever had murdered Jean Craig hadn't just picked up the weapon on the spur of the moment.

Behind us, the two men in white were transferring the body of the girl from the chair onto the stretcher.

"If you want an educated guess as to the cause of death, I'd say a knife like this probably penetrated right to the heart," Murphy said.

"So we've either got a lucky murderer or one who sees in the dark." I glowered at the weapon. "Could a girl do it?"

"Wouldn't need much strength with a knife this sharp. A schoolgirl could have done it." He smirked. "So that gives you about fifty possible suspects for a start, eh, Wheeler?"

"Stick to your medicine," I said. "As a cop all you'd be able to do is run yourself in for obstructing justice."

The men had finished moving the girl's body, had covered it with a heavy piece of canvas, and were now strapping it into place. One of them walked over and handed me a receipt.

"What a waste, eh, Loot? She was quite a dish."

"I prefer mine warm," I told him. I initialed the receipt and handed it back. He winked at me, rejoined his buddy, and they wheeled the stretcher toward the door.

"I'll be in touch," the doc said. He followed his men out. I stood long enough to take one last look around and to express my opinion of the kind of luck that would bring me back onto the job just in time to inherit this headache. Then I exited too.

The photographer and Slade, a short guy with rimless glasses and little or no chin, were waiting for me.

"Got anything else for me, Lieutenant?" the photographer wanted to know. He glanced around and grinned. "Must be some real art studies in a place like this. Not that the blonde wasn't a dish. But me, I don't go for still life."

"If anything occurs to us, we'll send for you," I told him. We waited while he headed down the hall and let himself out the far door leading to the parking lot.

That left just Slade and me—the closest thing to being alone. I tugged a pack of cigarettes out of my pocket and offered him a smoke.

"No, thanks, Lieutenant," he said. "I never smoke."

"Sorry I can't offer you a drink," I said with a grin.

"That's okay," he said. "I never drink." He looked around wonderingly. "What did he mean—art studies? What sort of place is this?"

"It's a finishing school for young ladies," I told him. "But it wouldn't interest you, of course."

I heard footsteps and a moment later a man appeared down the hallway heading toward us. He was young with hair that was three months overdue for a cut and his straggling mustache was the same way. He wore a silk coat and corduroy pants and underneath the coat a bright red silk shirt with a floppy black velvet bow tie.

"Holy Toledo!" Slade said in an awed voice. "Is this one of those young ladies you were telling me about?"

"Don't shake my faith in the female of the species," I said. "I'll take a bet with you right now he's the character that teaches art."

"Art who?" Slade asked.

"Let's just get a couple of things straight," I said. "I'm the Lieutenant and if anybody is going to be witty it'll be me!"

"I don't get it," Slade said blankly. "I only asked who this Art—"

"Why don't you have a cigarette?" I asked him. "It might do something for you—any change would be an improvement."

The overlong hair and mustache stopped in front of us. "Would one of you gentlemen be Lieutenant Wheeler?" he asked in a high-pitched voice.

"Sure," I said.

"Which one?"

"Him," Slade said.

"I don't need to ask who you are," I said with a grin toward Slade. "You're Mr. Pierce, the art master."

"Why, no," he said blankly. "I'm Dufay, the language master. Augustus Dufay. Whatever gave you the idea I taught art?"

Slade sniggered, then remembered just in time that I was a lieutenant and stopped abruptly.

"It must have been the gray flannel suit," I said. "Was there something you wanted?"

"Miss Bannister asked Edward and me—that's Edward Pierce of course—to stay here until the police arrived," he said. "A most unpleasant task, Lieutenant. The proximity of a corpse unnerves me, I'm afraid, and when the doctor arrived, we left. It occurred to me we should have obtained permission, so I came to apologize for leaving." He blinked at me hopefully. "I do hope you don't mind?"

"That's all right," I said. "Where's Pierce now?"

"In his room, I think," he said distastefully. "I imagine he's smoking those foul cigarettes of his and probably drinking whisky!"

"You don't smoke or drink?" I asked him.

"Disgusting habits!" he said.

"You and Detective Slade here should really hit it off," I said. "You've both got clear lungs and healthy livers. Really a helluva lot in common."

They gave each other an alarmed look and confirmed their mutual repugnance. Then Dufay did a neat job of dismissing Slade with a twist of his shoulders and turned his attention on me. He put both hands together, pressing his fingertips together like a man making his first dive into the ocean, and murmured politely, "May I go now?"

"I'd like to ask you some questions while you're here," I said. "You knew the girl?"

"The Craig girl?" he said. "As a student, of course."

"Do you know any reason why anyone should want to kill her?"

"Some of them may have been jealous of her," he said doubtfully. "She was quite a good-looking girl, you know, and she came from a particularly wealthy family. Always had far too much money to spend."

"Any other reasons?"

"Well—" He glanced over his shoulder nervously for a moment before he spoke. "This is in the strictest confidence, you understand, Lieutenant? I know she was friendly—very friendly with Pierce. I'm afraid Edward is always transgressing the boundary between tutorial and personal relationships."

"Would that give him a reason to kill her?"

"Really, Lieutenant!" he said in a shocked voice. "I have no idea. I always keep my own master-to-student relationships within the proper bounds. And besides," he said with a smirk, "I am already engaged."

"What does she look like?" Slade asked in an awed voice.

"You've probably met Agatha already," he said proudly. "She stands out in a crowd. Definitely the outdoors type, you know. She really shines with health."

I closed my eyes for a moment, seeing the vision, then opened them again. "You wouldn't be talking about Miss Tomlinson by any chance?"

"So you've noticed her!" he said in a pleased voice. "Isn't she wonderful?"

"Top-hole!" I said. "I think the idea is jolly good. My congratulations and all that sort of rot."

"You feeling all right, Lieutenant?" Slade asked anxiously.

"Spiffing, thanks," I said.

Heavy feet came pounding down the hallway and the next moment Polnik appeared. He slowed down to a trot and stopped in front of us, panting for breath.

"You found Mephisto?" I asked him.

He nodded, still getting his breath back. "I found him all right!"

"Fine," I said. "Why didn't you bring him along with you?"

"Only one thing stopped me, Lieutenant," he said soberly. "When I was doing my rookie training they told me never to move a corpse from the scene of the crime."

CHAPTER FOUR

I stared at Polnik, trying to persuade myself I had heard differently. "Mephisto's *dead*?"

"Unless he always wears a knife handle between his shoulders. And it sure plays hell with the way his coat hangs!" He swabbed at his gleaming jowls with the back of his hand. "Come to think of it, I don't know why anyone would have a coat on in the first place when he's doing acrobatics in a gym," he muttered. "He's lying on one of those horse things, Lieutenant, right between the handles. A vaulting horse!—right? You want to come to the gym now and see for yourself?"

"I've already seen a corpse," I told him. "And they don't do a thing for me. Not even the athletic kind. Take Slade back there with you and make sure nobody disturbs the body. I've got to make a phone call."

Polnik swallowed heavily. "The Sheriff?"

I nodded. "The Sheriff. Or maybe you'd rather make the call."

He paled at the thought. "No, sir, Lieutenant. Not me." He suddenly seemed itchy to be doing something. "After I show Slade where the body is, why don't I have a talk with somebody? Anybody. Anybody but the Sheriff."

"All right. There's an art teacher named Pierce. Edward Pierce. Seems his appreciation of the form divine may not be restricted to the kind that's on canvas. Why don't you have a talk with him? Find out how well he knew Jean Craig."

"Yes, sir, Lieutenant," he said, perking up. "I'll get right at it." He turned and headed back down the hall to the short staircase that led down to the gymnasium in the back. Slade had to run to catch up with him.

I waited until they had disappeared, then I walked over to the door to Miss Bannister's office, turned the knob, and pushed it open.

She looked up with a frown as I walked in without knocking. When she recognized me, the frown drained away. "Oh, it's you, Lieutenant."

"Who were you expecting?"

"I'm not sure. It's been such a terrible evening—"

"Oh, I don't know. I thought my talk got across very well."

She smiled wanly. "Of course it did. I was referring to the murder—"

"Oh, them."

She stared at me, her eyes widening. "*Them?* You mean there's more than one?"

I nodded. "Our friend Mephisto had another trick in his act. Sword swallowing. He did it the hard way—between the shoulder blades."

She swayed a little and grabbed at the desk for support. "How awful." Her eyes hopscotched around the room, came to rest on the bottle. "I know you're on duty, Lieutenant, but this has been a most trying evening. Would you be insulted if I offered you a drink?"

"I've got a thick skin."

She pointed to the bottle. "I'll join you, if you don't mind."

"I'd love it. But I'd prefer you pour. That way I won't feel quite as guilty for breaking regulations."

She worked on a smile and almost made it. She walked over to the bottle, and when she bent over to pour the drinks, the effect was still devastating. The neckline was fighting a losing battle and with any luck I'd be around when it gave up the unequal struggle.

She straightened up, looked around, and frowned. "The ice seems to have melted. If one of your men—"

"They're sitting up with a dead friend." I took the glass from her hand.

"This will do nicely for the job I have at hand."

She raised her eyebrows. "Job?"

I swallowed the drink neat and set it back on the table. "I have to call the Sheriff and tell him we have another corpse cluttering the premises. It upsets him when somebody uses his jurisdiction as a shooting gallery." I dragged myself to the phone and stared at it for a moment. "If I were you, Miss Bannister, I'd hold my ears. Lavers doesn't really need a phone when he gets upset." I sighed. "And this is bound to upset him."

This time Lavers let the phone ring seven times before he picked it up. "You've got the wrong number," he roared.

"Sorry to contradict a superior, sir," I told him in my most formal tones, "but I have the right number."

There was a strangled gasp from the other end. "Wheeler?" From the tone of his voice it was evident he was hoping it was a delusion.

"The same, sir. Checking in to report a murder."

"You crazy, you clown? You've already reported it. I sent—"

"Oh, that one?" I asked airily. "That's an old one. We've got a brand new one."

"Anyone I know?" he snarled.

"Mephisto, the magician." I lowered my voice. "Not too much of a loss. His act was lousy."

"I don't care how bad his act was. The DA gets narrow-minded about citizens getting knocked off. Besides, when did you become a critic?"

"I thought you'd like my opinion," I told him mildly. I waited until he ran out of adjectives to describe my effect on him. "I wonder if you'd mind asking Doc Murphy, the ambulance, and the photographer to come back again when you can reach them, Sheriff?"

"Wheeler,"—there was a pleading note in Lavers's voice—"you are drunk, aren't you?"

"No sir," I said.

"I was afraid of that," he said. "And now this conjuror's been murdered!"

"Magician, sir," I said.

"All right," he growled, "magician! Stabbed, you said, like the girl?"

"Check. Polnik found him."

"Where, exactly?"

I had been afraid he was going to ask that. "Polnik found him, sir. Would you like him to tell you—"

"I'd like you to tell me. Now!"

I took a deep breath.

"In the gymnasium," I said. "On a vaulting horse—lying between the pommels."

"Wheeler," he said gently, "it's not April the first?"

"No, sir."

"This really isn't your idea of a practical joke?"

"No, sir."

"Then you handle it, Lieutenant," he said in a tired voice. "You phone Homicide and tell them to send out a call for the doctor and the rest of them. I can't really be bothered with it. I am going to retire to my bedroom and quietly go mad!"

There was a clunk from the other end as he slammed his receiver down. I rubbed my ear and hung up.

"He does have rather a penetrating voice," Miss Bannister told me. "And I now feel that my education is complete." She wrinkled up her nose. "He has a rather colorful vocabulary, doesn't he?"

"He makes his point," I conceded. My eyes wandered toward the Scotch bottle. "Like you said, it's been a pretty trying evening—"

Her eyes followed mine to the bottle. "Help yourself."

I poured a fresh drink, had a quick slug of it, and phoned Homicide. I'd just hung up when a knock came at the door.

"Come in," she called.

The door opened and Slade came in. "Yes, Lieutenant?" he said.

"Yes what?" I asked him.

"I don't know, Lieutenant," he said. "You're supposed to tell me what."

I glared at him.

"Lieutenant!" Slade persisted. "What do you want?"

"It would take too long to detail the list," I said. "A million dollars—a collection of Hollywood starlets—a what the hell are you doing up here, anyway? I told you to stay in the gym with the corpse!"

He stared at me for a moment, then took off his glasses, polished them vigorously, replaced them on his nose and stared at me again.

"Maybe you forgot, Lieutenant," he said in a cold voice. "Maybe you don't remember phoning me at the gym a couple of minutes back and telling me you were in Miss Bannister's office and for me to come up here on the double."

"Frankly, I don't," I said. "But get a referee—Miss Bannister's been here all the time. Do you remember that call Miss Bannister?"

"Why, no," she said. "You called the Sheriff and then Homicide. They're the only two calls you made."

"You see, Slade?" I said. "If anybody is hearing bells ringing it's you, not …" Then I started running. I ran down the hall, down the short stairway in two jumps, and along a corridor to the gymnasium.

It looked like any other gym—that was the trouble. Vaulting horse standing empty and ready for action like always. The body of Mephisto had disappeared.

Slade arrived a couple of seconds later and stared disbelievingly at the empty vaulting horse. "It's gone!" he said. "It can't have! How can a dead man walk?"

"If it's gone it can have gone," I said. "And your last question is a little too complicated for me to try and answer. But taking a wild guess, I'd say someone carried it out of here—maybe the same guy who phoned and told you to go up to the office. That would have given him time to get in and out of here without any trouble!"

"I guess you're right, Lieutenant," he said.

Everywhere I went, I heard tramping feet. Right then I heard more tramping feet and then the doctor followed by the ambulance men followed by the photographer came in.

"Hey, the service around here is improving! How'd you get here so quick, doc?"

"Modern electronics is wonderful," Doc Murphy said sourly, "and we were buzzed before we were hardly out the driveway. Where is it?"

"That brings up a delicate point," I said. "Your guess is as good as mine."

"Don't horse around, Wheeler," he said. "I've had enough for one night!"

"The body has vanished, to coin a phrase," I said. "I don't have the slightest idea where it could be, except it can't have gone very far!" I turned to Slade. "Get hold of Polnik—he's somewhere in the staff living quarters talking to Pierce. Make a search—look in every room in the building. Don't come back till you've found that corpse again!"

"Yes, Lieutenant," he said weakly.

"And what do I do in the meanwhile?" Doc Murphy asked.

I walked over to the horse and stood looking at it for a moment. "Why don't you try a few push-ups, doc? You're badly out of condition."

"Listen!" he erupted. "If you don't present me with a corpse within the next five minutes I'm going to present the Sheriff with a detailed report that'll make you a candidate for my next post-mortem!"

"No blood," I said.

"What!"

"On the horse—no blood."

Murphy peered at the leather seat of the vaulting-horse. "No— That's right."

"Apparently he was stabbed in the same way the girl was stabbed—would he have bled much?"

"No—if the knife was placed as accurately as the first one," Murphy said. "How was he lying when he was found?"

"Across the horse, lengthwise," I said. "The pommels kept him on, Polnik said."

Murphy went down on his hands and knees on the floor and sniffed loudly.

"If you'd like a bone why don't you be a brave dog and come right out and say so?" I asked.

He got to his feet again hastily and dusted the knees of his pants. "No blood on the floor either," he said. "That's odd. I wouldn't expect any on the horse from the way you described his position, but there should have been at least a few drops on the floor." He looked at me nastily. "You're sure he was dead?"

"Polnik thought so," I said. "But maybe knives are being worn in the back this year?"

Murphy grunted and looked at his watch. "You've got about three minutes left, Wheeler!"

"Have you met Miss Bannister, the head of this joint?" I asked him.

"No," he said.

"Like Ava Gardner," I said casually. "Except she wears her hair a little shorter."

"Really?" Murphy looked interested. "She's not in need of any medical attention is she? An examination, perhaps? I mean, while I am here ..."

"I'll find out," I told him.

There was a phone on the far wall and beside it was a list of extension numbers. Miss Bannister's office was 23. I dialed it and she answered almost immediately.

"Wheeler," I said in a low voice. "I'm in a spot. Would you do something for me?"

"Anything, Lieutenant," she said. There was a moment's pause. "Anything within reason, that is," she added.

"If I send a doctor, two ambulance attendants, and a police photographer up to your office, would you give them a drink?"

"Of course," she said, "if it will help."

"That—and you looking the way you look will help quite a lot," I said and hung up.

I went back to the doc. "She's not in need of any medicine," I said.

"Too bad," he said, disappointed. "Like Ava Gardner, you said?"

"But she is dispensing medicine," I said. "Medicinal alcohol. You're invited—so are these other gentlemen."

"Well!" Murphy brightened. "How do we get there!"

I gave him instructions on how to find her office and they marched out of the gymnasium, leaving me alone.

I lit another cigarette after they'd gone and crossed my fingers that Polnik or Slade would turn up the missing corpse. I walked over to a large rectangular box in the corner of the gym. The sort of box they use for handstands and rolls and springs and that sort of stuff. The box had a heavily padded leather top and I sat down on it gratefully. I wanted to try and sort things out in my mind.

The groan sounded hollow and I thought that it summed up exactly how I felt. That was only logical anyway—the groan had been completely subconscious; I hadn't even realized I was doing it. I put the cigarette into my mouth and took a deep drag on it and the groan came again. I exhaled in the middle of inhaling and coughed furiously for ten seconds. Then I stood up. This thing had me worried. How can you consciously not notice yourself subconsciously groaning when you were consciously inhaling smoke at the time you subconsciously groaned? It was a question I passed up, too.

Then there was a third groan and I thought the hell with my subconscious and stooped down and threw back the lid of the box.

The Great Mephisto sat up slowly, rubbing the back of his head and still groaning. I practically swallowed my cigarette.

He looked at me accusingly. "Somebody slugged me!" he said. "If I find the—"

I held up my hand warningly. "Don't be tempted to use coarse language," I told him. "You may not be in a proper condition to indulge in coarse language."

"What the hell are you talking about!" he said.

"You don't feel anything in your back?" I asked carefully. "An itch? An irritation, maybe, as if someone stuck a pin into you?"

"Are you crazy?" he said. He looked around the gym with a blank expression on his face. "How did I get down here?"

"Don't worry about it!" I said, and patted him on the back encouragingly and then slid my hand down between his shoulder blades. There was no knife protruding from his back, there was no blood, no tear in his coat even.

He hauled himself to his feet and stepped out of the box. "I want to know what happened!" he said. "Last thing I remember the lights went out in the auditorium. I thought maybe it was that dumb assistant of mine so I started out to get to the fuse box and I just got into the hallway when … somebody must have hit me!"

"Think yourself lucky you weren't murdered," I said. "Stabbed like the girl!"

"Why would anyone want to murder me?" he asked thickly.

"I don't know," I said. "They'd all seen your act …"

He got his mouth wide open to say something but then Slade came hurrying into the gym and Mephisto's opportunity was gone.

"Lieutenant," Slade said breathlessly, "we've been through every room in the place and there just isn't a sign of the body anywhere!"

"Too bad," I said.

"You know every student has a room of her own?" he went on. "I'd covered five when the Sergeant realized it,"—his voice went sour—"then he took over those rooms and let me go through the lockers and the bathrooms!"

"Too bad," I said. "You haven't met The Great Mephisto formally, have you?"

"No," Slade said curtly and nodded to Mephisto.

"Hi, there. Well, I can't figure it, Lieutenant, I ..."

He stopped suddenly, his mouth opening and closing regularly but no words coming out. He looked at Mephisto and his face turned a chalky color and he started to back off uncertainly.

"What's with him?" Mephisto asked.

"The last time he saw you he was convinced you were a corpse," I said. "Now he's not quite sure what you are and it's worrying him. He's very insecure."

"Is everybody crazy around here!" he demanded.

"I know four people who are going to be," I told him and went over the phone. I rang Miss Bannister's office and she answered. I asked could I speak to Dr. Murphy.

A couple of seconds later Murphy came on the line. His voice sounded almost benevolent. "You were right for once in your life, Wheeler," he said. "Definitely Gardner."

"You know I wouldn't try to fool a Gardner expert like you, doc—"

"About the same height, same planes in the face, maybe a little fuller here in the—" I could hear the yelp of pain clearly across the wire. I wondered whether she had brought those stiletto-sharp heels of hers down on his instep, or had slapped him across the face. I sympathized with him. I had a terrific curiosity myself as to whether that skirt concealed or implied her true fullness.

When his voice came back on the line, the good nature was gone. "That does it, Wheeler. I'm getting out of here and when I do—"

"By the way, doc—that body we were talking about—want to talk to it?"

"I suppose you think that's funny?" he snarled.

"A corpse talking?" I considered. "Maybe not funny, but you'll admit it's kind of unusual. But then it's an unusual corpse. Now you see it, now you don't. First it's dead, then it's alive. Real unusual."

"Are you trying to tell me," he asked slowly, "that the whole thing was your idea of a joke?"

"Not my idea," I said, "somebody else's idea. Don't ask me why, I don't know. That's the hard part—I'll have to find out."

"You brought me—an ambulance—a photographer—out here for the second time because it was some halfwit's idea of a joke and you took it seriously!" His voice rose to a scream. "Wheeler, if it's the last thing I ever do, have you broken for this! I'll tell the Sheriff and the Commissioner that I refuse—you hear me—refuse point blank to answer a call that originates from you. You're an incompetent fool with the brains of a quartered amoeba and—"

"Thanks, doc," I said, "I knew you'd see it my way," and hung up carefully.

Mephisto was still glowering at me as I walked back toward him. "I wish somebody would tell me—"

"What it's all about?" I finished for him. "I'll tell you something, Mephisto—you're not the only one."

A moment later, Sergeant Polnik pounded into the gym. "Lieutenant!" He stopped suddenly and looked at Slade, who was over by the wall, nervously mopping his brow. "What's with him?"

"He lost his nerve," I said. "I introduced him to the walking corpse here beside me and he couldn't take it. I don't know what the Department's coming to."

"Walking …" Polnik looked at Mephisto for a long moment. Then he took a deep breath. "So it was a fake?"

"He got slugged over the back of the head," I said. "I found him in that box over there."

"But the knife in his back!"

"I guess nobody looked very closely at it," I said.

"It must have been one of those trick knives—you know, you plunge them into somebody's back and the blade just disappears into the hilt?" Polnik swallowed hard. "Maybe I didn't look too close," he admitted. "But you know what the book says. You don't touch nothing until the ME and his boys are finished. I was afraid I'd smear the prints, you know?"

I turned away from him and gave Mephisto one of my long searching glances—the kind that's supposed to make a reluctant witness break down and tell everything he knows. "That strike a note, magician? A phony knife with a blade that goes back into the handle?"

"Kid's stuff," he growled.

"Or magicians' stuff. How about it?"

He shrugged and raised his hands, palms up. "I don't know what the hell anybody around here is talking about. None of it makes any sense to me and I've given up trying."

Polnik rubbed his face with the palm of his hand and groaned. "When Doc Murphy and his boys—"

"The doctor and his ambulance are on their back to Homicide," I said to Polnik. "I don't think the doctor cared for the whole thing at all. He was quite rude."

"That's too bad!" Polnik said.

"Sure," I said, "but who cares?"

"Doc Murphy will care," he said thoughtfully, "when he just gets back, then has to turn around and come out here again."

"What are you talking about?" I asked him.

"I was checking the students' rooms, Lieutenant," he explained carefully. "Cheez, you should see the stuff some of them have!" He noticed the look on my face and went on hurriedly: "Like I say, I'm checking the rooms and I find one of the girls lying on her bed."

"So she has a headache," I said. "With the way things have been happening round here that doesn't surprise me at all."

CHAPTER FIVE

Polnik shook his head. "I took a close look this time, Lieutenant. It wasn't no headache made her a corpse—the knife in her back is definitely for real!"

The body belonged to the brunette with the tight curls around her head—the one who had been interested to know if there was a way to commit murder without signs of violence. Whoever had murdered her hadn't worried about that detail.

She lay face down across the bed, still wearing the clothes she had worn in the auditorium. There was a knife buried between her shoulder blades and, as Polnik had said—she was very definitely dead. There was no sign of a struggle in the room, nothing disturbed.

"I guess we better get the doc back, Lieutenant," Polnik said.

"Guess again," I said. "He wouldn't come out if we found a new wing of Bluebeard's honeymoon cottage. So far we've been run around like a souped-up stock car at Daytona. Somebody has handled us like a trio of jerks from Birdsville and, friends, we've lived up to it! So now we stop running around and start making other people run around. We're going to solve this case by morning."

"Lieutenant," Slade asked simply, "how?"

"That's a good question," I admitted. "For a start, you search this room—go through it with a fine-tooth comb—see if you can find anything unusual, anything that points to somebody else here—staff or student. And when you've finished here go along to the Craig girl's room and do the same thing. Then come down to Miss Bannister's office and report to me there."

"Yes, Lieutenant," Slade said.

I looked at Polnik. "Sergeant—I want everyone in this building sitting in that auditorium fifteen minutes from now—that's an order—you don't take no for an answer from anybody. That covers all staff, all students, Mephisto—and his assistant."

"Yes, Lieutenant," he said.

"I'll be in Miss Bannister's office—you can report to me there when you've got them all collected. And fifteen minutes is the absolute maximum."

"Sure, Lieutenant," Polnik grunted and went out of the room. I looked coldly at Slade, who pulled open the nearest drawer and started going through it at a frantic pace.

I walked back along to Miss Bannister's office, knocked on the door, and went in.

"I wondered what had happened to you Lieutenant," she said brightly. "Come back for another drink?"

I made an heroic effort. "Not just now," I said. "Who is the girl with the dark hair in tight curls—the one who asked me the question about murder without violence?"

"That's Nancy Ritter," she said without hesitation. "She hasn't been bothering you with any more foolish questions, I hope?"

"No," I said, "she's been murdered."

Miss Bannister looked at me, not quite sure whether to laugh or not.

"True," I said.

"But this is ..." she muttered, "... it's unbelievable!"

"Check," I said. "Sergeant Polnik is getting everybody into the auditorium. When he's got them all there, I'm going to start questioning them—one at a time. I'd like to use your office here for that, if you don't mind?"

"No," she said. "I don't mind."

"Thanks," I said. "Where did you get The Great Mephisto from?"

"I beg your pardon?"

"You hired him for his performance tonight," I said. "Did you know him personally—get him through an agency—what?"

"Oh! I see what you mean," she said. "As a matter of fact, he was recommended to me by one of the staff."

"Which one?"

"Miss Tomlinson," she said. The corners of her mouth quirked upward for a moment. "She said he was absolutely spiffing!"

"I asked you this question about the Craig girl," I said. "Now I'm asking it about the Ritter girl—do you know of any reason why anyone might want to kill her?"

"None at all," she said. "I think this is the work of a madman, Lieutenant!"

"You're sure of the sex?"

"I don't quite ..."

"A madman. Why not a madwoman?"

"I'm sure it's a man," she said.

"Why?"

"I don't have a definite reason—just a feeling. I can't explain it, Lieutenant."

"Women never can," I agreed. "That's it for now, Miss Bannister—would you mind going into the auditorium now?"

"You're going to put me on the same level as the students?" she asked coldly.

"That wasn't the idea," I explained. "This questioning could take a long time. I think if you're there they will behave themselves a lot better than if you aren't."

"Yes," she nodded. "I see what you mean. Very well, Lieutenant." She went out of the room, closing the door behind her. I lit myself a cigarette and then sat down in her chair behind the desk. A couple of minutes later, there was a knock on the door and Slade came into the office.

"Nothing in the Ritter girl's room, Lieutenant," he said. "But look what I found in the Craig girl's room!" He dropped an antique on the desk in front of me. A pearl-handled Colt, single action .44-40. The Frontier Colt. It would have been over a hundred years old. It didn't excite me.

"Too late to ask her if she had a permit," I said. "Anyway, this is probably an old family heirloom of no use at all. Her old man is a rich rancher in Nevada—probably gave it to her as a going-to-college present."

"He's certainly an original father then," Slade said with a smirk. "That thing's loaded!"

"You're nuts!" I said.

I picked up the gun and cocked the hammer and saw it was me who was nuts. I very gingerly rammed my thumb against the hammer and slowly lowered it again. I put the gun back quickly onto the desk and made sure the barrel was pointing at Slade and not me in case of accidents.

"What do you make of that, Lieutenant?" Slade asked triumphantly.

"I'll grow a beard and call myself Buffalo Bill if it'll make you happy, Slade," I said. "Tell me, what do *you* make of it?"

"I got it figured, Lieutenant," he said. "It's simple! This doll knows she's in danger, she's brought up on a ranch, knows how to handle a gun—this one—maybe she's played with the gun since she was a kid. So she brings it along to school with her. How about that?"

"Slade," I said, "you've been watching television again! When Polnik's got everybody inside the auditorium, I want you to search some more rooms. Do you think you can remember three or four names?"

"Sure," he said, looking hurt. "Just give 'em to me."

"Bannister, Partington, Dufay and Pierce," I said.

"Bannister?" his eyes widened. "But that's the dame who owns the joint, isn't it?"

"Nobody can fool you, can they?" I said. "You got it. Go down to the auditorium first and see if you can see Polnik." I looked at my watch. "Tell him he's got exactly two minutes left."

"Yes, Lieutenant," he said resignedly and walked toward the door. "You know something, Lieutenant? For an unorthodox cop you can be the most orthodox cop I ever met at times!"

"I have to take care of an orthodox doctor as well as an orthodox sheriff," I said. "And a couple of unorthodox corpses—three, if you count Mephisto, and he was the most unorthodox corpse of the bunch!"

He reached the door and had it half open.

"I just remembered," I said. "Add one more name to the ones you already have—Tomlinson. Search all five rooms thoroughly—but be neat!"

"Yes, Lieutenant."

The door shut behind Slade with a crash. I lit another cigarette from the butt of the one I was smoking and thought I must have been out of mind to refuse that drink Miss Bannister had offered me.

Polnik arrived five minutes later.

"You got them all out there?"

"Sure," he nodded. "All of them, Lieutenant."

"Good." I nodded toward a chair. "Sit down."

He sat down looking at me curiously. "What happens now, Lieutenant?"

"I'm going to question them in here," I said, "one at a time. You got Mephisto's assistant?"

"Sure," he said. "Funny little guy—doesn't talk much."

"Maybe he's too frightened to talk," I said. "Maybe he used to stooge in the guillotine stunt of Mephisto's once and one time it went wrong and cut his throat. Wouldn't you be too frightened to talk with a cut throat? You'd have no idea anything was wrong until you tried to turn your head, and then—" I ran my finger across nay throat. "Scary, huh?"

"Yes, Lieutenant," Polnik agreed politely.

"I think I'd like to meet Mr. Pierce first of all," I said. "Bring him in and, while I'm talking to him, check with Miss Bannister and get a list of the names of all the students and the teaching staff. If we don't get any satisfaction out of them I guess we'll have to start on the kitchen staff."

"Yes, Lieutenant," Polnik said, dispiritedly and went out.

A couple of minutes later, Mr. Pierce, the art master, was in the office. He was a big guy, good-looking the way movie stars are good-looking. He wore a nicely tailored gray suit, a white shirt, and a matching gray tie. His hair was neither long nor short and he didn't have a beard—he didn't even have a mustache.

"It's all wrong," I told him. "You should be Mr. Dufay, the language master, and he should be Mr. Pierce, the art master."

He grinned, showing nice even teeth. "You're out of date, Lieutenant. These days the creative boys wear gray flannel suits. The long-hairs in the camel-haired coats and jeans are clerks trying to assert their personalities in their spare time!"

"You could have something there," I said. "I spend most of my spare time in jeans."

He grinned again obligingly.

"You know that Jean Craig was murdered earlier this evening," I said. "You may not know that subsequently Nancy Ritter was also murdered."

His face sobered. "No," he said in a low voice, "I didn't know that."

"You knew them both?"

"Of course," he said. "They both took my course. Jean had the makings of a fine commercial artist—Nancy had no talent at all."

"Did you tell her that?"

"Sure," he said.

"I wonder she continued with the course," I said.

"You can't make 'em out," he said. "Women!"

"I hear you try hard," I said.

"Just what does that mean, Lieutenant?"

I looked at him for a couple of seconds before I answered. "I hear that your relationship with Jean Craig was a lot closer than that of teacher to student."

He took a pack of cigarettes out of his pocket, selected one carefully, and lit it with equal care.

"You know how it is, Lieutenant," he said easily. "Here there are fifty young and mostly highly attractive girls—and only four men. Three, really—you can't count Dufay in, and he's engaged to that English hunk of health in any case."

"I don't know how it is," I said. "But I'm willing to listen."

"I was friendly with Jean," he said. "We had interests in common."

"I'm with you," I said encouragingly.

"Well—that was all there was to it. There was nothing serious in it."

"But you would have known her better than most of the others probably?"

"I don't know about that."

"Did she have any problems?—anything worrying her, anyone she was frightened of? Did she mention anything like that to you? Take your time about it—think it over. Anything, anything at all, however small."

He thought for about five seconds. "There was one thing," he said slowly. "Maybe it's just crazy but still … it happened this afternoon about five. I met her in the grounds and she asked if I was going to be at the Sheriff's lecture tonight, and I said sure, I was commanded along with the rest of the students and teaching staff.

"Then she told me she was going to ask the Sheriff a question and, if I wanted to see somebody really warned, I should watch the audience when she asked it and I'd see quite a reaction on one particular face."

"She didn't say whose face?"

"No—although I suppose she was expecting me to ask her. One can hardly look at fifty faces at once and pick out a reaction, after all. But the whole thing seemed silly to me, so I didn't bite. And then she asked that nutty question about Lizzie Borden anyway."

"Yeah," I said. "It doesn't exactly make the picture clearer, does it? You don't know anyone who could have reason to kill her?"

"No, Lieutenant," he said soberly. "She was a nice kid—a little bit wild in places, I guess, but she would have grown out of that."

"What about Nancy Ritter?"

"She was just a student."

"Who had no talent but kept on trying even after you'd told her she had no talent?"

"That's right, Lieutenant."

"Okay," I said.

"Is that all?"

"It's your story and I'll believe it—particularly if it stands up under checking."

He walked out of the office and Polnik stuck his head around the door. "Who next?"

"Mephisto's assistant," I said. "Does he have a name or is he just a number?"

"He's got a name—Spike."

"Spike what?"

"Just Spike."

"That is the sort of routine that killed vaudeville," I told him, "and is killing television comics. Are you sure you're carrying enough insurance?"

"I'll get him," Polnik said hastily and closed the door. Spike was about five feet nothing and there was a clean, honest look about him that reminded you of a dope pusher or a lesser exponent of the badger game.

He stood there awkwardly looking in any direction but mine and a tic in his cheek throbbed to the soundless beat of a San Quentin tom-tom.

"You're Spike?"

"Sure, that's me." His voice was husky as if his vocal chords had been bruised beyond recognition.

"You're an ex-con."

"You goin' to make a Federal case out of it?"

"I might try," I said. "How long have you been assisting Mephisto?"

"Maybe six months, Lieutenant," he said. "When he's working, that is."

"He's not working regularly?"

"Maybe two nights a week—private parties—shows, places like this, Lieutenant."

"They all get their quotas of two murders a night?"

Spike's gray face turned a deeper shade of gray. "I don't know nothin' about that," he said.

"What do you do as his assistant?"

"Handle the lights mostly. You know—change the colors of the foots, angle the spots, kill the—"

"House lights?" I supplied. "Maybe accidentally knock off the main switch?"

"I don't know what you're talkin' about," he said sullenly.

I got up from the desk and walked out of the office, closing the door shut behind me. Polnik looked at me questioningly.

"Go back into the auditorium and find out if any of the women lost any valuables tonight while the magician's show was on," I said. "Make a list if there are any and bring it back to me—just hand it to me. If there's nothing, still hand me a list."

"Huh?"

"A piece of blank paper," I said wearily. "And hurry."

I went back into the office, back behind the desk, and stared at Spike. It's almost the lousiest of a cop's bag of tricks. When you don't have anything to say because you can't think of anything, you just give the guy the cold freeze. If they're really nervous, after a couple of minutes of it they'll confess to anything you care to name.

Spike didn't go for it much. He wouldn't look back at me, but every now and then he'd shoot a quick glance in my direction to see if he was still getting the treatment. And he couldn't keep his hands still either. They twitched at his tie, dug fingers inside the neckband of his collar, and rubbed the lapels of his coat.

Polnik came in with a piece of paper in his hand and put it down on the desk in front of me. "That's the list you wanted, Lieutenant," he said and gave Spike a significant stare on his way out.

I looked down at the list. There was one name on it. Caroline Partington—the languid blonde, I remembered. She was missing a pair of pendant diamond earrings. For the life of me, I couldn't remember if she'd had the earrings on when she'd thrown herself into my arms after Mephisto's—and her own—act, but I could guess.

Spike was beginning to sweat freely. I looked at him.

"Tell the Sergeant outside to go and get Mephisto and bring him in here," I said, "and then come back in here yourself."

"Sure, Lieutenant," he croaked and shuffled toward the door.

It didn't take Polnik more than a couple of minutes to bring Mephisto back with him. He let the magician into the office first, then closed the door and leaned against it.

"What's all this about now, Lieutenant?" Mephisto said angrily. "I've about had enough for one night!"

"Who's got them?" I asked him.

"I've given up trying to make sense out of you," he grunted. "I told you that before."

"Diamond pendant earrings," I said. "Who's got them? You—or Spike?"

"Earrings?" Mephisto said blankly. "What earrings?"

"We can search you," I said. "Both of you. It would be easier to hand them over."

"I don't know—"

"Shut up!" Spike said to him out of the corner of his mouth. "The copper's wise! Quit stallin', it's only trouble. You got 'em, give 'em to him!"

Mephisto glared murderously at him, then slowly put his hand into his pants pocket. He took a pace forward and then placed his hand on the desk-top and opened his fingers slowly. The earrings dropped onto the desk.

"That's better," I said.

"Hey, Lieutenant!" Polnik said incredulously, "how did you figure that one?"

"It's a racket that some of the ancient Romans probably pulled at one of Nero's banquets," I said. "Entertainer entertains—assistant handles lights. They case the audience and then at the right moment the lights fail—everything's in darkness for a couple of minutes. Long enough for the light-fingered magician and his assistant to move around and pick up a few trinkets. They'd aim to pick up the good stuff and only a little of that. With any luck, the owners don't even notice their loss until after the party's finished. Sometimes, they even amaze me. They learn one racket when they're still at reform school and they stick to it for the rest of their lives—what time they have outside a pen, that is."

"You talk a lot but you don't say nothing," Spike growled.

"The Partington girl was a cinch!" I said. "He picked her out for those earrings, got her on stage, put her through his act, grabbed her earrings when the lights went out—nothing to it if you're clever with your hands. She probably never felt it at all—"

"I never touched her!" Mephisto said indignantly.

"Maybe it was Spike's big rock-splitting paws, then?" I sneered. "Don't kid me, magician! He can hardly tie his shoes, much less peel an earring off a lady's ear lobe! Besides, he was busy dousing lights and prowling around the audience in the dark, weren't you, Spike? Unless you want to tell me it was your boss here who was commuting between the stage and the audience when the lights went out each time?"

"I was on stage the whole time!" Mephisto said. "I swear it."

"Me too!" Spike said. "And if it comes to a point, the second time the lights went out I didn't have nothing to do with it—somebody pulled the main switch for the whole building!"

"While we're at it," I said, "who's got the diamond necklace?"

"Diamond necklace!" they said together.

"The one the Craig girl was wearing," I said. "It wasn't around her neck when the lights went on again. Who got so enthusiastic he had to plunge a knife into her back before he grabbed the necklace?"

The color of Mephisto's face was beginning to match that of Spike's.

"I never touched the girl!" he said. "I swear it! I never left the stage either time the lights went out!"

"It must have been you!" Spike said tightly. "It wasn't me!"

"Why, you lying, dirty four-flusher!" Mephisto made a grab for the little man. He missed and was discouraged from any further demonstration of his physical prowess by Polnik giving him an almost gentle rabbit punch which paralyzed his nervous system without knocking him unconscious.

I shrugged my shoulders. "It doesn't matter right now. We've got plenty of time to find out—plenty of time to sweat both of them when we get them back to Homicide. In any case, whoever murdered the Craig girl, the other is still an accessory before and after the fact."

I pointed an index finger toward the door. "Take them away, Sergeant," I said. "Lock them in the boiler room—any place with a key and no windows. They'll keep."

"Sure, Lieutenant." Polnik took the gun from his shoulder holster. "All right, you guys!" he said. "Let's move."

Spike seemed to have shrunk a couple of inches as he slouched out of the room and Mephisto had the look on his face of a magician who's just been successful in turning a lump of gold into an egg.

It didn't take long for Polnik to come back.

"Got them in the boiler room, Lieutenant," he said and dropped the key on my desk. "Hell! I got to hand it to you. That was nice work. I hate to admit it, but I never even noticed that diamond necklace!"

"You don't have to apologize for not noticing it, Sergeant," I told him, "There's a perfectly simple explanation."

"There is?" he asked blankly.

"Sure," I said. "There never was a diamond necklace."

CHAPTER SIX

The languid blonde gave me a warm smile. "Thanks a lot, Lieutenant. I couldn't figure out what had happened to them. You can lose one earring without noticing it—but two! Did you pick them up somewhere?"

"You could say that," I said. "They're valuable, aren't they?"

She shrugged her shoulders. "Around five hundred, I guess. Daddy gave them to me last birthday."

She sat facing me. She'd changed her clothes since the last time I saw her. She was wearing a pearl-colored dress of wool jersey that clung to her the way it must have clung to the original sheep—only now it was twice as interesting.

"You knew Jean Craig and Nancy Ritter?" I asked her.

"Natch," she said. "Nancy was a very good friend of mine."

"You can't think of any reason why anyone should want to kill them?" It was the routine question again and this time I didn't really expect anything but a negative in answer.

"I can dig up a dozen!" Caroline Partington said calmly. "There were times I could have killed either of them myself!"

"Why?"

"Lieutenant—" she smiled at me lazily "—you're cute! This is a hen college with just four men around permanently. Prof Coleman is something over sixty and senile, so that really leaves only three. Lane is forty-five and married, so that leaves two. Two eligible men to fifty female vultures! And every one of those potent pigeons looking for co-education!"

"I hadn't thought of it that way," I said. "I guess Pierce is the dreamboat?"

"He's dreamy," she agreed. "And so is Dufay."

"You're joking!"

"Lieutenant," she said and shook her head slowly, "don't be a square! All the girls drool for Dufay. Maybe he appeals to our maternal instinct—he sure appeals, anyway!"

"That's what you meant when you said you could have murdered either of the girls?"

"You got it," she said. "The competition is intense. When one of them pulled a drag—"

"Did what?"

"Made a date." She lifted her eyebrows. "Don't you understand English, Lieutenant?"

"You're shaking my confidence," I said. "Go on."

"Dial me and call me phoney!" she said. "You fracture me, Lieutenant. You should get out of the rut and into the groove!"

"I should get out of this college and into a nuthouse!" I said. "And I probably will before the night's out!"

"You're a mellow fellow, Lieutenant," she said. "You're my cheezle-peezle. I'll help you as much as I can."

"Thanks. If you'd just remember I'm in my dotage …"

"You look old enough to be thirty!" she said frankly, "but you're kind of handsome still. You carry your age well, Lieutenant."

"I have built-in crutches," I said. "The toupee helps, of course—if you'd like a close look at my teeth, I'll take them out for you."

"You're still my flutterbump," she said sweetly.

I lit a cigarette and sucked smoke deep into my aged lungs and wondered if I should go out and buy me a headstone because it was so much later than I'd thought.

"Please," I said carefully. "I have to talk to a lot more people tonight. Let's stay with the facts!"

"Facts, Lieutenant. Competition for those two boys is hot! And believe you me, passions run high, too!"

"Are you seriously suggesting that one of the girls would have committed two murders just to eliminate the competition for a date with one of the masters?"

"Now you're plugged in," she said. "Sure—that's just what I've been saying all the time!"

"Okay," I said resignedly. "Anything else you know?"

"I don't know anything about the murders," she said. "I'd just left the stage when the first one happened and was with my roommate when Nancy must have been …"

"Sure," I said, "Do you own a diamond necklace by any chance?"

"Don't tell me I've lost that too!" she said.

"I wondered if you're lend it to me for a little while," I said.

"It would look kind of cute with your jacket."

"You wait outside for a couple of minutes," I said, "and then I'll come with you and get it."

I escorted her out of the office and took Polnik back in with me.

"I've got an idea," I told him. "Not much of one, but I'm going to be busy for a while. I want you to carry on questioning them. Ask them if they know any reasons why either of the girls should be murdered. See if anybody recognizes the knives that were used—they all saw the one in the Craig girl's back. You know what to ask them."

"Sure, Lieutenant." Polnik brightened up a little. "I'll do that."

I went out of the office and Caroline Partington smiled warmly at me. "This is like a date, Lieutenant," she said. "It'll be cozy up in my room with everybody in the hall. Not a chance we'll be interrupted."

The students" rooms were in a separate wing of the building. Caroline led me down a thickly carpeted hall, pushed open a door, and motioned for me to enter. The room was almost as big as my entire apartment.

She followed me in and closed the door after her. The only light in the room came from an indirect fixture. She leaned against the door for a moment, a sleepy smile on her face. "For a minute, I thought you were going to disappoint me, Lieutenant," she told me. "But you came through. Borrowing a diamond necklace—that is a new one." She walked over to where I stood and slid her arms around my neck. As she pasted her body against mine, her moist lips found my mouth. She gurgled deliciously as her mouth moved against mine, and her nails dug into my back. I finally broke her hold and held her away from me.

"I really did come to talk—about a diamond necklace," I told her. Her eyes were heavy-lidded, her breath was warm against my face; I could smell the fragrance of the scent she wore. For a moment, I tried to figure how important it was that I get the necklace. After all—a man can always lay his hands on a necklace!

She licked at her lips with the tip of a pink tongue. "You needn't worry, Lieutenant. I'm over eighteen—and nobody would think of walking in on us."

"About this necklace—" I told her weakly.

"Damn the necklace!" She broke out of my grip, stamped over to the dressing table, and opened the top drawer. She took out a flat, expensive-looking jeweler's box and opened it. A necklace of matched diamonds shot red and blue glints at me from a lining of blue velvet. I whistled appreciatively.

"Most men reserve that kind of a whistle for me," Caroline pouted. "I guess you're just T.D. and G."

"T.D. and G?"

"Tall, dark and gruesome!"

Served me right for asking. "If you think you can trust me with the bauble, I'd better be getting back to the ranch."

She held the box out indifferently. "Trust you with the necklace? From the way you resisted my advances I'm sure you don't have the ambition to try to run away with it." She looked me up and down. "You sure can't tell by appearances. I'd have said you were a wolf first class."

My pride was hurt. "I like to play house like the next guy. More so, maybe. But with somebody my own size."

She grinned at me impishly. "If you haven't tried it, don't knock it." She took my arm. "Would you like me to help you back?"

I shook my arm free and headed for the doorway with all the dignity I could muster. It didn't do me any good to hear her giggling as I slammed the door behind me.

I stamped down the hall in the direction of the boiler room. Somebody was sure going to catch hell to make up for this!

Mephisto and Spike were sitting on a steam pipe and they both leaped to their feet when I came in. I closed the door carefully, locked it, and dropped the key into my pocket.

"This is an outrage!" Mephisto said.

I leaned my back against the door and smiled at him. "It's not an outrage yet, chum," I told him. "But it will be!"

"What do you mean?"

"I took the diamond necklace out of my pocket and looped it over the index finger of my right hand, then spun it slowly around. The diamonds winked blindingly as they reflected the light. Their eyes bulged as they watched.

"Where did you get that?" Spike asked with a note of longing in his voice.

"You should recognize it," I said. "That's the necklace the Craig girl was wearing when she was stabbed—the reason she was murdered."

Spike licked his lips, which seemed to have gone dry suddenly. "Where did you find it, Lieutenant?"

"In your pocket," I said.

He jerked convulsively. "That's a lie! And you know it, Lieutenant!"

"I could be wrong," I said. "Maybe it was in Mephisto's pocket?"

"What are you trying to do?" Mephisto asked hoarsely. "Frame an innocent man?"

I spun the necklace for a few more seconds before I answered him. Both of them watched it, fascinated like rabbits by a snake. "I'll tell you how it is, boys," I said, grinning at them. "I've got a red-hot case here and the Sheriff will want it cleaned up fast. So I'm going to clean it up fast for him."

"How?" Mephisto said.

"You two," I said. "Spike is an ex-con—maybe you've got a record, too, wonder wizard. Working this racket around private parties where you entertain. I've got the Partington girl's earrings as evidence—Polnik will back that up and so will she. All I have to add as a clincher is this necklace. I tell a jury that it was around the Craig girl's neck but was missing directly after she was killed. Then I tell them that when you were searched, the necklace was found in the pocket of one of your coats. It doesn't really matter to me which one. Any way you cut it—one faces a murder rap and the other an accessory rap—and as you damned well know, they amount to about the same thing."

"You dirty, rotten—" Mephisto started.

"Shut up!" Spike said in an ugly whisper.

"Don't you tell me—"

"Shut up!" Spike repeated. "You ain't really got any brains, Mephisto.

Now I'm seeing it clear. And you don't know coppers the way I know coppers. This one is looking for a deal."

I nodded to Spike. "You're right!"

"Okay," he said slowly. "What is it?"

"It's this way," I said. "I tell a few lies about this necklace and the case is wrapped up. That's the easy way. The hard way is to keep on looking for a killer. And you two make it harder by telling me a lot of lies."

"What lies?" Mephisto demanded.

"Don't give me that," I groaned. "Lies about the light, about who was down in the audience in the darkness …"

"My story was the gospel truth!" he said.

"Can it!" Spike told him wearily. "Is that the deal, Lieutenant? The straight story and then no frame?"

"That's the deal, Spike," I agreed.

"Okay," he said, "Sure—I pulled the lights both times. The first time was to get 'em used to the idea that the lights weren't working right— the second time meant business, like always. I stuck by the board then and waited till Mephisto got back on stage. He gives me a jab with his elbow as he goes past to let me know he's back. Then I give him five more seconds before I hit the switch and put the lights on again."

Mephisto looked murderously at his assistant. "You're trying to talk me into the gas chamber!"

Spike shook his head. "I'm trying to talk us both out of it, pal. Get smart! Do the same!"

There was a silence which lasted five seconds.

"That's the point," Mephisto said finally. "If I told him the truth he wouldn't believe me!"

"Try me," I suggested, "you won't be any worse off."

"All right," he said. "I knew it was going to be a lousy night as soon as I saw the audience. I cased them from the wings while you gave them your spiel. I figured they'd all be dressed up, but they were wearing anything—jeans and stuff you saw 'em! Sports clothes—you saw!"

"I saw them," I agreed.

"There was nothing worth grabbing—except the kid who was wearing those earrings. I figured they were worth half a grand, maybe more. So when I ask for an assistant I'm hoping she'll make it easy by coming forward and she does. That way I had her right there on the stage from the beginning, and when the lights went out the first time, I took that opportunity to lift the earrings." He smirked in spite of his troubles. "I have a light touch—they never feel a thing! When Spike killed the lights the second time, he was just going through our usual plan. It wasn't really necessary—I had the earrings in my pocket, and the girl had left the stage anyway. So I just stayed there, and then I gave

Spike the nudge he was expecting, and he put on the lights again, and that was that."

The smirk vanished from his face. "But I guess you aren't going to believe that, Lieutenant."

"I'm going to surprise you, Mephisto the Great," I said to him. "I might believe you—after I've heard the rest."

"The rest?"

"The gym. The playing corpse with a knife in your back—what really happened?"

"I don't know," he said.

"Okay—" I nodded and took the necklace out of my pocket again. "Then I guess this belongs to you."

"Wait a minute!" he pleaded. "I'm telling you the truth. When the lights went on and I saw the girl had been murdered, I was worried! I figured that if the other one woke up to the fact that her earrings were gone and set up a squawk about it and they were found on me, things would look bad. So Spike and I took a walk, looking for a safe place to stow them. Somewhere we could pick them up later."

"And you found the gym?"

"That's right," he said. "I told Spike to go back and pack our stuff while I hid the earrings."

"That wouldn't be because you didn't want him to see where you hid them?" I asked brightly.

He gave me a sour look. "No!" he said too loudly and it didn't fool Spike either. "Anyway—Spike beat it back to the auditorium and I was looking around for somewhere to hide the earrings and wham! Somebody slugged me. The next thing I knew I woke up in the dark." He shivered and beads of sweat appeared on his forehead. "So I started feeling around," he went on, his voice shaking a little, "and I tried to sit up and I hit my head!" He fumbled for a cigarette and found one, then lit it. "You imagine how I felt. It was dark, and I was trapped in what felt like a wooden box. I thought that somehow I'd been buried alive. I never was so glad to see a cop in all my life as when the lid opened and I saw you!"

"I just might buy that," I told him.

There was a sudden hammering on the door.

"Lieutenant!" I heard Slade's voice, muffled through the thickness of the door but losing none of its urgency.

I unlocked the door and Slade burst in, quivering with excitement. "Lieutenant! We found out where those knives came from!"

"We?" I asked.

"Well,"—his glasses glittered coldly at me—"that is, the Sergeant did."

"All right—where?"

"Belong to one of those teachers."

"Which one?"

"The good-looking punk—Pierce!"

CHAPTER SEVEN

The instructors in Bannister College did all right for themselves. Edward Pierce, the art teacher, had a small suite at one end of the building with two exposures onto the spacious grounds. There was a small combination study and living room with a bedroom beyond. Both were empty when we walked in.

The living room looked like an antique shop or a seventeenth-century armory. Over the fireplace against the far wall, there was a pair of dueling pistols crossed; a complete suit of armor stood in the corner. I was tempted to lift the visor and look inside, but the regularity with which we were finding corpses tonight deterred me.

Pierce was obviously a collector of exotic ways to commit murder. In addition to the dueling pistols, I recognized a murderous-looking machete, a Malay creese, and a bola from the Argentine. The place was stacked with weapons.

Slade looked at me triumphantly. "What did I tell you, Lieutenant? The guy must be a homicidal maniac."

"Where is Pierce?"

"Polnik went to get him. He's down at the other prof's room—the one who looks like an ad for a Greenwich Village espresso joint."

"Dufay," I filled in the name. I turned my back on Slade, wandered around the room. On the desk was a knife case, its cover open, its interior showing where two knives should have been—but weren't.

"That's the box they came from," Slade breathed over my shoulder. He punched a stubby forefinger at the unmistakable depressions in the lining of the box. "You can tell it's them."

There was a sharp rap at the door. "Come in," I said.

Polnik opened the door, pushing the Madison Avenue type instructor in front of him. "Here he is, Lieutenant."

Pierce frowned. "Now, really, Lieutenant, I must protest this invasion of my privacy and—"

"Maybe we ought to take you down to headquarters and ask the questions." I watched while his mouth fixed in a stubborn thin line. "What do you do around here, run a museum?"

"I collect old weapons—museum pieces. It's my hobby."

I picked up the empty box. "And this?"

He hesitated for a moment. "There were a couple of matched stilettos in there. I—I haven't looked lately, but the last time I did they were in there." He tried to meet my stare, and dropped his eyes. "I—I did wonder a bit when I saw the handle of the knife that killed Jean. I thought it might be one of mine—" He shrugged. "You know how it is. No one wants to get mixed up in a murder if he can avoid it."

I studied the plush royal blue velvet lining and the indentations made by the knife. "When did you see them last?"

"I can't be sure. A week, ten days maybe—" his voice faltered. "You have to believe me, Lieutenant. I never—"

"You mean to tell me that after the idea struck you that maybe it was your knife in Jean Craig's back you didn't come back here and check for yourself—"

Perspiration started to pop out in small beads on his forehead. "I didn't have much chance. First, Miss Bannister asked me to help herd the girls out of the auditorium, and then we were all asked to meet there for questioning—"

"You didn't answer the question."

He brought a handkerchief from his hip pocket and swabbed at the beaded perspiration. "I—" He broke off, shrugged helplessly. "I did run in for just a moment. Both knives were gone!"

I shook my head. "Maybe if you'd leveled with us, the second one wouldn't have turned up in Nancy Ritter's back." I watched him swabbing his face. "Give me a description of these medieval switchblades."

"They were stilettos, actually. Quite valuable, really." He replaced the handkerchief in his hip pocket. "Narrow triangular blade, made in Brescia—a very famous name in the seventeenth century, Lieutenant. They were designed as thrusting weapons primarily, of course, and their temper—"

"I'm not interested in their moods, just their description," I snapped at him. "They're the shivs, all right. And you say you saw them in this case about a week ago and didn't look again until tonight."

"And they were gone," he said, bobbing his head.

I turned to Polnik and Slade. "Sergeant, you'd better get on back to Miss Bannister's office. Finish questioning the girls and the faculty."

He nodded and left.

"And me, Lieutenant?" Slade wanted to know.

"You remember the find you made when you were searching the girls' rooms?"

He scowled in concentration for a moment, then his brow cleared and a broad smile lit up his kisser. He nodded.

"Good," I told him. "Get it and bring it up here."

He touched his finger to the brim of his hat like a Warner Brothers cop in a 1920s movie. Then he turned and hustled out of the room. I was beginning to think we ought to make it mandatory for the men to watch the *Late Late Show*. Those cops sure showed Edward G. Robinson a lot of respect in those days. Maybe we could use some of it today.

After Slade had left, I fumbled through my pockets for another cigarette. The way things were going I was on my way to becoming a chain smoker. I just hoped I wouldn't run short of chains.

Pierce looked at me anxiously. "You think the murderer stole those knives from me, Lieutenant?"

"I think he used them," I said.

"What do you mean by that?"

"If they were his own property, he wouldn't have to steal them, would he?"

A dull flush crept over his face. "Are you accusing me of—"

"Not yet," I said.

Slade came back into the room and handed me the Frontier Colt. He looked disappointed when I told him to go down to help Polnik.

I handed the Colt to Pierce. "Maybe you recognize that, since you're an authority on ancient weapons."

"Of course," he said. "It's a Frontier Colt, single-action."

"Even I know that," I said. "Have you seen it before?"

"Of course," he said. "It was mine."

"Was?"

"Yes—I gave it to Jean Craig."

"Why?"

"A present, that's all. She came from Nevada, you know—lived on a ranch—I thought it might appeal to her."

"And did it?"

"I think so."

"Were you hoping she'd blow her brains out with it?"

He jumped, then tried to smile. "With this?"

"Didn't you look to see if it was loaded?"

"Loaded!" His laugh sounded genuine. "Really, Lieutenant, this gun hasn't been—" He stopped laughing suddenly and cocked the trigger. His face paled. "But it couldn't! That cartridge couldn't have been there all the time!"

"For a century you mean? I'll go along with that. But it's easy enough to drop in at your friendly neighborhood gun shop any day of the week, as you well know, and get the bullet to fit this toy. You don't have to be an expert to know that, but it helps."

"But you don't think for a moment that I … what on earth would I want to do it for?"

"You might have wanted her to have an accident," I said. "A convenient accident—if she'd looked down the barrel and pulled the trigger, that would have been a convenient accident. It's the sort of warning story the papers like—never trust a gun, however old."

Pierce blinked at me. "That's a crazy thing to say! Why would I want to kill Jean?"

"I don't know yet," I said. "But I'll find out. There could be plenty of good reasons. You were fooling around with her—and the Ritter girl. You admitted that yourself. Maybe things had gone farther than you'd intended—maybe she was taking you seriously. Maybe she was threatening to talk to Miss Bannister or her father. That would ruin your career, wouldn't it? Maybe she was blackmailing you—or maybe you were blackmailing her and she threatened to expose you."

"This is fantastic!" he said, his voice tremulous. "It's something out of a nightmare!"

"You had the opportunity," I persisted. "The weapons belonged to you. You killed her to keep her mouth shut and then you had to kill the Ritter girl to keep her mouth shut. They were close friends—you'd also fooled around a little with the Ritter girl—you knew she'd realize you had killed Jean Craig so you killed her too. Or maybe a big operator like you was getting trouble—or blackmail money—from both girls."

"No!" he said. "No!" He sat down suddenly in a chair and put his hands to his face and began to cry.

I picked up the phone and rang Polnik in Miss Bannister's office. I glanced at my watch and saw it was only ten after midnight. It felt like four in the morning.

"How's your questioning going?" I asked him when he answered.

"Slow, Lieutenant," he said. "I'm questioning the sixth one right now."

At that rate it was going to take about another twelve hours to get through all of them.

"Fold it up," I said. "Take whoever you've got there now back to the auditorium and wait for me. I'll be down there in a couple of minutes. And send Slade up here again."

I waited in silence for Slade to appear while Pierce finally managed to regain control of himself and blew his nose loudly. With the noise he made it was just as well the Walls of Jericho weren't close by.

Slade came in, slightly out of breath. "You keep this up, Lieutenant, and I'm going to lose ten pounds!"

"I'll try and figure out how," I said, and handed him a key. "You've got another candidate for the boiler room."

Slade lifted his eyebrows. "Him?" He jerked a thumb in Pierce's direction.

"Him," I agreed. "When you've locked him in there, come back to the auditorium—that's where I'll be."

"Sure, Lieutenant," Slade said. "Okay—on your feet!" he snarled at

Pierce.

I walked out of the room and back down to the auditorium.

Polnik met me outside the door. "They're all back in there now," he said. "And they're beginning to raise hell about being kept there."

"They won't be there much longer," I said, "I'm going in to talk to them. Don't look surprised at whatever I say."

"Lieutenant," he said, "I'm way past being surprised at anything you do."

I walked into the hall with him and a nasty growling sound came up from the people seated there as they saw me. I walked up onto the stage and stood there facing them.

"Ladies and gentlemen," I said, "I'm sorry we've had to keep you here so long. It was necessary so that we could conduct a complete investigation into the two murders. Not only that—by having you all together in the one place, we hoped to prevent the possibility of a further murder occurring."

A bald-headed gentleman whom I imagined was Professor Coleman, remembering Caroline's description, bounced onto his feet. "May I ask, sir," he said heavily, "if you propose to keep us here forever on those grounds?"

"No, sir," I said. "You all may leave within the next five minutes."

"I should think so!" he thundered. "This has been an outrage, sir! An intolerable outrage!"

"So were two murders," I said.

He sank back into his seat, still muttering to himself.

"Ladies and gentlemen," I started again, "you'll be glad to know the reason why I am letting you leave the hall. There is no longer any danger—the murderer has been caught!"

An excited roar went up from the audience—I was really wowing them tonight. I waited patiently until it subsided. "He has been charged with first-degree homicide and has already left the building on his way to Police Headquarters by car. So I wish you good night and hope you sleep soundly."

Coleman bounced to his feet again. "You mean to say, sir, that after making an announcement like that you aren't even going to give us his name!"

"I thought you would have guessed, Professor," I said. "He's the one member of the college not here—the gentleman who included murder among the arts."

"Pierce!" he said. "You're mad!"

There was a cry of agony from someone three seats away from Coleman. She half-rose from her chair, her face twisted with pain. "No!" Miss Bannister moaned. "No, it can't be!" Then she swayed on her feet for a moment before sliding gently to the floor.

I can only say it was absolutely spiffing the way Miss Tomlinson took charge from then on. She held them back to give the Head some air, and then picked up the Head in her arms as if she was a babe rather than around a hundred and ten pounds of delectable femininity, and carried her out of the auditorium and into her office.

I followed them inside and closed the door firmly.

Miss Tomlinson put Miss Bannister down gently on the sofa along the far wall and patted her hand briskly. "She'll be all right, you know," she said. "It was just the shock, that's all."

"It was quite a shock too," I said. "I wonder why?"

"School secrets," Miss Tomlinson said briskly. "Shouldn't tell but you're a policeman, after all, so it's not blabbing to tell you, really, is it?"

"Positively not," I agreed.

"She was sweet on him," Miss Tomlinson said. "Can't for the life of me see why. I always thought Pierce was an underhand sort of chappie, you know. I've seen the look in his eye when he's watched some of the students walk past in the corridors." She shook her head. "Unhealthy, I call it. What he needed was more exercise and more cold baths in the mornings—that would have stopped that sort of rot. Now, you take my Augustus—we're going to be hitched, you know. I'm looking forward to it, rather jolly and romantic and all that sort of thing, and he needs someone to look after him, poor lamb. But you wouldn't catch my Augustus leering at the students. He knows the difference between good clean feelings and the other kind!"

Miss Bannister's eyes fluttered open. "Edward?" she said in a dazed voice, then fainted again.

"Shock," Miss Tomlinson said. "Better she takes her time to come out of it, don't you agree, Lieutenant?"

"I agree," I said.

Suddenly Miss Tomlinson beamed at me. "Congrats, old boy! Mighty fast piece of work!"

"Huh?"

"Finding out it was Pierce who did it. Jolly good. Better than the movies even. It's certainly been a thrilling evening for all of us. When I think of those two poor girls …" She shook her head. "He's nothing but a monster! A depraved monster I'd call him, Lieutenant, and I'm not normally given to strong language. Don't believe in it. If you have a healthy mind in a healthy body, graceful speaking is simply inevitable. Don't you agree, Lieutenant?"

"I can only come fifty per cent of the way with you," I said. "I have a healthy body."

She snorted and went on patting Miss Bannister's hand. There was a timid knock on the door. I opened it and Dufay smiled at me weakly. "Is Agatha—that is, Miss Tomlinson—still inside, please, Lieutenant?"

"Sure," I said. "Come in."

"Thank you," he said and came in.

His fiancée threw him a brief smile. "You were worrying about me, dear heart!" She looked at me. "Augustus has some beautiful character traits, Lieutenant! I'm only out of his sight for two minutes and already he's worrying about me."

"He's probably practicing to be a husband," I suggested. "It's a marriage cycle. First the husbands worry about their wives and then it's the wives' turn."

"I think you're being cynical," she frowned. "Cynicism is our worst enemy, Lieutenant. You should fight it—have a jolly bout of fisticuffs with it. You'll be surprised at the results."

"I don't think my cynicism would be," I said.

Miss Bannister moaned softly without opening her eyes.

Dufay cleared his throat. "My love?"

"Dearest?" Miss Tomlinson answered, and I shuddered.

"I want to have a talk with you, sweetheart—"

"Augustus," she said benevolently. "You can see I'm busy now. I'll talk to you later—now run along."

Dufay hesitated for a moment, then walked toward the door. He closed it gently behind him and a moment later Miss Bannister sighed deeply and opened her eyes again.

"There, there, Head," Miss Tomlinson said maternally. "You'll be all right now. Perhaps the Lieutenant would get you a glass of water?"

"I'll fix it," I said. "I have to talk to Miss Bannister too. Thanks for your help, Miss Tomlinson." I held the door open for her.

"I don't think I should leave her," she said. "But I suppose I can't defy the long arm of the law, can I?" She smiled roguishly as she walked past me. "I wouldn't like to do a stretch behind bars, would I?"

"I guess not," I said.

"Well," she said, pausing outside, "be a good sport, won't you, Lieutenant? I mean—play the game and all that—the Head's had a nasty turn and it's up to you to help her put her best foot forward, isn't it?"

"Oh, sure," I agreed.

"1 knew I could rely on you," she said. "You're the type that we call 'Public School' at home—always keep a stiff upper lip and never think of being unkind to animals!"

I closed the door gently in her face before I was tempted to stronger action. I turned around and saw Miss Bannister was sitting up on the couch and I remembered the glass of water. I got her half a glass of water, the other half of the glass being filled with Scotch, and gave it to her.

She drank it down quickly and gave me back the empty glass.

"Thank you," she said in a quiet voice. "I'm afraid that was a shock."

"Miss Tomlinson explained it to me," I said. "You are sweet on Pierce, she tells me."

"If she means I'm in love with him the answer is yes," she said. "And to think that Edward could kill anyone—let alone those two young girls—is ridiculous."

"The evidence isn't," I said.

"I don't believe it," she said. "You see, Lieutenant, I know Edward—and you don't. If there is evidence against him it's false—or else you are putting the wrong interpretation on it."

"What makes you so sure?"

"I told you—I know him."

"A court won't accept that sort of evidence."

She got to her feet. "I see no point in discussing the matter any further," she said coldly. "And since your business in my school is apparently finished, I should be glad if you would leave the building at your earliest convenience, Lieutenant."

"I still have some things to check on," I said. "It'll take me quite a while."

"Then at least I can ask you to leave my office."

"Sure," I said. I opened the door and looked back at her. "If you think Pierce is innocent, who would you pick?"

"Dufay," she said without hesitation. "That man is a monster. How he's gulled poor silly Tomlinson into thinking he loves her and means to marry her, I don't know. The only thing that's stopped me telling her is that I know she wouldn't believe me."

"If he's that bad, why haven't you fired him?"

She looked at me for what seemed a long time, then looked away. "That's a fair question, Lieutenant. You'd better close the door and come inside again—and I'll show you why."

CHAPTER EIGHT

She opened the bottom drawer of her desk with a key and took out a folder. Her face was stiff as she straightened up and handed me the folder.

"I think you'll find the answer inside, Lieutenant," she said. "I am going to have another drink—I need it. Can I offer you one?"

"That's the kindest thing that's been said to me in hours!"

I put the folder on the desk and opened it, hearing the welcome sound of a bottle tinkling against glass in the background.

The folder contained a few newspaper clippings. The first one had a large headline: "Con girl gets two years!" and underneath a picture of Miss Bannister. A very young-looking Miss Bannister. The clipping was dated four years back and it was from a Baltimore newspaper.

The story told how the girl—Edwina Bannister—had conned a thousand dollars from a prominent businessman. She had sold him a half-share in a mythical oil well by producing forged documents of ownership and fake reports that claimed the well was loaded with oil and needed only some money spent on plant and equipment to reap the owner a fortune.

Fortunately, the newspaper recalled, the businessman's attorney had heard of the project and, being suspicious, he had investigated and, subsequently called in the police.

The story was routine—what had made it a front page story was the fact that Edwina Bannister was the disinherited daughter and only child of a Connecticut millionaire. She had been thrown out of her home at the age of nineteen because of some undisclosed rift with her father and he had publicly stated he never wanted to see her again and she would never get a penny of his money.

I finished reading the clipping and the others which were on the same theme, covering different stages of the affair, the arrest, the court verdict and so on. Then I looked up and saw Miss Bannister standing beside me, holding out a glass.

"Thanks," I said automatically and took it.

"My father had a change of heart at the last moment," she said in a toneless voice. "Revoked his will and left me everything—of course the millionaire bit is a typical newspaper exaggeration—it was a lot less than that."

I drank the Scotch down and began to feel that maybe my stomach would stay in one piece until morning.

"I served eighteen months in the women's penitentiary. When they released me I heard from his lawyers that he had died six months before and I inherited the estate. I sold up everything and came to California. The one thing I wanted to do was forget the past and make sure that no one else remembered it.

"I got the idea of running a college like this. I had the money to establish it—I knew I could do it. And it would be a perfect cover. Who would ever dream that the principal of an exclusive finishing school for girls could have been a criminal and served a sentence in the penitentiary?" She laughed without any humor. "Then a year ago I had a vacancy for a language teacher and Dufay was one of the applicants. His qualifications were good, so I hired him. What I didn't know at the time was that he'd taught in Baltimore for a year, around the time those headlines hit, and he remembered me."

"And he produced the clippings, and threatened to expose you if you didn't pay up?"

"Exactly."

"And you paid up?"

"I paid. Some thirty thousand dollars so far. I would have gone on paying if this hadn't happened. He could ruin me entirely—not only my college and my social standing in the community—he could have ruined my future with the man I love—Edward."

"Why did you show me these clippings?"

"Because it's gone too far," she said. "I can't see Edward falsely accused of murder. I don't care what happens to me but I won't see anything happen to him."

I lit a cigarette. "It looks like you've proved Dufay to be a blackmailer, but that doesn't necessarily mean he's also a murderer."

"Once he knew I wouldn't dare say anything to him, he became a different man," she said. "I knew he was always trying to date the students and meeting with some success, but I didn't dare put a stop to it. I couldn't fire him and he would have only laughed at me if I'd told him to stop."

She leaned forward, her face tensed. "I'm sure you'll find he had a very good reason for killing both those girls, Lieutenant. He's a genius in some things—an evil genius! That front he puts on—the meek and mild, bewildered manner. You've seen how it's got poor Tomlinson fooled. Underneath that, he's as hard as nails!"

"I'll have a look at it," I said. "This blackmail—you're prepared to give evidence in court against him?"

She bit her lip for a moment, then nodded. "Yes, I'll give evidence against him."

"Okay," I said. "I'll have a talk with him."

I went out of the office and found Polnik and Slade waiting for me.

"Lieutenant," Polnik said wearily, "what gives? You tell 'em in there you arrested this guy Pierce and he's on his way to Headquarters and everything is wrapped up, so I get outside the place and first thing happens, Slade tells me that Pierce is locked in the boiler room along with the other two! They're transferring Homicide to the boiler room, maybe?"

"If I explained it, it would sound just as stupid to me as it does to you," I said. "So I'm not going to explain it. See if you can find the kitchen—it shouldn't be hard—and make some coffee. I'll see you there in about twenty minutes. Okay?"

"Okay, Lieutenant," Polnik said in a resigned voice.

I left them and went along to the residential wing. I knocked on the door bearing Dufay's name and heard a furtive scuffling inside.

"Who is it?" Dufay called out in a nervous voice.

"Wheeler," I said. "Open up! I want to talk to you."

"It's very late, Lieutenant and—"

"Open up," I said, "before I bust the door in!"

There was the sound of a key scraping in a lock and then the door opened.

Miss Tomlinson stood there, her face a fiery red.

"Augustus was upset," she said. "So I thought I'd just stop by and talk to him for a moment, Lieutenant. He locked the door in case any of the other masters dropped in. We didn't want any—" she gulped "—well, nasty-minded surmises, if you know what I mean."

"I have a faint idea," I said. "But we Public School types don't go in much for that sort of thing. You know—Rugger, cold baths, walks in the country, and cricket, of course—they keep our minds much too busy for any unhealthy surmises and all that sort of rot."

She brushed past me, her face an even deeper shade of scarlet, and ran down the corridor.

Dufay blinked at me nervously. "What is it, Lieutenant?"

"I've been talking to Miss Bannister," I said, stepping inside the room and pushing the door shut behind me. "Or anyway—she's been talking to me."

"Oh?" he said. "About me?"

"About you."

"Really, Lieutenant, I can't see what possible interest I could be to you—or Miss Bannister, apart from the work of the college, naturally."

"Come off it, Dufay. Miss Bannister has a very special interest in you, purely extracurricular, just as you have in her—and I'm speaking of finance, not romance, in case you think I'm confused."

"I'm afraid I don't follow you, Lieutenant."

"I think you're ahead of me, pal," I said. "I'm talking about that unfortunate lapse of Miss Bannister's that you capitalized on. I'm talking about—to be coarse—blackmail, the money you've extorted from her. I hope I make myself clear?"

He shook his head, a bewildered expression on his face. "It's Greek to me, Lieutenant."

"Okay," I said. "Then you have five minutes to translate it, or I'll send you down to Headquarters and have you booked on an extortion charge."

His mustache quivered like a suspension bridge. "I think you must be mad, Lieutenant," he said. "You come bursting into my room accusing me of blackmail!"

"You have four and three-quarter minutes left, Dufay," I said. "If you run out of adjectives before the time's up—ask me. I smoke in my bath, too."

"You're insane!" he said. "A manic depressive!"

Someone pounded on the door. There must be something about me and doors—every time I get behind one, somebody starts to pound it.

"Lieutenant!" It was Slade again.

"Keep the coffee hot," I said. "I'll get it later."

"Never mind the coffee, Lieutenant! The Sheriff's on the phone and he's raising all hell!"

That was different.

"Come in here," I said.

Slade opened the door and rushed in, looking eagerly around him, then looking disappointed that there was only Dufay and myself in the room.

"Just watch this character until I get back," I said.

"You don't want him in the boiler room with the others?"

"It's a wonder the Intelligence Service didn't snap you up!" I said. "You'd be just the boy to keep an official secret!"

I walked back to Miss Bannister's office. She had gone but her perfume lingered. I picked up the phone off the desk and said who I was.

"Wheeler!'—the word buckled my eardrum. "I have an official complaint—what's this about you calling out a doctor, an ambulance and two attendants, and a police photographer too—all for a corpse that wasn't a corpse!"

"The doc drinks too much, I guess," I said. "I've got a corpse here for him—with a knife in her back."

"He's already doing an autopsy on that one!" Lavers shouted.

"Uh huh!" I said. "He's doing the autopsy on the first one—Jean Craig. The second one is Nancy Ritter and her body is still here."

"The doctor said the second one was a man—the conjuror, Mephisto or whatever his name is!"

"I told you Murphy drinks too much, it's another girl. And he's not a conjuror—he's a magician."

"Sorry," Lavers said. "I meant the mag— Who the hell cares what he is! Just how many corpses do you have down there anyhow, Wheeler?"

"Just the two," I said. "Business had been lousy the last couple of hours."

There was a noise like somebody chewing uncooked spaghetti.

"I'll keep you informed, Sheriff," I said politely.

"Wheeler, I know you like to handle things your own way. You like to be secretive about things. I don't mind that—not at all. Just so long as you produce results—and you *are* producing results"—his voice hit a rising inflection of hope—"aren't you?"

"Two corpses already!" I said.

"Let me put it to you another way," he said, nearly choking on the words. "I told you the pupils of that school come from some of the most influential families in Pine City. And so help me, Wheeler, if you can't come up with something ..."

"I get the picture, sir," I interrupted. "Let me put it to you another way. Murphy says I called them out to a corpse that vanished. I say he drinks too much. It's only his word against mine, and I have a genuine corpse to back up my statements."

"Was he really drunk?" Lavers asked incredulously.

"Confidentially, no," I said. "What he told you was true—it's too complicated to explain, but what I've just told you now is true too. I do now have that second corpse and—"

"Wheeler!" he said hoarsely. "You didn't kill somebody just to put one over on Doc Murphy!"

"If I'd been going to do that it would have been Murphy himself!"

"Well, that's something, anyway. But what in hell's happening out there?"

"I'm not too sure myself," I admitted. "But give me till morning, anyway, Sheriff. Blackmail Murphy—tell him I've got a real corpse out here and he's going to look pretty stupid telling everybody I haven't."

"You know the thing that really depresses me," he said in a trembling voice. "If I'd gone out there to give that lecture, I'll guarantee nothing would have happened. No murder—nothing. And I'd be sleeping peacefully in my bed right now instead of twisting my ulcer!"

He hung up, bending my eardrum again. I put the phone back onto the rest and crossed all my fingers carefully that Dufay would be ready to talk when I got back to him. I stepped out of the office and cannoned into Polnik.

"Why don't you—" He recognized me and gulped. "Sorry, Lieutenant."

"That's all right," I said. "I still have most of me left—I think. What's new?"

"The coffee's wasting," he said. "That Bannister dame came looking for us, said there was a phone call for you, so I sent Slade back to tell you. Then as neither of you came back to the kitchen I thought I'd come look for you."

"And you found me, you lucky sergeant, you," I said. "You might as well tag along—I left Slade watching Dufay."

"What for?"

"To see he didn't get away."

"Why would he want to get away?"

"I'm hoping he'll tell me," I said.

"Sure, Lieutenant," he said slowly.

"Does that make sense to you?" I asked him.

"Not a word," he said. "But I've given up worrying now."

"It must be a relief," I said.

We reached the door of Dufay's room again and I opened it. The room was empty.

"Looking for somebody, Lieutenant?" a voice asked from a little way down the corridor.

I turned around slowly and saw Caroline Partington leaning against the wall. She wore a silk robe over silk pajamas—at first glance you got the impression that she had a silken skin. "They went thata way, partner!" she said and pointed back the way we had come.

I counted to ten slowly, then told Polnik to take a look and see if Slade had taken Dufay down into the boiler room. If he had, I promised myself that I'd feed him limb by limb into the furnace before the night was through.

CHAPTER NINE

Polnik hurried down the corridor and I walked in the opposite direction toward Caroline. She yawned gently as I came close to her.

"I can't sleep," she said. "I'm a nervous, mixed-up kid!"

"Do tell," I said.

"I've lost my fatal allure," she said. "I can't sleep nights any more. I throw myself at a man and what happens?" Her voice took on a slight edge. "He gets out of the way—that's what happens—and I fall flat on my—"

"Face?" I offered.

"Of course, Lieutenant," she said. "You don't think that any student attending Miss Bannister's College would be so unladylike as to fall on her—"

"The idea is unthinkable," I said. "How long ago did Dufay and Slade leave that room?"

"Slade is the funny little man with glasses?" she asked.

"It depends on your sense of humor whether you think he's funny or not—but the rest of the description is accurate."

"About three, four ... five minutes ago."

"They just walked out of the room into the corridor and went thata way?"

"You've got it," she said. "That's exactly how it was."

"Did they see you?"

"I don't think so," she said. "Neither of them looked this way at all."

"And you're out here because you can't sleep?"

"Check," she said. "And what is your story, Lieutenant?"

"I need a reason?"

"The last I heard I thought you would have rushed into town to see your murderer being brought face to face with justice."

"I'm just naturally soft-hearted," I said. "The thrill of the chase is enough for me."

"I've seen that already," she said tartly. "I'll say this for you—you're certainly unorthodox. You must be the only guy in the world who ever fought his way out of a girl's room!"

"The call of duty," I said. "And while I'm waiting around here, give me a quick rundown on Dufay."

"Haven't I done that already?"

"Try again—and stay clear of that double-talk. This time I want to be able to understand it."

She yawned again. "Okay. Well, he's an egghead for a start." She paused then and gave me a sharp look. "You do understand that word, don't you? Not too new for you is it?"

I sighed heavily. "All right, comedian. Of course I know that one—I've been an egghead myself for years. And what's more, everyone over twenty-two on a college campus is an egghead—everybody knows that. So make with the news already."

"Well, eggheads have a certain irresistible appeal for women of all ages—"

"You're telling me?"

"—while non eggheads appeal only to the very young and the very old."

I waited. She'd finished. "You should write a book," I said finally.

"Who would dare print it?" she said disdainfully. "Is that what you wanted to know about Dufay?"

"Hardly."

"What else do you want to know?"

"What's his attitude to the students generally?"

"Wolfish, definitely W.F.C."

"Spell it out!"

"Wolf First Class—you must have been behind a rock for years!"

"You know something?" I said. "You intrigue me—in a macabre sort of way."

"In any way and I'm thankful," she said. "Would you care to see my etchings, Lieutenant?"

She leaned toward me and I got another whiff of the scent she wore. I found myself thinking how nice it would be to relax and just be sent by the scent.

The silk gown had a sway of its own as she moved closer to me, her tip-tilted breasts tracing little designs on the silk. I caught myself asking myself what was the rush? Nancy Ritter and Jean Craig weren't going anyplace anyhow—and a few hours wouldn't make much difference to them …

"Lieutenant!" a hoarse voice bawled from the other end of the hall. It blasted its way into my consciousness, broke the fascination of the scent and the shimmering silk.

I turned to see Polnik beckoning to me from the far end of the hall.

"Damn!" Caroline Partington said in an unladylike tone. "You must have some kind of a distress signal that when your temperature gets to a certain point, bells go off and your minions come charging in to rescue you."

"It's just that Providence watches over me. It's like Miss Tomlinson says—if you take enough cold baths—"

"You get pneumonia," the blonde told me coldly. "Whereas I've never lost a patient to pneumonia yet. High blood pleasure, maybe—but pneumonia never."

"Well, I must be off—"

"You certainly are."

I passed up the chance for some clever repartee and hurried down the hall to where Polnik stood waiting, his eyes bulging. From the look of him there was more trouble. "Don't tell me somebody wiped out the whole second floor?"

He shook his head. "I haven't been up there yet. You sent me to check if Slade took the fancy pants guy to the boiler room."

"You were right. He took him, there. He's still there."

"Dufay?"

Polnik swallowed hard and shook his head. "Slade."

I groaned. "And the others?"

"The door's wide open and the boiler room's empty. Somebody clouted Slade behind the ear and he's sleeping it off on the floor."

"Still among the living?"

The sergeant nodded. "He's out like a light, but he'll live."

"Oh well, we can't have everything," I told him. "And the rest—Mephisto, Spike, and the two teachers—all gone?"

"Not a sign of them. By now they're probably making tracks for four corners of the earth."

I tossed it around in my mind. "Maybe. Maybe not. Mephisto and Spike probably won't stop running until they hit the Pacific Ocean and then they'll only stop long enough to take a deep breath before they dive in. They've got too many strikes against them."

Polnik frowned. "And the teachers?"

"They have women in their lives and those women are right here. My guess is that they won't get too far away from them. I'll bet right now you'll find Dufay hiding behind Miss Tomlinson's skirts."

"Miss who?"

"The one with the healthy mind and the absolutely spiffing sense of humor."

"Oh, that!"

"Go search for that," I told him. "When you find that, you should find Dufay. I'll find Pierce."

"Okay, Lieutenant." He shook his head. "This job is sure different then I had it figured out before I signed up."

"How's that?"

"I had it figured that by being a cop there was one thing you could count on getting."

"Flat feet?"

"No, respect." He looked at me sadly. "I never figured I'd be spending all my time looking for criminals behind a woman's skirts." He snorted. "Most of them couldn't hide a midget behind the skirts they wear." He wandered off down the hall, muttering to himself.

I figured if I was right in telling Polnik Dufay would be hiding behind Miss Tomlinson's skirts, I would find Pierce doing likewise with Miss Bannister. I tried her office first. It was empty. It figured that it'd be more interesting to hide behind her skirts in her apartment than in her office, anyhow.

I retraced my steps into the residential wing. Caroline was still leaning against the wall outside her door.

"Tell me if you move away the roof will fall in and I'll probably believe you!" I said.

"There must be a leak in the roof," she said to no one in particular. "Here comes a drip!"

"Where do I find Miss Bannister's room?" I asked her gently. "And if you say something funny, so help me I'll take your arm and break it!"

"It's number twenty-eight," she said, "around the corner and down at the far end of the corridor." She looked at me and her eyes were wide open for the first time since I'd met her. "My!" she said. "You almost frightened me then!"

"Sometimes I even frighten myself," I said. "Most times it's shaving— I get a candid picture of myself when I'm not expecting it."

I walked on down the corridor and heard mules shuffling hurriedly behind me. I look back and saw Caroline was half running after me.

"You go back and look after that wall," I said. "Who wants the roof to fall in!"

"Let me come with you," she said breathlessly. "I just know it's going to be exciting!"

"No," I said.

"I don't care what you say!" she said. "I'm coming with you anyway."

I stopped at the next door along and thumped on it. It was opened about twenty seconds later by a redhead in a pair of baby-doll pajamas which proved she was certainly a doll, but anything more remote from a baby you couldn't imagine. And I do have an imagination for that sort of thing.

"Why," she said sleepily. "It's that crime-buster in person!"

"You have a key to your room?" I snapped.

"Of course."

"Give it to me—quickly!"

"But what …" She fumbled on the inside of the lock for a moment, then handed me the key.

"Stand back!" I said fiercely.

She backed off quickly, her hand to her mouth. "What are you going to do?" she quavered.

Caroline stepped up close beside me. "What are you doing, Lieutenant?" she asked interestedly. "What's going on?"

"Not on," I corrected her, "in!"

I caught hold of her arm, swung her off balance, then gave her a push. She stumbled forward helplessly into the room and into the arms of the redheaded doll.

I swung the door shut and put the key into the lock and turned it. I removed the key, dropped it into my hip pocket, and continued on my way down the corridor.

I found number twenty-eight and stopped for a moment outside the door while I debated if I should knock. I decided against it.

I turned the handle gently. The door moved inward, so I swung it open hard and stepped inside quickly.

The living room was empty, and so was the bedroom, except for Miss Bannister. She stood in the center of the room, a frozen tableau with a slip halfway over her head.

She gave a jerk and the slip came right over her head and dropped to the floor. She looked at me with frozen-faced indignation.

She wore nothing under the slip. The décolleté gown that had given a hint of the full bosom hadn't been misleading. Her waist was narrow and swelled softly to well-rounded thighs. Her legs were long and perfectly shaped.

For a moment, she stood frozen with surprise. "What are you—"

"You make a charming picture, Miss Bannister," I told her.

My words seemed to bring her out of her trance. She looked down, saw her state of nakedness, and colored becomingly. She grabbed a robe from the back of a chair, shrugged into it, and tied it tightly around her waist. It didn't spoil it for me—I have a photographic memory.

She turned toward me angrily. "What do you mean by bursting into my private quarters like this? Are you in the habit of entering a room without knocking?"

"No," I admitted. "But if I can expect results like this, it's a habit worth cultivating." I looked around the room carefully—Pierce was either under the bed or inside the wardrobe or he wasn't there at all. That's the sort of snap deduction I can make any time—given a room with a bed and a wardrobe and no other furniture than could possibly hide anybody bigger than a lapdog.

"I was looking for a friend of yours," I said. "Name of Pierce."

"Edward!" she said eagerly. "You mean they let him go—that he hasn't been charged after all!"

"Well … yes and no," I said.

"You're wonderful, Lieutenant!" she said excitedly. "You went and saw Dufay and got the truth out of him that he killed those girls! I know it! You're a genius and I could kiss you—and I will!"

Before I could stop her—not that I would have tried—she flung her arms around my neck and kissed me passionately. I kissed her back—passionately. It seemed the only fair thing to do.

So there we were, kissing each other—passionately. And there, as far as I was concerned, we would have stayed till the middle of the following week but like always, I got interrupted.

"Just relax, Lieutenant," Pierce's voice said from behind me. "Don't try and go for your gun—I'll blow a hole right through you if you do."

"I'll let you into a secret, Pierce," I said. "I never wear a gun under a dinner jacket—it spoils the line."

"I'm not taking any chances on that," he said.

Miss Bannister looked at me scornfully. "I suppose you thought we'd do something stupid, like have Edward hide behind the door or under the bed or something."

"Something like that," I agreed. "Where did he come from?"

"The room across the hall is empty," she said, smiling with triumph. "Edward has been waiting in there—we knew you would think he'd come to me as soon as he was free. So we waited for you to come to us—you're very necessary to us, Lieutenant Wheeler."

"I'm flattered," I said. "Most nobody wants a cop."

"We do," she said. "You're going to be our passport out of here and across the state line."

"Whatever makes you think that?" I asked her.

"This!" Pierce said and jabbed me painfully with the barrel of the gun.

"Where did you get that gun?" I asked him.

"You can't see it, of course, Lieutenant," he said. "I was forgetting that. It's my own property—you remember it, surely?"

It wasn't that Old Black Magic that fingered my spine icily.

"Have you ever fired it before?" I said in a strangled voice.

"No," he said. "It only has the one bullet in it, remember, Lieutenant?"

"I'm remembering all right," I yelped. "And it only needs a light pressure on the trigger. Just don't take a sudden deep breath or anything!"

"Just so long as you do as you're told, Lieutenant," he said evenly, "I won't pull the trigger."

"It's a better than even bet that the bullet won't leave the barrel in any case," I said, not in the least convinced or convincing. "It'll probably blow up in the barrel—how do you think you'll look without a face, Pierce?"

Miss Bannister was giving me a nasty look. "When I think how you got up on that stage and lied your head off!" she said. "Telling everyone that Edward was a murderer and already on his way to Police Headquarters when all the time you had him locked up in that boiler room!"

"That leads me to a point," I said. "Edward—you don't mind me calling you Edward, do you? After all, we're so close at the moment."

"I don't mind," he said. "What was it?"

"How did you get out of the boiler room?"

"That little cop of yours—the one with glasses—he opened the door and pushed Dufay inside, and while he was busy getting Dufay in, the magician hit him. Then we all ran."

"It has the simplicity of all great strategy," I admitted. "Hit and run!"

"We're only wasting time," he said. "You've got your own sports car parked outside, Lieutenant. We're going out of the building and walk to your car. If we meet anyone on the way, you see that they don't become suspicious. If they do, it will be too bad for you."

"The funny thing is," I said, "that right up to now, I hadn't seriously considered you as the murderer at all!"

"What!" Miss Bannister gasped.

"Why do you think I had him put into the boiler room out of sight while I told everyone else he was on his way to Headquarters?"

"Don't ask me to try and explain your actions," she said tartly. "I think you're—"

"Raving?" I said. "I know—most people do. I do sometimes. But you aren't trying very hard to make a decent guess."

"He's only stalling for time," Pierce said impatiently. "We ought to start moving right now."

"I wouldn't," I said. "That's the point I'm getting at. I figured that if I announced an arrest, the murderer would feel safe—and inquisitive. So if I stuck around for awhile, I might with any luck get a lead on him— or her. How do you think the murderer is going to feel if he sees you marching me through the building? Even if you don't hold that gun in my back, you'll have it in your pocket and it will make a very obvious bulge.

"You're giving the murderer a perfect setup for another murder. He shoots you—probably in the back—and then expects to be treated like a hero because he believes, from what I said in the auditorium, that you have been arrested for murder and must have somehow escaped. He sees you marching me outside at gunpoint, so he shoots you to save my life. The Police Department would have to give him a medal!"

Miss Bannister bit her lip. "If he's telling the truth, Edward …"

"Yes," Pierce said nervously. "And he could be—I hadn't thought of that. I don't fancy being shot in the back."

"Very painful," I muttered. "Blood everywhere."

"Don't!" Miss Bannister said tearfully and then came to a decision. "We can't do it, Edward," she said briskly. "We can't afford to take the chance. Now I've got you back, I'm not going to risk losing you, forever."

"If you take that gun out of my back, Edward," I said, "I am prepared to forget the whole thing."

"And put me back into the boiler room! No thanks!" he said bitterly.

"The boiler room has lost its point," I said. "Remember three others got out of there as well as you, and they'll have spread the good word. Just don't turn your back on anybody in a corridor, Edward!" I felt the pressure of the gun removed and my pulse came down to only twenty above normal. I heaved a sigh of relief.

"These lieutenants are really tough, aren't they?" Pierce sneered.

"It's always the amateurs that frighten you," I said.

"If it had been a professional torpedo holding that gun I wouldn't have worried half as much. I'd know he wouldn't kill me accidentally—only deliberately if I tried anything."

I found a cigarette and lit it thankfully. "No," I said, "the boiler room is out, finished! I don't care what you do now, so long as you don't try and leave the building."

"I'll stay right here," Pierce said, grinning at me. "I couldn't think of a better place to stay." He looked down at the Frontier Colt in his hand and laughed. "I never really did put this thing in shape," he said, and before I could stop him, he pointed the gun at the outside wall of the room. "And you thought it could—" I lost the rest of his sentence. There was a violent explosion that nearly took care of my eardrums for good, then a stream of black smoke drifted up from the barrel of the gun. About a foot beneath the window sill there was a hole in the plaster, but no sign of the slug.

I walked over to the hole and found I could get my thumb into it without any trouble at all. I looked around at Pierce and scowled at him. "Just imagine what that slug would have done to my backbone!"

"I am," he said weakly, "and I think I'm going to be sick!" He tottered a couple of paces toward the door and then buckled at the knees and slid gently to the floor, out cold.

"Now look what you've done!" Miss Bannister wailed at me.

"He'll be all right," I said. "Couldn't have happened at a better time. I wanted to ask you something."

"You're a fiend!" she said. "A cruel, heartless fiend!"

"That story you told me," I said. "It wasn't true, was it?"

"Of course it was true about what happened in Baltimore," she said. "You read the newspaper clippings yourself."

"I didn't mean that," I said. "You lied to me about who was blackmailing you, didn't you?"

She moistened her lips with the tip of her tongue for a moment, then looked at me steadily. "Blackmail, Lieutenant?" she said casually. "You must have been dreaming! I never said anything about blackmail!"

CHAPTER TEN

At first it sounded like the chatter of a machine gun spiced by the screams of its victims. Then it sounded like the banshee wail of a wounded tigress screaming defiance at the high-powered rifles popping away at her. It finally narrowed down to the screaming of two girls who were trying to knock a door off its hinges.

Rather guiltily, I remembered the key in my hip pocket that had locked Caroline Partington in with the redhead. I started down the hall to the redhead's room and found Sergeant Polnik getting ready to put his shoulder against the door.

I ran up. "What are you doing, Sergeant?"

"Sounds like the killer's in here with one of the girls. Can't you hear her screaming?"

"Her screaming?" I echoed. "That's a full chorus. I think it's the *Massacre of Bloody Ridge* in there." I took the key from my pocket, stuck it in the door, and opened up.

Caroline Partington stood behind the door, glaring hatred at me. Her face was white with fury, her full lips compressed into a straight line. I looked past her to the redhead. "I'm returning your key. Thanks for the use of the building," I said and replaced the key in the lock on the inside of the door.

"Very funny!" Caroline Partington pushed past me and high-tailed it up the hall in the direction of her room. The redhead grinned at me as I pulled the door closed.

"What was that bit?" Polnik wanted to know as we stood outside in the corridor.

"I keep mislaying my blondes," I told him, and before he could make any cracks, I added, "I just wanted to know where this one was when I wanted her."

He nodded sagely as though he understood, which he didn't. "Find the art teacher, Lieutenant?" he said, changing the subject.

"I found him, for all the good it did me. How about Dufay?"

He shrugged. "That character has stepped off the earth. No sign of him. Disappeared completely."

"You looked in the Tomlinson girl's room?"

"I looked. But I wouldn't expect anybody in his right mind to be cozying up to that female moose. I outweigh Dufay by plenty and I wouldn't want to go up against her."

"No accounting for tastes," I said. "How's Slade?"

"Okay. He's got a sore head, but then he's a natural sore head anyway," Polnik grunted.

"Why, Polnik!" I exclaimed, clapping him on the shoulder. "That's good—that's very good! You keep improving that way, and you'll be a lieutenant like me someday!"

He muttered something under his breath that I didn't catch. I figured it was probably just as well so I didn't press him to repeat it.

"You and Slade better keep looking for Dufay." I answered the unasked question in his eyes—"I want to have a little talk with the redhead in here."

He nodded sourly. "It figured." He turned and headed back down the hallway. It might have been interesting to hear what he was muttering to himself—not very flattering, just interesting.

I rapped my knuckles on the door and the redhead opened it.

"Mind if I come in?" I asked.

"I'd be disappointed if you didn't." She didn't seem to mind the inventory I was taking of her assets. She stood aside. "In fact, I was listening to see if you were leaving. If you were I was going to call out to you."

I walked past her and closed the door behind me. "I'm glad I didn't have to put you to all that trouble."

"No trouble at all," she told me sweetly. "Are you going to give me the third degree?" She shivered deliciously. "I've read all about it, and—"

"Nothing like that," I told her. "I just thought you might be willing to answer a few questions."

"Would you like me to say yes to them?" She smiled brightly. "I think you're quite a guy—handling Caroline the way you did. It's about time somebody pushed her around—she's been unbearable the last few months."

"In what way?"

"In every way," she said. "Upstaging everybody all the time and spending lots of money and everything."

"Her parents must be wealthy," I said.

"I guess they must be," she said. "Though Caroline never talks about them."

"Too proud?"

"I don't know." The redhead wrinkled her nose thoughtfully. "If it comes to that, Caroline never does talk about herself—only about how much she paid for a dress or some jewelry—things like that."

"Thanks," I said and opened the door. "Thanks very much."

"Hey," she said. "Wait a minute! I thought you wanted to ask me some questions!"

"You answered them all for me," I told her. "I think you're gorgeous, too. How old are you?"

"Eighteen," she said.

"Come around and see me when you're twenty-two," I told her. "We could have a date."

"But I'll be married by then!" she said despondently.

"Bring your husband," I said. "And then we'll ditch him in some bar."

"Already I hate him," she said. "I'm considering divorce."

We grinned at each other and I backed out into the corridor and closed the door behind me. I looked at my watch again and saw it was two-twenty. The long night was turning into a longer morning.

I went back to Miss Bannister's office, closed the door carefully, and regretted the fact that the key was missing. I dug into the filing cabinets and after ten minutes or so, found what I wanted—the list of pupils, their home addresses, and the names of their parents. I looked up Caroline Partington and found she was an orphan. Her home address was an apartment in New York, and it was followed by the word "sister" in parentheses.

I put the file back and walked down to Caroline's room and knocked on the door.

"Who is it?" she called out.

"Wheeler," I said. "I have a diamond necklace of yours to return."

"Oh?" she said. "That can wait till morning."

"It is morning."

"Then it can wait until after breakfast!"

"I wanted to talk to you."

"We have nothing to talk about, Lieutenant, not after the way you pushed me around a little while ago!"

"I'm sorry, honey," I said. "But I didn't want you running into any danger and—"

"Say that again!" she said, her voice decidedly warmer.

"I didn't want—"

"Not that part—the beginning!"

"I'm sorry, honey ..."

The door opened and she stood there with a welcoming smile on her face. "Honey!" she said. "That's what you called me. Could it be I'm getting to first base with the Lieutenant at last?"

"It certainly could," I said and stepped into the room, kicking the door shut behind me.

The next moment we were in a clinch and we'd still be in it except after a while my feet began to ache. I gently disengaged her arms from around my neck and dug my hand into my pocket and took out her necklace.

She held out her hand and I dropped the necklace into her palm.

"That must be worth a fortune," I said.

"Oh,"—she shrugged her shoulders carelessly under her robe—"a few thousand, I suppose."

"I can see I don't have much of a chance of competing with the competition on a police lieutenant's pay." I smiled at her.

She laughed. "Don't be silly … Al, isn't it? That necklace wasn't bought for me by any admirer!"

She walked over to the wall cupboard and opened it. "What would you like to drink?"

I stared, goggle-eyed, at the array of bottles displayed inside. "Don't tell me students are allowed to keep liquor in their rooms!"

"Only me," she said, "and it's sort of unofficial, really—but I'm a little bit older than most of them, Al. I'm twenty-two!"

I lit myself a cigarette. "I'll have a Scotch, thanks. Water with it."

"Don't worry," she said, "the lower half of the cupboard is refrigerated— I have ice."

She poured the two drinks and then looked at me. "Come and sit down on the divan over here, Al. It's more cozy."

I did as I was told. She came and sat beside me and handed me my drink.

"Here's to our better acquaintance," she said and drank.

"Agreed."

She moved toward me a little so that we sat like Siamese twins on the divan. "Tell me, Al," she said. "You were kidding weren't you, when you made that announcement about Mr. Pierce being the murderer? You must have been or you wouldn't still be here."

"You're too smart," I said. "Sure—I was kidding. Hoping to lull the real murderer into a false sense of security. It's done in all the best mysteries."

"And have you?"

"That's the trouble," I said. "I don't know. All I know is I've lulled myself into a night without sleep."

"Never mind," she said softly. "I'll try and make it up to you."

"That would be wonderful," I said, "if I could remove that lurking streak of jealousy that's still inside me."

"You—jealous?" Her eyes sparkled as she looked at me. "Who of?"

"The guy that gave you that necklace."

She laughed. "Then you can stop being jealous, my pet! Daddy gave it to me."

"That sounds better," I said in a relieved voice. "What for?—your twenty-first birthday?"

"Oh, no," she said. "As a matter of fact he only gave it to me last week—he just felt like giving me a present. He always does whenever he comes to see me."

I finished my drink and looked at her over the rim of the empty glass. "Where does he park his wings?"

"What?" She looked at me blankly.

"Or his halo?"

"Al Wheeler," she said. "What on earth are you talking about?"

"Nothing on earth," I said. "I'm talking about your father."

"I don't get it." She shook her head, a puzzled expression on her face. "Sorry, Al, but I just don't get it."

"Forget it," I said. "A corny sort of joke that didn't come off. Would you like to play games?"

"Yes," she said, "with you, Al!"

"This might be a little different," I said. "You play it with words."

"Words!" She got to her feet. "I need another drink. Get you one?"

I gave her my glass. It took her half a minute to refill both glasses and come back to the divan with them again. She sat right beside me and I took the glass out of her hand.

"All right," she said. "Games! With words yet! I suppose we could wait until we've finished this drink, anyway."

"It's a very simple game," I said. "But sometimes it's quite funny. I say a word and you say the first word that comes into your head in answer—it's the sort of thing the tame industrial psychologists amuse themselves with for hours."

"All right," she said doubtfully, "if this is your idea of fun."

"I think it's terrific," I said. "Okay—I'll start ... Black!"

"White!" she said promptly.

"Up!"

"Down!—This is stupid!"

"We haven't gotten started yet, Boy!"

"Girl!"

"Sister!"

"Brother!"

"Baltimore!"

Her mouth opened but no word came out. She smiled at me.

"It often happens," I said. "Don't worry—we'll just keep on going. Father!"

"Mother!"

"Orphanage!"

"Lilyfield Home For—" She bit down on her lower lip.

"You're doing fine!" I said encouragingly. "I guess you've had enough now, though. I did have a few more—it was an amusing sequence I thought, but I can see you're bored with the game. I had a sequence something like orphanage, poor, Baltimore, finishing school, rich, diamonds, blackmail ..."

She finished her drink slowly and deliberately, then looked at me. "I think you're here under false pretenses, Al," she said reproachfully. "I think that underneath you're still going right on being a policeman."

"Could be," I said. "Right now it's such a fascinating problem I can't forget it."

"What?"

"This set-up inside the college," I said. "On the one hand there's the head of it, loaded with money, and on the other the orphan girl who hasn't got any but was lucky enough to be in Baltimore at a time when the conviction of a con girl hit the front pages. The rest of it is like Cinderella. The orphan girl is suddenly rich with beautiful clothes and diamonds ... Don't you care for that story?"

"No," she said coldly, "I don't!"

"That's a pity!" I said. "I hoped you would. It would be so much easier if you did."

"I'm very tired, Al," she said. "Thank you for returning my necklace. Will you please go now?"

I got to my feet and walked over to the cupboard and helped myself to a third drink. "I'll put it on the line," I said. "I can prove the blackmail without any trouble—and get a conviction."

"Then why don't you go ahead!" she said.

"I might make a deal," I said.

"A deal?" She looked up at me suspiciously. "What sort of deal?"

"I want the truth from you—and this time, you make sure it is the truth because it's your last chance!"

"Well," she said in a small voice, "ask your questions then."

"How much have you blackmailed out of Miss Bannister?"

She hesitated a moment. "Five thousand," she said finally.

"Miss Bannister says it's about six times that."

"Then she's lying! Five thousand is all I've had!"

"You were in Baltimore when it happened?"

She nodded. "Working—as a waitress! That's what I was doing here in Pine City when I first arrived. Then I saw Miss Bannister driving past one day and I recognized her right away."

"So you found out what she was doing here and contacted her?"

"Sure," she said. "My folks died when I was six and I was put into an orphanage. That was the first time I'd ever had three meals a day. All my life until I left the orphanage I was determined about one thing— I was going to be rich, Al. And not only rich, but a social success." She got up and poured herself another drink. "It's not that hard to marry money if you move in the right circles. And seeing Edwina Bannister again was my Fairy Godmother at last coming through! I didn't want to blackmail her, I didn't like the idea much, but it was the only way I could get what I wanted. So I made a deal with her. She admitted me here as a student, and I didn't pay any fees, of course. And she paid me five hundred dollars a month as an allowance while I was here. I told her I'd stay a year and then, if she introduced me around the social circles she moved in, the quicker I got a husband with money in the bank, the quicker her payments to me would stop."

It made sense. In some ways I didn't blame her. Blackmail, as they say, is an ugly word, but murder is uglier. I'd made a deal with her to forget the blackmail in return for information. If the information led me to the murderer, I figured it was worth it.

"Okay," I said, "I'll believe that. What about the set-up between Pierce and Miss Bannister?"

She had a look of genuine surprise on her face as she lifted her head. "I didn't know it even existed!"

"It exists all right," I said. "They're crazy about each other—to coin a phrase."

"That's a new one on me!"

"What about the murdered girls? What about Jean Craig and Nancy Ritter? What can you tell me about them? This is the real part of the deal, Caroline. Make it good."

She thought for a moment. "That's the trouble, Al, there isn't anything about them. I can't see any reason why anyone should have wanted to kill them."

"You'll have to do better than this," I said tightly.

"I'm trying to think—honestly," she said in a worried voice. "They were a couple of bright kids, always boasting about their conquests. It was quite funny, really—the only conquests a student can make here are Pierce or Dufay."

I lit a cigarette. "Pierce and Dufay?"

"The only two eligible males around the place," she said. "And naturally those boys certainly make conquests!"

"Even Dufay?"

"Particularly Dufay!" she said. "I told you that before and it was the truth then—he's got a lot of appeal. Not to me, but I'm an exception. I like my men to be a combination of egghead and muscles!"

"I'm enchanted," I said. "Go on about Dufay."

"There was a sort of rivalry between Jean and Nancy—they'd argue with each other about who'd had the most dates with either or both of the men during a week. Some of the other girls used to run a sweepstake on the result!"

"Didn't Miss Bannister know about this?"

Caroline shrugged. "How could she miss it? Everyone knew it."

"Did she try to stop it?"

"She gave Jean a bawling out a couple of days ago—I suppose it was about that. I don't know whether she said anything to the men about it."

"I might be able to find out," I said. "This is the craziest case I ever had!"

"One thing," she said, "they sure picked the right lieutenant to handle it."

"I'm not necessarily the smartest lieutenant in the Department," I said.

"I didn't mean that," she said sweetly. "I meant you're certainly the craziest!"

"Thanks," I said. "Anything else you can tell me?"

"It's just girls' gossip," she said. "And I suppose it's not worth any more than that. You heard about Dufay getting engaged to Miss Tomlinson, I guess?"

"She told me—with bells on."

Caroline giggled. "That's the silliest thing I ever heard! She must think he's still a babe in the wood or something. She'll fuss around him like a mother hen, even in public—and if anybody said anything about him to her, she'd blow her top right away!"

"Yeah," I said. "None of this stuff is helping me at all. For almost any crime you find a motive, and murder usually has the strongest motive of all. But so far I can't find one damned motive for either of these girls being killed."

"I'm sorry, Al," she said. "I wish I could help."

"I wish you could," I said. "I made a lousy deal for myself, but that's my bad luck."

Someone pounded on the door. "Lieutenant Wheeler?" It was Polnik. "You in there?"

"What is it?" I called back.

"The Sheriff's on the phone again. Wants to speak to you."

"See you later," I told Caroline as I headed toward the door. "Right now

I have to go and talk to trouble!"

CHAPTER ELEVEN

Sergeant Polnik walked me to the door of Miss Bannister's office. "If it's okay with you, Lieutenant, I'll wait out here. I can't stand to hear a strong man cry."

"Don't worry about that. I have no intention of crying."

"I'm not talking about you, Lieutenant. I'm talking about the Sheriff. He is."

I gave him one of my special sneery looks, walked into the office, and slammed the door after me. The receiver was lying off its hook and I picked it up. "Here I am, Sheriff," I chirped in my cheeriest tone.

There was a brief pause and then the Sheriff told me clearly and concisely that he wasn't interested in where I was but had rather definite ideas about where he wished I was.

"Something wrong, Sheriff?"

His voice broke in a sob. "Something wrong, he asks." He waited a moment to regain his composure. "My whole world is crashing down around my head and he wants to know if something is wrong. And all because I wanted a quiet evening at home!"

"They can't prove a thing, Sheriff. Doc Murphy can do all the yelling he wants and the DA can make all the guesses he wants, but guesses aren't proof and—"

Lavers's voice was frighteningly calm. "They caught them, Wheeler. They caught them miles away from the college and still running."

"Oh." I had a sinking sensation in my stomach. "They caught them? They caught who?"

He raged on as though he didn't hear the interruption. "They brought them into Homicide because of the story they were telling. The story was so interesting they were shipped right over to the DA's office. And they're still telling the same story."

"You wouldn't be talking about Mephisto and Spike?"

"That's exactly who I am talking about! The magician and that refugee from a horror movie he calls his assistant. Right this minute they're singing like a couple of stage-struck canaries that went on a bird-seed binge." He paused for breath, I could hear it whistling through his clenched teeth. "The lyrics go something like this—you locked them in a boiler room and threatened to frame them with a murder rap unless they agreed to confess to thieving jewelry during the performance. Can you imagine—"

"That's pretty close to being right. They did lift the jewelry."

"What?" I had to hold the receiver away from my ear. "You mean you actually threatened to frame them for murder?"

"It was just a figure of speech."

"You sure cut a fancy figure. Right now the DA's trying to set up a case against you so that you'll be right in style with the new trend toward stripes. Only yours will run the wrong way. On top of Doc Murphy's charge that you were either drunk or crazy when he saw you, this will really wrap you up. My guess is that you're neither drunk nor crazy. You're both!"

"I could make sense out of it if I had the time," I told him. "Only I don't think I have. I need all the time I can get to tie up the loose ends."

"You mean you think you know who the killer is?"

"No, sir," I admitted. "All I've got is loose ends. No proof, no motive, no nothing. But you can be sure I'm giving it everything I've got."

"I'll tell you how it is, Wheeler," he said. "The pressure is on right now. There are great screams going up from the DA's office as to why I haven't replaced you with a team of regular men from Homicide. The Commissioner and DA thought this was important enough for them to get out of bed and come to their offices—The DA's got a couple of his own investigators with him and they're scribbling down every word that bum of a magician and his assistant tell them."

"I can imagine," I said.

"So if you don't crack this one wide open, we're both in trouble!"

"How much time can you give me?"

"That's some more of the trouble," he said. "Not much. I can stall off sending a Homicide team out to you for maybe an hour—at most. That's all you've got, Wheeler—one hour."

"It's not long. You just stall them as long as you can, Sheriff. I'll call you as soon as anything breaks."

"If it doesn't break within an hour, don't bother," he said. "I'll be out there with that Homicide team!"

I hung up and stood looking at the telephone for about half a minute, wondering if they needed any good cops in Paraguay.

Polnik and Slade came into the office and stood there just looking at me. "Lieutenant," Polnik said dully, "would you tell me just one thing? What are we supposed to be doing here? All I do is go around knocking on doors to find out if you're behind one of them!"

Slade rubbed the top of his skull gingerly. "And all I do is keep on getting slugged over the head!"

"You!" I said. "The bright boy who let them out of the boiler room. Mephisto and Spike got picked up by a prowl car a mile from here— they're down in Homicide right now.

"Well!" Slade brightened up. "That's good news, isn't it?"

"Oh, fine!" I said. "And they're busy telling the DA right now how we kept them locked up in the boiler room and the DA is lapping it up, I have that on good authority—that's what the Sheriff just phoned about!"

Polnik winced. "Well, Lieutenant," he murmured gently, "I guess now is as good a time as any to buy into a chicken farm!"

"Don't let Slade in on the deal," I warned him. "Before he's been there a week the chickens will be laying square eggs!"

"You know, Lieutenant," Slade said enthusiastically, "you could have something there—square eggs! They'd never roll off a table!"

"Couldn't you take him out somewhere and lose him?" I pleaded with Polnik.

"I tried," he said, "but he keeps on finding his way back."

"You still haven't found Dufay?"

"No, sir," he said, shaking his head. "I searched that Tomlinson dame's room, but he wasn't there."

"Okay," I said. "Keep on looking, will you?"

"Sure," he said. "Come on, Slade."

The two of them went out again. I went along to Jean Craig's room and went inside. It had been searched once by Slade, who'd found the Frontier Colt there. It was doubtful if he'd missed anything, but I thought I might as well check—it was better than just standing around waiting for Lavers and the Homicide boys to arrive.

A quarter of an hour later I'd finished the search and found exactly nothing of any interest. There was a record player in one corner of the room and I went over and had a look at it. There was a record on the turntable—*New Faces of 1952*. That was the show that rocketed Eartha Kitt into the limelight, I remembered, and incidentally this was a good recording. I looked at the numbers on the table. The last one was Lizzie Borden.

Lizzie Borden? It rang a bell and then I remembered. When I'd finished that fateful lecture of mine and questions had been asked from the audience, Jean Craig had asked if I considered Lizzie Borden had been justified. The connection was obvious now—she had probably played the record just before the lecture.

I switched on the record player and then lifted the pickup, finding the start of the Lizzie Borden track. I grinned as I listened to it—it was beautiful burlesque. The endearing line about Lizzie meeting her mother in the street and cutting her dead ...

When it was finished, I switched off the record player and went along to Nancy Ritter's room. I hurried it this time and seven minutes later I was finished and had found exactly nothing.

I went back toward the office and I remembered for no good reason that somebody had put Mephisto when he was unconscious inside that box in the gym. The gym would be a good place to hide someone, I realized. Particularly a little guy like Dufay.

I hurried along until I got within about fifty yards of the door that led into the gym, then I slowed down, cat-footing with no noise the rest of the way.

The door was shut. I tried gently and found it wasn't locked. I turned the handle and eased the door open a couple of inches. There was a light on inside and I heard the murmur of voices.

"Augustus, darling!" Miss Tomlinson cooed, "does you love your little precious?"

"Of course, Agatha," Dufay's voice sounded strained. "You know I do!"

"Then tell your little precious how much you love her!"

"I love you, Agatha!" Dufay said irritably. "Surely that's enough!"

"Not for your little precious, Augustus! She will be hurt if she doesn't hear from her precious' own lips that he really lovey-doves her!"

I inched the door shut again and walked back down the corridor, grinning to myself. I was willing to bet Dufay was wishing he was back inside the boiler room.

I got back to Miss Bannister's office and checked my watch. It was a quarter to four. I had about half an hour before Lavers and the rest of them arrived.

I sat down in Miss Bannister's chair and put my feet up on Miss Bannister's desk and tried to think. I went over everything in my mind and got exactly nowhere.

"I couldn't sleep," an apologetic voice said from the doorway.

I looked up and saw Caroline standing there.

"Come on in," I told her. "I'm not sleeping either."

"You wouldn't like another drink?"

"That sounds like a good idea," I said.

"Then follow me, Lieutenant," she said briskly.

"Just before we go," I said, "you collect things, Caroline?"

"Only diamonds," she said with a grin.

"I bet you hoard all sorts of useless things!" I said. "All women do."

"Not this one," she said firmly. "I'm against it! I never keep anything I don't have an immediate use for."

"You're sure of that?"

"Of course I am—what's this all about, anyway?"

"I was just wondering," I said. "Wondering why you kept all the newspaper clippings of the trial of a con girl in Baltimore who you'd never even heard of before until you read the papers—kept them for two years until you saw her by chance in Pine City and could use the clippings to blackmail her. Honey, that's what I call foresight!"

She smiled wanly. "Oh, well. That was a case of hoarding, I guess."

"Second sight, I'd call it," I said. "Look! I'm running out of time—level with me now, Caroline. You're no blackmailer. No blackmailer would ever reason the way you did to me. They're greedy and they get more and more greedy as they go along. Miss Bannister was closer to the truth when she said she'd been taken for thirty thousand to date. No blackmailer would fool around with a deal like the one you told me about."

She bit her lip. "You're really a detective, aren't you?"

"I'm not at all sure of that at the moment," I said. "What's the real pitch, Caroline?"

"I suppose you'll find out anyway," she said. "I am an orphan—and so is my sister. But my name isn't really Partington—it's Bannister."

"Bannister!"

"That's right," she said.

"Why the secrecy?"

"Because the blackmailing has been going on for six months now," she said. "Poor Edwina was nearly out of her mind. She didn't know who it was doing it—and she still doesn't know. I was in New York—modeling. She flew in one weekend and told me about it. She was nearly frantic, she felt she didn't dare go to the police. Everything she'd built up here would be torn down.

"So we talked it over and decided I'd come to the college as a pupil. Living here, I might be able to get some idea of who the blackmailer was—hence the fake surname and so on." She pulled a face. "Not that I've had any success!"

"One thing is for sure," I said. "Your sister is crazy about Pierce. When she thought I'd really booked him for the murders, she told me about the blackmailing, showed me the clippings, and then told me it was Dufay who was doing it."

"I can't get over it," Caroline said. "Until you told me, I had no idea she felt that way about him. She must be really hooked to spill the beans to you that way."

I nodded. "It looks as if she'd do anything to protect him. Anyway, once I felt sure it wasn't Dufay, I remembered you and your diamonds." I grinned at her. "And I checked into your background and found there wasn't any on record. So when I accused you of being the blackmailer, you thought the smartest thing you could do to protect your sister was play along with it?"

"Check," she nodded.

"It doesn't get us very far," I said. "No nearer the murderer—or the blackmailer."

"I guess not," she said.

"Interesting speculation," I said. "Your sister would do anything to protect Pierce when he was accused of murder and Miss Tomlinson would do anything to protect Dufay when he was accused. But neither of the men thought of accusing someone else when they were accused."

"What does that prove?" she said. "That men have nicer instincts than women? Or merely that women love more deeply or are more possessive!"

"Or jealous?"

"You're just trying to prove the superiority of the male sex now," she said. "And everybody knows that's been disproved beyond all doubt!"

"Maybe you're right," I said.

"Are you coming to have that drink now?"

"No," I said. "If you don't mind—I've just remembered I should see Polnik about something."

"Okay," she said with a shrug, "that's your boss, Lieutenant!"

"I might knock hopefully on your door a little later on," I said.

"And I might be asleep!" she said firmly.

I watched her walk out of the office and then I went out. I had a fair idea where I could find Polnik and Slade and I was right.

"Nobody tells me these things!" I said as I came into the kitchen, where they both sat down at the table, drinking coffee.

"Slade was just coming up to tell you we had some coffee made, Lieutenant," Polnik said with an insincere smile. "Weren't you, Slade?"

"Oh—sure!" Slade said heartily. "Square eggs—I figure that's a lulu of an idea!"

"You guys can stop drinking coffee and start working again," I said. "Slade, you go to Miss Bannister's room and bring her back to her office. I'll be waiting for you there. I don't want Pierce along with her—got it?"

"Yes, sir, Lieutenant," he said briskly and marched out of the kitchen.

I looked at Polnik. "Miss Tomlinson and Dufay are in the gym. Jump 'em there. If you frighten them a little, it won't matter. Put Dufay into Miss Tomlinson's room and lock the door, then bring her along to the office."

"Sure, Lieutenant." He looked at me with a peculiarly glazed look in his eyes. "Could I ask a question?"

"Go ahead."

"Why are we doing this?"

"I just think it's immoral for people of mixed sexes to be together at this time of night," I said.

"I never figured you'd crack under a case, Lieutenant," he muttered as he went out.

I walked leisurely back to the office, sat down behind Miss Bannister's desk, and lit myself a cigarette. About a minute later Slade brought Miss

Bannister herself into the office and looked at me inquiringly.

"Just keep an eye on Pierce," I told him and he went out again.

Miss Bannister knotted the cord of her robe tighter around her waist and glared at me. "What now, Lieutenant?"

"Sit down, please," I said. "It won't take very long."

She sat in one of the two chairs for visitors and tapped her foot impatiently.

Another three or four minutes went by and then Polnik appeared escorting Miss Tomlinson, who wore a white sweater and a plain black skirt.

"Lieutenant!" she said. "Really! This persecution is intolerable. I shall jolly well write to my Senator about it!"

"Sit down, Miss Tomlinson," I told her. "I'll be with you in a moment."

I took hold of Polnik's arm and pushed him outside the office, closing the door behind me for a moment.

"Sheriff Lavers and the boys from Homicide should arrive any time now," I said. "Get out in front of the building and stall them as long as you can. Give me as much time as you can. When they get into the building, keep them away from this office—and keep them away from both Pierce and Dufay if you can. Play it a little dumb—you don't know where I am, I seem to have disappeared …"

Polnik looked dubious. "Sure, Lieutenant, I'll try—but the Sheriff!"

"Do your best," I told him. "Tell Granny I died with a smile on my face!"

I closed the door behind me and walked slowly around the desk and sat again in the chair behind it.

Both women facing me sat bristling in their chairs.

"I demand—" Miss Tomlinson started to say.

I shook my head solemnly and she closed her mouth firmly.

"Ladies," I said, "I have something to tell you—something about the investigation into the murder of the two girls—something not pleasant, I'm afraid."

They both leaned forward in their chairs simultaneously.

"I know that my methods of carrying out such an investigation are open to criticism," I said, "but they do get results. That's why I've had you brought here now—to tell you those results."

Miss Bannister took a deep breath. "Go on."

"Two things a murderer must have," I said slowly. "Those are motive and opportunity. Now when the Craig girl was murdered in the auditorium during the period the lights were out, everyone there had the opportunity to do it. Anyone could have slipped into the Ritter girl's room and killed her. So the question of opportunity is not going to narrow the field for us."

"I say!" Miss Tomlinson couldn't help being enthusiastic in spite of herself. "This is absolutely ripping! The real thing!"

"So I had to look for motive to narrow the field," I said. "And that's done it—narrowed it to two."

"Two?" Miss Bannister said breathlessly. "Which two?"

"I warned you my news wasn't pleasant," I reminded them.

"You mean …" The enthusiasm in Miss Tomlinson packed up its bag and left. "You mean … we are the two you suspect of the murders?"

I shook my head. "Of course not. The field is narrowed down to two men. And I have to tell you the facts concerning them, unpleasant as they may be to you both."

Miss Bannister lifted her head a little. "Please go on, Lieutenant," she said quietly.

"Yes," Miss Tomlinson said and squared her chin. "Tell us everything."

"You will have to accept what I tell you as the truth," I said. "It has been sifted and analyzed and then verified by statements from everyone in the college. It has been checked and double-checked."

"We understand," Miss Tomlinson said.

"I hope you do," I said. "Here in this college you have a preponderance—naturally enough—of females to males. Apart from the female teaching staff, there were fifty girls as students. As far as they are concerned, and this is from their own statements, out of the four men on the staff, only two were considered to be attractive and eligible. They were Mr. Pierce and Mr. Dufay."

"Disgusting!" Miss Tomlinson snorted. "If I'd known this sort of loose thinking was rife in the college I'd have seen to it they worked harder at their volleyball! There's nothing like a stiff neck or a bruised shin to take the mind off more impolite matters!"

"That was the situation," I said quickly as she stopped to take a breath. "Now with two of the girls—with the two murdered girls in fact—it was a game they played. They used to compete with each other to see who could make the most dates with either of the two men during the course of a week. It had got to a point where, apparently, even bets were being wagered."

"Arrant nonsense!" Miss Tomlinson said loudly.

"You can't expect us to believe this!" Miss Bannister said angrily.

"Remember what I said in the beginning," I told them patiently. "And please listen and concentrate—this is most vital to everyone concerned. Both men would willingly date any of the attractive students, and as the majority of them are very attractive young women, the two men were in the perhaps pleasant situation of being in very heavy demand and being able to pick and choose between the girls."

"I can't stand it any more!" Miss Bannister said.

"I'm afraid you'll have to," I said, "I didn't bring you here and tell you all this for you to let me down at the end of it. Coming to the hours preceding the murders, my feeling is that the Craig girl had threatened one of the two men concerned. What exactly the threat might be, I don't know—anyone can hazard a number of guesses—but it must have been a terrifying threat for a man to commit murder because of it.

"And I think that, having killed the Craig girl, he realized that her closest friend and partner in this dating game would probably know of her threat to him, so he had to kill her to prevent her telling the police."

Miss Tomlinson was halfway out of her chair. "Are you trying to tell me, Lieutenant, that my Augustus would dare to look at another girl when he was already engaged to be married—to me!"

"In a word," I said evenly, "yes!"

She dropped back into her chair. "I can't believe it," she whispered. "I can't believe that dear Augustus would betray me like that."

"Is this your idea of an elaborate joke of some sort, Lieutenant?" Miss Bannister asked. "Something that amuses you?"

"It doesn't amuse me at all," I said. "The only reason I took such pains to tell you about it, is because I need your help. You two are the closest to them both now, now that the Craig and Ritter girls have been disposed of, of course. And you may, I hope, be able to tell me any remarks they may have passed in the last few hours which, in the light of what you know now, may be significant."

I looked hopefully at them.

"Augustus ran to me like a little lamb running to its mother," Miss Tomlinson. said. "He needed protection, poor lamb, and I gave it to him." She glared at me, "It's absolutely monstrous to imply be could even as much as look at another woman!"

"As far as Edward is concerned, I wonder you need ask, Lieutenant!" Miss Bannister said. "You saw to what lengths he was prepared to go to protect me. The way he even handled a gun to protect me!"

"I'm afraid I must disagree with both of you," I said. "I've only seen the lengths to which both of you are prepared to protect them!"

There was a knock and the door opened suddenly; Slade stuck his head in. "See you a minute, Lieutenant?" he asked anxiously.

"Sure," I said, and got to my feet. I followed him outside the office and closed the door behind me.

"They've just arrived," Slade whispered. "The Sheriff and Lieutenant Tighe and half a dozen more from Homicide. Sergeant Polnik went out to meet them a couple of minutes ago. He'll stall them the best he can, but he said to tell you not to rely on more than a quarter of an hour at the most."

"Thanks, pal," I said. "You get out there and see if you can help Polnik distract them. Try and keep them outside the building as long as possible."

I went back into the office and sat down behind the desk again.

"Have either of you thought of anything yet?" I said.

They both glared at me with their lips tightly compressed.

"I have to remind you of the dangers that one of you is subjecting herself to," I said. "A man who has murdered twice won't hesitate to murder again. And the next time it may well be either of you."

Miss Tomlinson got to her feet. "Lieutenant Wheeler," she said, "I cannot believe that a man in such a position of trust as a Lieutenant of Police would stoop to telling such a tissue of lies! If I hadn't heard it with my own ears, I would never have believed it." She walked toward the door and stopped for a moment when she reached it.

"I am going back to Augustus," she said. "He needs me, he has faith in me. And I, faith in him!" She walked out, her head held high, her shoulders well back. I figured she was lucky she hadn't been born a couple of hundred years before or some pirate would have slapped her on the bows of his ship. The door slammed shut behind her. I lit myself another cigarette and hoped Polnik had persuaded Lavers and the rest of them to fall down a deep hole somewhere.

Miss Bannister rose to her feet and looked at me. "I wonder if it has occurred to you, Lieutenant Wheeler," she said in a low voice, "that the arguments you applied to Edward and Dufay could be equally well applied to the two women who are so deeply attached to them …"

I didn't answer that one.

She still looked at me steadily and I thought there should be a law against women being equipped with brains as well as all their other formidable weapons.

"If it did occur to you," she went on slowly, "then you must have calculated this meeting very carefully indeed … not only the meeting but the inevitable result of the meeting and—" Her eyes widened. "You devil!" she whispered, then turned around abruptly and walked toward the door.

"Give my regards to Mr. Pierce, Miss Bannister," I called after her and the door slamming shut answered me. It was ten minutes later when the door opened again and Lavers stormed into the office, followed by Lieutenant Tighe from Homicide, who was followed by Polnik. I could see the rest of them standing in the corridor outside.

"Wheeler!" Lavers said, his face a deep scarlet. "Is that sergeant of yours a complete idiot!"

"Polnik?" I said.

"Yes, Lieutenant?" Polnik asked wearily.

"Are you a complete idiot?"

"No, Lieutenant."

I looked at Lavers with polite attention. "He says he isn't a complete idiot, sir."

Lavers pursed his lips. "All right."

"Where do we start? That fool of a sergeant took us on a tour of inspection around the place! We've seen the pool, the tennis courts ... ah!"

He took out his pipe and crammed it between his teeth, biting savagely on the stem. "First things first, I suppose. Where's this second body there's been so much argument about?"

"Still in her room, Sheriff," I said. "Polnik will show you the way."

"Oh, no!" Lavers said firmly. "Not him again!"

"I'm quite sure he'll be able to take you directly to it, sir," I said. "Isn't that right, Sergeant?" I nodded slightly to Polnik as I asked the question.

"Yes, Lieutenant," he said, and closed one eye slowly, then opened it again.

"Well, let's move then!" Lavers said sourly. He took two paces toward the door, then stopped and glared at me. "And what are you intending to do while we see the corpse?"

"I am meditating, Sheriff," I said.

"Some blonde?"

"The infidelities of man," I said.

Lavers shook his head and carried on toward the door. "I think Murphy may be right," he said in a loud voice to Tighe. "He's acting like a maniac right now!"

A couple of minutes later there was a gentle knock on the door and Polnik came in.

"They're all too busy up there doing nothing to notice I left, Lieutenant," he said. "I was sort of wondering if I could help in any way?"

"That's very kind of you, Sergeant," I said. "Take a chair."

He looked at me blankly. "If you don't mind me saying so, Lieutenant, you don't have much time left. I don't like to see them doing to you what they're doing! I was sort of hoping that maybe you had an idea up your sleeve. Working with you is ..." He groped hopelessly for a word to describe it, then gave up. "Different," he finished lamely.

"Thanks again," I said. "Sit down and wait with me."

"For them to come back?"

I shook my head. "For another three minutes or the sound of violence."

He looked hard at me, then edged his chair back a little away.

"You know, Sergeant," I said, "the trouble with being a cop is that you get hidebound. You get the routine running a roller over you every day for years and you can only think about the roller."

"Sure, Lieutenant," he said heartily and edged his chair back a little further.

"Because ninety-nine cases have the same motives, we expect the hundredth to conform," I went on. "We're used to finding that money is the prime motivation of nearly all crime, so we expect it to motivate all crime. It's a mistake. If I'd thought about this a little earlier, we could all be home in bed by now—or having a comfortable drink someplace anyway."

"Is that right, Lieutenant?" he said.

"You did a good job in stalling the Sheriff," I said.

"Thanks, Lieutenant." He didn't sound happy about it. "I got a nasty feeling the Sheriff noted it, too!"

"He'll get over it," I said. "He always does."

"Those three minutes nearly up, Lieutenant?" he asked restlessly.

I glanced at my watch. "About forty seconds to go."

"What do we do then?"

"Take a look around," I said.

"You listening for something, Lieutenant?" Polnik couldn't bottle his curiosity.

"The crack of Doom!" I said.

"Oh—sure!" The back of his chair hit the far wall.

"Sure, Lieutenant. I meant, were you waiting for something to happen that sort of connected with the case, not—"

The sound of a shot sounded loud, even inside the office.

"That's it!" I told Polnik. "The crack of Doom."

CHAPTER TWELVE

I was first through the doorway, into the room, with Polnik close behind me. I could hear other footsteps racing down the corridors, all converging toward the room, and I had a moment's regret that Murphy wasn't there to receive his third corpse.

Then I heard the soft voice crooning: "Hush-a-bye, baby, on the ..."

I stopped where I was and looked at her, hearing Polnik's sharp intake of breath behind me.

Miss Tomlinson was down on her knees on the floor, holding Augustus Dufay in her arms and crooning her lullaby gently to him.

It really wasn't going to help Mr. Dufay much because there was a powder-burned hole in his left temple and a gun dangled from the limp fingers of his right hand.

Miss Tomlinson glared at me, her lips curling back from her teeth for a moment, then resumed her song, clutching his unresisting head tighter to her breast.

"Shot himself!" Polnik said huskily.

Then everyone seemed to crowd into the room. There were Lavers and Tighe, both with blank expressions on their faces, Caroline showing only keen interest, Pierce with a fixed stare of horror, and Miss Bannister with a look of compassion in her eyes as she looked down at Miss Tomlinson.

Then she looked across at me. "So I was wrong about you, Lieutenant," she said softly. "It was one of the men, after all!"

I shrugged my shoulders without answering.

"Someone had better do something!" Lavers said. "Move that woman away from the body for a start!"

Miss Tomlinson looked up at him with such incredible ferocity showing in her face that even Lavers blinked.

"No one shall touch him but me!" she said in a low voice. "He's mine, he always was mine, and the rest of it was lies—foul lies!"

It was my turn for the look.

"You made them up!" she said. "You—a Lieutenant of Police, you made up all those foul lies about my little precious and those other women!"

She cradled Dufay's head in her arms and rocked backward and forward. "There, there, my precious," she said. "Nobody's going to hurt you."

"Wheeler," Lavers said with faint disgust in his voice. "Do something!"

"I'm glad you're here, sir," I said politely, "to vouch for the body before Dr. Murphy makes it vanish again."

Tighe grinned, then sobered when he saw Lavers's beady eyes directed at him.

I took a step toward Miss Tomlinson and she bared her teeth at me. "You shan't touch him," she said.

"It's all over, Lizzie," I said. "come on, Lizzie, Lizzie Borden!"

She screamed thinly, coming to her feet, Dufay's body forgotten so that his head slid from her protecting arms and bumped down onto the floor. The gun slipped from the still fingers and slithered a couple of feet across the polished floor before it hit the edge of a rug and was stopped.

She came toward me in a slightly crouched position, both arms held out in front of her, the fingers hooked into talons.

Suddenly she was at me, her nails scratching at my face. She moved so fast, she took the rest of them by surprise. They could only stand and gape. "I'll kill you for that!" Saliva glistened in a thin stream from the corner of her mouth.

I caught her by the wrists and it didn't take a second for me to know that I had two hands full of raging, struggling female. Those hours under cold showers and taking long, bracing walks left her in better condition than I was. She fought wildly with feet, teeth, and nails.

Finally Polnik came to life, caught her around the waist, and pulled her off me. And not a moment too soon. I had the impression of a broad smile on the Sheriff's face, which disappeared when he realized I was looking at him.

"You all right, Wheeler?" he asked.

"Oh, sure. I just go three rounds with a crazy female twice a day to keep in shape." I turned to Polnik. "Thanks, Sergeant."

He was still holding Miss Tomlinson, but the fight had drained out of her. She sagged in his arms.

"It was all true, wasn't it, Lizzie?" I said to her in a soft voice.

She stared at me as though she didn't hear.

"It was all true what they said. The Craig girl and the Ritter girl. You wouldn't believe them, but it was true, wasn't it, Lizzie?"

She continued to stare for a second, then consciousness slowly seemed to light up her eyes. She looked into my face and shook her head. "It was lies, all lies."

"It was true, Lizzie. You know it was true."

She came to life with a vengeance, tried to break free of the Sergeant's grasp. "They lied," she said in a rasping whisper. "They told dirty, filthy, horrible lies about my poor Augustus. And when I warned them to stop, when I told them what would happen if they kept on telling their filthy lies, they started calling me Lizzie Borden. Lizzie Borden! They kept taunting me with the name."

"And you had to put a stop to it?" I asked her in a conversational tone of voice.

"Of course," she said. "Of course I had to stop them. I couldn't have them telling those lies about Augustus—he couldn't defend himself against them."

She smiled and it was suddenly the smile of a very small child who has taken a cookie from the plate without being noticed.

"I knew Pierce had those knives and things in his room," she said. "I took them—I made sure he was a long way away when I slipped into his room and got them. I carried one of them with me—ready. Tucked into the top of my stock—" She blushed. "I shouldn't name part of a lady's wearing apparel in front of a gentleman. But when the lights went out the first time in the auditorium, I thought if I'd only been ready to take the chance then. But I was ready the second time …"

I nodded. "What about the magician?"

"Him!" she snorted contemptuously. I nodded for Polnik to let her go. The momentary spasm of violence had passed. "I'd seen his act before. It was stupid. He was stupid."

"But it gave you an idea," I said. "When the lights went out, you could act. Is that it?"

She grinned shrewdly. "I knew all about the guillotine that didn't cut their heads off and the knife that looks like it's buried in someone's back and isn't." She chuckled. "Sure, he gave me the idea. The knife in the back and the lights going out. It worked, too."

"You did stab Jean Craig."

"That's right." She looked around as if proud of herself. "And no one knew it. No one."

"And Mephisto?" I wanted the whole story in front of witnesses. "You used his trick knife on him. Why?"

"I was afraid he saw something. I had stolen the prop knife from his gear. When he came off the stage, I knocked him out." She looked around proudly. "I carried him into the gym. It's physical fitness, you know—equips you for any emergency. I picked him up like he was a baby and carried him into the gym and put him on the vaulting horse."

I remembered how she'd lifted Miss Bannister in the auditorium when she'd fainted and carried her so effortlessly across to the office.

"Then I put the trick knife onto his back," Miss Tomlinson continued quickly, "and I rang before, of course, phoned the funny little detective with glasses and told him I was Lieutenant Wheeler, making my voice sound gruff, and he believed me!" She went into peels of laughter.

"And afterward?" I said.

"Afterward?" She looked at me and blinked. "Afterward it was so easy. I knew the police would be rushing about because they'd think the magician had been murdered—for a little while, anyway, until they took a good look. So I went along to the Ritter girl's room." A look of cold satisfaction came into her eyes. "And that was that!"

"It was very clever," I said. "And then you went back to the gym?"

"Just to see how things were getting on," she said and giggled. "You see, they wouldn't think there was anything odd about me visiting the gym because I'm the sports mistress at the college and I must say I am a firm believer in the old adage that a cold bath every morning followed by a bout of hard exercise is always good for the moral as well as physical fibers! And another thing—"

"You went back to the gym!" I said quickly. "And what happened then?"

"They'd all rushed out and left poor Mephisto on top of the horse," she giggled again. "So I thought I might make it even funnier and I took him off the horse and put him inside the equipment box and closed the lid on him!" She looked around expectantly as if she expected applause, and her mouth turned sullen when no one clapped.

"It was a very clever scheme," I said.

"And how about Augustus?" I glanced down at the body on the floor.

"I suppose you were going to make it look as if he'd shot himself?"

"I was going to," she whispered confidentially, "but I don't think it's worth the bother now, do you?"

"Not really," I said.

"No," she said, shaking her head. "Not worth the bother."

"And the blackmail," I said. "You must have made a lot of money!"

"Fifteen thousand dollars," she said. "We had to have it, you see, Augustus and me, because we were going to be married."

"Of course," I said. "You never were in Baltimore, were you?"

"Oh, no," she said. "Never. Although I believe it's absolutely top-hole and one can have an absolutely spiffing time there."

"It was your partner who told you about Miss Bannister's trouble in Baltimore, then?" I said.

"Yes." Miss Tomlinson nodded slowly. "Oh, yes. She gave me the clippings to send to Miss Bannister to let her know we meant business. And I've been quite fair to my partner, mark you, she's had exactly half of the blackmail money—she has fifteen thousand dollars exactly as I have."

"Why don't you say hello to her, now she's here?" I suggested gently.

"What a nice idea!" She beamed at me, then her eyes shifted focus across the packed figures grouped just inside the door. Her face looked anxious as she scanned the faces for maybe ten seconds, but then a broad smile of relief appeared. "Hello, Caroline!" She said loudly. "I couldn't see you for a minute—you looked as if you were trying to hide behind Mr. Pierce's back!"

"I think we should be getting along now, don't you?" I said, and reached out to take her arm.

She reared back. "Please don't touch me! Augustus—he's my fiancé—wouldn't like it. He's a terribly jealous man, you know! He won't even look at another girl and he expects me to be exactly the same about other men—and I am, of course!"

She looked down at the floor. "Augustus!" she said, laughing fondly. "Look at him playing games on the floor. Come on, Augustus! Really!"

There was a strangled sob in her throat as she spun round toward me. "He's dead! You tricked me! He's been dead all the time and I had it all arranged so that it would look as if he had shot himself and now you've spoiled it all!"

She threw herself at me again, her fingernails hooking toward my eyes. Polnik stepped forward and hit her with a brief, merciful judo chop to the neck and caught her before she fell to the floor.

CHAPTER THIRTEEN

I had finished telling the story from the beginning and my throat was dry.

Lavers looked at me and nodded. "You must have the most incredible luck, Wheeler, or—"

"I was saying to Sergeant Polnik before she killed poor Dufay," I said, "that we get too used to being coppers. We get run over with the routine roller and nothing is ever simple any more. That's where I goofed on this one. I found a blackmail plot, so I was convinced automatically that blackmail or something closely connected to it was the motivation of the murders. I forgot a simple, elemental passion like jealousy—jealousy in a woman who was deeply inhibited and off balance so that one push sent her over the cliff."

Lavers snorted. "What was this Lizzie Borden business you started her off with?"

"A wild guess," I said. "Another piece of luck. Jean Craig got up after I'd given—er—your lecture, sir, and asked a question: Did I think Lizzie Borden was justified? A gag on the surface. But I found a recording on the record player in her room of the Lizzie Borden track from *New Faces*. Then I heard about the girls boasting of their dates with Dufay. I wondered if they had boasted to her—taunted her with it. If she'd threatened violence to them, they could have called her Lizzie Borden to show their contempt. The question could have been another rather cruel joke directed against Miss Tomlinson and not, as I thought at the time, the poor lecturer!"

Lavers looked at his watch and grunted. "Seven o'clock—another day. We might as well go, everything's cleared up here. I can't wait to get into the DA's office and tell him the whole case is finished." He got onto his feet. "You'd better take the day off, Wheeler, you must be tired."

"Thank you, sir," I said. "And Sergeant Polnik and Detective Slade?"

"Of course," he said. "They'll be tired too. Can we give you a lift back to town? Oh, no! Of course! You've got that red monster with you."

They filed out of the door and I lit a cigarette. A few seconds later Miss Bannister came into the office and stopped abruptly when she saw me. "I thought everyone had gone," she said.

"I'm just going," I said.

"I should thank you for proving my younger sister a party to the blackmail, I suppose," she said tonelessly. "You will forgive me, Lieutenant, if I say I find that a hard thing to do at the moment."

"Sure," I said. "What are your plans now?"

"I am going to close the college," she said. "It would be hopeless to continue."

"I'm sorry," I said.

"Mr. Pierce left ten minutes ago," she said. "Traveling to all points north, I believe."

"But you're seeing him again?" I said.

"Not in this life." She walked around the desk and sat down in her chair and looked at me. "I could hardly marry him now, could I?" she said evenly. "He was as unfaithful to me as Dufay was to Miss Tomlinson. I was very lucky it was Miss Tomlinson who shot her lover and not me. The way you had it worked out, there was a fifty-fifty chance either way, wasn't there?"

"The odds were slightly in your favor," I said. "I had a feeling about Miss Tomlinson. She was too eager-beaver all the time. The way she fussed around you when you fainted, for example. She didn't want to miss anything that went on. Her approaches to me all full of enthusiasm about police work, hoping to get me to open up on what I knew. Most of the time I knew nothing."

She nodded. "Most interesting. Now, if you'll excuse me, Lieutenant, I have work to do."

I looked out of the window behind her chair.

"I have been given a day off today," I said, "it's a lovely day—the sun's up. Why don't you play hooky with me and we'll really have a day out."

She dropped her pen onto the desk and got to her feet, her fingers gripping the edge of the desk so hard that they turned white.

"Lieutenant Wheeler," she said in a low voice. "Twelve hours ago I had never even heard of you! Now, just twelve hours later, you have been instrumental in destroying my college, which was dear to my heart—and the social prestige that went with it. The love I had for a man you have turned to hate! You have shown me my sister as a treacherous snake whom I can never speak to again. And then—" her voice broke for a moment—"and then you have the gall to stand there and blithely invite me out to spend the day with you!" She drew herself up straight. "I wouldn't go out with you if you were the last man left alive, Lieutenant Wheeler! I wouldn't give you a drink if you were dying of thirst right now in this very room! I have only one interest as far as you are concerned, Lieutenant! And that is to see the last of you as quickly as possible. I never want to see you again. I hate you with every fiber of my being!" She took a deep breath. "Do I make myself clear!"

She did.

I sighed. During the night I had been making some interesting plans for Edwina Bannister and me. They had seemed particularly feasible when it turned out that Pierce had been playing her dirt from the start.

But some women don't like to face the truth. She hated me now more than she hated the man who'd played her dirt because I'd pulled the wool off her eyes instead of pulling it over them.

"I still have my memories," I said, smiling at her. "I'll never forget that brief interlude in your room."

"I wish he'd pulled the trigger then," she said. "He would have killed two birds with one stone—you and himself." She turned her back and stared out the window. "Now, will you leave, or will I call your superior and tell him you're harassing me?"

I left. I walked down the hallway of the main dormitory, stealing a page from Sergeant Polnik's book, muttering to myself. A policemen's lot is a sorry one, some English character named Sir Robert Peel once said.

I headed across the parking lot where I'd left the car the night before— was that only last night? It was still there and Miss Bannister had overlooked the opportunity to slash my tires. Or maybe she was too anxious to get rid of me to do anything that would keep me around. I climbed into the Healey, put the key into the ignition, and turned it.

"Excuse me," a familiar sultry voice said.

I looked up. It was the redhead who wore the baby-doll pajamas, who was a doll but didn't resemble a baby at all.

"Eighteen, you said?" I asked.

She batted her carefully tinted eyelids at me. "That's right—but you've been looking at it all wrong, Lieutenant. You want more positive thoughts about eighteen and less about twenty-two. Here I am, in the bloom of my youth, unmarried and carefree, at the age of consent, too, remember. What's twenty-two got that I haven't, except four more years?"

"And clear sailing with the bartender, I'll bet you have one hell of a time getting a drink served to you!"

"I know of one bartender who wouldn't think of questioning my age, or anything else! His name is Barney. He works at the Blue Oasis." Again the eyelashes fluttered. "That's a motel." She let it sink in. "I'm looking for a lift. Going my way?"

"You just know it, baby. Hop in."

She climbed in beside me and I must say that one advantage of a sports car is that when a girl gets settled into the seat, she's settled and that's that. Even if her skirt has ridden up four inches over her knees. The redhead and I looked at her knees with equal interest.

"They dimple," I said.

"Do you really think so?" She sounded delighted. "I can never tell—I always hoped they did."

"What are you going to do when you get to town?" I asked her as I gunned the motor.

"Love that exhaust note!" she said. "In town? I don't know really. I felt depressed in the college this morning, so I thought I'd get an early start and have a day out."

I went down the driveway in first, changed into second at forty miles an hour as we turned onto the macadam highway, built it up to seventy in third, then just slid it through into high and relaxed. Hell! I wasn't in any hurry! I looked at the redhead and smiled. She smiled back, her eyes warm and friendly, her lips full and inviting.

"It so happens," I said, "that I have a day off today, by some happy co-incidence …" I took another look at her knees—dimples, all right. "This friend of yours—this bartender named Barney. I'd like to meet him some time."

She grinned at me. "Why don't we put it on the agenda for today?"

I couldn't think of a suitable argument against it.

THE END

Death on the Downbeat
- - - - -
by Carter Brown

CHAPTER ONE

Annabelle Jackson did a double-take: "Is this the place?"

"This is it," I agreed.

"I realise, Lieutenant," she said coldly, "that on your salary you might not be able to afford to take me to the most exclusive club in town—but this!" She stared at the doorway, almost speechless. "Could I offer you a loan?"

I had to admit I'd seen better doorways. This was just a door that was open and that made it a hole in the wall. There was a battered neon that would have spelled out the Golden Horseshoe if all the letters had been lit, and underneath it said, Midnight at Midnight.

I took her arm and pushed her gently through the doorway.

"You'll love it!" I said hopefully and we went down the stairs into the cellar.

We found a table against the wall and sat down. It was a big cellar but still just a cellar, and it didn't have any air-conditioning. It was hot and the place was thick with smoke. A consciously-unkempt waiter lolled up against the table and leered at Annabelle.

"What'll it be, folks?" he asked.

"Scotch," I said, "over the rocks."

"And please wash the glasses before you pour!" Annabelle said tartly.

The waiter grinned amiably at her then wandered away. Annabelle looked around her distastefully. "This I presume, is the natural habitat of the criminal element of the city?"

"Such big words," I said admiringly. "Look around, honey. You'll see the criminal element all have high foreheads and wear heavy horn-rims. This is the intellectuals' hide-out."

"Why would they come to a dump like this!"

"One word—jazz. As she is played, Chicago-style. It's only a trio but they've really got what it takes. Clarence Nesbitt on the bass-fiddle, Cuba Carter on the hides and Wesley Stewart playing his horn. Nobody ever heard of them till three weeks ago and now everybody in town is talking about them."

"I'm not," she said, unimpressed.

"There's a second reason," I said. "Midnight at midnight, like the neon says outside."

"Is that a quote from Gertrude Stein?"

"Midnight O'Hara is her name," I said. "To be blatantly obvious, she sings at midnight." I checked my watch. "Around fifteen minutes from now. She's quite something."

"I don't like jazz," she said.

The scotch arrived which saved me trying to think of an answer to that.

"This is practically the first date you've given me," I said, lifting my glass. "I drink to your beautiful blue eyes, Annabelle Jackson!"

"I was just wondering," she said, "what are you going to do with all the money you've saved tonight?"

"Pay off another instalment on my Jaguar," I said. "This is not the way I planned things, honey-chile. But wait till you hear this combination—they'll send you."

"A long way from here, I hope!"

"You wait till you hear them," I said, not very hopefully.

"But I don't like jazz," she repeated. "I know—I tried listening to a man called Brubeck once and you can't even hear the melody except just for a few bars at the beginning and end of the number. There's a great big chunk in the middle that doesn't make sense at all."

I winced.

"Brubeck plays something they call progressive jazz," I said, still in there, pitching. "Chicago-style is a variation of New Orleans ... it's ... never mind, but what you'll hear tonight is distinctly different from Brubeck."

"I hope so," she said without any enthusiasm at all.

The conversation waned sharply after that. The trio hit their stride with, "I Found a New Baby."

I looked at Annabelle after they had finished.

"What did you think of that?"

"Very noisy," she said carefully.

Somebody announced Midnight O'Hara and there was a storm of applause. I concentrated on the spotlight which wavered for a moment, then picked up Midnight making her entrance. She was quite a girl, Midnight O'Hara.

She was tall and blonde and she had dark eyes—as black as Midnight. She had a full figure and the black strapless put a very definite emphasis on her curves—the rhinestones on the bodice flashed as they reflected the spotlight. She was a nice-looking dame in a world populated with nice-looking dames—right up to the moment she reached out a gloved hand and took hold of the microphone. And started to sing.

When she sang, she was all the women you had ever known and the only woman you ever wanted to know. She hit you right where you lived.

You could say she had style, she had personality, she had depth ... her phrasing was perfect. You could use up all the words to describe it, explain it, analyse it—and her voice still reached out casually and melted your insides.

She sang "Reckless Blues," then followed it up with "Bewitched, Bothered and Bewildered." The clincher was, "The Lady is a Tramp."

And when the applause died away and she had gone and the trio were digging into "China Boy," I looked expectantly at Annabelle.

"How was she?" I asked.

"Quite competent," she said coolly. "Have you noticed how hot it is in here, Lieutenant?"

"I feel a certain chill in the air," I said. "But I get your message loud and clear. The next step is Roger and Out!"

A character who didn't qualify in the intellectual stakes leaned against our table and looked at Annabelle admiringly.

He was around thirty and fat with it. His sports-coat was cut wide enough to shelter a team of adagio dancers and he hadn't shaved in a couple of days.

"Man!" he said admiringly. "I dig you the most, you crazy chick, you!"

"Blow!" Annabelle said coldly.

"A sometimey chick, huh?" he said, straightening himself up with an effort. "Sleep with your glasses on, huh? Okay, so I'll nix out!"

He weaved his way unsteadily through the tables towards a door at the end of the cellar.

"What language was that?" Annabelle asked.

"Jive-talk," I said. "Liquor, or more probably dope in some form. Pay no particular attention."

"It really is a charming place, isn't it?" she said. "Kind of grows on you—like a fungus."

"We can leave?" I suggested.

"Don't let us hurry—I'm having a whale of a time."

"Like Jonah?"

It was Annabelle's turn to wince.

"You know something?" she said. "You intrigue me, Lieutenant! For some months now I've sat at my desk in Commissioner Lavers' office, fighting you off with both hands—and feet!"

"Now that's a wild exaggeration and you know it," I said coldly.

"I was speaking figuratively," she admitted.

"And that's where you can speak with assurance, honey," I said, taking a long, steady, admiring glance at her ample curves.

"There you go again," she said, "if you see what I mean. I've been fighting off that down-to-earth approach of yours. I'll swear you have eyes in the back of your head—even when you're faced in the opposite direction I can feel you looking at me. I have the feeling that whatever I wear doesn't make any difference—you can see right through it in any case."

"I'll wear dark glasses around the office from tomorrow morning on,"

I said. "But weren't we talking about tonight?"

"That's exactly what I'm talking about," she said.

"Tonight. When I was finally worn down to a point of no resistance ..." She must have seen the gleam in my eye. "... well, almost," she corrected herself. "I said I'd have a date—so here we are!"

She looked at me with an air of triumph.

"So here we are?" I muttered. "Look, honey, I know I'm just a dumb, flatfooted cop but ..."

"So here we are," she repeated. "Am I in your apartment, fighting the good fight the girls in the Confession magazines fight? Am I in your apartment being plied with good liquor and insidious hi-fi renditions of "I Surrender"? No! I'm sitting here in a rather smelly cellar listening to something you tell me is Chicago-style jazz and being insulted by somebody you tell me probably takes dope!"

"It can all be rectified," I said apologetically. "The apartment, the good Scotch, the Peggy Lee, Julie London, Como, Sinatra and King Cole discs are already stacked. I just thought you might like some jazz first. There are girls," I confided in a confidential whisper, "whom jazz sends!"

"I think you are nothing but a bluff, Al Wheeler," she said. "Or a fool. Or both. I think I would like to go home."

"Not even a cup of coffee on the way?"

"Not even a hand held on the way!" she said firmly.

"Annabelle Jackson," I said, "you are the sort of girl who destroys man's faith in the Confession magazines!"

She opened her mouth and replied to that. I didn't hear what she said because the trio were beating their way into the middle of "Rampart Street Parade."

What I did hear was the sudden scream followed by the sound of a shot and then a moment afterwards, the jive-boy who had whispered sweet words of endearment into Annabelle's pink ear appeared suddenly in front of the trio.

He looked the same as he'd looked the first time except for the blood staining his sky-blue shirt. He stood for a moment, swaying on his feet, his eyes not focussing too well.

"Crazy!" he giggled.

Then he pitched forward on his face and lay still right in front of the trio and from where I sat, he looked very dead indeed.

CHAPTER TWO

By the time I reached the corpse, the trio's audience had thinned by about fifty per cent and I could hear most of the other fifty per cent tramping up the stairs so fast you could believe Orson Welles had just made a replay of his "Men From Mars" radio epic.

I knelt down beside the cat and discovered he'd run out of his ninth life. There was a bullet-hole through his white sports coat and from the way it looked it had gone straight into his chest. I wondered how he'd managed to stay alive long enough to give us his finale to "Rampart Street Parade."

The trio watched me impassively as I got onto my feet again and dusted the knees of my pants. The waiter who had served us and looked as if he needed tidying up, walked up to me uncertainly.

"Are you a doctor?" he quavered.

"Just a cop," I said, and showed him my shield to prove it.

"That's a break," he said. "I didn't know what to do. I couldn't figure it whether to call a doc or a cop first. Now I got no decision to make."

"Who owns the place?" I asked him.

"I do," a husky voice said from behind me. "What goes on here?"

I turned around and saw Midnight O'Hara standing there right behind me. I took a deep breath and closed my eyes for a moment.

"That perfume," I said huskily. "It has a name?"

"Midnight—of course!" she said crisply. "I asked what goes on here?"

"Murder," I said. "Unless he shot himself and swallowed the gun quickly afterwards. That wouldn't surprise me." She looked at the past-tense jive-merchant with an expression of distaste on her face.

"Who was he?"

"No friend of mine," I said. I looked at the waiter hopefully: "Your brother?"

"I never saw him in here before," he said quickly. "I don't know the guy from nothing!"

"And you won't get the chance now," I said. "That's for sure."

"If you're a police officer aren't you going to do something about it?" Midnight O'Hara demanded. "This is ruining my business!"

I took a look around and saw there were about half a dozen people left in the cellar and they looked as if they couldn't move without some assistance. And they also looked as if they were earnestly hoping that assistance would be forthcoming fast. I noticed that Annabelle Jackson wasn't among the half-dozen.

"Where's the phone?" I asked.

"In my office," Midnight said. "I'll take you there."

"You stay right here," I told the waiter, "and see that nobody touches him."

He shuddered: "Who would want to do that?"

I followed Midnight through the door at the back of the dais where the trio still sat, staring into space and looking as if they'd like to render "Oh, Didn't He Ramble," for the cat who was really gone.

Midnight's office had a business-like desk and chair in one corner, a dressing-table in the other. On the floor was a tiger-skin rug. The glass eyes of the tiger had a sort of contented look and I thought that was understandable. Most tigers didn't get the chance of lying around a girl's office cum dressing-room all day—and all night, too.

I picked up the phone from the desk and dialled Homicide. Hanlon was on duty and I spoke to him, giving him the score.

"I'll come over right away," he said. "What are you going to do about it, Al?"

"I'll wait till you get here," I said, "then go home."

"Have you spoken to the Commissioner?"

"No," I said quickly.

"Would you like me to call him?"

"Whatever for?"

"Well—you're his boy, aren't you? Seeing that you were Johnny-on-the-spot, he might like you to handle it."

"I'm sure he wouldn't!" I said firmly. "You just get out here fast and it's all yours."

"What's your number there?"

I got the number from Midnight and repeated it into the mouthpiece of the phone.

"Right, Al," Hanlon said. "See you soon."

I hung up and saw Midnight looking at me with a look of impatience on her face.

"Well," she said tersely, "aren't you going to get on with it?"

"With what?"

"The investigation or whatever it is you have to do. And how long is that body going to stay there, ruining my business?"

"It'll have to stay for a while," I said. "Till the doctor's had a look at it and we've had some photographs taken. And a Lieutenant Hanlon will be taking care of the investigation. I just happened to be here when it happened, that's all."

"Oh," she said coldly.

I lit myself a cigarette: "Seeing that your waiter is occupied with official business, do you think I could pour myself a drink?"

"You'll find most things in that cabinet over there," she said. "Do you always drink on official business?"

"Only when I get the opportunity," I admitted. I opened the cabinet: "Can I get you something?"

"Vodka and tonic," she said. "I need something for my nerves."

"But not your curves," I said. "They're perfect just the way they are."

"That's a typical policeman's approach," she said, "flatfooted!"

"I can only try," I said. "I'll probably get better with practice."

The phone shrilled and she walked over to the desk and lifted the receiver.

"It's for you," she said a moment later. "That is, if you're Lieutenant Wheeler?"

"I'm Lieutenant Wheeler," I admitted and took the phone from her hand and said a not very bright "hello" into it.

"Wheeler," it was the voice of doom—Commissioner Lavers. You could pick his bark even at a dog-show.

"Yes sir," I said politely.

"Hanlon just phoned me. Somebody dropped dead?"

"With a bullet through them."

"So he told me. Homicide is having a busy night. I told Hanlon to stay there—he's sending a squad out to you."

"I'm off-duty, Commissioner," I said quickly. "I just happened to be here, having a drink and ..."

"Emergency," he said crisply. "You handle it. Give you something to do. There's a beautiful woman around somewhere, isn't there?"

I looked at Midnight appraisingly: "I wouldn't say beautiful, exactly. Much too exciting to be beautiful—perfect figure, big black eyes ... and you should hear her sing!"

"There wouldn't be another reason for you being there," Lavers said. "And Wheeler—this looks like a nice, orthodox murder by what Hanlon told me. Just handle it that way, huh?"

"Lieutenant Hanlon has a gift for handling these matters in an orthodox fashion," I said hopefully. "Now, if you ..."

"I want a full report on progress by nine tomorrow morning, Wheeler!" he said coldly. There was a click as he hung up.

I replaced the receiver back on the rest and felt conscious of two bright pieces of steel boring into me. I looked up and caught them full blast as I met Midnight O'Hara's eyes.

"What was that you said about not beautiful, exactly?" she asked.

"It was a compliment," I said. "You are atomic fission with a fuse that's been counted down to the last second. Beauty is a static thing, it's ladylike and ..."

"So now I'm a tramp?"

"I mean ..."

"I understand very well what you mean!" she said. "I suppose you use your official position to insult people all the time! Well, let me tell you, Lieutenant ..."

There was a knock on the door and a small procession came into the room. Heading the procession was Sergeant Polnik, and following close behind him was Doctor Murphy. The doc looked at me longingly.

"One of these days when I get close enough to you with a scalpel in my hand, I'm going to carve right into your skull and find out what blocks your ears inside," he said.

"Nothing blocks my ears, doc," I said. "I have a hundred per cent hearing."

"Don't give me that!" he sneered. "If there's nothing blocking your ears on the inside, how come you keep that vacuum inside your head!"

"This is Doctor Murphy," I said to Midnight. "Unofficially known as Little Murder Incorporated. He owns two graveyards of patients already."

"She isn't the corpse," Murphy said, eyeing Midnight appreciatively. "She's breathing." He sighed deeply. "And you can say that again!"

"What a nasty little man he is," Midnight said. "He's nearly as bad as you are!"

Polnik coughed gently: "Lieutenant?"

"Sergeant?"

"I got the team outside—can we get started?"

"I guess so," I said. "It's the taxpayer's money we're wasting."

We left the office and went back to the dais. Murphy knelt down beside the body and made his examination.

"I'd like to move him," he said. "You want photographs first?"

"I guess so," I said. "It's the orthodox thing to do."

So the photographer took pictures and then Murphy rolled the body over. He got onto his feet and dusted his hands together briskly.

"Bullet through the left lung," he said. "Probably entered the heart. Death would be instantaneous."

"Crazy!" I said.

Murphy bristled: "What did you say!"

"It wasn't me who said it," I told him. "It was him." I pointed to the corpse. "I heard the shot and heard him scream. Then he got up on the dais in front of the trio, said, 'Crazy!' and keeled over."

Murphy muttered nastily to himself: "How long from the time he screamed to the time he keeled over?"

"Maybe five seconds," I said. "Maybe less."

"And how long do you think instantaneous is? Five seconds is virtually instantaneous!"

"You're the doc, doc," I said politely.

"I'll do an autopsy as soon as the meat-wagon brings him in," he said.

"Anything else you want?"

"His personal effects," I said. "It doesn't matter if I go through his pockets now, does it?"

"Help yourself," he said. "I suppose you would in any case."

"You should wear a shroud," I said, "more in keeping with the ghoul that you are."

I through the cat's pockets and got an assortment of junk which I turned over to Polnik to take into Midnight's office.

The meat-wagon arrived and the body was taken away, Murphy going with it. The three musicians still sat staring steadily into space.

Polnik came back. "The dame in there don't seem any too happy about us using her office, Lieutenant."

"We'll have the Commissioner send her an official apology," I said. "In fact I'll go and make her an interim apology right now. That should last her till the Commissioner gets around to the official one."

"Sure, Lieutenant," Polnik said vaguely.

"I'll talk to her," I said. "When I've finished talking to her I want to talk to these three guys," I nodded at the musicians.

"One at a time?"

"All at once to start with," I said. "And after that the waiter."

"Which waiter?"

"The one who played the shaggy dog in that story about a waiter and a shaggy dog," I said. "You can't miss him. He's the only cocker spaniel inside the place that's wearing a stiff shirt."

I walked back into Midnight's office.

"Didn't anyone ever tell you it's polite to knock?" she asked coldly as I came in.

"Opportunity did once," I admitted. "I'm taking over this office as my headquarters for the time being, if you don't mind?"

"I do mind," she said. "But I don't suppose it makes a damn of difference!"

She had what looked like a new glass of vodka and tonic in her hand. I went over to the cabinet and helped myself to another Scotch and dropped a couple of ice-cubes from the tray into it. Then I walked over to the desk and sat down.

Polnik had left the contents of the corpse's pockets in a neat pile on the desk-top. I went through them. A half-empty pack of cigarettes, a match-folder which had Golden Horseshoe printed on the flap, and underneath was Midnight at Midnight. There was a handkerchief, crumpled into a ball, a roll of ten-dollar bills which added up to a hundred and sixty dollars, a pocket-comb, a nail-file.

The last item was a creased, dirty envelope with some words scrawled across the front of it in pencil. The words read: Knock a fade on Oscar hype tea-man.

I went back to the cigarettes, took one out of the pack and sniffed it. It was marihuana all right. The tea-man was self-explanatory, marihuana cigarettes being commonly known as tea-sticks as almost any high-school kid can tell you.

"You know anybody called Oscar?" I asked Midnight.

"You'll do!" she said.

That hit the gong inside my vacuum. Oscar—quote, a narrow-minded character, unquote. I thought Annabelle would be proud of my jazz education and knowledge of jive-talk which is more the addicts than the musicians these days. Hype was a build-up to shaking somebody down—in this case an oscar—lined up as a sucker.

So my hep-cat had been mixed up in a scheme to take somebody for some money and the note on the envelope told him to lay off. Maybe he hadn't laid off and maybe that was why somebody had put a bullet into him.

So I was a little genius and I still knew nothing from nothing. I drank some of the Scotch, opened the top drawer of the desk which was empty, and swept the pile of junk into it, then closed it again.

"Make yourself at home, Lieutenant," Midnight said. "Can I get you a cushion?"

"It would be nice," I admitted. "But I have to go through the motions of doing some work. I have to ask questions and listen to answers. How about I start with you?"

"Make it quick, Lieutenant," she said. "I want to organise the cleaning-up of my place before everybody goes home!"

"I'll make it quick," I said. "Important things first. You work here every night of the week?"

"We're closed Sundays and Mondays," she said.

"That's fine," I said warmly. "What are you doing next Monday night?"

CHAPTER THREE

The trio sat in a line on the other side of the desk and for a time I looked at them as individuals.

First in line was Clarence Nesbitt who looked sort of lost without his bass-fiddle. He was fat to the point of grossness and he still wore the brown bowler-hat he always wore when he was playing in the trio.

In the centre of the three was Wesley Stewart, the horn-player, the leader of the trio. Wes was tall and thin to the point of emaciation. He had large blue eyes which were dreamy-looking and his nose was half-an-inch too long for the rest of his face.

The last one was Cuba Carter who was short and dark and looked as if he had some Filipino blood in him, but that was only a guess. He had a thin black moustache and gleaming white teeth which showed in a perpetual grin of what was probably embarrassment.

I lit myself a cigarette and looked at them. Cuba shuffled his feet nervously and Clarence's fingers plucked invisible strings and I half-expected to hear his bass-fiddle start to play although I knew it was propped against the wall outside. Only Wesley Stewart sat without movement, his eyes dreaming and in some place that was a million miles away from Midnight O'Hara's office.

I cleared my throat gently: "You boys must have seen it happen," I said. "How about telling me the score?"

They looked at each other for a long moment.

"I guess we didn't see nothing, Lieutenant," Clarence said in a high-pitched voice. "We were beating out Rampart Street and we weren't in a mind to worry about anything else. First thing I hear is some guy yell and I figure we sent him good. But then I hear this bang and while I'm trying to figure that and not lose the beat, that hophead wanders on in front of us and I figure he's some dummy trying to horn into the act and I'm about to give him the business over his skull with my l'il old pink-a-pink when he keels over and then I see the blood on his shirt and, Man! I'm off-time!"

"He says it right, Bloodhound," Cuba nodded his head quickly, his teeth flashing the smile in my direction. "He says it right—we know nothing from nothing till the guy becomes a cadaver right in front of our eyes!"

I looked at Wesley Stewart: "What's your story?"

Slowly his eyes focussed on me: "What was that, Lieutenant?" His voice was quiet and pleasant.

"I asked if your story was the same as theirs," I said.

"I'm sorry," he smiled vaguely. "I wasn't listening. I was trying to work out an idea on Weary Blues and maybe use a tenor sax instead of ..."

"I hate to interrupt your musical arrangements," I said. "But a guy was murdered here about half an hour back. If I'm not disturbing your musical genius too much, I'd like to hear your impressions of the event. Stuff like did you see who killed him and so on ..."

"Sure, Lieutenant," he smiled his quiet smile again.

"I'm sorry—I didn't see a thing—not till he got right up in front of us. Whenever I'm playing I get carried away, I guess. I never heard any yell or shot although Clarence told me about it afterwards. All I saw was this guy standing up in front of us, and then saw him fall down."

"Did any of you know him at all?" I asked and all three of them shook their heads.

"Did you ever see him before in here?"

They shook their heads again.

Again a strict negative.

"None of you saw anything. You didn't see anybody with a gun in their hand? You didn't see anybody behind you or off to the left or right—somewhere close where they could have pulled a gun out and shot him?"

"Sorry, Lieutenant?" Wesley Stewart said finally. "I guess we were all too busy at the time."

"Okay," I said. "Thanks for your help."

They got up from the chairs together and walked towards the door in step. After they had left the office, Polnik came in.

"How are things going, Lieutenant?" he asked hopefully.

"The girl knows nothing—she said," I told them. "Those three knew nothing—they said. Let's try the waiter."

So half a minute later it was the waiter sitting opposite me, with an empty chair either side of him.

I looked at him closely. He was tall and heavily-built with it. He had thick dark hair which needed cutting six weeks back and needed mowing right now. He sat slouched in the chair with a look of defiance on his face and I had the feeling that being questioned by the law was no new experience for him.

"Where were you when it happened?" I asked him.

"I was in the kitchen," he said. "Had an order for a party of four bums at a table near yours. Joe was pouring 'em for me when I heard the yell and the shot, so I raced back into the room just in time to see the guy put on an act before he knocked off."

"You didn't see anyone behind the dais?"

"There was nobody there," he said firmly. "Nobody else in sight except those three hopheads making a noise up there on top of the dais."

"You don't go for Chicago-style jazz?"

"I don't go for any type of jazz, Lieutenant," he said. "I go for silence!"

"The man who got himself shot by nobody," I said. "You ever see him before?"

"Sure," he said. "He was in here a couple of times last week. Smoking reefers—you could smell them five tables away!"

"You served him before?"

"Both times," he said. "Midnight believes in getting value for her money. She only has two waiters working any night—that gives us fifty per cent each of the tables to look after. I was the lucky guy—I got him both times."

"He never told you his name?"

"No," he grinned. "We never got that well acquainted. He did tell me he could fix me up if I needed any reefers and I told him I didn't use them. Then he called me a square and a lot of other names as well."

"Did he stay long, either time?"

"The first time maybe an hour," the waiter said. "The second time only ten minutes. The first time he looked like he was waiting for somebody to arrive, but I guess they didn't. The second time he was really floating and I was going to ask Midnight whether I should rush him out of the place—maybe he got the idea because he beat it off his own bat after about ten minutes."

"What did he drink while he was here?"

"A small beer," the waiter said contemptuously. "And smoking those stinking reefers all the time. He never even tipped a dime!"

"You sound like you really appreciated him!" I said.

He grinned, "I didn't hate him that much to knock him off, Lieutenant!"

"Can you think of anything else about him, you haven't told me? Anything at all?"

The waiter thought hard for a few seconds: "There was something he said to me the second time—when he was really freewheeling, but it didn't make any sense."

"Let's try it for size?" I suggested.

"He said I was an oscar, whatever that meant. He said I was an oscar then he laughed like crazy and said I'd never have the dough to be an oscar!"

"That makes sense," I said. "But it doesn't help any."

"I figured an oscar was one of those Hollywood awards," he said slowly. "You know—a piece of bronze about twelve inches high and shaped like a man."

"That was what your friend thought too, I imagine," I said blandly.

His face darkened, "Why, the dirty, fat ..."

"Call him a liberal," I suggested. "That's still a dirty word."

The waiter went out, and I followed him. The trio were back on the dais again, Clarence plucking a muted rhythm from his strings, Cuba tapping a gentle beat from a snare-drum and Wesley just sitting there peacefully with his eyes closed.

Midnight was watching two guys carefully scrubbing the blood from the floor. The customers who hadn't got out before Polnik and his boys arrived, sat around looking unhappy and cold sober.

"I got all their names and addresses, Lieutenant," Polnik said. "You want to question 'em, or should I let them go now?"

"You can let them go now," I said.

I walked onto the dais and just stood there looking around. Polnik came back to me and stood beside me.

"They're on their way, Lieutenant. Anything else I can do?"

"You can join me in looking baffled," I said. "Here we have a dais, right?"

"Right!" he said enthusiastically.

"Behind it a clear space of about six feet to the wall, right?"

"Right!"

"Off to the left are two doors—one leads through to Miss O'Hara's office and the other straight into the kitchen. There are no other doors, right?"

"Right!"

"The corpse, before it was a corpse, must have been standing behind the dais when someone fired a bullet into him. Then he stepped up onto the dais, walked around in front of the three musicians and died. Right?"

"Right!"

"The musicians never saw him, they were facing the other way in any case and all of them playing their instruments at the time. Miss O'Hara was inside her office, the waiter was inside the kitchen when it happened. Nobody could have shot over the heads of the musicians and had the bullet follow a curved line so that it dropped five or six feet into the guy's chest, right?"

"Right!"

"So who killed him?"

"R ..." Polnik blinked a couple of times.

"Just so long as you're baffled as well," I said. "I feel happier."

"There was no gun on the floor any place," Polnik said, "so he couldn't have killed himself, could he?"

"I already had the theory that he did and then swallowed the gun," I said. "The autopsy should show whether the theory's any good."

"Maybe the doc already found the gun and ..." Polnik frowned at me. "You're kidding, Lieutenant?"

"Maybe it was a small gun," I said. "And I just remembered something, get that waiter back into the office, will you?"

I walked back into Midnight O'Hara's office and sat down behind her desk again. A few seconds later the waiter reappeared.

"You wanted to see me, Lieutenant?"

"I have a memory," I said. "Not a very good one but sometimes it functions. You told me about the guy coming in here a couple of times and sitting around drinking small beers, smoking reefers and not tipping even a dime."

"That's right," he said.

"Just after it happened you asked me if I was a doctor or something—remember?"

"Sure," he said.

"I told you I was a cop," I said. "I asked who owned the place. Miss

O'Hara appeared and said she did. I asked you if you knew the corpse and you said you'd never seen him inside the place before. You didn't know him from nothing."

"That's right, Lieutenant," he said slowly. "I guess I was upset—it all happened so suddenly and ..."

"Let me save you some time," I suggested. "I don't believe you."

He licked his lips, "Anybody can make a mistake at a time like that, Lieutenant!"

"No."

"But honest, Lieutenant ..."

"Which story was the truth—you'd never seen him before or he'd been in a couple of times?"

"He'd been in a couple of times, like I told you. The first time I wasn't thinking straight—not even seeing straight! A guy suddenly gets himself murdered, it's not easy to ..."

"Let's try another routine," I said. "Let's say you like working here. Maybe you even need the money, most people work for that reason, including me. So when you see your boss right behind me, you think maybe it would be better to say you'd never seen the guy before?"

He swallowed hard, "You're making it tough for me, Lieutenant!"

"If I am, I'm not even trying," I said. "You should see me when I'm trying."

"I figured he could be trouble," he said, "and Midnight wouldn't be any trouble. I thought if anybody was going to tell you about the guy it would better be somebody else. Then I cooled down a little and when you asked me the second time, I figured for sure somebody else would have told you about him, so I'd better tell the truth about him having been inside the place a couple of times."

"The truth but not the whole truth?"

He licked his lips again, "That's about it. He looked like trouble the first time I ever saw him. The reefers—maybe more than reefers, he looked hopped-up all the time."

"What was his name?"

"Landis," he muttered. "Johnny Landis. He used to talk to Midnight and I could see when he did that she wasn't liking any part of it, but it looked like she had to stay with it for some reason."

"He had something over her?"

"I wouldn't know, Lieutenant," he said quickly. "Maybe he did and maybe he didn't. It just looked that way, that's all."

"How often was he in here?"

"Four, maybe five times altogether. The first time was around six weeks ago. He'd come in about once a week, sit around for a while, the way I told you before. The first couple of times he asked for Midnight and she'd come out and sit with him at a table, the times after that, he'd walk through into the office—he'd watch her sing first, then about five minutes later he'd get up and just walk through into her office. He'd stay there maybe twenty minutes then leave."

"Did she ever leave with him?"

He shook his head, "Midnight never leaves till the joint closes and that's not till three in the morning. He'd be out of the place by one at the latest."

"Do you know where he lived?"

"No, Lieutenant. He told me his name the first time—he said to tell Midnight that Johnny Landis was out front and wanted to see her. He never told me anything else."

"You're sure?" I asked him. "If I find out you're lying to me this time, the next time I question you will be down at Headquarters."

"Believe me, Lieutenant," he said earnestly. "That's the whole truth!"

"Okay," I said. "What's your name?"

"Booth," he said. "Eddie Booth."

"All right, Eddie," I said. "That's all for now."

He got onto his feet then hesitated for a moment.

"You won't tell her it was me who gave you the story?" he asked anxiously.

"Not unless I have to, Eddie," I said. "And I would think unkindly of you, if you happened to tell her about it, most unkindly."

"I won't tell her," he said, "and that's for sure!"

"Then we might both be happy," I suggested.

"You going to talk to her right away, Lieutenant?" he ventured.

"No," I said. "I don't think so."

CHAPTER FOUR

I sat facing Lavers across his desk at nine the next morning. I'd got to bed around five and up again at eight and I was tired. I tried to keep an orthodox look on my face as he scowled at me.

"All right, Wheeler," he grunted. "Stop trying to look like a plaster of Paris saint, it doesn't become you! Tell me what progress you've made—if any."

I told him in sequence. Everything went all right up to the point where I told him that when I'd finished questioning Eddie Booth, I folded up the investigation at the Golden Horseshoe and went back to Homicide, taking Polnik and the remainder of his posse with me.

"You mean you didn't question the woman again!" he gargled.

"That's right, sir."

"When she'd told you the first time she knew nothing of the man!"

"You're right again, sir."

"If I asked you were you out of your mind, that would be a stupid question, I suppose!"

"Or an orthodox one."

He gave me a vivid impression of a starving cannibal as he bit off the end of a cigar. "All right, genius! Why didn't you question her again?"

"I thought I'd like to find out a little more about the corpse first," I said. "That might show up the connection between him and the girl. If I questioned her right then she could have said she lied because she didn't want any trouble with the police over her place—that Landis was just a reefer-smoking nuisance who she tried to humour, so he wouldn't bust up her cellar."

"You wouldn't believe that sort of nonsense!"

"But I wouldn't be able to throw her on it, Commissioner. I'd rather wait until I know something more about Landis, and when I know that I might know something about the connection between them."

"And meanwhile, suppose she's hopped a plane to South America!"

"If you'll give me leave of absence," I said hopefully, "I'll hop another plane and chase her!"

Cigar-smoke made a fog between us. When it disappeared, his face was only a medium shade of red.

"All right!" he said. "What else?"

I put the stuff I was carrying on the desk in front of him.

"There's the autopsy report," I said. "Landis was shot through the lung, the bullet just missed his heart. He died of internal hemorrhage—it took long enough for him to get up onto the dais and give his soldier's farewell. The slug was a point two-two."

Lavers tossed the autopsy report aside irritably.

"What else?"

"No trace of narcotics—apparently he hadn't gotten beyond the reefer-stage."

"What else?"

I put the morgue photo on his desk. "That's him," I said.

Lavers glanced casually at the picture.

"No trace of him with the bureau," I said. "I checked the name, description and fingerprints through R. and I. of course."

Lavers wasn't listening to me. He was staring fixedly at the photo in front of him. I thought if he wanted to go into a trance around now, it was his privilege. I lit a cigarette and leaned back in my chair.

"It can't be!" Lavers said in a low voice.

It was what is commonly known as a cryptic remark. I let it pass—if the Commissioner was going to play crystal-ball, I wasn't going to play stooge.

He pressed the buzzer at the side of his desk and Annabelle Jackson came into the office a couple of moments later with a pencil in one hand, a note-book in the other and a blank look for me in both her eyes.

"Get me Joe Randle of the *Tribune* on the phone," Lavers told her.

"Yes sir," she said.

"Good morning, Miss Jackson," I said brightly. "I hope you enjoyed yourself last night?"

"Oh, I did, Lieutenant," she said frigidly. "Chicago-style!"

I waited while Lavers spoke to Randle, asking him to come over right away. When he'd replaced the receiver, he looked at me.

"I have a nasty feeling about this," he said. "We'll find out soon enough!"

"Yes sir," I said, because he was obviously expecting me to say something.

I knew Joe Randle who was the police roundsman for the *Tribune*. He said hello when he arrived at the office and looked at us expectantly.

"I'd like you to see something, Joe," Commissioner Lavers said. "You'd better come with us, Wheeler."

So fifteen minutes later we were inside the morgue and the attendant opened the refrigerated drawer that held the body of Johnny Landis.

I saw Joe Randle's face go white as he looked down.

"It is?" Lavers asked him gruffly.

"It certainly is," Randle said in a subdued voice. "When did it happen, Mr. Commissioner?"

"I'll fill in the details later for you, Joe," Lavers told him. "Right now I've got to see Landis hears about it first, you understand? You don't know anything till he tells you. You never saw me, you were never down here."

"Sure," Joe nodded. "I understand."

We went back to Lavers' office. Joe left almost immediately and Lavers got back behind his desk and I got back into my chair. I watched him light himself another cigar carefully

"He will not only mystify but amaze you!" I said. "There is nothing up his sleeve but we defy you to see how the trick is done. We even defy you to know what the trick is!"

"All right!" Lavers grinned bleakly. "I thought I might give you a little of your own treatment, Wheeler! And if you didn't devote all your spare time to blondes of doubtful origin you might know that the owner of the *Tribune* happens to be a man called Landis, Daniel Landis. He has ... had a son named John."

"I'm feeling exactly the same way Aimee Semple MacPherson must have felt," I said, "I'm beginning to see the light."

"You do possibly know that the *Tribune* is the most influential newspaper in this city?" Lavers continued. "And when the son of the proprietor has been murdered, that newspaper is going to be most anxious to see the murderer caught—and quickly."

"I see exactly what you mean, sir," I said.

"I hope you do," he grunted. "We are going to be roasted over this one, Wheeler. Landis is a most difficult man at the best of times. With this ..." He shook his head somberly. "I don't like to even think about it."

"Who is going to tell him?"

"I think I'd better do that," he said. "I'll have to get him to formally identity the body. He'll expect every man in the Bureau to be working on this. All hell is going to break loose on this one, Wheeler!"

"Yes, sir," I said.

"Don't just sit there saying, 'Yes, sir!'"

"No, sir."

"Get out!" he said. "Get out of my sight! But don't go past your desk!"

"Yes, sir," I said, and got.

I went through into the outer office and sat at my desk that so conveniently faced Annabelle's desk. A minute later Lavers walked through.

Half an hour later he came back with a tall, lean character in tow. The tall lean character was Daniel Landis, I guessed. He had neat grey hair, a hooked beak of a nose and very thin lips. He also had a look of confident arrogance on his face that went well with his immaculate suit, handmade shirt and Italian silk tie. I thought I could see exactly what the Commissioner meant by all hell breaking loose.

Landis left the Commissioner's office about twenty minutes later and thirty seconds after that I was called into the office. "Sit down, Wheeler," Lavers said. "You saw Landis leaving?"

"Yes, sir."

"How did he look?"

"Exactly the same as when he came in with you."

"That's right. He's got ice in his veins instead of blood. He identified the body with as much interest as he'd identify an ant. He doesn't seem to give a damn about his son being dead but he gives a whole lot of damns that we catch who did it—and quick!"

I waited for the fast break to follow the slow curve.

"I'm assigning Hanlon to the case," Lavers said abruptly.

"It does need an orthodox cop," I said coldly.

"That is, officially," he continued. "I think you might employ your peculiar talents more efficiently if you tackle it from the outside."

"Yes, sir."

"Don't let us start that again!" he said wearily.

"No ..." I stopped in time.

"Landis implied that he almost expected to see his son end up that way. I could almost swear he was faintly pleased at having been proved right! The only information I could get out of him was that he virtually disowned his son some three months ago when he discovered he was smoking marihuana."

"Next week he's playing East Lynne?" I suggested.

"He means it!" Lavers said. "He says he has no knowledge of his son's activities during the last three months. He paid him an allowance of three hundred dollars a month into a bank account and that was that. He says he doesn't doubt that his son had degenerated completely during the time and was probably murdered for not paying his bills for the marihuana."

"Mr. Landis sounds like any warm-blooded father," I said. "What about Mrs. Landis?"

"She's dead."

"That figures!"

"But there is a daughter," Lavers continued. "About five years younger than John was. She lives at home with her father. He was going home to tell her the news, then guess what?"

"He was going back to his office."

Lavers looked at me sourly, "You're so smart! That's exactly what he was going to do." He glanced at his watch. "He'll be back there by two. If you call around three, you should find the daughter alone. She might be able to give you some information."

"Shouldn't Hanlon do that?"

"Certainly not!" Lavers said. "I don't want Hanlon who's officially in charge of the case to be accused of not informing Landis of every move on the case he makes. If the daughter tells her father about your visit, you'll be explained as a misguided junior who didn't understand his instructions clearly, and went straight to the house instead of arranging an appointment first with her father."

"I am to be demonstrated as a moron?"

"For once you will have the privilege of appearing in your true colours," Lavers said kindly.

"What about the Golden Horseshoe?"

"What about it?"

"Is Hanlon going to take over questioning the O'Hara girl, that is," I qualified the question, "if she hasn't taken off for South America?"

"I'm prepared to leave Miss O'Hara to your tender mercies," Lavers said. "And I have no doubt they will be tender. Hanlon will make all the routine checks you should have made already. But I'll see he stays clear of the leads you have. For a time, that is. We won't have much time at all, Wheeler, with Landis breathing down our necks. So I'll have to review the situation every twenty-four hours."

"You mean if I don't come up with something good fast, I might find myself back behind my desk?"

"You might find yourself back in a precinct," Lavers said evenly. "This is one homicide we solve, and I don't particularly care how many Lieutenants I have to break to do it!"

"That's the thing I like most of all about working for you, Commissioner," I said admiringly. "Job security!"

"You could always go back to being a bum," he said.

"Thank you, sir," I said as I got onto my feet. "Thank you for the confidence you've just expressed in me. I won't let you down and if I do, I promise it will be deliberate."

Lavers grinned amiably, "Get out of here and go chase your blonde suspects!" he said. "And may I offer you a suggestion concerning technique?"

"You may," I said.

His grin widened, Cheshire-wise, "Chicago-style is out!" he said.

CHAPTER FIVE

It was five after three when I parked the Jag outside the Landis home.

The Landis home was Olde Englande. It was two storeys high and had big gables and fake thatch on the roof and Elizabethan beams everywhere. It stood in the middle of a small, five acre plot which had neat trimmed hedges and a pond with seven swans placed carefully on the surface.

I was disappointed when I pressed the button beside the timber-panelled front door. All I got was chimes when I was expecting the first chorus of John Peel on a hunting horn.

The door was opened by a butler who looked Olde Englande too, and spoke as if he'd just cut his mouth on a bottle.

"Good afternoon, sir," he said.

"A bright tally-ho to you," I said. "I would like to see Miss Landis."

"I'm afraid that is impossible, sir," he said stiffly. "There has been a sudden bereavement in the family and ..."

"I saw it this morning in the morgue," I said brutally. "I'm Lieutenant Wheeler from the Homicide Bureau and I insist on seeing Miss Landis."

"Very good, sir," he said. "If you will follow me."

I followed him. Through an oak-panelled hall, past the suit of armour that stood rusting at the foot of the wide staircase and into an oak-panelled ante-room, tucked away under the staircase.

"If you will wait here, sir," the butler said. "I will announce you."

"The place is so big you have a public-address system?" I asked with admiration.

He went out closing the door behind him with a terrible gentleness. I lit a cigarette and waited. I had a nasty suspicion that the ante-room was normally used for hanging coats.

Around about five minutes later the butler returned.

"Miss Landis will see you in the sitting-room, sir," he said.

"You have rooms for sitting and rooms for standing?" I asked him.

"If you will follow me, sir."

The sitting-room was panelled in cedar. There was a big fireplace with polished irons standing in front of it. On one wall was a seventeenth century musket and on the opposite wall a picture of a non-laughing cavalier. I could understand the way he felt—laughter would be indecent in this house.

There was a thick-piled, flower-patterned rug in the centre of the floor. Around it were grouped a settee and four armchairs chintz-covered and uncomfortable enough to be either genuine antique or reproduction antique.

I looked for the daughter of the house—something with straight hair drawn tight across her head into a bun at the back of her neck. Something that wore a neck-to-ankle, eighteenth-century milkmaid's gown and wore steel-rimmed spectacles. Something that wept gently into a lace handkerchief and squeezed it out into her milkmaid's bucket which would be made of china and have roses painted on the outside.

I didn't see her.

"Miss Landis will be with you in a moment, sir," the butler said. "If I may make a request—the rug is very valuable. Would you mind using an ashtray, if you smoke, sir?"

"I would prefer to use a cigarette," I said with equal politeness. "But if you insist ... you can light an ashtray for me."

I heard a distinct click this time as he closed the door. I walked over to the settee and sat down on it. To be accurate, I sat on it—the springs didn't give one eighth of an inch. I wondered if the bowl that stood on the spindly-legged side-table beside the settee was an ashtray or an heirloom. I thought in any case the best things about heirlooms is that they can be converted so I lit a cigarette and dropped the dead match into the bowl.

I had deposited about an inch of ash into the bowl before the door opened again and in came the milkmaid. I looked at her and dropped my cigarette onto the rug.

The cows would never give milk while she was around—it would curdle with jealousy.

She was around average height but that was the only thing average about her. She was a brunette with her glossy, rich hair drawn back loosely into a horse's tail. She had the face of an elf—a beautiful elf. Her lips were full and a deep red and the lower lip curled slightly into a pout which could only be described as provocative.

She wore a mandarin gown of a dark grey silk that shimmered as she walked. It was high-necked and fitted her closer than any glove could fit and was split up one side to mid-thigh so she could walk in it and when she did, there was a glimpse of suntanned, perfectly-shaped legs.

Her violet-coloured eyes looked huge behind the lenses of her glitter-framed glasses. Her earrings were two golden dragons ready to spit fire and flame.

"I'm Rena Landis," she said a high-keyed, breathless voice.

I picked up my cigarette from the valuable rug and got onto my feet.

"I'm Lieutenant Wheeler," I said. "From …"

"I know," she said. "Talbot told me."

"The butler?"

"That's what he's supposed to be," she said. "He's a fascinating study in repression, really. If he had a wife, I'm sure he would beat her!"

"I'd think it would be the other way round," I said. "There's a limit to what any woman can endure!"

"What's your Christian name?"

I blinked. "Al," I said, a trifle hoarsely.

"Call me Rena," she said. "I don't think people can possibly get to know one another when they use surnames and are formal all the time. Don't you agree, Al?"

She sat down beside me on the settee. The split in her gown was on my side and she might just as well have been wearing shorts. It was disconcerting.

"You want to talk about John," she said. "Father told me about it this morning. Do you know he smoked marihuana?"

"There were marihuana cigarettes in his pocket," I said weakly.

"I tried it," she said seriously. "But I gave it up."

"I'm glad to hear it," I said.

"Childish," she said. "But then John was childish. Besides, reefers are only the start. After a while you start taking heroin or smoking opium and before you know where you are, you're a slave to habit. I don't believe in habits, do you, Al? I like to feel I'm free of convention and I can do what I like. Don't you like doing what you like, Al? You look very young to be a police lieutenant, I thought they were all dried-up and not emotionally stimulating at all. I find you quite emotionally stimulating, Al. Do you find me emotionally stimulating?"

"I …"

"You don't have to tell me," she smiled brilliantly. "I can see you do because you're uncomfortable and that's the fourth time you've looked at my legs since I sat down. I have a special name for this gown, I call it, Impact! Quite a good name, don't you think? Would you like to kiss me, Al?"

I choked on a lungful of smoke and stubbed out the butt of the cigarette in the bowl.

"Father would just love to see you do that," she said. "That bowl is seventeenth-century Doulton. You're the first person I've seen find a practical use for it."

"About your brother," I tried again. "Can you tell me why ..."

"You don't have to worry about Talbot," she said, "it's more than his job is worth to disturb us in here. The other servants are in the kitchen and that's right at the back of the house. You can make love to me, Al, if you want to. I've never been made love to by a police officer before. It's rather an exciting idea. Of course you'll have to be discreet. You can kiss me and put your arms around me but nothing more than that. I'll need a little time to know whether I like you making love to me."

I got up quickly from the settee and walked around the back of the armchair opposite. I felt a little safer there, not much.

"Please," I pleaded. "All I want to do is to ask you some questions."

"Don't you want to make love to me?" Her violet eyes grew even larger. "Don't you think I'm attractive? Would you prefer I put my arms around you and kissed you to begin with?"

"I'd prefer you to sit right where you are and shut up," I snarled.

Her lower lip curled into a definite pout, "Now you're being rude and shouting at me, Al. Don't you like brunettes?"

"I think you are beautiful," I said. "I like brunettes as beautiful as you. I would like very much to put my arms around you and kiss you—but this is an official call on official business. I'm a cop, working on the time they pay me to be a cop. Some questions?"

"I can see you have a sense of duty, Al," she said. "I don't want to confuse your sense of values—it could set up all sorts of irritating complexes and compulsive neuroses. You ask the questions first and when you're finished we can make love then."

She settled herself back against the cushions of the settee and re-crossed her legs.

"Go ahead!" she said.

"Do you have any idea why your brother was murdered?" I asked slowly, having difficulty in regaining my breath. "I know these questions must be painful for you, but I hope you'll realise that ..."

"Painful?" she laughed politely. "I think I should put you right at the beginning, Al. I hated my brother from the time I could walk and long before I could talk. He was cruel and nasty. You know how some little boys pull the wings off flies?"

"Yes," I said, "but ..."

"John was the type who'd prefer to pull the arms of the boys who were pulling the wings off the flies," she said. "That way it would be as good as a double-feature to him."

"Well," I said doubtfully, "in a way it makes it easier for me to ask the questions if you are not mourning your brother's death."

"I'm not mourning, I'm celebrating," she said. "I would be drunk now if I hadn't given up alcohol. Alcohol is a weaker form of narcotics, you know, Al. Habit-forming and I like to be completely free of habits and repressions."

"Good for you!" I muttered.

"I don't smoke for the same reason," she said.

"But you don't mind making love—in a discreet sort of way?"

"That has nothing to do with habit," she smiled slowly. "That's to do with biology. It's dangerous to repress the chemical reactions, you know, Al. It ..."

I gritted my teeth, "I know," I said. "It causes repressions and compulsive neuroses!"

"Exactly."

"Questions?" I almost whimpered. "Do you have any idea who would want to kill your brother or why he was murdered?"

"Of course I do," she said firmly. "Anybody who knew him at all would want to kill him, and knowing him would be enough reason why to murder him."

"You can't think of anyone in particular?"

"Well," she said reflectively, "there's me, and Father and Talbot. Then there's Cook, and Elsie, the maid, and Jannings, the gardener. There's the mailman, the ..."

"That's very funny!" I said coldly.

"Is it?" I would have sworn there was genuine surprise in her eyes as she looked up at me. "It wasn't meant to be."

"Outside your immediate family and your servants," I said. "Do you know of anyone else?"

"I don't think so," she said. "John hadn't been living with us for the last three months, you know. Before that I always saw as little of him as possible. It was safer."

"Safer?"

"He'd generally indulge in some little pleasantry when we met," she said, a metallic edge to her voice. "He'd twist my arm up behind my back or kick my shin ... things like that."

"He sounds charming," I said.

"He was," she said, "the complete adolescent. He had a mania for anything depraved ... the way he dressed, the way he talked in some slang gibberish, the music he liked—some peculiar variation of jazz he called Chicago-style."

I winced.

"So you think you can take your choice of anybody who knew him, Al," she said brightly. "I wouldn't have minded killing him, it would have been a new experience."

"And the electric chair would also be a new experience," I said. "The final experience."

"That was the one thought that probably stopped me," she said musingly. "Did you have any more questions, Al, or can we make love now?"

She lifted her legs onto the settee and stretched out, her hands behind her head. The Japanese surrender at Tokyo Bay couldn't have been more obvious.

It was at that moment the door behind me opened and someone walked into the room. I thought for a moment that the butler had just lost his job but it wasn't the butler who spoke.

"Rena!" a cold voice said. "Go to your room!"

She sat up with a jerk, one hand futilely clutching the skirt of her gown, trying to close the slit. Her lower lip quivered uncontrollably.

"Father!" she said in a shaking voice. "I didn't know you were ..."

"Go to your room!" he repeated. "This instant!"

She got onto her feet and scuttled towards the door. She didn't look at me as she went past. I could see the tears starting to fall down her cheeks underneath the lower rims of her glasses.

The door closed behind her and I heard footsteps running down the hall.

"And you, sir?" the cold voice said. "May I enquire the name of the man I find trying to seduce my daughter under my own roof!"

"Smith?" I said hopefully.

CHAPTER SIX

Landis stood in front of the bureau and lifted the phone in one hand.

"So," he said, "you come to my house to question my daughter about her brother's murder—within a few hours of her being told of the tragedy! You ignore completely the fact that such questioning could have a serious effect on a highly-strung, sensitive girl grieving badly for her brother! You don't choose to see me first. To even grant me the courtesy of asking my permission to question her! Well, let me tell you something, Lieutenant. You aren't dealing with some poor, helpless immigrant family this time! You happen to be dealing with the most powerful newspaper in this city! And I shall see that the public are acquainted with the loutish, third-degree tactics employed by our so-called guardians of justice!"

He dialled a number carefully then looked at me steadily.

"This is Daniel Landis," he said into the phone. "Connect me with Commissioner Lavers." He looked up at me. "What was the name again?"

"Wheeler," I said.

Four seconds went by—I counted them.

"Commissioner?" he said. "Landis here. I have just arrived home. Arrived home to find one of your men terrorising my daughter ... terrorising is the word I used. The poor girl is half out of her mind with grief already. The brutal questioning she has been subjected to may have done incalculable damage to her mind. I demand that this man who forced his way into my house shall be severely disciplined—and immediately!"

A faint marble of red showed on each of his cheekbones as he listened for a few moments.

"Commissioner!" he said abruptly. "I don't presume to tell you how to run your department, but this third-degree method of interrogation cannot be tolerated ... in any case I intend to devote tomorrow's editorial in the *Tribune* to the subject. And I give you fair warning now—if any of your men approach my house again I shalt have them forcibly ejected from the grounds!"

He put the receiver back into place with a sharp click.

"I hope this will be a lesson you remember, Wheeler," he said. "I have a strong feeling that the Commissioner will take heed of my words, even before he reads tomorrow's editorial!"

"You think I'll be directing traffic before nightfall?" I suggested.

"Shall I say I think that's the direction in which your talents lie?" he said. "And I think the Commissioner will probably take the fullest advantage of your talents in the near future."

I lit myself a cigarette and flipped the dead match neatly into the Doulton bowl. He looked down at the bowl, seeing the ash and the butts inside it, then looked up again at me. The red marbles grew until they were silver dollar size.

"That bowl," he said in a choked voice, "is ..."

"Genuine seventeenth century," I finished for him. "But the match was genuine twentieth century."

"Get out!" he said. "Get out before I have you thrown out!"

I turned around and walked towards the door. I had my fingers on the handle when he spoke again.

"And don't think I won't break you, Wheeler," he said softly. "Before I'm finished with you I'll have you out of the Police Department and blacklisted throughout the city! You'll finish up right where you belong,

Wheeler—back in the gutter!"

"Tell me," I said politely, "do you write the comic-strips as well as the editorials?"

I opened the door and stepped out into the hall. I made my way along to the front door but the butler was there before me.

He opened the door and bowed slightly, the look in his eyes ironic to make an understatement.

"Good afternoon, sir," he said. "May I wish you a bright tally-ho?"

"Tally-ho is the cry of the hunter, Talbot," I said gently, "not the hunted."

"Sir?" he raised his eyebrows a fraction.

"I was merely suggesting that in this house you are the hunted?" I said. "I may be wrong. But after meeting Miss Landis this afternoon, I don't think I'm wrong."

"I'm afraid I don't understand, sir!" he said coldly.

"I think you understand me very well, Talbot," I said. "I think it could make a very fascinating story—for, say, the *Tribune's* chief rival."

"What ..."

"Don't let us argue about it," I said pleasantly. "Your master desires my presence removed from this house as quickly as possible."

I took a card out of my wallet and gave it to him. More factually, I pushed it into his unresisting hand.

"That phone number will probably find me either in the early morning or late evening," I said. "I'd like to meet you again, Talbot, soon. But not here. Somewhere else—a bar, perhaps. I'd like to have a quiet chat about this house and its occupants."

"I could never abuse the confidence bestowed on me," he said stiffly.

"You're a free agent," I said agreeably. "I wouldn't dream of trying to force you into breaking any confidences. I'm just hoping you might feel a desire for justice and to help me solve a murder. If you do get that feeling, then call me."

"Impossible!" he said.

"All those old jokes about what the butler saw!" I said. "Most unfair. But it would make a wonderful story for a paper that didn't particularly care for the *Tribune*, and that covers all the other papers in town. The newspaper proprietor's household. He, being a tycoon is very rarely there, working most days and nights as he does. The only permanent occupants being the butler, young enough to photograph well—and the publisher's daughter—who dresses as if she's the strip-queen of burlesque and makes passionate advances to any man within reach. Headline: What went on behind closed blinds?"

"But it's not true!" he said frantically. "It's all lies, dreadful lies!"

"You can convince me," I said, "by ringing that number. And a final bright tally-ho to you, Talbot."

I walked down onto the drive and got into the Jaguar. I gunned the motor, pushed the gear-stick into first and spun gravel from the drive in all directions.

"Wheeler," I said to myself, "you are nothing but a dirty, blackmailing louse! You don't really believe that smear-story you gave to Olde Englande at all."

"That's right," I said back to myself, "but then Landis is nothing but a dirty louse and the only way to beat him is to find out who killed his son."

"Okay—rationalise it!" I sneered out loud as I hit the roadway and headed back towards town. "See what good that does you when you're directing traffic!"

When I got back to town my watch said it was four-thirty. I had a definite disinclination to go back to the office and see Lavers. I had a definite disinclination to go back to my apartment in case he rang and in an absent-minded moment I picked up the phone.

So I went to a bar instead and stayed there until six. Then I had a meal in the restaurant next door and that made it seven, and by the time I drove leisurely down to the Golden Horseshoe, it was seven-thirty.

There was a notice on the door which said, Open, 9 p.m. I tried the door and found it wasn't locked. I walked down the steps into the cellar.

A couple of waiters were busy setting out tables and on the dais, Clarence Nesbitt sat plucking the strings of his bass-fiddle idly.

The waiters looked at me, recognised me, and looked the other way. I walked down to the dais. Clarence looked up and saw me and stopped plucking the strings.

"Hi, Lieutenant!" he said.

"Hi, Clarence," I said. "Business as usual tonight, eh?"

"It's all over the evening papers," he said. "Midnight figures we'll have to beat 'em off with a stick. She figures this is the best publicity the joint ever had."

"She ought to set up a dummy corpse in front of you, with tomato-sauce all over the shirt-front," I said. "That would really send them."

Clarence rolled his eyes: "Man!" he said. "Don't bug me!"

"You probably read the guy's name was Johnny Landis," I said. "He was a Chicago-style fan, he came here a lot. You sure you don't remember ever seeing him?"

"Lieutenant," he said, "all we ever see is a lot of faces out front there. We play up here because we dig that Chicago-style and we got to eat so we can go on playing. There ain't no other reason—faces out there are just faces."

"I see what you mean," I said. "Miss O'Hara in?"

"Sure," he said. "In her office, Lieutenant."

I went through the doorway and knocked on the door of her office.

"Come in!" she called out.

I went in. She was sitting in front of the mirror, putting on some lipstick. She was wearing a scarlet gown which was identical with the black one she had worn the night before—down to the last rhinestone.

"Oh!" she said, looking at my reflection in the mirror in front of her. "It's you!"

"You sound as though you've missed me," I said.

"Like a pain in the neck!" she said. "What do you want?"

"A talk," I said. "A nice confidential talk, man-to-woman, which is almost so much more interesting than man-to-man, don't you think?"

"No, I don't," she said flatly. "And I'm busy. Tonight's going to be a bust for us after all that publicity in the papers. All the goons within a radius of fifteen miles will be here with their mouths wide open."

"Giving your waiters a chance to toss liquor down their throats at an exorbitant price?" I said.

"I run this place to make a living," she said shortly.

"I'm a very easy-going character," I said. "We can talk now, or after you've finished your act."

"I told you," she said, "I'm going to be very busy tonight!"

"But I'm not that easy-going," I said. "Make up your mind when we'll have our talk or I'll take you down to the Bureau right now and we can talk there, for hours probably."

She glared murder at my reflection: "All right! After I've finished my act."

"In here?"

"I'd rather not," she said. "I'll have to leave early, I suppose. You could drive me home if you own an automobile."

"I own an automobile."

"I'll meet you outside at twelve-fifteen then."

"Fine," I said. "See you."

"There's just one thing, Lieutenant!"

"Miss O'Hara?"

"This is strictly business—not funny business. I want that clear from the start."

"Strictly business, Miss O'Hara," I said. "I'd call you Midnight but I'm four hours too early. But strictly business."

I got outside again and wondered if I was going soft in the head and thought maybe I was, but who could blame me. I thought the hell with it, the hell with Johnny Landis, the hell with his father and the hell with Commissioner Lavers. Thinking like that gave me the courage to go home.

It was sometime after eight when I got into my own apartment. I stacked Ellington's "A Drum is a Woman," and "Early Ellington" onto the turntable and let the hi-fi roll. I poured myself a drink and sat down in an armchair.

It was halfway through "Carribbee Joe" when the phone rang and without thinking I lifted the receiver and answered. "Where the hell have you been!" a familiar voice bellowed into my ear.

"Writing out my resignation?" I said doubtfully.

"You were there when Landis rang me?"

"I was there," I said.

"I've got to do something," Lavers said. "He'll plaster it all over his front page tomorrow morning. So far I've been saying, 'No comment,' to all the reporters, but I'm going to have to say something once the *Tribune* hits the streets."

"How about, 'Nuts to Landis?'" I suggested.

"How about, 'Wheeler to Sergeant!'" he snorted.

I couldn't think of an answer to that one.

"What I don't understand is how he went back to the house to find you there," the Commissioner went on.

"I can," I said. "It's the classic solution to all crimes, it was the butler who did it! He rang Landis and told him I was there."

"Did you get anything worth knowing from the daughter?" he asked.

"Nothing very definite," I said. "She didn't like John, he was a number one louse. Noboby liked John. That's about it."

"That doesn't help much!"

"I'm hoping to find out more," I said.

"You'd better find out fast," he said. "And be in my office by nine in the morning—without fail, Wheeler!"

"Yes, sir," I said and hung up.

The phone rang again a minute later. I lifted it off the hook and said: "Yes, sir. Nine o'clock in the morning."

There was an unlike-Lavers silence the other end. Finally a voice said: "Lieutenent Wheeler?"

"That's right," I said. "Who's that?"

"Talbot here, sir," he said. His voice was so soft, I could hardly hear him. "I've been thinking about your ... suggestion this afternoon. I think perhaps it might be better if we had a little chat."

"I'm glad you feel that way," I said. "Where can I meet you?"

"I was wondering if I might call on you at your apartment, Lieutenant?"

"Sure," I said and gave him the address. "What time?"

"About an hour from now, sir. If that's convenient?"

"That will be fine," I said. "Tally-ho, Talbot."

There was a faint click as he replaced the receiver.

I sat there for a while feeling the way a blackmailer must feel when his first client is about to part with some genuine money.

After a while I got myself another drink and settled down into the chair again. I had "Creole Love Call" piping through the five speakers strategically situated around the wall and I couldn't have asked for anything more expect a blonde, maybe. Maybe?

Half an hour later I had a third phone-call. I recognised the voice right away. I recognised the high-pitched breathlessness that sent my nerve-ends twanging the way hers must always be twanging.

"Al," she said. "I'm dreadfully sorry about what happened this afternoon. It was so mortifying I could have died. I really could. I don't know why Father came back when he did. It's no use trying to explain things, to him, he just doesn't listen. He ... he frightens me all the time. He always has, ever since I can remember."

"Don't worry about this afternoon, Rena," I said.

"But I do worry about it, Al," she said. "You know your emotional impact was quite disturbing and I never had a chance to find out whether ..."

"Quite," I said.

"Father's out," she said. "He's at the paper and he won't be back for hours and hours. I'm all alone in the house. You couldn't come over and see me, Al? The butler went out about ten minutes ago and I don't think he'll be back for awhile. We'd be quite alone, Al."

"I'm sorry, honey," I said. "But it's impossible."

"I'm sorry, too," she said. "I had quite a primitive feeling about you this afternoon and if I don't express it, I'll sublimate it and get a repression. I don't believe in repressions, Al, I think ..."

"I know," I said hastily, "you told me this afternoon."

"I know!" she said triumphantly. "Why don't I come over and see you?"

"Sounds like a wonderful idea," I said. "How soon can you make it?"

"In about three-quarters of an hour," she said. "What's your address, Al?"

I gave her the address and she hung up.

I checked my watch. It was just on nine o'clock. At nine-thirty Talbot was due to arrive, and Rena was expected at nine forty-five. I had a date with Midnight at a quarter after midnight.

It looked like it was going to be a busy evening.

I flipped the two discs and got the second side of "Drum is a Woman." I also got myself another drink—I thought I was justified with all the hard work ahead of me. It was going to be what Annabelle would call a piquant situation when Rena found her butler baring his soul to me already, when she arrived.

It was five minutes after nine when the buzzer sounded and I got up from the chair to open the front door.

I opened the door and said a bright, "Tally-ho!"

Talbot collapsed into my arms and I staggered backwards a couple of paces with his unexpected weight. The door swung shut and I lowered him to the floor awkwardly.

There was bullet-hole through the back of the coat of his neat, pin-striped suit and he wasn't breathing.

So maybe the butler had seen too much after all.

CHAPTER SEVEN

Five minutes later I was back in my apartment but my breath wasn't—it took about a minute longer than I had to return. I was now in possession of three things. Firstly, the fact that whoever had shot Talbot wasn't in the building, second the fact that as I hadn't heard the shot, whoever had fired it must have used a silenced gun. And thirdly, of course, I was still in possession of Talbot's corpse.

It was embarrassing. I never have had a collector's enthusiasm for corpses. They're awkward things to dispose of, and you can't just leave them lying around. I was still looking at it, wondering what I could do with it, when the buzzer sounded again.

I opened the door quickly and Rena stood there, blinking at me from behind her glasses. I pulled her inside the apartment, slammed the door shut and grabbed her purse.

I went through the contents quickly and didn't find any gun inside.

"Al!" she said. "You're so impulsive! But why grab my purse instead of me?"

Then she saw Talbot's body lying on the floor.

"Terence!" she said in a range at least an octave higher than usual. "What's he doing here? What's the matter with him?"

"He's dead," I said, "that what's the matter with him. Somebody shot him in the back while he was waiting for me to answer the door."

She keeled over in a faint. I caught her before she hit the floor—I was getting to be an expert. I carried her into the living room and put her on the divan. She was wearing another of those mandarin gowns, this time gunmetal in colour with small black dragons rearing their way across the skirt. The slit was just as high as it had been in the first one, and just as disconcerting.

I poured some Scotch into a clean glass and when she came around and fluttered those violet eyes up at me, I handed her the glass.

She drank and coughed a little. "Alcohol," she said. "I suppose it was a necessary stimulant."

"If you don't want it, don't drink it," I said. "It would be a criminal waste."

She sat up and handed me back the empty glass.

"Sit down here, Al," she said, patting the empty space beside her on the divan.

I sat down there. She leaned her head, against my shoulder. "Put your arm around me," she said.

"This is no time to test your primitive reactions!" I said.

"I'm not," she said. "I need comforting, Al."

So I comforted her. She comforted very well. So well, that it took me five minutes to fight my way off the divan and onto my feet again.

I straightened my tie and ran a hand through my hair.

Her violet eyes looked at me reproachfully: "Your instincts are just as primitive as mine, Al," she said. "Why fight them?"

"Maybe Talbot didn't fight them," I said. "And look what happened to him."

She remembered Talbot all over again and her lower lip dropped. "Poor Terence!"

"Who do you think might have killed poor Terence?"

"I don't know," she said. "I can't think why anyone should want to kill him. Why was he here?"

"He rang me half-an-hour before you did," I said. "He came to see me."

"What about?"

"He was going to tell me about John," I said.

"Terence would never divulge a confidence!" she said firmly.

"Terence was persuaded," I said. "I suggested that if he didn't tell me about the set-up in your house, I might suggest to one of the *Tribune's* rivals that it could have an interesting feature in what went on while Daddy was at the office."

"Just what do you mean!"

"Talbot wasn't a bad-looking guy," I said. "I'd say the odds were you tried your primitive reactions on him, too."

She stood up suddenly and slapped my face.

"I gave him the choice," I went on, "either he arranged to see me or I made the suggestion. He arranged to see me. That speaks for itself, doesn't it?"

"Father was right about you!" she said breathlessly. "You're nothing but a fiend! A depraved fiend who preys on young and ..."

"Innocent?" I lifted my eyebrows.

"I shall tell Father about this!" she panted. "I'll see he makes you wish you'd never been born! I'll see he ..."

"You'll tell him how you came to be visiting me in my apartment, of course?"

Her mouth hung open for a long moment.

"I said you were a fiend!" she repeatedly shakily.

"Fiend Wheeler," I agreed. "Just what was the set-up inside that Shakespearian mansion of yours?"

"Father and John never got on well together," she said. "I think a lot of it was Father's fault. He bullied him, bullied both of us. John lost interest in everything when he was still at college and when they had thrown him out, he came home and just hung around."

"Until your father tossed him out? What caused that?"

"They had a fight about something," she said listlessly. "I don't know what it was—then John left and I didn't see him again. Not that we liked each other very much."

"What about Talbot?"

She picked up her purse and walked towards the door.

"I'm leaving," she said. "I don't care what you tell Father, I'm leaving!"

"Was there anything between you and Talbot?"

"Yes!"

She swung around to face me, her eyes glittering behind the opaque lenses.

"Yes, there was something between me and Terence. But nothing you'd understand! Nothing like you're thinking now! He loved me, he wanted to marry me and take me away from that house!"

"And you didn't want to marry him?"

Her face puckered like a little girl's: "I don't know," she whispered. "I wasn't sure. And it's too late now, isn't it? I'll never know!"

Her hand reached blindly for the doorknob, found it and pulled the door open. She stepped out into the corridor, then looked at me, her face wet with tears.

"I hate you, Al Wheeler," she whispered. "I'll hate you as long as I live!"

Then she went, stumbling as she ran on heels that were too high and made her look pathetic and ridiculous at the same time. I stepped back to my apartment and the corpse that now went with it.

I got the number from the directory and dialled it. I heard the steady ringing tone but no-one bothered to answer. I thought maybe Midnight was having such a hell of a good night with a crowd of rubbernecks at the Golden Horseshoe that it would cost her ten dollars' worth of business to answer the phone so she wasn't bothering. It was a pity.

I hung up again and looked at Talbot still stretched out on the floor. He was becoming my number one problem. I didn't want to do the right thing by the manual and report the killing—not yet, anyway. It would involve too many awkward explanations about what he was doing calling on me and I hadn't got my answers that would save my badge—

or skin.

I thought maybe the easiest way would be to just walk out on him and pretend I was seeing the corpse for the first time whenever I came back into the apartment. I could say somebody dumped him on me.

From blackmail to perjury, to withholding vital evidence. I poured myself another drink and tried to stop thinking about it. It was getting close up to ten o'clock, still two and a half hours to go before my date with Midnight. I drank some of the Scotch then lit myself a cigarette and at the same time the door buzzer sounded again.

I nearly swallowed the cigarette. It could be Rena come back with her primitive emotions uppermost again and a meat-cleaver in her hand. It could be Opportunity or maybe Commissioner Lavers. While I was thinking about it, the buzzer sounded again which let out Opportunity.

With a mental apology I got hold of Talbot's feet and dragged him into the kitchen, and closed the door. On my way back towards the front door I took a close look at the carpet. One advantage of Talbot lying on his face was that the blood from his back hadn't dripped down onto the carpet to leave stains.

I opened the door and a large round face under a brown bowler hat looked at me anxiously.

"Hi, Lieutenant," Clarence Nesbitt said anxiously.

"Hi, Clarence," I said. "What did you lose—your bass-fiddle—you should see the F.B.I. That's a Federal case!"

He grinned weakly and I saw his fingers were still plucking away at invisible strings.

"Midnight asked me to drop over, Lieutenant," he said. "She says the date is nix."

"She's a foolish little Midnight to say that," I told him.

"Don't dig me wrong," he said quickly. "She figures maybe you'd better see her at her apartment and she says there ain't no point in her waiting up all night so maybe you'd travel now?"

"Business is that bad she's closed down early?" I asked him.

He stared at me blankly for a couple of seconds.

"You ain't hep, Lieutenant. Midnight's about ready to fracture her toupee!"

"What happened?"

He shook his head wonderingly: "Then you ain't heard! The cops closed down the joint an hour before it was due to open."

"They what!"

"That's right," he said. "They got a bar and padlock across the door and Man! we ain't gonna jam there no more!"

"Who did it?"

"A cat called Hambone?"

"Hanlon?"

"You dig the most!" he said in a gratified voice.

"Thanks, Clarence," I said. "Thanks for the news. Where do I find Midnight?"

He gave me the address.

"I'll be on my way in about ten minutes," I said.

"Sure, Lieutenant," he said. "I'll give Midnight a buzz you're coming."

"So long, Clarence," I said.

"Solid, Lieutenant!"

I closed the door and went back to the phone. I rang Homicide and got Hanlon.

"Al!" he said. "Where you been? Lavers has chewed through a box of cigars already waiting to hear from you."

"I'll send him a postcard," I said. "I heard you closed down the Golden Horseshoe tonight."

"That's right," he said. "Suspected centre for narcotics distribution. Didn't find anything. We went through the place with the proverbial toothcomb."

"What does that mean?"

"That they can open up again tomorrow night."

"Why raid it tonight?"

Hanlon's voice sounded tired: "I understand, unofficially of course, that Mr. Landis said his son was never a marihuana smoker and as there were reefers found in his possession the night he was murdered, he must have got them at the Golden Horseshoe. Mr. Landis demanded the Police Department should raid the place at once."

"So the Commissioner said raid it?"

"It was something he could do that wouldn't matter very much," Hanlon said. "I think he's still trying to do a deal about that editorial Landis promised for tomorrow morning's *Tribune*."

"You mean Lavers is trying to spoil my publicity?" I said.

"You'd better speak to him, Al," Hanlon said. "He went home half an hour ago, you'll get him there. He's worrying."

"He's worrying?" I said. "You should see me."

"No thanks, Al," Hanlon said. "I've done that too often already. You getting any unorthodox breaks on this case?"

"Strictly nothing," I said. "You getting any orthodox breaks?"

"Strictly nothing," he said. "We make one hell of a team, don't we?"

"Sure," I said. "Do me a favour, will you? Forget that I called."

"Okay," he said. "But you call Lavers soon or you'll have to make it long-distance somewhere over the State line."

"You don't know how true that is," I told him, thinking about Talbot in the kitchen. "Be seeing you." I hung up.

I had one more drink before I left the apartment. Then I picked up the Jaguar from the kerb outside the apartment block and started on my way to my date with Midnight O'Hara.

Rena Landis had been all mixed up. First she liked me then she didn't like me and finally she hated me. I wouldn't have any of that uncertainty with Midnight O'Hara—she'd hated me from the first time she met me.

CHAPTER EIGHT

She opened the door and looked at me coldly. I looked back at her warmly. She was wearing a negligee which was made out of black lace, rhinestones and Midnight O'Hara. I thought if she was feeling cold, the warmth of my look should fix it.

"Come in," she said abruptly and turned around, walking back inside the apartment.

I followed her inside, closing the front door behind me. It was a nice apartment about three times the size of mine and nicely furnished in the modern manner.

She lit herself a cigarette then turned around to look at me again.

"I suppose you're still laughing yourself sick!" she said.

"About what?"

"That brilliant gag of yours—making a date to have a talk with me tonight after I'd finished my act when you knew all the time you were going to close the place down!"

"I didn't know you were going to be closed down," I said. "I didn't know anything about it until Clarence told me. It wasn't my idea, it was the Commissioner's idea."

She didn't look impressed.

"If you still want to talk to me, you could make it quick—I'm tired!" she said.

"I'm in no hurry," I said.

I sat down in a fibreglass chair and lit myself a cigarette. "Were you going to offer me a drink?" I asked hopefully.

"No," she said firmly.

"It was just a thought," I said.

"You didn't come here to waste my time fooling around like this?"

"Not really," I agreed. "I came here to ask why you lied to me about Johnny Landis."

"Johnny Landis—the man who was murdered? I didn't lie to you about him."

"Midnight," I shook my head reprovingly. "You told me you'd never seen him before and all the time you knew him quite well. He came into your place at least half-a-dozen times before he was murdered. You sat at his table and talked to him a couple of times. A couple more times you even took him into your office to talk to him."

"You must be crazy!" she said.

"I have witnesses," I said. I did have one witness anyway.

"You're lying," she said. "You're trying to make out I had something to do with the murder! You're trying to frame me! You're trying to trick me into making some sort of confession!"

"I'm trying to get you to tell me the truth," I said. "What time was it Hanlon closed you down tonight?"

"Eight o'clock!" she said bitterly. "It would have been our best night ever!"

"What happened exactly?"

"They bust into the place," she said. "They told me it was a raid and they were going to search the place—and all the employees."

She took a deep breath which threatened the security of several rhinestones. "They even brought a policewoman along to search me! They went through everything!"

"What happened after that?"

"They searched everyone first and when they didn't find anything, they said they were going to search the whole place, but the people could go home because the place wouldn't open tonight anyway."

"And they all went home?"

"All except me."

"About what time was that?"

"About twenty after eight, I suppose."

"You stayed?"

"Of course I stayed!" she said. "I've seen coppers at work before! If they can't find what they're looking for, they would plant it on you if you give them half a chance. I stayed to make sure they didn't!"

"What time did you leave?"

"Just after nine."

"I wouldn't worry," I said. "Hanlon says you can open up for business again tomorrow night."

"Thank you!" she said coldly.

I stubbed the butt of my cigarette in a bronze ashtray beside me.

"Now tell me the truth about Johnny Landis."

"I already have!"

"Have it your way," I said.

I got onto my feet and looked at her for about five seconds. "It's a pity," I said finally, "but you'd better get dressed."

"What do you mean?"

"Magnificent as you look in that outfit, you'll catch cold down at the Bureau if you don't put some more clothes on."

"Bureau?" she faltered.

"I'm taking you down there now," I said. "I'm holding you as a material witness. You're lying about Landis, I can prove it with no trouble at all."

"Material witness?" she was distinctly worried.

"I can hold you almost indefinitely on that," I said. "Days ... weeks."

"But I've got to be there tomorrow night to open up the place again!" she said.

"That's your worry, not mine," I said. "You'd better get dressed."

She made no movement. Her face was white under her make-up.

"Lieutenant?"

"Midnight?"

"I don't know ..." she said desperately. "I'm scared!"

"No need," I said. "They're nice people down at the Bureau. You'll have plenty of time to get to know them really well."

"I'll go broke if my place stays closed for a few days," she said. "It has to stay open five days a week to show a profit."

"You're breaking my heart, Midnight," I told her.

"If I tell you about Johnny Landis," she said hesitantly, "you'll give me protection?"

"That would be a pleasure," said. "I'll make it my own personal chore. In fact, I'll move right in here with you, if you like."

"You said something about a drink before. Scotch?"

"Sounds nice," I said.

She went into the kitchen and came back with two drinks. She handed me the Scotch and sat down in a chair opposite me. The negligee stretched tight in all directions as she sat down and I wondered what the breaking-point of lace was and thought with any luck we must be close to it.

"You were right, of course," she said. "I knew Johnny Landis. He did come in half a dozen times and I spoke to him most times he was in."

"That's better," I said. "You're doing fine. Go on."

"Would you do a deal with me?" she said slowly. "You have to believe me that I didn't know it was going on until it was too late."

"If I could figure that in English I could give you an answer," I said.

She drank from her glass: "The dope," she said.

"Dope?"

"Johnny Landis came in to buy his reefers. I was a fool, didn't even know about it until he told me."

"Somebody in your set-up was selling him reefers?"

She nodded: "Not only him, either. And not only reefers, but heroin, cocaine … opium. Anything and everything. We were doing a roaring trade and I didn't know anything about it!"

"Until Johnny told you."

"Until he told me."

"Why did he tell you—was he paying too much for his reefers?"

"Johnny was ambitious!" she laughed bitterly. "He had a bright idea. This guy has you set up as an oscar, he told me, using your place as a distribution centre. String along with me and we'll set him up as an oscar."

"How did he plan to do that?"

"Blackmail. Pure and simple. He'd buy a lot of narcotics from the man, then make a sworn statement saying from whom he got them. We'd tell the man that we'd turn the statement over to the police if he didn't kick in with sixty per cent of the profits. Johnny would take forty per cent, he told me, and me twenty per cent."

"What did you think of the idea?"

"I didn't want any part of it," she said. "I was running a legitimate place, or I thought I had been. I wanted it that way again. The first couple of times we talked, Johnny was very reasonable. He tried to convince me there was no risk. He told me about his father owning the *Tribune*. He said the man wouldn't dare touch him because of the outcry the *Tribune* would make about it.

"Every time I saw him, he kept on trying to persuade me. Then one time, in my office, he told me I was a fool. If I didn't want any part of it, that was all right with him, he'd do it alone.

"I said I'd go to the police and he laughed at me. 'They wouldn't believe you didn't know about it,' he said. 'They'll close you up, you'll probably end up in the pen for a couple of years.'"

"And you thought he might be right?"

She nodded: "The more I thought about it, the more right I thought he was. Who would believe it had been going on under my nose and I didn't know. I found it hard to believe myself."

"And what about Johnny?"

"He told me to go on as usual. He told me he'd handle it his way from then on and if I tried approaching the police, he'd swear that it was me who had first introduced him to the man who supplied him with reefers. There was nothing I could do about it. The last time he came in—before the night he was killed—he showed me an envelope that had been given to him. It was in jive-talk …"

"Knock a fade on oscar hype, tea-man," I said.

"You've seen it?" she looked surprised.

"He was carrying it on him when he was killed," I said.

"Johnny didn't take it seriously," she said. "He laughed about it. Nobody would dare try and get tough with me, he said, not with my con-nections!"

"His old man had tossed him out of the house three months before," I said.

"I didn't know that," she said. "You mean—he was bluffing about his old man and what his old man's paper would do if anything happened to him?"

"I guess so," I said. "Go on."

"There isn't anything more to it," she said helplessly. "I thought he had me right where he wanted me, so I did as I was told. I tried to carry on in the usual way and pretended I knew nothing about the narcotics be-ing sold."

"There's the sixty-four thousand dollar question," I said. "The man's name?"

She bit her lip for a moment: "You're sure you'll give me that protec-tion!"

"You'll be protected," I said. "I guarantee it."

"All right," she said. "It's ... Wes Stewart."

"The dreamy character," I said. "Thanks, Midnight. Now you don't have to get dressed."

"The deal, Lieutenant," she said in a small voice. "Do you think you might ..."

"I might," I said. "Are you prepared to sign a statement saying every-thing you've just said to me. Tonight—right now?"

She nodded: "I'll do that, Lieutenant."

"You do that and I think I can guarantee you won't be involved in the narcotic charges," I said. "In fact, if you can find yourself another horn-player, you'll still be in business."

"Thanks, Lieutenant!" she said warmly. "I don't know how to thank you enough!"

"I'll give you a practical demonstration when we have the time," I mur-mured. "Do you know where Stewart lives?"

"No," she said. "But I think I know where he is right now. After Clarence delivered my message to you, he asked me could they use the Horseshoe tonight as it wouldn't be open."

"What were they going to do—buy themselves a drink?"

"They were going to have a jam-session. You know what they're like. All musicians are crazy! They like playing for free. I told him it was all right with me and gave him the keys."

"You've got another set?"

"In the drawer."

"Where's the phone?" I asked her.

"Over there, behind the table-lamp."

I rang Lavers' home and he answered finally in a tired snarl.

"Wheeler!" he shouted when I started to speak. "I've been trying to locate you for the last two hours! Where in creation have you been! I've had Landis riding me for ..."

"Take it easy, Commissioner," I said. "Remember all your friends who died with a coronary occlusion!"

He stopped talking for a moment to think about that and it gave me a chance to tell him the story.

"I suppose you're expecting congratulations!" he said sourly. "You could have done this twenty-four hours ago—you could have broken down a couple of hours after the murder when that waiter told you the story! But you had to be bright and unorthodox and leave it till now!"

"Yes, sir," I said.

"You'd better go down to the Horseshoe and pull him in," he said. "Wait outside. I'll have Hanlon join you—I wouldn't trust you to make an arrest on your own. You're not capable of handling it!" He slammed down the receiver.

I hung up and looked at Midnight. She handed me the keys.

"We're going down there now to take him in," I said. "I'll call you as soon as we've booked him, then you won't need any protection."

"Thanks, Lieutenant," she said.

"Call me Al," I told her.

"Thanks, Al."

The lace lifted sharply as she took a deep breath. "If you aren't too tired after you've booked Stewart, maybe you might like to come back here and have a drink to celebrate?"

She smiled slowly: "You could tell me some more about that practical demonstration."

"It will be a pleasure," I told her. "This will be the fastest arrest ever made."

She walked with me to the door and opened it for me. She put her arms around my neck suddenly and kissed me warmly.

"That's just so you'll hurry back, Al," she said huskily and then closed the door gently.

I went down to the car and drove the fifteen blocks to the Golden Horseshoe and parked the Jag about half a block away from the entrance. Five minutes later a prowlcar pulled into the kerb behind me. Two men got out and I joined them on the sidewalk.

"This is the break we needed, Al," Hanlon said. "And am I glad we got it! I brought Polnik along with me. I thought the three of us could handle it without any trouble."

"I hope so," I said. "There's only one of him."

We walked along to the door of the Horseshoe. The bar and padlock had been removed. I inserted the key in the lock and turned it gently. The door swung open and we stepped inside and started down the stairs.

It was going to be a pity to break it up. They had the joint jumping. They were hitting something which vaguely resembled "The World Is Waiting For The Sunrise."

Wes Stewart was hitting a solid riff, with lots of quarter-tones and glissandos and Cuba Carter was right with him, while Clarence Nesbitt was holding the basic rhythm.

"A guy who can play a horn like that deserves to get away with murder!" I said to Hanlon as we came to the bottom of the stairs.

"I care for opera!" he said stiffly.

We threaded our way past the empty tables until we stood in front of the dais.

Clarence was the first one to see us and he stopped playing suddenly. Cuba was next and he stopped playing as well. But Wes was real gone with both eyes shut and he went on talking with that horn for another thirty-two bars before he realised his partners weren't with him and he opened his eyes to find out why. Then he stopped playing as well.

The three of them sat, looking at us with blank expressions on their faces. Clarence's fingers were plucking invisible strings again and Cuba shuffled his feet nervously. Only Wes was calm.

"Anything we can do for you gents?" he said softly.

"Sure there is," Hanlon said coldly. "You could sell me a pack of reefers for a start."

"I don't understand?" Wes crinkled his forehead.

"Or maybe some coke. Some H? Some hops," Hanlon went on. "I'm not particular—just so long as it's narcotics."

Wes sat there, open-mouthed, staring at him.

"It's all over, Stewart," Hanlon said. "We know the score. You were using this place as a distribution centre. Then Johnny Landis got the bright idea of blackmailing you. You even sent him a note warning him to lay-off but he wouldn't. So you killed him!"

Wesley shook his head slowly like a man coming out of a dream.

"Narcotics?" he said. "Blackmail! Me kill Landis? I never even knew the guy!"

"There's no point in stalling us," Hanlon said. "We've got proof of the narcotics, proof of Landis' blackmail threats, we've even got the note you wrote to him. We're taking you in, Stewart, on a narcotics charge for now. By tomorrow it will be homicide."

"I'm not going!" Stewart said nervously. "It's all lies, you're trying to frame me for it because you can't find out who really did it. I'm not going. Once you get me down there, you'll never let me go!"

"On your feet," Hanlon said, "we're going now!"

"No!" Stewart said desperately.

He hurled his trumpet suddenly at Hanlon who ducked to avoid it hitting his head.

Stewart made a wild jump that took him off the dais and ran for the kitchen door. Polnik dived his hand inside his coat for his gun. He got it in his hand and levelled it carefully as Stewart reached the door.

I took a pace forward, tripped and cannoned heavily into Polnik. His gun exploded and the slug chipped plaster out of the ceiling. Then Stewart was through the doorway.

"Hell!" Polnik said furiously, "I would have got him if you hadn't hit me!"

"I tripped," I said humbly. "I'm sorry."

"Don't stand there and argue!" Hanlon said, his face livid, "let's get after him."

We ran towards the door. The kitchen was deserted. The far door that led out into the back-alley stood open. When we reached the alley it was also deserted.

"All right!" Hanlon dropped to a walk. "He got away. We'll put out a general alarm for him. They'll pick him up sooner or later!"

We walked around the corner and then into the main street, towards the prowlcar.

"Damn it, Wheeler!" Hanlon said furiously. "If you hadn't knocked into Polnik, this would never have happened. What will Lavers say about this! Two Lieutenants and a Sergeant sent to arrest one man and we let him get away!"

CHAPTER NINE

Hanlon had radioed in the alarm from the prowlcar. When we got back to Homicide, Lavers was waiting for us there.

He looked at us for some fifteen seconds before he spoke.

"It's my fault," he said finally. "I shouldn't let you out alone at night. Not just the three of you, you aren't safe! I should see you get some police protection!"

I winced.

"Who knows," he went on, "who knows but what you might meet up with some six-year-old desperado armed with a shanghai and all drop dead from fear!"

"It was ..." Hanlon started to say.

"Shut up!" Lavers snarled. "I hadn't finished! Three men sent to arrest one man and you let him get away. I don't blame Sergeant Polnik—it's the two senior lieutenants I blame. And out of the two senior lieutenants I blame you, Wheeler, most of all! You could have arrested him twenty-four hours ago as I told you on the phone earlier on if you'd acted logically."

He took a deep breath: "I've been fighting Landis all day for you. But now I'm beginning to think he's right—you'd look good directing traffic!"

"Yes, sir," I said.

"I'll think about it," he said. "About where the traffic's thickest—and that's where I'll send you!"

"Yes, sir," I said.

"Meantime you're suspended from duty as from now."

"Yes, sir."

"So get out of my sight!"

I walked out of the Bureau back to my own car. If I'd had the time I would have worried about the suspension, but I didn't. I had my own private corpse and I wanted to get rid of it as soon as I could. And now I had an idea where I could leave it.

I drove back to my own apartment. I staggered down the corridor, half-carrying, half-dragging Talbot and hoping I wouldn't meet anyone on the way and if I did I'd have to tell them how drunk my friend was, but would they believe me?

I was lucky—I didn't meet anybody on the way. I got Talbot into the Jag and he sat there, his body slumped backwards into the upholstery. I drove the car away and every time I went round a corner, his head would roll from one side to the other.

I was glad when I reached the Golden Horseshoe.

There was no-one in sight on the street. I unlocked the front door again and then pulled Talbot out of the car and carried him inside.

I carried him down the stairs and along to the dais and I dropped him onto it. I was just straightening my aching back when a quiet voice said from behind me.

"I guess you were too smart, Lieutenant. I'd been thinking about it, and I won't make any trouble."

When my feet touched the ground again, I turned around and saw Wesley Stewart standing there.

"I figured this might be the last place you'd look for me," he said. "Seems like it's the first."

"You came back here?" I said. I couldn't think of anything less obvious to say.

"I ducked over a fence in the alley," he said. "I heard you go past. When I was sure you'd gone I sneaked back into the kitchen. I stayed there till I heard Clarence and Cuba leave, then I came in here. But like I said, I got to thinking. I didn't do any of those things that other officer said,

Lieutenant. And when I got to thinking straight, I thought the Law wouldn't convict an innocent man, and the sensible thing would be to give myself up. Then I heard you coming."

He looked down at Talbot's body and his face paled. "What's wrong with him?" he asked.

"He's dead," I said. "Somebody murdered him the way Johnny Landis was murdered. I'm leaving him here for somebody else to clean up."

"I don't understand this," he said feebly. "Has everyone gone crazy?"

"Understand?" I said. "You mean dig, don't you?"

He smiled wanly: "I never use jive-talk, Lieutenant. I don't like it. I think it's rather childish. What's wrong with Webster's English any-way?"

"You'd have to ask Mr. Webster about that," I said, "I wouldn't know. How about we leave this place?"

"Sure, Lieutenant."

We walked up the stairs and out into the street. I closed the door behind me carefully and locked it again. We got into the car and the next time Stewart showed any surprise was when we arrived at my apartment. I switched on the light and stood to one side to let him pass. He walked into the living-room and stood there, looking around him.

"Where's this place, Lieutenant?"

"I live here," I told him.

"I thought we were going down to the Homicide Bureau—I thought you were arresting me, Lieutenant?"

"Not me," I said. "Would you care for a drink?"

"I don't get it," he said bewilderedly. "Why did you bring me here?"

"Scotch?" I asked him and he nodded vaguely.

I poured a couple of drinks and handed him one. We sat down facing one another. I went over to the turntable, switched the speed back to 78 and put on my prize disc of Sidney Bechet and Mezz Mezzrow's "Gone Away Blues."

At the first note, Wes closed his eyes and he didn't come back to me until five minutes after the disc was finished and I was onto my second glass of Scotch.

"That was Pappa Snow White on trumpet," he said. "If I try real hard maybe in another twenty years or so I'll get to play like him. Not as good of course, but good enough that folks will stay around when I play."

"Why are you staying with Chicago-style?" I asked him.

"It's the in-between land," he said. "It's where I belong right now." He blinked his eyes a couple of times. "I keep forgetting I don't belong any-where right now outside of a cell!"

"Which reminds me," I said. "You told Hanlon you didn't know any-thing about narcotics or about Johnny Landis getting himself shot."

"That was the truth, Lieutenant," he said. "Nothing but the truth!"

"I could even believe that," I said. "But if you weren't selling narcotics, then who was?"

"I don't know anything about anybody selling narcotics," he said. "I know that both Clarence and Cuba smoke reefers sometimes—you can always tell if they've been using them when they play."

"They hit the wrong notes?"

He shook his head: "They play better, much better. They get kind of relaxed inside and the music flows out of them."

"Were they hopped up the night Landis was killed?"

"I think so," he said. "They were playing fine all the time except after that shot then Clarence got a different tone entirely out of the fiddle— I guess the noise unnerved him. I didn't even hear it." He smiled with embarrassment.

"When I'm really with it I guess I wouldn't notice if the roof fell in."

"I still think you're telling me the truth, Wes," I said. "But you aren't being much help to me—not much help at all."

"I'm sorry, Lieutenant," he said.

"After the police closed down the Horseshoe tonight," I said, "where did you go?"

"I went home," he said. "I've got a room about four blocks from the Horseshoe."

"You stayed there?"

"Till around ten."

"What then?"

"Cuba called around, he said Clarence wanted to have a session and we could use the Horseshoe. So I picked up my horn and went around there. You know the rest, Lieutenant. We were still playing when you and the other two guys came it."

"I guess so," I said.

"We going down to the Bureau now?" he asked.

I shook my head: "I want you to do me a favour, Wes. I want you to stay here for awhile."

He looked at me as if I was crazy and maybe I was.

"You're kidding?"

"I'm being very serious about it," I said. "I want you to stay here in my apartment. I don't think anyone will look for you here and you'll be quite safe as long as you don't go out. There's a good supply of food, Scotch and L.P. records. It won't be too hard."

"I'd certainly prefer that to a cell!" he said. "What are you doing all this for, Lieutenant? You don't even know me!"

"I'll be honest, Wes," I grinned at him. "I'm doing it for me, not for you."

The buzzer sounded and he jumped.

"Get into the kitchen," I told him, "stay there till I get rid of whoever this is—and take that glass with you."

He did as he was, told, shutting the kitchen door carefully behind him.

The buzzer sounded again, irritably and I walked across to the front door and opened it. Joe Randle stood there, a sheepish grin on his face.

"Hope I didn't get you out of bed, Al?"

"You think I always sleep with my clothes on?" I grinned at him. "Come on in. I never have worked out how a square like you became a police roundsman!"

He followed me into the living-room and helped himself to Scotch with the help of an automatic reflex.

"I hoped I'd find you home, Al," he said. "I just wanted you to know that none of tomorrow's *Tribune* is my idea."

"You mean the ceremonial killing of Al Wheeler and the ritual dismembering of his corpse?" I said. "I heard it was coming. I didn't think you had any part of it, Joe."

"He's a monomaniac or something," Joe muttered. "I never met a guy even remotely like Landis in all my life."

"Nobody could be that unlucky to meet two of them in one life-time," I said.

"He's got a lot of bugs," Joe said. "But the biggest bug of all is the way he hates people. He doesn't trust anyone, not even his own family. You know something, Al—he's even got the phone-wires tapped into his own home. They're monitored into his office at the *Tribune*. Anybody makes a call in or out of his place while he's not there, he listens in at the office."

"Supposing they make a call while he's on the way into his office?" I suggested. "He can't be in his office all the time."

"That's taken care of," Joe grinned bleakly. "You don't think Mr. Daniel didn't think of that? It's all automatically put onto a tape recorder, so he can play it back and listen at his leisure. That was the main reason his son was tossed out neck and crop. The old man heard some of his confidential calls when young Johnny thought he couldn't."

"How confidential are his confidential tapes?" I asked.

"I'm not sure I'm quite with you, Al," he said cautiously.

"I mean do you have any idea what those calls of Johnny Landis' were about?"

"Something to do with dope, I think," he said. "He was smoking reefers—I don't know whether he took anything stronger than that."

"You don't know definitely?"

"Not definitely," he said. "That was what the grapevine said. I doubt if anybody heard those tapes other than the old man."

"He double-locks his office every time he leaves it and if anybody walks in when he's there unannounced, they're fired. And that goes for any-body, including the city editor."

"It's a wonder Daniel stays so healthy with the milk of human kind-ness flowing out of every vein all the time," I said.

"I wouldn't work for him if it wasn't for the money!" Joe grinned again. "This edition tomorrow is really a lulu. The only truth is the fact he spelled your name right."

"I wish he'd spelled it wrong," I said. "You heard what happened later on tonight?"

"Sure," he nodded. "They arrested Wes Stewart, the horn-player down at the Golden Horseshoe and he escaped. Every op in town is out look-ing for him—except you. And I know why you aren't out there looking for him—that's one of the headlines in tomorrow's paper, your suspen-sion."

"I imagine," I said.

Joe shook his head. "I never thought Lavers would do it—toss you to the wolves like that. Give Landis your hide in the hope of saving his own."

"I don't think he did," I said. "He suspended me because I didn't do what he thought I should have done."

"That makes a lot of sense," Joe looked at me blankly.

"It's sort of complicated," I admitted. "He thinks I should have asked some questions when I first had the opportunity, but I didn't. And that made a lot of difference to the case."

"I see, I think," Joe said still doubtfully. "But you're still Old Loyal Wheeler paying homage to Old Loudmouth Lavers?"

"You could put it that way," I said. "Have another drink, Joe, there's still some left in the bottle, I think."

"I'd like to know where that Stewart character is hiding out," he said. "What a scoop that would be! If I knew that I could trade that job of mine with Landis for another with a reasonable newspaper around the town and get myself some more money!"

I lifted my foot and kicked the table-leg hard.

Joe looked up with a puzzled frown on his face: "You hear that knock, Al?"

"It was Opportunity, Joe," I said soberly. "Sit down while I talk to you."

He sat down on the divan, a glass in one hand, the bottle in the other. I managed to prise the bottle out of his hand long enough to pour my-self another drink.

"Joe," I said. "How would you like an exclusive interview with Wesley Stewart?"

"How would I like an exclusive interview with the President!" he said. "Are you kidding?"

"It could be arranged," I said.

He stared at me for a moment then relaxed.

"They must have grabbed him when I was on my way up here—that's why I didn't hear about it," he said. "Lavers wouldn't give me an exclusive with Stewart. If I know Lavers, none of the newspaper boys will get a chance to get within ten feet of Stewart."

"Stewart hasn't been picked up," I said. "He's still a free man."

He swallowed hard, "Then what the heck are you talking about?"

"How would you like to find a corpse?" I said. "An exclusive corpse—exclusive to you. One that nobody else has found yet and is wrapped up with the Johnny Landis killing."

"I know it's been a hell of a strain, Al," he said gently. "Why don't you go to a farm somewhere way out in the country for awhile. Take it easy and relax—watch the chickens!"

"Have you ever seen a rooster relax?" I asked him. "And I'm not talking out of the top of my head. I can give you both exclusives—one with Stewart and one with a brand-new corpse."

He nearly fell off the divan, "You mean it?"

"I mean it."

"Okay," he took a deep breath. "Just tell me who I have to kill first and I'll go out and get it over with quickly, then you can take me to Stewart!"

"Your feeling is right, Joe," I said. "I want something in return."

"Diamonds?" he said. "Three Cadillacs—a bank? You name it—it's yours!"

"Firstly, when you've got your interview with Stewart, I still want him kept clear of the police."

"That's a logical thought for a cop to have!" he said. "What goes, Al?"

"Let's call it Lavers' favourite word, unorthodox," I said. "You can write your interview and Wes will sign a statement for you, proving it's the truth—but I don't want the cops finding him until I'm ready for him to be found."

"That's fair enough!" Joe said enthusiastically. "What about the corpse?"

"One thing at a time," I said. "Let's fix the interview first."

"Sure!" Joe even forgot about the Scotch in his eagerness. He jumped on his feet and headed for the front door. "You lead the way, Al!"

"Wes!" I called out. "I'd like you to meet a friend of mine."

The kitchen-door opened and Wes came into the room slowly, a look of polite interest on his face.

"Well," Joe said slowly, "I'll be triple-damned!"

CHAPTER TEN

It was three in the morning and Joe was halfway through the second bottle of Scotch. I'd told Wes Stewart to take over my bed and he'd gone to the bedroom five minutes before.

"Okay, Al," Joe said enthusiastically. "I've got Wes' story and his signed statement. What now?"

"What do you mean?"

"What's the angle? Wes says he innocent, he didn't know anything about the murder, anything about the narcotics. Do you think he's telling the truth?"

"Yes," I said.

"So that's the way I angle the story?"

"It's your story, Joe," I said. "It's your angle. I'd like to see you say that Wes was framed. Framed deliberately by whoever really killed Johnny Landis. I'd like to see you say that the police department was pressurised into making a hasty and wrongful arrest by a certain newspaper publisher."

"Oh, brother!" he said. "Landis is going to have a stroke when he reads this!"

"You go and make your deal with the other paper," I said. "And don't forget that once that story is published or the department gets to hear about it, you'll be hotter than Wes already is around the town."

"That's right," he said. "They'll know I know where they can find Stewart."

"Check," I agreed. "So you'd better come back here as soon as you've made your deal and written your story for your new employer—and make sure you aren't followed. I don't trust another newspaper proprietor any more than I'd trust Landis!"

"The trouble with you is you're biased!" he grinned. "But I'll watch it."

"I'll give you my keys," I said. "If I'm going to start running a rooming-house I'm damned if I'm going to keep answering the buzzer all night!"

It was around six that Joe came back. I'd had nearly three hours' sleep on the divan so I didn't feel ghastly, just dreadful. I made some coffee and we drank it while he enthused about the deal he'd made with the *Gazette*.

He poured Scotch into his cup and laced it with coffee.

"How about this corpse?" he asked.

"It will keep," I said. "I'm going to have some sleep—you need some sleep. And that corpse might kill your exclusive with Wes Stewart, so you don't want to find it till your first story has hit the street."

"True!" Joe said. "Very true!"

He finished his Scotch and coffee and curled up in an armchair. Two minutes later he was fast asleep. I went back to the divan and beat Joe's record by at least half a minute.

The next thing I knew was a polite hand shaking my shoulders. I opened my eyes and saw Wes Stewart standing there, looking down at me.

"It's two in the afternoon, Lieutenant," he said. "I've cooked that steak you had in the ice-box and it's about ready for eating."

"You're nothing if not a genius, Wes!" I told him and staggered off the divan and into the bathroom.

By the time I'd shaved, had a shower and got dressed in fresh clothes I felt almost human. Joe passed me on the way to the bathroom. His eyes were still tight shut.

By the time we'd finished the superb steak Wes had cooked, even Joe was looking human.

"I was looking through your discs this morning, Lieutenant," Wes said. "You mind if I play some this afternoon for a while?"

"Help yourself, Wes," I told him.

After Wes had gone out into the living-room, Joe lit himself a cigarette.

"The early editions will have hit the streets by now," he chuckled. "I bet Landis is offering a reward for me dead or alive!"

"I doubt if he's worrying about that 'alive' part," I said.

"So now we can do something about that corpse of yours," Joe suggested.

I nodded, "It's getting around time. Did you ever interview Midnight O'Hara, the owner of the Golden Horseshoe?"

He shook his head, "No, I was too busy following Hanlon around hoping he'd give with some information."

"That's a good thing," I said. "She won't know your voice."

"What am I going to do—haunt her?"

"Just call her," I said. "Tell her there's a corpse in the Horseshoe. It used to answer to the name of Talbot, then hang up."

"Talbot?" he thought for a moment. "You don't mean Talbot the butler? Landis' butler!"

"I mean Talbot the butler, the butler of Landis," I said. "If we go on like this we only have to put it to music and we've got an opera!"

Joe shuddered at the thought.

"Well, okay. So I ring her and tell there's a corpse at her place. What then?"

"You ring your new owner and dictate your story. That the corpse of Talbot, the butler of Landis—there I go again!"

"Landis' butler, a butler named Talbot!" he chanted. "I have that bit clear, Al!"

I uncovered my ears, "The body was discovered on the dais at the Golden Horseshoe—lying in the exact spot that Johnny Landis' body lay. Talbot was shot through the back at close range. The body was discovered by Midnight O'Hara, the owner of the Horseshoe. There is, you hint—if it's possible for a newspaperman to hint—some connection between the two deaths."

He got up from the table and followed his nose to a new Scotch bottle. When he'd poured himself enough drinks for four people he came back again with the glass.

"I've already dictated an interview with a man wanted for murder," he said. "Now I'm going to file a story on a corpse which nobody knows about yet—presumably the first thing the cops will know about it is when they read the late editions of the *Gazette* tonight?"

"You win the cigar," I agreed.

"I can also win myself about fifteen years in the pen!"

"That, too," I said. "Do you want another scoop or don't you?"

"I want!" he said. "What's this Midnight dame's number?"

He made the call the way I'd told him to, short and to the point. Then he rang the *Gazette* and dictated his story. When he finished that he poured more drinks for four people—into his own glass.

"All right, master-mind," he said. "What do we do now?"

"I'm going to listen with Wes," I said as the strains of "Go 'long Blues," filtered into the kitchen. "You can sit here and get drunk, if you like. Or if you prefer it, you can come and sit in the living-room and get drunk."

"I'll sit in the living-room," he said. "If I fall onto the floor in there it's got a carpet!"

We went into the living-room and sat down. I fast-talked Joe into letting Wes and I have a drink, so he grudgingly poured it for us without letting go of the bottle even once.

We sat around listening and drinking—or Wes and I did anyway—Joe just drank—for about an hour.

It looked like being a pleasant afternoon. Right up to the time the buzzer sounded. Joe and Wes disappeared fast into the kitchen, taking their glasses with them. I lit a cigarette and put on a nonchalant look and went to the front door and opened it.

"Well!" I said. "Why didn't anyone tell me it was going to be a party?"

"You don't mind if we come in, Wheeler?" Lavers said coldly as he walked past me into the living-room. He was followed closely by Hanlon, Polnik and two uniformed cops. That left two more uniformed cops outside.

"Why don't you two guys come in?" I said to them. "There's bound to be some left-overs."

I got a blank stare in return.

I followed the coppers' convention into the living-room. I was just in time to see Polnik walk into the bathroom, Hanlon walk into the bedroom and Lavers walk into the kitchen. There was nothing much I could do about it except scream and that seemed hardly worthwhile.

I poured myself another drink instead. Hanlon and Polnik returned with disappointed looks on their faces, just in time to see Lavers ushering Wes Stewart and Joe Randle out of the kitchen, with a look of triumph on his face.

"A jackpot!" he said. "We got both of them!"

Hanlon's face showed no expression but Polnik's face had a regretful look.

"That's too bad," he said, looking at me, "I kind of liked the Lieutenant!"

"Take them down to the Bureau," Lavers said to the two uniformed cops. "Polnik, you'd better go along with them. And if you lose either of them this time I'll personally shoot you and plead justifiable homicide!"

"Yes, sir!" Polnik said.

"Are you arresting me, Lieutenant?" Joe asked in an injured voice.

Lavers gave him a filthy look all for himself, then looked at Polnik.

"You can book Mister Randle on a charge of withholding vital evidence," he said coldly, "obstructing the police in the execution of their duty ..."

"Keeping a dog without a licence?" Joe asked interestedly.

"Get him out of here," Lavers bellowed. "Before I leave myself open to an assault charge!"

Polnik and the two uniformed men hustled Joe and Wes Stewart out of the apartment. That left Lavers, Hanlon and l'il ole me. I wondered how Annabelle Jackson would look by the time I got out of the pen— like Whistler's mother, maybe?

Lavers growled at me, "Like to try and explain it, Wheeler?" he barked.

"Ask me something easy," I said, "like what do the people do in New York."

"I don't get it, Al?" Hanlon said. "You picked up Stewart and didn't turn him in ... why?"

"I didn't think he killed Johnny Landis," I said.

"You didn't ..." Lavers gurgled for a few seconds. "Since when have you been the Police Commissioner!"

"Did I get promoted?" I said brightly. "That's nice."

"If you didn't turn him in," Hanlon said slowly, "then when we went out to bring him in and Polnik drew a gun on him and ..."

"I deliberately stumbled into him so the slug would go wide," I finished for him. "Give that man a cigar, Commissioner."

Lavers' right hand fumbled absently inside his top pocket for a moment and the cigar was halfway out of the pocket before he realised what he was doing and dropped it as if it had suddenly lit up in his hand.

"You know what this means, Wheeler?" he said. "You're not only finished as a cop, you're going to pick up five years for this!"

"All I need is a little more time," I said, "and I can clear this whole thing up."

"Time!" Lavers snarled. "I'll see you get plenty of time, Wheeler. Would five years be enough? If it isn't I'd be happy to see they make it longer!"

"About five minutes would be enough," I said.

"Five minutes for what!"

"To show you exactly how Johnny Landis was murdered."

He glared at me for a few seconds, "If this is just a stall, Wheeler ..."

"What good would it do me to stall for five minutes?" I said. "Or don't you care how Landis was shot?"

"All right," he said finally. "Five minutes—but not one second longer."

"I knew you'd listen to reason, Commissioner," I said. "You always do sooner or later even though it is mostly later."

I saw his face about to erupt again so added hastily: "Shall we go into the bathroom?"

The two of them walked into the bathroom and I followed them, carefully palming the key from the inside of the lock as I did so.

They stood there with their backs to the bath, Lavers still glaring, Hanlon puzzled.

"I'd like your co-operation in a recapitulation of the crime," I said.

"He's just read *The Thin Man* for the first time!" Lavers said. "Tomorrow he's going out to buy himself a wife and a dog!"

"Please!" I said severely. "Do you want to see this, or don't you?"

I realised that was a stupid question as soon as I'd asked it.

"I can see that you do," I said. "So we'll get right on with it. I want the three of us to pretend for a few moments that we're the trio at the Golden Horseshoe, the night of the Landis murder."

"You want me to sing?" Lavers asked in an awful voice.

"Just play trumpet," I said apologetically. "Hanlon is Clarence Nesbitt playing the bass-fiddle and I'm Cuba Carter playing the drums."

"What do you want to do, Al?" Hanlon asked. "This?"

He plucked imaginary strings with the fingers of one hand while supporting the imaginary fiddle with the other.

"That's it, exactly!" I said. "Now, Commissioner, if you play horn ..." I put both hands in front of my mouth and moved the fingers up and down.

"And I'll play drums," I started beating it out on imaginary hides.

Lavers took a deep breath and gave his imaginary trumpet a tune-up.

"You're doing fine, Commissioner!" I said admiringly. "Loud and clear—a second Beiderbecke yet!"

"Don't push me too far, Wheeler!" he said hoarsely.

"No, sir," I agreed politely. "Well, the night it happened, they were playing "Rampart Street Parade," so I guess we might as well get started. One, two, three!"

I hummed the music as the silent trio went to work. After a few moments I stopped.

"What now?" Lavers demanded.

"You're off-beat," I said. "We'll have to go back to the beginning again."

"Stop sniggering."

Lavers looked at Hanlon speculatively.

"Wheeler is going to the pen in any case," he said.

"He can afford to insult me. But you ..."

"I never sniggered, sir!" Hanlon said nervously. "I just had an irritation in my throat."

"Just be careful it doesn't turn into a demotion!" Lavers said nastily.

"Are we ready?" I demanded. "One, two, three!"

So the three of us got to work again beating out no music but having ourselves a time doing it. I broke off my humming for a moment about halfway through.

"Johnny Landis is right behind us now," I said. "Behind the dais—the audience is out there in front of us. Wes—you don't mind me calling you Wes, Commissioner, you are Wes Stewart for a moment."

"Go on!" Lavers grunted, his four fingers of his left hand hitting a magnificent discord.

"All right," I said, letting the excitement mount in my voice. "The time is coming right now. Wes! Johnny Landis is right behind us. Get a gun and shoot him!"

Lavers looked at me blankly.

"But don't miss a note, will you, Wes?" I said softly. "Because the audience is going to notice it."

Laver's fingers were frozen in mid-air in front of him.

"What ..."

"That's the way it was that night," I said. "I was there, out front in the audience watching them play. Wes Stewart was building up a succession of riffs at the actual moment the shot was fired. He didn't even miss a beat, I don't think he heard the shot at all. It would have been impossible for him to go on playing his horn and at the same time take a gun out of his pocket and shoot Johnny Landis!"

Lavers blinked at me a couple of time then recovered himself.

"I thought you were going to show us how Landis was killed," he snorted, "not how it was impossible for Stewart to kill him!"

"And so I am," I said, "right now."

I dropped my voice to an urgent whisper.

"If you will both keep absolutely quiet and watch the bathroom window ..."

"The window?" Lavers said blankly: "What on earth has a window ..."

"You'll have to keep absolutely quiet," I said coldly. "Or I can't show you how it was done."

"All right!" he gritted his teeth. "Get on with it."

"Concentrate, please," I whispered.

The two of them turned their heads and looked hard at the window. I took three delicate paces backwards, then slammed the bathroom door shut and locked it quickly.

I went quickly across to the hi-fi controls. The discs that Wes had stacked on the turntable were still playing, and I turned the volume-control up, so that the sound was loud enough to drown the noise of Lavers and Hanlon hammering on the bathroom-door.

I dived into the bedroom, collected my wallet, car-keys and gun out of the drawer, then ran back to the front door.

I jerked it open and yelled: "The Commissioner wants you both— quickly! The bathroom!"

The two uniformed cops who had been standing outside the door, lumbered past me into the apartment. I didn't wait to explain. I went out of the apartment and down the corridor and then down the stairs three at a time.

The Jaguar was at the kerb and I got into it, started the engine and was doing thirty-five in first gear by the time I reached the first intersection.

CHAPTER ELEVEN

The one snag about owning a scarlet sports-car was that people noticed it. I might just as well go around with a blinking neon on top of my head which said "Al" in blue lights then "Wheeler" in red.

I left the car in a parking-station in the centre of the city and started walking. I walked five blocks then collapsed in the nearest bar and drank some Scotch over the rocks to recover.

I didn't hurry about recovering. About three-quarters of an hour later I left the bar and started walking. I bought a copy of the *Gazette* at a news-stand and saw Joe Randle's story of the discovery of Talbot's corpse was spread right across the front page.

I kept on walking until I came to the street where the Golden Horseshoe was situated. From a block away I could see the crowd on the sidewalk that was just starting to disperse. Outside the door were two prowlcars and as I came up to the edge of the crowd, the first prowlcar pulled away from the kerb and about ten seconds later the second one followed.

"What gives?" I asked the guy next to me.

"Nothing!" he said in a disgusted voice. "One of them papers has a story about another body in that place," he nodded towards the door of the Horseshoe.

"The cops beat it down here and give the place a going-over. I've been standing here twenty minutes waiting to get a look at the body and nothing!"

"Nothing?"

"False alarm!" he said bitterly. "They ought to do something about them papers. Make a law against them! If they don't have a story they make one up."

"There wasn't any body?"

"No!" he said contemptuously. "No body nothing!"

"Tough," I said.

"You're telling me it's tough," he growled. "Twenty minutes I'm standing here and what do I get to see?"

"Nothing?"

"Nothing!"

"You never know your luck," I told him. "On your way home you might get to see an old lady run over by a bus."

He brightened for a moment, then the habitual scowl took over.

"If I did," he said morosely, "I bet she wouldn't even bleed!"

"You could always trample on her a little," I suggested and left him thinking about it.

I walked on for a couple of blocks, crossed over the street and came back down the other side. By the time I got back the crowd had thinned away to nothing. I kept on walking slowly until I reached the end of the block, then I turned back.

About ten minutes later it started to get dark and ten minutes after that the neon sign came on. I checked my watch and saw it was six-thirty. Five and a half hours to midnight and Midnight at Midnight.

I stood in the doorway of a drugstore and lit a cigarette. As I watched I saw the door of the Horseshoe open and Midnight O'Hara came out. She walked down about twenty yards to where a dark sedan was parked and got into it. I watched it pull away from the kerb and watched till it disappeared from sight.

I watched for another fifteen minutes. If the cops were also watching the place they'd got a lot smarter than they were up till yesterday, because I couldn't see one of them anywhere. I thought the odds were they wouldn't leave anyone watching the place. Lavers and Hanlon would think Joe Randle's story was a wild goose chase and they'd be more worried about proving their case against Wes Stewart and getting their hands on a certain lieutenant who had locked them in a bathroom when they had no need to be locked in a bathroom.

I walked across the street, past the Horseshoe and into the alleyway that led around the back of the place. The alleyway was deserted I was glad to see. I made my way up to the back door of the Horseshoe and opened it with the keys that Midnight O'Hara had given me some twenty-four hours before.

There were no lights on in the kitchen but the failing daylight coming through the window lightened the gloom enough for me to see my way without falling over anything.

I made my way to Midnight's office and closed the door behind me once I got inside. I found the light-switch on the wall and flicked it on. The office was in the centre of the area and had no windows so the light wouldn't be seen outside.

I stooped down and patted the tiger's head and his glassy eyes looked back at me unwinkingly.

"The neon jungle is no substitute, I guess, pal," I said.

I walked around the desk and sat in the chair behind it. I opened the drawers of the desk, one by one and went through their contents systematically. I didn't find anything exciting.

When I'd finished I went over to the drink cabinet and poured myself a whisky. I took it back to the desk with me, sat down on the chair again and put my feet up on the desk. I lit a cigarette and thought about life in general and Annabelle Jackson in particular.

It was seven-thirty by my watch when I heard the front door close and then footsteps that sounded hollow as they came down the stairs into the cellar. A few moments later the door of the office swung open and Midnight O'Hara stood framed in the doorway, a look of complete surprise on her face.

"Come on in and close the door, honey," I said, "there's a draught."

She moved forward slowly, pushing the door shut behind her. She was wearing a black Orlon sweater with a diamond clip on the right shoulder and a full white skirt to match, made of taffeta that rustled as she walked.

"Lieutenant!" she said. "You frightened me! What are you doing here?"

"I thought you were going to call me Al," I said.

"Al," she smiled. "How did you get in here?"

"Your keys you gave me," I said. "I came to return them. You remember giving them to me, the night we came down and arrested Wes Stewart."

"Of course," she said. "You needn't have bothered, Al, you could have dropped them in the mail."

"Or in the ocean," I said.

She put her purse down on the dressing-table and then walked over to the liquor cabinet.

"I see your glass is empty," she smiled. "How about a refill?"

"Just what the coroner ordered," I agreed.

She refilled my glass, poured herself a Vodka and tonic and brought both drinks back to the desk.

"You were coming back to my apartment to give me some protection," she said. "You never did. I waited up an awfully long time for you, Al."

"I'm sorry about that," I said sincerely. "I got caught up. But if you're still in need of protection I'll be glad to take up my duties as from now."

"I understand they caught him," she said. "There was some crazy story of another body being found here, in one of the evening papers, and we had a couple of carloads of police down here about an hour ago."

"And was there any body?"

"Of course not," she said. "The police were most annoyed about it. But they told me they had Stewart, they caught him sometime this afternoon."

"I'm sorry you don't need any more protection."

She smiled warmly: "So am I, Al," she said softly. "You're the sort of guy who can make an apartment cosy."

"Turn a house into a home?" I said. "That's better than the other way round."

"The kitchen staff will be here soon," she said. "I think we're going to have a big night tonight. The publicity over poor Johnny getting himself shot was enough, but after that story tonight!"

"It should be very good for business," I said. "The kitchen staff can manage on their own, can't they?"

"I like to be here to see things are done right," she said.

"I'm afraid this is one night you'll have to trust them," I said mildly.

She lowered her empty glass carefully and put it on the desk. "What do you mean, Al?"

"I want you to take an hour off and come with me," I said.

"But that's impossible!"

"Nothing's impossible," I said tritely. I slid the gun out of my pocket, looked at it thoughtfully then slid it back again.

"How can I persuade you?" I said.

She licked her lips slowly: "Where are we going?"

"I thought your apartment would be nice," I said. "I like this office, I'd like to sprawl on your tiger skin rug, but your apartment is more private, isn't it? We aren't likely to be disturbed there."

She laughed nervously: "I never know with you," she said. "Whether you're kidding or not."

"I'm not," I said and got up onto my feet. "Shall we go?"

"If you really mean it, I guess I don't have any choice," she said. "But what's it all about, Al? Why are you being so mysterious and pulling guns out of your pocket!"

"Only one gun," I said. "I'm not really being mysterious, I just want a private talk and I think your apartment is the best place for it."

"A private talk about what?"

"Just a few points," I said. "Like what did you do with Talbot's body— stuff like that."

"Talbot!" she stiffened. "That was the name they mentioned in that crazy newspaper story. You don't believe that crazy story, do you, Al?"

"Yes," I said.

I took her arm and walked with her to the door. I opened the door with my free hand; she walked out in front of me. She had switched on the lights in the cellar when she first came in and the empty tables stood around like the guests at a wake.

"You have your car out front!" I said. "We'll travel in that."

"All right," she said. "But I still think you're crazy!"

"Like a fox," I said. "You weren't very smart removing Talbot's body, you know."

"I still don't know what you're talking about!" she said. "I think you must be crazy or you're making a dreadful mistake. I told you the truth about Wes Stewart last night. You went to arrest him and he got away, but you've got him again now. What more do you want!"

"Let's save it till we get to your apartment," I said.

We were two-thirds of the way across the floor, about twenty feet away from the foot of the stairs when there was the faint noise of a key being inserted in the front door. The door started to swing open and Midnight suddenly flung herself away from me and yelled, "Wheeler!" at the top of her voice.

I made a grab for her and missed and then the lights suddenly went out, plunging the place into complete darkness.

I stayed where I was, listening. I couldn't hear anything. I got the gun out of my pocket and held it in my right hand. I strained my ears but still there was no sound. Then I thought I heard one of the bottom stairs creak.

"Stay right where you are!" I said harshly. "I've got a gun and I'll use it! Get back up the stairs and hit that light-switch again if you want to stay on living."

Then there was no sound again.

Ten long seconds ticked away and then I could smell perfume. A moment later a soft hand touched my face.

"Al!" Midnight said tremulously. "I'm sorry—I lost my head. Now I don't know who it is and I'm frightened!"

"Shut up or I'll plug you!" I snarled and the next second I realised it was too late. I should have hit her when she started to speak. I should have hit her or moved quickly away from her. I should have ... but I hadn't.

I'd stood there, flatfooted like a dummy and let her finger my exact position with her voice. And she'd done a good job of it. I had the proof right then with the two locked hands around my throat squeezing my windpipe with brutal pressure and squeezing the life out of me at the same time.

I lashed out desperately with one foot and felt it connect with a shin. I heard a low grunt and then fireworks were exploding in front of my eyes and the pain in my chest was a red-hot poker searing my lungs into hot ashes.

There was a final brilliant display of pyrotechnics and then complete and utter darkness.

CHAPTER TWELVE

I opened my eyes and would have screamed if the soreness in my throat and the gag around my mouth hadn't prevented me. I was staring into cruel, yellow eyes only a couple of feet from mine, seeing the striped head and the bared fangs. Then I realised I was on the floor of Midnight's office, almost face to face with the head of the tiger skin rug.

I could hear movement in the office somewhere to the side of me. My hands were tied behind my back and my feet were also tied. I thought from here on I would be known as the undignified cop instead of the unorthodox.

I twisted my head and saw Midnight was sitting facing the dressing-table, putting her make-up on carefully. I watched until she finished, then she stood up and took off her sweater and skirt casually. She stood there in a nylon slip and reached into the wardrobe and brought out one of those rhinestone-bodiced gowns that she always wore when she sang.

Then she must have felt that burning sensation my eyes were making between her shoulder-blades. She turned her head and looked down at me.

"Naughty Lieutenant!" she said. "You mustn't peek!"

She pulled the gown over her head and wriggled her way into it, then zipped it tight.

"I hope you're comfortable, Al," she said and she primped her hair in front of the glass again. "Sorry this is such a one-sided conversation but I wouldn't like you to start yelling, it might upset the customers. They're starting to arrive already."

She looked down with a smile. "You took quite a while to come round—you needn't have hurried, though, there's plenty of time. You're going to stay here until I close up the place again. Then I'm going to do you a favour, I'm going to show you what I did with Talbot's body—I expect he'll be glad to have company."

She took a final look in the mirror then opened a drawer and took out a black, chiffon scarf and walked over towards me and knelt down. She put the scarf around my eyes, wound it tight and knotted it securely at the back of my head.

"See no evil and speak no evil," she said lightly. "But you can still hear some. You're a fool, Lieutenant! I gave you Wes Stewart on a plate and you wouldn't have him. Now you're going to wind up dead and it won't make any difference to anyone except you!"

I heard her heels tap across the floor, the sound of the door open and close and then the click of the key in the lock.

I never knew a night as long. I could hear the hush of conversation from outside. I heard the trio play their numbers—whoever was substituting for Wes couldn't play trumpet the way he could. I heard Midnight sing her three numbers and then the trio play again. I would have given a year's pay and the Jag for a drink—water, even!

But after what had felt like ten years, I heard the door open again and her heels tapping across the floor towards me.

"Getting bored, Lieutenant?" she asked softly. "It won't be long now, we're closing down in half an hour. I'm just going to get changed, ready for our journey."

I listened to some tantalising rustling sounds and then her heels tapped across to the door again. Time drifted on meaninglessly. The trio stopped playing, the buzz of conversation died away to nothing to be followed by the sound of glasses and crockery being carried into the kitchen. Finally even the noises from the kitchen faded and died away into silence.

Then the door opened and I heard her heels, followed by a slower, much heavier tread.

"We're on our way, Al," Midnight said lightly.

Strong hands gripped me and lifted me without any apparent effort. I heard Midnight walking ahead of us, doors opened and closed and then there was the click of a car-door opening and the guy who was carrying me let me fall onto the floor of the car. I hit my head against the edge of the seat as I fell and somebody discovered a couple of rockets left over from last time and let them off in my head.

The motor started and the car moved away. I didn't know how long the journey took except it was much too long. Then the car was stopped and I was lifted out again and carried.

It seemed a long time before I was put down again—this time onto stone which was rough and cold against my face.

"We'll leave you here for about an hour," Midnight's voice said. "Don't worry—you can't do any damage in here so you can sing and dance as much as you want," she chuckled at the thought. "Then we'll be back with you for the grand finale. You and Talbot hand in hand, Al."

The sound of her footsteps receded and I heard a door close. That left the world to darkness and to me as a poet once said, but he only thought it—I was living it.

I moved my feet around and touched nothing. I started to squirm my way across the stone floor, swinging my legs as much as I could. I kept on doing that without touching anything at all with my feet, until the back of one hand which was against the stone floor was scraped almost raw and my shoulder was in the same state.

I wondered if they'd left me at the bottom of an empty swimming-pool and were coming back later to turn the water on. It wasn't exactly an encouraging thought. It was a spur to keep on shuffling along. So I kept on shuffling along and finally my feet did hit something which hurt like hell.

I squirmed a bit closer and pushed my feet out more cautiously and touched whatever it was. It was solid and also rounded by the way my feet slipped from it. I drew them back under me as far as I could, then lashed out so the soles of my shoes hit the thing and it gave a loud clanging noise. So it was made of iron or steel and rounded in shape. Maybe it was the bucket they were going to have me kick, or maybe it was a pipe or some sort.

Genius said if it was a pipe it probably went from somewhere to somewhere. Genius hoped illogically that if I kept on kicking that pipe, somebody, somewhere, where that pipe went to or came from, would hear it. The odds were, I realised, that if anyone did hear it, it would be either Midnight or the character who had done the carrying of Wheeler on the way here. But what did I have to lose—apart from a couple of feet.

So I kicked the thing again and heard the loud clang as I did so. I kept on kicking it until my legs ached so much I couldn't lift them anymore. Then I just lay there for about five minutes and then started again.

After the third session I knew I'd never walk again—my legs were all used up. I was trying to work out an arrangement with wires that could lift one foot at a time and place it down in front of the other, when I heard the door open and somebody take one cautious step.

The hope that it wasn't Midnight or her helper was as good as a couple of hours with a masseur. With what felt like no effort at all I lifted my legs again and kicked the thing once more.

Footsteps started again, coming closer and closer. I could feel someone so close that I could hear their quick breathing. Then soft, cool hands fumbled at the back of my neck and I felt the gag pulled away from my mouth. A few moments later the scarf was pulled away from my eyes and I looked up into a pair of enormous violet eyes only a couple of feet away from mine and they were a distinct improvement on the tiger's yellow ones I had seen the last time.

"Al Wheeler!" Rena Landis said slowly. "What on earth are you doing playing silly games in our cellar!"

I licked my lips, trying to overcome the dryness in my mouth and throat enough so that I could speak.

"I heard that bang, bang, bang until I thought I'd go crazy!" she said. "Then I came down here to find out what was causing it and it's you!"

"Could you untie my hands?" I croaked.

She looked at me thoughtfully for a few seconds.

"I don't know that I should," she said. "I hate you!"

"They're going to kill me!" I said.

"Who are?"

"Midnight O'Hara and somebody else I never saw," I said. "She said she'd be back in an hour and maybe the hour's up already."

"She's the girl who runs that Horseshoe place," Rena said. "How could she put you into our cellar?"

"She said she would put me with Talbot's body," I said. "Then she'd get rid of me the same way as she got rid of him!"

It wasn't exactly the truth but it was calculated to put Rena on my side—I hoped.

"Terence's body?" she whispered. "In here? I must look, I have to know."

She got onto her feet and walked away from me. The cellar, I saw, looking around hopelessly, was a wine cellar. There were rows of bins that stood some six feet high, running around the walls and two rows in the centre. They had put me between the centre rows and I saw Rena disappear around the corner of the left-hand row.

Ten seconds later she was back, with the tears welling out of her eyes and running down her cheeks.

"You were right!" she said as she knelt down beside me and started to loosen the cord that held my wrists. "It's ... he's just around the corner there. How could they do a thing like that!"

"It was quite easy," a dry voice said from behind her and Rena gave a sob of fear as she jumped up onto her feet.

Midnight stood there, watching us, a gun in her hand.

"Little girls should be seen and not heard," she said. "Little girls should mind their own business if they want to stay out of trouble!"

"You killed him!" Rena sobbed. "You killed my Terence!"

"Terence?" Midnight looked taken aback for a moment. "Oh! You mean Talbot? So that's what Wheeler told you?"

"You killed him!" Rena repeated bitterly.

"No," Midnight said softly. "It was Wheeler who killed him."

"You're lying!" Rena said hysterically.

"Why should I bother to lie to you," Midnight said casually. "The police will be here within the half-hour and they'll tell you. Wheeler invited Talbot to his apartment and killed him there. Then he took the corpse and put it into the Horseshoe, hoping to divert suspicion away from himself and onto me.

"That's why I had Talbot's body brought here. When Wheeler found his body hadn't been discovered at my place, he came to find out why with a gun in his hand—so that's why I had him brought here—with Talbot's body to prove he's a murderer!"

Rena took her hand away from her face: "Did you say the ... police will be here?" she whispered.

"Within half an hour," Midnight said calmly.

Rena looked down at me, her fingers curling into talons. "You lied to me again," she said. "And I nearly believed you!" Her fingers started to rake down towards my face.

"Rena!" Midnight said sharply and the fingers stopped six inches from my face.

"Rena," Midnight repeated in a softer voice, "don't give yourself any more pain. I'll wait here till the police arrive and they will take care of everything, including Wheeler. You go up to your room. I'll come and tell you when it's all over."

"All right," Rena said dully. She walked slowly past Midnight and out of the cellar.

Midnight smiled at me: "Busy little beaver, aren't you? I heard the last of the pipe-banging as I came back into the house so I thought I'd better come down and investigate again."

"Another couple of minutes would have made a difference," I said. "But there's been enough difference made—Rena saw me here—and she saw Talbot's body here, too. You sold her that crazy story about me having killed him but she's not going to believe that forever. She's going to get curious again when the police don't arrive. Do you aim to have her join Talbot and me as well?"

"It won't be necessary," she said. "The police will arrive, you see."

"You don't have to kid me," I said, "I'm not going any place."

"I wouldn't dream of kidding you, Al," she said. "The police will be here.

They'll find the body of a certain Lieutenant who unfortunately went berserk and for some unknown reason killed a butler."

"You'll need to do better than that!" I said.

"Why?" she said. "They're looking for you—they've put out a general alarm for you, even. They're showing your picture on television and broadcasting your description on radio."

"That's because I was rude to the Commissioner and locked him in a bathroom when there was no need. But I'm not wanted for murder."

"You are the brilliant cop whose brain became unhinged," she said easily. "The brilliant but unstable mind that went round the loop when a case didn't work out the way you thought it should. So you intended to have it work out your way even if you had to make some circumstances fit your theories. So you murdered a man and planted the corpse in my place and gave the story to a newspaper, being determined to blame me for the first murder at any price.

"Luckily for me I found the corpse in time, and removed it—here. It wasn't the right thing to do but I was scared to death you would pin the murders onto me. Then you came into my office, forced me to show you where I'd taken the corpse—at the point of a gun—and brought me here."

"Then shot myself, just to embarrass you further?" I asked politely.

"Then said you were going to shoot me and make it look like suicide," she said. "In desperation, I struggled with you—the gun went off!" She shook her head sadly. "No more Wheeler!"

"It wouldn't stand up for five seconds," I said. "I proved to Lavers and Hanlon that Wes Stewart couldn't have possibly killed Johnny Landis!"

"Quite right," she said gravely. "I only made that statement about Stewart being involved in narcotics distribution and Landis trying to blackmail him, because you forced me to."

"You sound even more stupid the more you say!" I said. "Why would I do that?"

"Because you killed Landis," she said patiently. "The whole thing started when you first came to the Horseshoe which was about two months ago."

"I was only there once before the night Landis was murdered," I said. "And that was a week ago!"

"I'll produce witnesses to say you were there at least four nights a week, every week for the last two months," she said. "You were crazy about me, Wheeler! You couldn't stand it that I wasn't attracted to you at all. You threatened me that you'd commit the perfect murder and involve me in it. I laughed at you, I thought you were drunk. But you weren't!"

She took a step closer to me: "I've wasted enough time already. I've got to shoot you and make it look like a struggle and I'm wasting time!"

She stretched out her hand and I found myself looking down the barrel of the gun which looked like the mouth of a gaping canyon.

"Farewell, Wheeler!" she said tautly and I saw the bottle rise in the air behind her and closed my eyes.

I heard the thud and opened my eyes again just in time to see Midnight hit the floor beside me.

Just behind the spot where Midnight had stood, was Rena, the bottle still in her hand.

She looked at me broodingly: "I got upstairs and got to thinking about it," she said. "And I wasn't quite so sure—so I tiptoed back down the stairs again and listened."

She looked dispassionately at Midnight: "She must have thought I was dumb or something!"

I rubbed the circulation back into my wrists and ankles after Rena had freed them from the cord, then climbed onto my feet. The bin closest to me held half a dozen bottles of hock. I grabbed the nearest one and broke the top of it off against the side of the bin and drank half the bottle.

It cured my thirst, anyway.

I stooped down and picked up the gun Midnight had dropped and looked at Rena.

"You see anyone else at all?"

"No," she said. "Was there someone else with her?"

"She didn't carry me down here," I said. "Whoever he was, he'll be back."

"Then we ought to leave here?" she said.

"I think we'll wait till he arrives," I said. "I'd rather meet him down here than on the stairs."

"But he might be dangerous!" the violet eyes widened again.

"Not as dangerous in here as on the stairs," I said. "You get over to the far side of the cellar behind those bins and stay out of sight—I'll wait for him by the door. And don't talk!"

"All right," she said nervously.

She moved away behind the row of bins which would conceal her from the view of anyone coming into the cellar. I went across to the door which stood wide open and stood behind it, Midnight's gun in my hand. There was a kind of familiar feel about the butt and I took another look at it and saw it was my own. I had to hand it to Midnight, she hadn't missed a trick!

I waited for about five minutes. Then I heard a top stair creak and then the slow, heavy footsteps coming down the stairs. I heard his heavy breathing as he came in through the doorway. I saw his bulk pass in front of me as I watched him walk up between the centre row of bins then stop suddenly as he saw Midnight stretched out on the floor.

I stepped up behind him and rammed the gun hard into his kidneys.

"Why, Clarence!" I said. "Come to play me a lament on your pink-a-pink?"

CHAPTER THIRTEEN

They sat side by side on the period reproduction antique sofa. Clarence Nesbitt just sat there, his brown bowler hat stuck firmly on top of his head. Midnight had her elbows on her knees, her face buried in her hands. Maybe she was in despair or maybe she had a headache from the sock on the head Rena had given her with the bottle.

Rena was pouring me a second glass of Scotch and I needed it. I had a gun in one hand and a phone in the other, and the phone was running hot. But I figured sooner or later Lavers would have to take a breath or drop dead. Right then I didn't care much which alternative he decided on.

He turned out to be a natural piker and took a breath.

"Undoubtedly all you say is true, Commissioner," I said patiently. "But I have Talbot's body right here in the cellar and Rena Landis as a witness to the O'Hara dame's statements to me. All I want to do is a Thin Man—like you said, I only caught up with the book the other day, and a reconstruction of the crime with all the suspects there, appeals to me."

I listened to another torrent of words and waited till he had to take that breath again.

"Pick us up here at Landis' house," I said. "Bring Wes Stewart with you. Have somebody get Cuba Carter down there as well ..." I had a sudden inspiration. "Or do I let that locked bathroom story leak out to a certain well-read columnist?"

Lavers nearly crawled down the phone and bit my ear. Finally be had to stop for another breath.

"You'd better bring Joe Randle along with you, too, Commissioner," I said, and hung up before he started to use his new breath again.

I dialled the *Gazette* and got through to the editor and talked to him for five minutes straight, then I put the phone back onto the rest.

"You sure run off at the mouth, Bloodhound!" Clarence said in his high-pitched voice.

Rena gave me the new glass of Scotch which I drank gratefully.

"Is there anything else I can do, Al?" she asked in a soft voice.

"Not right now, honey," I said. "Where's your father, anyway?"

"He's at the paper," she said. "I don't think he'll be back before dawn."

I looked at my watch: "That won't be too long now."

Midnight lifted her head: "Could I have a drink, please?" she asked in a low voice.

"You!" Rena's voice cracked. "You're lucky I didn't split your skull with that bottle! I wish I had!"

"Poor little rich girl!" Midnight said savagely. "Locked up all day with the butler!"

The violet eyes grew luminous and their gaze fixed and trancelike. Slowly Rena picked up the Scotch bottle by the neck and walked towards the sofa with it balanced in her hand.

"Rena!" I yelled.

She stopped and turned her head slowly in my direction.

"Did you say something, Al?"

"Put the bottle down," I said gently. "The Law will take care of her."

"She said things," she pleaded. "Nasty, horrible things!"

"Pay no attention," I said. "Go and wait at the front door for the Commissioner and the other police to arrive. When they do, take them down to the cellar and show them where to find Talbot. And when they've seen him, tell them what you heard the O'Hara girl saying to me in the cellar. That will hurt her a lot more than hitting her with that bottle!"

"It will?" Rena said eagerly. "I'll go now, Al! Right away!"

She ran from the room into the hallway.

Midnight O'Hara's lips twisted into a sneer.

"She's going to give you trouble one of these days, Wheeler—professional trouble. One day she'll do a Lizzie Borden and make this town famous!"

"She'll have to do better than you first," I said. "And that will take some doing."

I heard the howl of sirens coming closer.

Midnight lifted her eyebrows as she heard them, too.

"Meanwhile," I said, "back at the ranch ..."

"The girl is still wanting a glass of whisky," she said. "Do the right thing by me, Al. I always gave you a drink, didn't I?"

"Sure," I said. "Help yourself—only don't do anything foolish."

"I've done all the foolish things I'm going to do," she said.

"If she gets to having a drink, Bloodhound," Clarence said, "do I get to smoking?"

"You can have a reefer, Clarence," I said. "But even that won't help you think your way out of this rap."

Midnight came over to the table and poured herself a drink.

"Here's to better days, Al," she said as she lifted the glass. "You and me and the tiger skin." Her lips were parted in a slow, provocative smile and her eyes were half-closed as she looked at me, taking a deep breath that threw an unnatural strain on the Orlon sweater.

"How about that, Al?" she said huskily. "You and me and the tiger skin?"

"I've seen better and prettier things than you crawl out of an apple," I said carefully.

Her face was suddenly frozen and the moment's silence was broken by a high-pitched giggle from Clarence Nesbitt.

"Doll," he giggled, "you're off-time! You don't lay your racket good for the Bloodhound."

I heard feet tramping down the hallway and Rena's excited voice say: "Down here!" and then the sound of heavy feet going down the stairs to the cellar.

Midnight looked at the gun in my hand pointing straight at her firm midriff and changed her mind about throwing the contents of her glass in my face.

The acrid smell of marihuana twitched at my nostrils as Clarence puffed contentedly.

"Man!" he said. "The great mezz! The glorious muta!"

"By any other name it still stinks!" I told him.

Midnight finished her drink and put the empty glass carefully onto the table.

"I hope, Lieutenant Wheeler," she said formally. "That you rot in hell!"

"It's a middling to better than even chance," I admitted. "You save me a place."

Feet stomped up the stairs again and a few seconds later Rena came back into the living-room, followed by Lavers, Hanlon, Polnik and half a dozen uniformed cops.

Lavers walked up to the table, looked at Midnight, Clarence, then me.

"All right, Wheeler," he said. "I've heard Miss Landis' story and I've seen Talbot's body. You can play Thin Man if you want. And after you've finished we'll have a little talk about your future!"

"You think I may get a promotion out of this?" I asked.

"I'll speak to the Commissioner for Sanitation about it," he said coldly. "Maybe he'll start you off working on one of the bigger trucks!"

I thought maybe it wasn't wise to press the point. "Let's get down to the Golden Horseshoe," I said. "Then we can play reconstruction."

Lavers nodded. "All right—always give a man enough rope is my motto. Hanlon, see these two," he gestured towards Midnight and Clarence, "are taken down there in one of the cars."

"Yes, sir," Hanlon said smartly.

"You can travel with me, Wheeler," Lavers said. "I want to surmise about your future on the way. Maybe I can even help you get started. I've got some old overalls in the garage that I can let you have!"

Half an hour later the Golden Horseshoe was open, if not for business.

Cuba Carter was there, rubbing the sleep out of his eyes and Wes Stewart gave me a warm smile as I walked into the cellar and Joe Randle winked heavily at me. Midnight O'Hara slumped into the nearest chair and looked bored with the whole proceedings.

"All right, Wheeler," Lavers said. "You've got what you wanted so go ahead, but make it fast. And if you suggest at any stage that I look at a window ..."

"I'd like to see the trio group up on the dais and play for us," I said. I saw the murderous look in Lavers' eyes and added hastily, "the tune they were playing when Landis was killed."

A beefy cop took the handcuffs from around Clarence Nesbitt's wrists and he walked over to where his bass-fiddle was propped against the wall and took the cover off. He rubbed his wrists thoughtfully a few times then hoisted the fiddle onto the dais.

A few seconds later Cuba had his drum-kit spread out and was ready. Wes fingered his horn lovingly and looked at me. "I guess we're ready, Lieutenant."

"Fine," I said. "I want just one more thing. Sergeant Polnik?"

"Lieutenant?"

"You're going to play Johnny Landis. After the music has started I want you to come out of that door there." I pointed to the door that led into Midnight's office, "and walk around the back of the dais."

"Sure, Lieutenant," he said.

I nodded to Wes and the trio started in on "Rampart Street Parade."

Polnik was standing just inside the office door, waiting. I nodded to him and he came out slowly and walked around behind the trio at the back of the dais.

"Hold it, Polnik!" I said and then thought that anybody could be a poet just so long as you didn't try.

I let Wes build up his succession of harmonic riffs then yelled for him to stop.

The three of them stopped and gazed stolidly at us.

"That's it," I said. "That's about where they were when Jonny Landis got his. You can see that Wes couldn't have shot—he was using both hands to play his horn, as I ... er ... did point out once before. And Cuba would have had quite a job with those drumsticks in each hand. But Clarence ..." I shook my head affectionately, "a very bright boy is Clarence," I said.

I stepped up onto the dais beside Clarence.

"You'll notice, gentlemen, that in playing his bass-fiddle, Clarence is only really side-on to the customers and as his right hand plucks the strings, he could quite easily point a finger in Johnny Landis' direction. A finger—or a gun. He could even have had a gun up his sleeve, ready for the occasion. I'll take an even bet that he took a four bars rest the moment before the shot was fired—Wes was real gone and wouldn't have noticed, neither would Cuba. He could have shot Johnny Landis and gone right back on plucking his pink-a-pink."

"Bloodhound!" Clarence said shrilly. "You're crazy!"

"You told me something, Wes," I said. "You said you did note that after the noise which you hadn't realised was a shot, the tone of the bass-fiddle seemed to change."

"That's right, Lieutenant," Wes agreed quietly.

"Are you trying to tell us that proves the fiddle player's nerves must have been bad, and that was because he'd just murdered somebody!" Lavers snarled.

"No, sir," I said politely. "I'm trying to prove something quite different."

"What about the gun, Al?" Hanlon said. "What did he do with that—use it to pluck the strings of that fiddle?"

"I thought nobody was going to ask me!" I smiled thankfully at Hanlon. "That's the most exciting piece in the whole show as Freberg might say."

I looked at Clarence and said, "Excuse me," in a gentle voice and took the bass-fiddle out of his hands. I stepped off the dais and walked towards Lavers.

"If you think you're going to play that thing to me!" he yelped.

"I have no intention of playing, sir," I said and lifted the fiddle over my head.

Lavers yelped again and ducked as I brought the bass-fiddle swinging down in a vicious arc. The centre of the fiddle hit the back of the empty chair I'd aimed for, and snapped clean in half.

I was left holding the neck and the beginnings of the sound-box in my hand, with the broken strings dangling limply into thin air.

The other half which consisted mostly of the rest of the sound-box dropped onto the chair, rolled, teetered on its edge for a moment then dropped onto the floor. And as it did so, something else fell from inside and also dropped onto the floor. I was glad about that, if it hadn't I would have made straight for Lavers' garage and those overalls.

Everyone stared blankly at the small pistol that lay there on a floor.

"Anyone care to bet?" I asked. "A point two-two with one slug fired and the slug the doc pulled out of Johnny Landis will match it.

"It's one of the smallest twenty-two's I've seen," I said. "Small enough for Clarence to slip it under the string of his fiddle and force it through the hole there in to the sound-box of the fiddle. One thing he didn't bargain for was the slight change in tonal quality it made being picked up by Wes Stewart's ear. But then Wes is a great musician and Clarence wouldn't know a great musician even when he played there right alongside him!”

Lavers picked up the gun gingerly with his handkerchief and looked at it.

“Amazing!” he said.

“Like Johnny Landis put it,” I said, “Crazy!”

CHAPTER FOURTEEN

Clarence came off the dais in one jump, heading towards me, his mouth working, his eyes wild, his great hands clenched into fists.

A couple of uniformed cops grabbed him, one from either side and he stood still for a moment as the veins stood out in his forehead, then he sort of shook himself and both cops catapulted away from him.

He kept on coming for me, and now he was making a curiously shrill grunting sound like a wild pig that’s just been stuck by a native’s spear.

I would have liked to clip him neatly under the jaw and drop him where he stood, but that stuff belongs to television. My fist would have hurt him about as much as a fly landing on his jaw.

I took my gun out of my pocket as he got real close and rammed the barrel into his stomach so hard that the first three inches of the barrel disappeared.

“Just say, Boo!” I told him. “And my nervous reflexes will pull the trigger.”

Clarence stood motionless looking at me. “Bloodhound,” he whispered. “You mean every word!”

“It would be a pleasure,” I assured him. “Just cough, why don’t you?”

Then the uniformed cops grabbed him again, twisting his arms behind his back and then slipping the handcuffs onto his wrists. I took the gun out of his paunch and put it back into my pocket.

“Take him away!” Lavers grunted. “Put him in one of the cars and get him down to the Bureau.” He held out the handkerchief-wrapped gun to another of the uniformed cops.

“Take this with you and have it fingerprinted then turn it over to the lab, and have them match the slug they took out of Landis.”

The gun and Clarence disappeared with four cops outside.

Lavers lit himself a cigar carefully: “All right, Wheeler, you hammed your act successfully. Now tell about Talbot and the why’s of it.”

“I’d rather start with the why’s of Johnny Landis being knocked off first,” I said. “If you don’t mind?”

“What difference would it make?” he said resignedly. “Go on!”

I looked at Midnight O’Hara who still sat slumped in her chair with an apathetic look on her face.

"Midnight's story about Wes Stewart had some truth in it," I said. I caught the startled look on Wes' face and grinned at him. "Not about you, Wes, but about the narcotics. This place was used as a distribution centre and it was a member of the trio who sold the stuff, not Wes, but Clarence Nesbitt of course. And Midnight knew all about it—she organised it."

"That's a lie," she said tonelessly.

"Johnny Landis progressed from being a customer to blackmailing the owner for a cut of the profits, or he tried to. One of the waiters, Eddie Booth, testified that Johnny Landis was in the place at least half-a-dozen times before he was murdered. And on at least four occasions he had long conversations with Midnight—twice at a table out here and twice inside her office."

"He's lying!" Midnight said again.

"Flip the disc, honey," I told her, "we've heard this song before."

"Save us the repartee, Wheeler!" Lavers grunted. "Go on with the story."

"Midnight realised that there was only one way to stop Johnny Landis and that was doing something to him that would be permanent," I said. "So she used her salesman-muscleman, Clarence, to take care of it. I don't think he would have had the brains to think of that bass-fiddle caper all by himself. But that was it. It got rid of Landis permanently."

"How did she hope to get away with it?" Lavers asked.

"I think she might have had the idea she was committing the perfect crime," I said. "No-one would ever discover how Landis was shot or who killed him. Maybe she thought we would be too busy ripping up the floors looking for a gun so that we wouldn't ask the sort of questions we did ask people like Booth, the waiter. Don't ask me, Commissioner, she's a dame, and who can tell what a dame thinks?"

I modified that: "Except under certain circumstances, of course."

"You still haven't told me about Talbot!" Lavers said.

"I was coming to that, sir," I said. "You see ..."

The sound of raised voices at the front door grew louder and louder, one voice topping the rest.

"I demand to see Commissioner Lavers immediately!" the voice shouted. "Let me inside there or I'll see you never wear that uniform again after tonight! Do you realise who I am! Do you realise I represent a million readers! I have a right in the public interest ..."

The door burst open and Daniel Landis appeared suddenly at the head of the stairs and glared down at us for a moment before he clattered down the stairs and almost ran across the floor towards Lavers.

"Commissioner!" he said crisply. "I demand to know what's happening here! I just got a call from my daughter and for a moment I thought she was out of her mind! She told me the body of our butler has been found in the cellar and that the Lieutenant you so rightly suspended for incompetency—Wheeler ..." He saw me and his eyes widened.

"So it's true!"

"Probably," Lavers said coldly. "If you don't mind, Mr. Landis, I ..."

"But I do mind!" Landis said. "You happen to be investigating the murder of my own son! I have a personal right, apart from the right of a newspaper proprietor, to be here and learn what is going on. It's true my butler is dead?"

"Quite true," Lavers said shortly.

"Then the story in the *Gazette* wasn't a tissue of lies as was first thought!" Landis said sharply. "This is very interesting, Commissioner! Very interesting, indeed. You are making a confidante of one newspaper at the expense of the others."

"I never gave that story to the *Gazette*," Lavers said, giving me a murderous stare. "It so happens, Mr. Landis that Wheeler ..."

"I have no wish to discuss that brutish oaf!" Landis said crisply. "I demand to know right now exactly what steps are being taken ..."

Lavers moved his shoulders irritably: "I'll give you a choice, Mr. Landis," he said. "Sit down and shut up or I'll have you forcibly ejected from this place!"

"You'll ..." Landis' mouth opened until his jaw nearly touched his chest. "I'll have you thrown out of office for this, Lavers! I'll have you ..."

"Polnik!" Lavers snapped his fingers. "See that Mr. Landis leaves this building—now!"

"Yes, sir!" Polnik said happily. He crooked his finger at two uniformed cops who came up, one either side of Landis, got hold of an elbow each, lifted him four inches off the floor and carried him towards the stairs.

Lavers tossed the butt of his cigar away and began to carefully open the wrapper on another.

"You were saying, Wheeler?"

"Talbot was Johnny Landis' associate," I said. "When Johnny was murdered, Talbot got cold feet and decided to tell me what he knew. He rang me and arranged an appointment to see me in my apartment. They got to know of it and Midnight sent Clarence after him and he just made it. When I answered the door, Talbot dropped dead in my arms."

Polnik came back down the stairs and Lavers looked at him questioningly.

"I put him in his car with a cop to chauffeur him home," Polnik said cheerfully. "That okay, sir?"

"An excellent plan," Lavers said without any expression in his voice.

"There are times when Mr. Landis takes himself too seriously."

He looked back at me, "Go on, Wheeler."

"I was saying that Clarence shot Talbot outside my apartment and made his getaway before I got to the front door, sir."

"Strange," he murmured as he lit the new cigar. "I don't remember you reporting this, Wheeler?"

"You might remember you had suspended me at the time," I said. "And I also had an idea who might have killed him. So as I still had a set of keys to this place, I brought the body back here and dumped it on the dais. I then told Joe Randle to give the story about the body to the *Gazette*.

"I also had him phone Midnight and tell her the body was here. I thought if she was on the level, she'd report the phone-call to the police and the body would be discovered. If she wasn't on the level, she would remove the body again, she wouldn't want it connected with her in any way."

"And she didn't report it," Lavers said.

"I wasn't so smart," I said. "I forgot she would have read Joe's first story in the *Gazette* about his interview with Wes Stewart. She put two and two together—it could only be me who'd tipped him off about Talbot's body, so he must be with me. And since he'd got an exclusive interview with Wes, then the three of us must be together and the obvious place for us to be was my apartment. So she tipped you off where to find Wes, the man you were hunting for."

"The tip-off came from an unidentified, obviously disguised, voice calling from a public paybooth," Lavers said.

"She hoped that once you'd got Wes back again, that would be the end of it," I said.

Lavers nodded, "It makes sense," he said grudgingly, "in a balled-up kind of way."

"Lieutenant!" Polnik said in a subdued voice. "If you hadn't knocked me that time I might have killed an innocent man!"

"I was hoping he was innocent at the time," I admitted.

"Hell!" Polnik swallowed. "I'm sure glad you did it!"

"I owe you an apology, Al," Hanlon said. "I hope you'll accept it."

"Don't let us start crying on Wheeler's shoulder!" Lavers snarled. "He's just about violated every rule in the book on this one. If you'd had a little faith, Wheeler, just a little faith in the rest of the Department, we could have made this thing a lot easier for everyone concerned."

"The trouble was," I said apologetically, "that I felt the Department didn't have any faith in me, Commissioner!"

Lavers' face slowly turned a deep purple.

"All right!" he shouted. "That wraps it up! Everybody back to the Bureau. I don't want to stay here all night!"

"It's all lies," Midnight said as she was lifted onto her feet.

"Commissioner," I said. "I'd like to ask you a favour. On the way back could I take a car and take Joe Randle with me?"

"You take a car on your own if you want," he grunted. "But you don't take Randle with you—he's not getting any more exclusives on this case—you heard Landis didn't you? How much trouble do you want to give me?"

"Supposing he gives you his word not to contact his paper before he gets to the bureau and you give him the okay?" I said.

Lavers thought about it for a moment. "All right," he said finally. "I never knew Randle to go back on his word before."

"Tell him, Joe," I said.

"You don't know what you're asking me, Al!" Joe said, his face contorted with pain. "Keep clammed up on a story like this!"

"Tell him, Joe!" I repeated.

"Okay," he sighed. "I won't contact the paper, Commissioner, not till you give me the okay!"

"Fair enough," Lavers grunted.

Midnight stopped in front of me on her way out between Polnik and Hanlon.

"All lies!" she said dully. "Selling narcotics here, was I? Then where are they? Did you ever find any—the place got searched often enough. Who found one single reefer inside the place!"

"I'm glad you reminded me, honey," I said. "I nearly forgot."

I looked at the Commissioner, "Inside her office you'll find a tiger skin rug, sir. I spent some time earlier this evening lying down on it ..."

I saw the look on his face, "... bound hand and foot," I added quickly. "It's a very lumpy tiger skin and maybe if someone puts a knife through it and looks closely ..."

"You dirty ..." Midnight screamed until Polnik quickly put a hand over her mouth.

"From a lady!" he said mildly. "What will the carriage-trade say?"

I turned away to Joe Randle. "Let's go, huh?" I asked him.

"Anything you say, Al," he said wearily.

Hanlon tossed me the keys to one of the prowlcars outside. "The last in line, Al," he said.

"Thanks," I told him.

"Don't be too long getting to the bureau, Wheeler!" Lavers said. "I'll want you there for some time yet."

"You mean I'm not suspended any longer, sir?"

He shrugged his shoulders helplessly. "What difference would it make?"

"Thank you, sir," I said politely.

I walked with Randle up the steps and out onto the sidewalk. We sat in the front seat of the prowlcar last in the line and I started the motor and wheeled it away from the kerb.

"You must have blown a gasket!" Joe said bitterly. "The biggest punchline I ever had to a story and you make me promise not to use it. You make me promise Lavers not to ring my paper!"

"I had a reason, Joe," I said.

"Reason! What reason could there be!"

"Because I already did," I said.

"Come again?"

"I already rang your paper and gave them your story from Landis' house," I said. "Right after I rang Lavers!"

Joe leaned back in his seat and started to laugh. He kept on laughing and after a while I joined in with him. We both nearly had hysterics.

"Al!" Joe moaned, punching me painfully in the ribs. "You're a genius! I can just imagine Lavers' face when he finds out!"

I stopped laughing abruptly.

So could I!

CHAPTER FIFTEEN

Joe had sobered down by the time we stood on the doorstep.

"I'd be as popular here as a locust in a vineyard!" he said. "What's the idea of stopping off here, Al?"

"A debt I owe somebody," I said. "I'd like to repay it, if I can."

I pressed the push and waited.

The door opened about twenty seconds later and Landis stood there. His eyes widened as he recognised us.

"Wheeler!" he rasped. "And Randle! I like your unmitigated gall in calling at my house!"

"Commissioner's order, Mr. Landis," I said with a poker-face. "He instructed me to give you a full account of what has happened tonight. In fairness, he instructed me to bring Mr. Randle along, too. He thought that both papers would then be equally represented."

Landis hesitated for a moment.

"All right," he said finally. "I suppose you'd better come in. But don't let Lavers fool himself this will make any difference. After his cavalier treatment of me an hour ago, I'll nail his hide to his office-door!"

We followed him into the living-room. I looked around hopefully but the bottle of Scotch had disappeared and it didn't seem likely Landis would produce it again.

He nodded towards the sofa and we sat down. I lit myself a cigarette and told Landis the story as briefly as I could, the same story as I had told Lavers.

He sat stiff-backed in a chair behind the table, watching me as I told him the story. There was a few seconds silence when I'd finished then he nodded stiffly to me.

"I find it hard to say this, Wheeler, but I must I congratulate you. I apologise for my former attitude, I was quite obviously wrong. You have done a good job, a very good job indeed and I shall make it my business to see that the special editions of the *Tribune* say so later on this morning!"

"I appreciate that, Mr. Landis," I said. "But that wasn't the only reason I came here."

He looked at me sharply. "There is something else?"

"A postscript, maybe," I said. "I didn't want to say anything about it to the Commissioner until I'd seen you first—not because of you," I said carefully, "but because of your daughter. She happened to save my life earlier on tonight and that's a debt I'd like to repay if I can. This is one small way of repaying it."

"My daughter—Rena!" he bristled. "What has this got to do with her?"

"Let's go back to Talbot for a moment," I said. "You threw your son out of this house about three to four months ago. You spend most of your time at your newspaper's office so that left only your daughter at home ... and Talbot, the butler."

He jumped onto his feet, his face crimson, "Are you suggesting ..."

"That anything indecent went on between them?" I finished the question for him. "No, Mr. Landis. But I'm suggesting, because your daughter told me so herself, that they had a much stronger relationship than that of employer's daughter to employee. So strong in fact that Talbot had actually asked her to marry him."

"Balderdash!" Landis shouted.

"I'm taking her word for it," I said evenly. "But we'll leave it at that for a moment. Why did you throw your son out of the house?"

"I'd suffered him for too many years," he growled. "I'd paid his debts, got him out of more serious trouble but it made no difference. He was a wastrel, a throw-back, rotten to the core!"

"It all sounds very convincing," I said. "But I'm sure you must have had an even better reason."

"What do you mean?"

"We'll leave that, too, for a moment," I said. "How is your financial state at the moment, Mr. Landis?"

"I won't tolerate any more of this!" he said wildly. "Get out, or I'll throw you out myself!"

"Not healthy," Joe Randle answered my question. "The *Tribune* is mortgaged up to the hilt and way beyond, they say. He spends five hundred thousand dollars on new presses just over a year ago and circulation and advertising revenue have dropped off since then."

I lit another cigarette. Landis was standing there at the table, his back rigid.

"I'll tell you how I see it, Mr. Landis," I said. "And you can tell me how right or how wrong I am. The way I see it is, you needed money desperately. You were having an affair with Midnight O'Hara and you heard her talk of the reefer-smoking musicians she employed. She told you about one in particular, Clarence Nesbitt, who had contacts who could supply him with narcotics. You began to think about it—you could finance the purchases and Clarence could handle the distribution through Midnight's place, the Golden Horseshoe."

He still didn't say anything.

"Because you've got a mental quirk about your family, you have the house phones tapped, and channelled into your office," I said. "You have the conversations taped, so you can play them back and hear everything that's been said on your phones. And one day you heard a conversation between Johnny and Clarence Nesbitt with Johnny arranging to buy some marihuana cigarettes from the musician. And that was when you tossed him out of your house, because if he was already in contact with Nesbitt, you thought it would be too dangerous to have him around, constantly, perhaps eavesdropping on your conversations with Midnight herself.

"You made a mistake when you tossed him out. Because he already knew about you and Midnight, but he didn't know the narcotics part. But my guess is, when Clarence Nesbitt suddenly expanded into a bigtime pusher of all kinds of narcotics that Johnny realised he must be backed by somebody. Who—it wouldn't be hard for him to work out it must be Midnight. He knew of your liaison with her so he went to her and tried to blackmail her.

"The ironic part of that was he probably tried to blackmail her by threatening to tell you she was mixed up in the dope racket. But both you and Midnight were frightened that sooner or later he'd hit on the truth. So you told Midnight to frighten Clarence into getting rid of your son.

"The other one was Talbot. Talbot could have heard your conversations with Midnight and spoken to the police of the connection. Maybe he'd already approached you about your daughter and you'd threatened him with all sorts of unpleasantness if he ever dared again to talk of marriage.

"So my bet is that after you'd tossed me out of your house, Talbot came to you. He told you he knew of your association with the O'Hara girl but he hadn't told me anything about it. And he wouldn't either—just so long as you gave him permission to marry Rena. And you laughed at him and told him he couldn't threaten you—something like that. But you went to your office and listened very carefully to that wire-tap and you heard him ring me and arrange a meeting at my apartment that night. So then you contacted Midnight and told her at all costs Talbot had to be prevented from speaking to me. And she sent Clarence to take care of him."

Landis shook his head slowly like a man coming out of a trance.

"It's completely absurd," he said. "And in a case you couldn't prove any of it."

"I see you have a smug look on your face, Mr. Landis," I said. "Which means you've probably wiped the tape clean that held the recording of my conversation with Talbot. But we can still prove it. Don't think for a moment that Midnight O'Hara won't talk to try and save some of her own skin.

"And we can prove you had that wire-tap on your phone—we can prove every call was put directly onto the tapes inside your office, and we can prove you would be the only person in this city who could have possibly known that Talbot was coming to visit me that night."

"You won't need to prove anything, Lieutenant," a soft voice said from behind me.

Landis looked like a puppet whose strings had been savagely jerked. "Rena!" he gasped.

I looked over my shoulder and saw her standing just behind the sofa. Her violet eyes were larger than I had ever seen before.

She wore a black negligee that fitted her loosely, like a shroud, and she looked like an Angel of Death with the gun in her hand.

"I heard everything," she said in a monotone. "So it was you who arranged Terence's murder, Father? It was you who arranged John's murder. It was you who was wallowing in the filth of narcotics—you," she took a deep breath, "you with your crusading editorials and your clean-up-the-city campaigns and your businessmen's luncheon talks and your cheques to the League of Purity!"

She walked past the end of the sofa where I sat, getting closer to the desk.

"I always hated you," she said. "Ever since I was quite small, and I never really knew why. I know now—because you were everything you accused John of being just now. If he was any or all of those things, it was because he bore your blood. It's you who are a wastrel, a throw-back, who's rotten to the core!"

"Rena!" he said fearfully. "Don't! Please put down that gun, it's dangerous, it's loaded, the safety-catch isn't even on!"

"I know," she said. "I made sure it was that way."

"Lieutenant!" she said, without taking her eyes away from her father. "You won't have to worry about making an arrest. It won't be necessary!"

"I knew it!" Landis said, with naked terror shaking his body. "You're mad! I always suspected it, now I know!"

"No," she said composedly. "I'm not mad, Father. I know that now for certain. Many times I wondered about it, but now I know if there's a streak of insanity in this family it runs through your veins. The vanity and greed and jealousy that consumes you is better off helpless. I'm doing Humanity a favour, Father, in shooting you down like a mad dog!"

I came up from the sofa and grabbed her wrist, twisting it sharply so that the gun dropped from her fingers noiselessly onto the thick-piled carpet.

"Not that way, Rena," I said. "There's a better way."

I picked up the gun and carefully wiped it clean with my handkerchief and then tossed it onto the table.

Rena was crying softly into a handkerchief.

I put my hands into the pockets of my jacket and hunched my shoulders.

"Like I said Landis," looking him directly in the eyes, "there's a much easier way out for everyone. Why don't you take it?" I nodded towards the gun that lay within his reach on the table-top.

He looked at me incredulously for a moment then his right hand moved towards the gun, shaking uncontrollably as it got close.

Then he made a grab for it and grasped the butt in the palm of his hand, the index finger curling around the trigger, and the shaking stopped.

The gun came up, the barrel swinging in an arc towards me. "You fool, Wheeler!" he said in a delighted voice. "You poor, crazy fool!"

I shot him twice and both slugs hit him in the chest. He dropped the gun back onto the table and it bounced once and then hit the carpet.

He went down onto his knees, both hands clutched to his chest, and the ferocity of his snarl as he died would maybe give me nightmares sometime, if I wasn't dreaming about a blonde at the time.

I looked down ruefully at the smoking hole in my pocket and hoped somebody would pay for a new suit.

Rena still stood crying quietly.

Joe Randle got onto his feet with an awed look on his face.

"You were holding that gun in your hand all the time, Al?" he said. "Inside your pocket! You never trusted him to do the decent thing for a moment!"

"Would you?" I asked him. "It's much better this way, nice and neat. D.O.A. Dead on arrival, shot while resisting arrest. I needed a witness, Joe, that's why I brought you along."

"You knew this would happen?"

"No," I admitted. "But I thought something like it might happen—if I could org ... well, just call it a cop's intuition?"

"Oh, sure!" he said.

I got hold of Rena's shoulders and shook her gently.

"It's over," I said. "You don't want to stay in this house. Is there someone you can stay with, a friend?"

She nodded, "Mrs. Kathman. She was a friend of my mother's."

"You know her phone number?"

She told me and I rang the number and after a long time Mrs. Kathman answered. I told her the story quickly and she said she'd come right over and pick up Rena and take her back to her own house.

I rang the Bureau and spent a painful ten minutes explaining to Lavers what had happened, then surprisingly enough he softened up enough to tell me to wait there until Hanlon arrived then get the hell out of there and back to the Bureau.

I put the phone down and lit a cigarette. I saw that Rena had disappeared and Joe had found the Scotch and was pouring us both a drink—enough for four people for me and enough for six people for him.

He caught my questioning look. "She went upstairs to dress and pack a suitcase," he said. "I think she'll be okay."

"She's had a tough run," I said.

"Here's your Scotch," Joe said. "Now would you mind moving out of the way and let me get onto my paper and give them the rest of the story."

"There's no real story, Joe," I said. "I gave them the lot when I rang them."

He stared at me open-mouthed, "You knew all this was going happen!"

"Not that Landis would get shot," I admitted. "But I knew just how he was involved and he'd be bound to crack."

"Well, I'll be ..."

"I don't doubt it," I said. "You could ring them and give them the postscript about Landis being shot dead while resisting arrest. But they've got the rest of the story—you were quite lavish in your praise of Commissioner Lavers, by the way.

"You pointed out how he'd strung Landis along all the time by pretending to play ball with him and have a certain Lieutenant suspended from duty and pretending he agreed with the vilification of said Lieutenant in the *Tribune*."

"I suppose Wheeler got an odd mention here and there?" Joe asked in a nasty voice.

"Not more than once to every paragraph," I said. "Don't push me, Joe, or I might ask for royalties on this. I even gave them a headline for it."

"A headline! What was that?"

"A DANIEL COME TO JUDGMENT!" I said soberly.

THE END

The Blonde

\- \- \- \- \-

by Carter Brown

CHAPTER ONE

"Wheeler Lonely Hearts Club," I said. "Give us a ring and we'll see you get one."

"Lieutenant Wheeler!" Sheriff Lavers' voice was surprised. "You sound alive and it's only nine-thirty in the morning. You couldn't have a blonde there, could you? Left over from last night or something."

"No, sir," I said, "no blonde here."

I waved good-bye to the redhead as she went out the door. She had a remorseful look on her face but it was her own fault. I had offered to get breakfast but she said she wasn't hungry.

I concentrated on the phone again: "I have a surprise for you, Sheriff," I told him. "You gave me a day off, remember! And this is it."

"I wouldn't let it worry me," he said. "I want to talk to you, it's important. You'd better come down to the office right away." He hung up before I could argue.

I would have ignored him but so long as he kept me detached from Homicide and attached to his office, he was my boss. Like the man says, the second quickest way to get fired is to be rude to your boss. The quickest way is to be rude to his wife.

I put down the phone and on some clothes. I drove my Austin Healey downtown and twenty minutes later was inside the County Sheriff's office. There always was one good reason for calling on Lavers. Her name was Annabelle Jackson and she was a blonde and his secretary, in that order.

"Hush my mouth, honey-chile," I said admiringly, "you get more beautiful every time I see you. You're nothing but a living doll!"

"Dope is the word you mean," she said coldly. "Haven't you noticed the difference since our last date, Lieutenant—I've aged!"

"You know how it is," I mumbled, "Homicide."

"I've been thinking about it!" she said. "You were going to call me, as I remember. I've been calling you."

"Busy line?"

"Names," she snarled. "The sheriff said you were to go right on in."

I walked into Lavers' office and he nodded toward a visitor's chair. I sat down without thinking and shot into the air again with a piercing yelp.

"What's the matter with you?" Lavers asked tersely.

"That loose spring," I said. "You should get it fixed. One of these days I'm going to walk out of here with a falsetto voice."

I carefully selected another chair, sat down and lit myself a cigarette.

"You ever watch television?" he grunted.

"Sundays," I said, "my day of rest."

"Ever pick up a show called 'Without Favor'—run by a woman called Paula Reid?"

"Once," I nodded. "It's one of those no-holds-barred interview shows, isn't it? She asked a lot of impersonal questions like, 'How regular is your sex life?' Whichever way you answer she wants to know why."

"Something like that," he said: "She also moves the show around the country, interviews personalities in their own city or home. She arrived here in Pine City this morning and her show goes over on Saturday night from the local station."

"I won't be there," I said.

"You will."

There was a tone of finality in Lavers' voice.

"Who's getting murdered," I asked him, "the rating?"

"She's interviewing Georgia Brown."

"Sweet?" I queried. "I thought she was a song title."

"I don't know why it is," he said wearily, "but I sometimes forget you're a moron! Cast your mind back three years or so, Wheeler."

"...There was a strawberry blonde," I said nostalgically, "and built like Fort Knox—to stay. She stayed about three weeks as I remember ..."

Lavers lit his pipe, handling it carefully like a time fuse. "You remember Lee Manning?"

"Came the dawn," I said. "The celluloid Romeo who wrote his own lines for a final exit, I remember. And Georgia Brown was the cause of all the trouble."

"That was the story," Lavers agreed. "But it was never proved. The tabloids made a big play with it and the scandal mags took care of the rest. The old story, liquor, orgies, the works."

"Ah, Hollywood," I said wistfully.

"Georgia Brown was a star in her own right," he went on. "She disappeared right after Manning suicided. Nobody ever heard of her again."

"You mean she worked in radio?"

"I mean she disappeared!" Lavers snarled. "I wish you'd stop being cute, Wheeler. Paula Reid claims to have found her. Claims she's going to interview Georgia Brown on her show Saturday night. She says Georgia was the innocent victim of the Manning scandal but now she'll break three years' silence and tell the truth.... I quote Miss Reid's own words, of course!"

"The truth about what?"

"About why Manning suicided, the orgies, and so on. The names of the other people involved."

"I might break a habit Saturday night," I said. "This should be worth seeing."

"Miss Reid claims that her life and Miss Brown's have both been threatened. She's been told her show will never make the air Saturday night."

"She wants protection?"

Lavers shook his head. "No, she thinks it's all wonderful publicity. This stuff has been headlines for the last couple of weeks. Don't you read the newspapers, Wheeler?"

"You know how it is," I said. "If I had time to read I'd be an educated man."

"Your stamina must be remarkable!" he said obliquely. "Anyway, whether these threats are real or just a publicity stunt, I don't intend taking any chances while she's in Pine City. That show goes on Saturday night!"

"What's the gimmick?" I asked suspiciously.

"There's no gimmick," he said. "This show is getting nationwide publicity. If anything happens to either of those two women before it takes the air, there'll be headlines coast to coast—"

"From the halls of Montezuma to the shores of Tripoli," I said helpfully.

Lavers glared at me: "I thought you were in Army Intelligence, not the Marines!"

"Sometimes when they were feeling generous they'd talk to us," I explained. "Well, nod, anyway."

"This is serious!" he said in a strangled voice. "That television station is almost plumb center in my area of jurisdiction, and that means I'm responsible. I can see what a story the papers would make of it. 'County Sheriff fails to prevent murder after beautiful woman's desperate appeal!'"

"Sheriff," I said, "you've been reading those paperbacks again. I thought you said this Reid dame liked the publicity?"

"But her secretary doesn't. A girl named Janice Jorgens. She's asked for protection—unofficially, of course. But she's the one to give you concrete details about the threats."

"It seems to be an uncomplicated assignment," I said bitterly, "like World War II."

"Just stay with it," he said harshly. "Remember, I want to see that show go over on Saturday night. That means that both Miss Reid and Miss Brown must still be alive then. I don't give a damn what happens to them from Monday on, when Miss Reid leaves Pine City."

"Yes, sir," I said resignedly.

He puffed his pipe complacently. "That's all there is to it, Wheeler. Let me know how you make out."

"If I find any corpses, Sheriff, I'll send them on to you, collect."

"Don't fall over my secretary on your way out!" he snorted.

"And damage one of those beautiful curves?" I asked in a horrified voice. "You must be out of your mind."

I checked and found that Miss Reid, her secretary, producer, and the rest of her staff had taken over suites at the Starlight Hotel that morning.

I arrived just after eleven-thirty and asked for Miss Jorgens at the desk. I took the elevator to the ninth floor, then walked down the corridor until I reached the right door and knocked.

The door opened about ten seconds later and a redhead stood there. She wore a sack in white shantung, overprinted with gold cartwheels. The red hair clustered in tight curls around her head, her eyes were blue and watchful, her lips a symphony yet to be played. The sack had no more chance of hiding her robust curves than I had of hiding my appreciation. Not that I tried.

"Well," she said finally, "if you're all through, I'll go take a shower."

"If I didn't look at you that way, you'd start to worry," I said. "My name's Wheeler. Sheriff Lavers sent me."

"Oh," she said. "Then you'd better come inside."

I followed her into the living room. There was a table in the center, piled high with papers, and a typewriter trying to make itself at home on one side. In a forty-dollar-a-day suite it was out of place.

"Are you from the Sheriff's office, Mr. Wheeler?" Miss Jorgens asked.

"Sort of," I said. "I'm also from Homicide when I'm not from the Sheriff's office. I double as a Lieutenant in both parts but they don't pay me any more."

"I can understand that," she said easily. "What do you want to know?"

"Sheriff Lavers tells me you want police protection," I said. "Not for yourself but for Miss Reid and Miss Brown. You also don't want Miss Reid to know anything about it?"

"That's absolutely right," she said. "I could be most embarrassed if Paula ever found out I'd asked for it. She might even fire me!"

"I'll remember that," I told her. "What exactly do you want me to do?"

"These threats worry me," she said, "but Paula won't take them seriously. I'd like you to make sure nothing happens to her—or to Georgia Brown."

"That won't be any trouble," I said. "I'll stay with Paula day and night, and Georgia, too. Are you kidding?"

"For what they must pay you, we could get about one-eighth of a writer," she said thoughtfully. "Even one-eighth of a writer could turn out better dialogue than that."

"Maybe Georgia Brown might feel differently about having official protection." I suggested. "If I could talk her into it, we could keep tabs on her all time up to the show. That would only leave Paula to worry about."

Miss Jorgens bit her lower lip gently with nice white teeth. "I don't know," she said. "If Georgia told Paula about it ..."

"There must be other jobs you can do in television," I said, "like standing in front of a camera and breathing deeply?"

"One-sixteenth of a writer would do," she said almost absently. "Georgia Brown's address is one of television's best-kept secrets right now. Only two people know it, myself and Paula."

"And Paula won't tell."

She looked at me for a long moment: "Lieutenant, if I give you the address, you'll handle it tactfully, won't you?"

"You'd be surprised how tactful I can get," I said. "Ask me back here tonight and I'll give you a demonstration."

"What did they have you doing before they gave you this assignment?" she asked. "Filing correspondence?"

"Give me the address and you can halve your problem."

"All right," she said abruptly.

She walked over to the desk and sat down. She lit herself a cigarette and the nails of her right hand beat a faint tattoo on the desktop for a few moments.

"All right," she repeated slowly. "I have a feeling I'm going to hate myself for this. She's in apartment 4-A at 1105 Lake Street. She's under the name of Jones, Miriam Jones. Say that I sent you or she won't open the door."

"Jorgens sent me," I said. "Do I knock three times and ask for Miriam?"

"You can—" She took a deep breath which made the sack a frame for the merchandise rather than a container. "Are you sure they couldn't send someone else, Lieutenant? It really had to be you?"

"They sent the best man available," I said modestly. "This is Pine City, not a metropolis."

"Handle her gently," she said, "Georgia Brown is a badly frightened woman."

"I always handle my women gently," I said. "It's a Wheeler trademark. I'll come right back after I've seen her and tell you all about it. We can have dinner," I looked around the suite appreciatively, "here."

"You can tell me about it in ten minutes," she said. "I'm going to be busy tonight. We've only got seventy-two hours before the show."

The door opened suddenly and a woman came in without knocking. "Janice, about that—" She stopped abruptly when she saw me. "Sorry," she said distantly, "I didn't know you had company."

"That's quite all right, Paula," Miss Jorgens said nervously. "This is Mr. Wheeler, he's a ... a ..."

"Cop," I said, and smiled gently at the hatred that suddenly shone in the redhead's eyes.

Paula Reid's fingers touched her smoke-blue hair, which wasn't one strand out of place, and her blue eyes had an arctic quality as she looked at me. "A police officer?" she queried coldly.

"Lieutenant," I explained. "I wanted to see you, but your secretary's been trying to stall me. Says you're too busy to be bothered with the police."

I saw the look of relief in Miss Jorgens' eyes.

"Oh?" Paula's voice was flat. "Why did you want to see me?"

"You've been threatened about your show," I said. "Frankly, it's not the possibility of you being murdered that worries us, it's all that publicity your murder would get."

"You're honest, anyway," she said. "I can give you five minutes but I don't think they will do you much good. You'd better come to my suite."

She turned toward the door and I followed her.

"Lieutenant!" Janice Jorgens said urgently.

"Yes?" I turned and looked at her for a moment.

"Don't ... er ... keep Miss Reid too long, will you?" Her eyes were asking all sorts of questions.

"That depends on Miss Reid," I said and smiled sweetly at her, the moment before I closed the door. We went into the suite next door.

"Please sit down, Lieutenant," Paula Reid said.

I sank into a comfortable armchair and she sat opposite me. She wore an orlon suit in vertical stripes of alternating shades of blue. It clung to her bold curves with the same sort of smug satisfaction I would have.

"Well, Lieutenant?"

"What about these threats?"

"There have been threatening phone calls," she said, "quite a few of them. But I'm used to that kind of thing, I don't take them seriously."

"How about Miss Brown—does she take them seriously?"

"No, she's hidden away quite safely. No one could find her."

"That's a sweeping statement."

"It's true."

"Don't you think it would be better if we gave you police protection—until after your show, anyway?"

"No, it's not necessary."

"Do you have any idea who's making the threats?"

She shook her head. "The caller doesn't give a name, of course. It's the same husky voice each time, sounds like a woman but I'm not sure. I don't think it's important. A good publicity gimmick, that's all."

"You aren't being much help, Miss Reid."

"Did I ask you for any help?"

"I guess you didn't," I admitted. "What exactly is Georgia Brown going to say Saturday night?"

She smiled momentarily. "Why don't you watch the show and find out?"

"She's going to name names?"

"I don't know," she said lightly. "We don't work to a script and the show isn't rehearsed, not the actual interview, at least. It goes over better that way, it's more authentic. The viewers like that."

"But you must have a pretty good idea what you're going to ask her."

"Surely," she said. "I'm going to ask her the truth about Lee Manning's death and the people associated with him at that time. And I think she'll answer by telling me the truth."

"O.K.," I said, "I quit."

I got onto my feet and looked down at her.

"You're a wise man, Lieutenant," she said. "Good afternoon."

"Good afternoon, Miss Reid," I said. "If you wake up dead one morning, I hope you won't blame the Sheriff's office."

I stopped at the desk downstairs and showed my shield to the clerk and told him who I was. He wasn't impressed. He started to fidget. I could see he thought that if I stayed around too long they'd have to knock five dollars a day off the price of their suites.

"How many people are with Miss Reid exactly?" I asked him.

He consulted his book. "She has a suite of her own, so does her secretary and her producer," he said. "There are three others with them, and they have rooms of their own. Six in all, Lieutenant."

He closed the book with a bang and looked at me hopefully but I didn't move.

"Anybody called on her since she arrived?"

"The reporters were here to meet her," he said. "There have been no other callers.... Excuse me," He turned to greet the man who had walked up to the desk and stood beside me. "Yes, sir?" the clerk said politely. "You have a reservation?"

The man was tall, wearing a dark-blue Brooks Brothers suit and a white carnation in his lapel. He had an ascetic's face and his carefully waved gray hair had recently been given a blue rinse.

"No," he said in an English accent, "I don't have a reservation. I would like to see Miss Reid."

"I'm sorry, sir," the clerk looked faintly regretful. "Miss Reid has given strict orders that she will see no one."

"But it's most important that I see her." He brushed the side of his head, fingering the wave into place. "Would you call her and say that Norman Coates—"

"I'm sorry, sir," the clerk said firmly. "I have strict orders—"

"You don't understand!" Coates said. "My business with Miss Reid is urgent and—"

"Quite impossible!" the clerk said and pointedly turned his back on him.

Coates hesitated for a fleeting moment; even the Brooks Brothers suit had an air of uncertainty. Then he turned and walked slowly away from the desk.

The clerk glared at his departing back for a moment, then turned to me. "Really!" he said. "Some people!"

"You got to expect all types when you're running a flophouse," I said, and left him impersonating a goldfish suddenly removed from its bowl.

I went out of the hotel to the Healey parked at the curb and drove over to Lake Street. It was a nondescript street and the nearest lake was about ten miles north. It consisted mostly of apartment buildings and they all had the same wilted look as if they'd been waiting too long for something to happen and had finally given up.

I stopped outside 1105 and got out. I walked up the steps to the front entrance and found that 4-A was on the second floor. I went up the two flights of stairs and then down the corridor to the door at one end. I knocked gently on the door—three times—and waited.

Nothing happened. I knocked again and said in a guarded voice: "Miss Jones? Miss Jorgens sent me. Miss Jones?" I wondered if she'd be wearing a false beard when she opened the door.

Some twenty seconds went by without my seeing them. I thought I heard a movement inside the apartment but I wasn't sure. Maybe she was allergic to knocks? I could try the buzzer for a switch in technique.

I put my thumb against the buzzer and pressed.

The door leaped out of its frame and hit me over the head. I was flung backwards about ten feet down the corridor with the noise of the explosion still ringing in my ears.

I sat up slowly and shook my head. "That's one hell of a way to answer the door," I said to nobody in particular.

Blue smoke drifted from the open doorway and I could see part of the way into the apartment. I could see the plaster floating down from the ceiling and the splintered matchwood which had once been a chair. A tongue of flame licked from the center of the carpet.

The front door lay in the corridor a couple of feet away from me. I looked down at it and slowly realized I must be looking at the inside panels, which were also splintered. But the handle was intact.

Attached to the handle was a human hand. I noticed vaguely that the nails were a bright carnation-pink.

CHAPTER TWO

Dr. Murphy came out of the wrecked apartment, rubbing his hands together. "Got a matchbox?" he asked.

I took my lighter out of my pocket and offered it to him.

"You know I don't smoke," he said. "Disgusting habit!"

"Then why ask for a matchbox?"

"It'll save the meat-wagon a job," he said.

"You ghoul," I said. "It's a wonder they don't save you for Halloween."

He shrugged his shoulders. "She was blonde, I can tell you that much; we found some hairs on one wall."

"Thanks."

"Saves an autopsy, anyway," he said and walked away whistling.

MacDonald, the explosives expert, came out along with Sergeant Polnik.

"Find anything exciting?" I asked him.

"You pressed the buzzer and the whole lot went up," he said. "That right, Lieutenant?"

"That's right."

"You were lucky—the bomb was rigged to blow inwards, if it hadn't been, you wouldn't be here now."

"What else?"

"Whoever set it up knew what they were doing," he said. "They wired it through the buzzer circuit. As soon as anybody pressed the buzzer they completed the circuit—and blooey!"

"How big was the bomb?"

"Not very big, I'd say the whole package would be around a foot square, maybe smaller. It didn't need a timing device and they're the things that take up the room generally."

"Anything else?"

"I've got a few bits and pieces to take back to the lab with me," Mac-Donald said. "Give you a report on it just as soon as I can, Lieutenant."

"Thanks," I said.

"Fixed the dame all right." His face was a couple shades paler than normal. "I wouldn't want to see something like the inside of that apartment too often—not and sleep nights, that is!"

He walked off down the corridor, and he wasn't whistling. But then MacDonald was a human being, which was the difference between him and Doc Murphy.

Polnik looked at me hopefully. "What do we do now, Lieutenant?"

"Scream," I said.

"Huh?"

"Sheriff Lavers particularly wanted me to look after the dame who was in there," I explained.

Polnik gulped. "You mean it was you blasted her?"

I lit myself a cigarette carefully. "Are the rest of the boys still working inside there?"

"Sure, Lieutenant."

"Stay here till they're finished," I said. "Seeing that I looked after the dame so well, Lavers gave me a bonus. This is now the Sheriff's homicide, as well as Homicide's homicide."

"You going to confess to yourself, Lieutenant?"

"I'll think about it," I said. "When the boys are through, check the rest of the apartments in the building. Find out if anybody knew the dame, if they saw her at all, if she had any callers—you know the routine."

"Whatever you say, Lieutenant."

"I'm going over to the Starlight Hotel," I said. "When you're through here, follow me over. Ask for me at the desk."

"Sure, Lieutenant." He blinked at me. "You were kidding about the Sheriff wanting you to take care of the dame, weren't you?"

"Why no," I said. "I thought I did it rather well—it went over with a bang."

I walked away, hearing the rasping sound as Polnik scratched his head. I went downstairs and out through the entrance hall. I pushed my way through the gaping crowd on the sidewalk and got into the Austin Healey and drove away.

Fifteen minutes later I knocked on the door of Paula Reid's suite. She opened it right away. She'd changed her suit for a pale-blue silk shirt and a pair of dark-blue tapered slacks. She didn't look pleased to see me.

"Really, Lieutenant!" she said. "I can't afford to waste any more time talking to you. I have to work on the show and—"

"There won't be any show," I said. "So you've got all the time in the world. Get Miss Jorgens in here, will you? It will save me repeating myself."

I walked past her into the suite and saw Miss Jorgens was already there. Her eyes grew wider as she looked at me.

"Hello, Lieutenant," she said nervously. "Nothing wrong I hope?"

"Nothing a jury can't fix," I said.

Paula Reid slammed the door shut and glared at me. "If this is a sample of the manners of Pine City Police Department I'm going to complain to the—"

I lit myself a cigarette. "Miss Jorgens was worried about those threatening letters," I explained. "She asked for our help, unofficially."

"You ..." Janice Jorgens stopped, trying to think of an adequate word.

"So I talked to her," I said. "And she gave me the address where you were hiding Georgia Brown."

"Janice!" Paula glared icily at her secretary. "What right had you to—"

"You can go into that later," I interrupted her. "She told me that only two people knew that address, one was herself and the other was you. Is that right?"

"It was right!" Paula said. "Now, I suppose you've told the papers or something equally stupid!"

"When did you last see Georgia?"

"I don't see what—"

I closed my eyes for a moment: "I'm having a long, hard day—don't make it any harder."

"About three days ago," she said. "I came here incognito to see her."

"Better than flying?"

"If you're asking me a serious question ..."

"I am," I said hastily. "Three days ago. You haven't seen her since then?"

"I haven't had the time. We only arrived here this morning, you might remember."

I looked at Janice. "How about you?"

"I saw her this morning," she said. "Paula wanted me to check she was all right."

"And was she?"

"Of course," she said in a puzzled voice. "She was still there when you called, wasn't she?"

"She was still there," I agreed.

"What have you done with her now?" Paula asked briskly. "If it's public knowledge where she is, that apartment is too dangerous for her now. You didn't leave her there, did you?"

"In a sense," I said.

"Will you stop being mysterious!"

"I knocked," I said, "but there was no answer. So I pressed the buzzer. That completed a circuit which blew up a bomb inside the apartment."

They both stared at me for a moment, open-mouthed. "Georgia," Paula said shakily, "is she ..."

"The doctor said she was a blonde," I told her gently. "He found a few hairs on the wall to prove it."

Paula Reid's face suddenly dissolved into tears.

"Oh," she said faintly. Then she crumpled into a chair.

"Get her a drink," I told Janice. "You could get me one too," I added hopefully.

Janice poured out three drinks, which proved she was more sensible than I thought. By the time Paula had got halfway through hers, she had recovered a little.

She dabbed her eyes gently. "If I hadn't publicized the fact she was appearing on the show …"

"If she was ready to talk, she would have talked anyway—your show was only coincidental," I said. "I want to ask you some questions."

"Of course," she nodded. "I'll do my best to help you, Lieutenant."

"Why did she want to appear on the show?"

"To clear her name," Paula murmured. "She was tired of living in obscurity. She had run out of money, so she wanted to get back into film business."

"Were you going to pay her to appear on your show?"

"Five thousand."

"I should be a cop," I said regretfully. "How did you find her?"

"She found me," Paula went on. "We did the show from San Francisco six weeks back. She came to my hotel there one night and told me who she was …"

"How much did she tell you about the Manning suicide?"

"Not a great deal. She was … well, a little cagey. I suppose she didn't trust me entirely. She thought if she told me too much I mightn't need her on the show at all and she wouldn't get the money."

"She must have told you something."

"Please, Lieutenant!" Janice said earnestly. "At a time like this! Do you have to keep on with these questions? Can't you see Miss Reid is all—"

"She's in much better shape than Georgia Brown right now," I pointed out mildly. "Why don't you do something useful like pouring us all another drink?"

She came over and took the glass out of my hand, nearly taking a couple of my fingers along with it.

"The Lieutenant is right, Janice," Paula said. "Georgia has been murdered and he's got to find the murderer, and I've got to help him."

"She must have told you something," I said. "What about names? Did she mention any names?"

"Yes, she did. She said she was prepared to tell the truth about the circumstances surrounding Lee Manning's death, and that would involve a number of prominent people. She also said she could prove her statement if necessary and she'd take full responsibility for any accusations made on the show."

"Fine," I said patiently. "What were the names?"

"There were four," she said. "Hilary Blain, Kay Steinway, Norman Coates and Kent Fargo."

"Fargo?" I said. "I know he's been mixed up in most of the rackets, but I didn't know the film business was included."

"He did back a number of films at one time," she said. "But it was kept very quiet. Coates produced most of the films he backed."

"That makes Coates a producer?"

"You're so sharp, Lieutenant!" Janice said.

"Kay Steinway is the girl who can't sing but everybody loves watching her try," I said. "I saw her last musical. And Blain is *the* Blain, the financier?"

"That's right," Paula agreed.

"Only those four names?"

"They were the only ones she mentioned. But they're all famous names, one way or another, Lieutenant. Enough to boost my Trendex another five points at least!"

I glanced at her contoured silk shirt. "It doesn't need boosting from where I sit," I said admiringly.

"Trendex," Janice said coldly, "is a rating service. A scientific measurement of a show's popularity."

"I'm disenchanted," I confided.

"That's all I can tell you, Lieutenant," Paula added. Janice handed me the new drink and I took it gratefully.

"It's a start," I said to Paula. "Now I'll have to find out where I can get in touch with these people."

"I can tell you that," she said. "Georgia was frightened to death that someone might kill her to stop her appearing on my show and, after what's happened, she was obviously right. I checked on where those people were only a few days ago."

"You're getting to be a help," I said.

"Give the Lieutenant a list of those addresses, Janice," she said.

Janice went out of the suite and came back half a minute later with a typed list which she handed to me. I thanked her and put it into my pocket.

"Is there anything else you can tell me?" I asked Paula. "Anything at all you think might help?"

She shook her head. "I'm sorry, I can't think of anything right now."

The phone rang and Janice lifted the receiver. She looked across at me a moment later. "It's for you, Lieutenant."

I took the receiver from her and said, "Wheeler," into the mouthpiece.

"Polnik, Lieutenant. I'm at the desk."

"Wait there, I'll be down in a moment." I replaced the phone on the cradle. "Thanks for your help," I said to Paula. "I'll let you know any developments."

"Thank you," she said dully. "This is a tragedy, Lieutenant!"

"Try not to think about it," I suggested. "Try and forget Georgia Brown ever existed, for a while."

"Georgia Brown!" she wailed. "I'm not worrying about her.... What am I going to do for a show Saturday night!"

Polnik smiled at me as I came up to the desk.

"Hi, Lieutenant! What's new?"

"My thirst," I said. "Let's go into the bar and get a drink."

I ordered Scotch on the rocks, with a touch of soda. Polnik let his head go and ordered a beer.

"What did you find out?" I asked him.

"I checked all the other tenants like you said, and the janitor. He helped her in with her bags and that was the only time he ever saw her. Said she was a blonde, not a bad looker, but she didn't say much."

"What about the other tenants?"

"They never saw her at all, she never went out."

"What about callers?"

"Two. Both dames, both had class. One was a redhead —she was there this morning—and the other was ..." he hesitated for a moment, "well, so help me, Lieutenant, this is what they say ..."

"She had blue hair and was dressed in blue," I said.

"You know?" Polnik looked disappointed. "They were the only two, Lieutenant."

"They were the only two with legitimate reasons for calling on her," I said. "You sure there was nobody else?"

"There's an old dame lives in the apartment opposite, and she told me for sure there weren't any others. The janitor said she's the nosiest old dame he's ever met and he's got forty years' experience in the business. If she says the blonde don't have any other callers, then she don't."

"It makes a depressing picture," I said.

The bartender served the drinks and Polnik looked worried until I paid for them.

"So she got bored, sitting around doing nothing," I said broodingly. "So she made herself a bomb and wired it into the buzzer circuit, then sat around waiting for somebody to press the buzzer."

"Suicide!" Polnik said admiringly. "Maybe you got the whole case sewed up already, Lieutenant!"

CHAPTER THREE

The style was twentieth-century Spanish in white stucco. "My adobe hacienda," they used to sing once and this was the place they sang about. It had a walled courtyard and six palm trees that weren't good for a date between the lot of them.

I tried the front door and got no answer. I walked back toward where I'd left the Healey on the driveway and heard a splashing noise from somewhere inside the courtyard. I stopped for a moment and heard a voice singing. A husky voice crooning gently, "Lover, come back to me."

It was off-key and Kay Steinway.

The courtyard had a door which was closed. I tried the handle and found it wasn't locked, so I opened it and stepped inside.

There was a swimming pool shaped like the sign of a bass clef. At the far end I caught a flash of whiteness, then there was a splash. I lit a cigarette and waited patiently.

She swam three-quarters of the length of the pool with a powerful crawl stroke before she noticed me. She stopped swimming suddenly and trod water.

"This is private property," she said in that husky voice. "Or didn't you notice?"

"You're Kay Steinway?"

"Get out of here!"

"I'm Lieutenant Wheeler, from the County Sheriff's office," I said. "I wanted to talk to you."

"Oh," she said. "Well, I'll have to get out of here first."

"I'll wait."

"But I'm not wearing a swimsuit!"

"Your loss is my gain," I said politely.

She laughed easily: "My robe is on that chair behind you. Could you be gentleman enough to hand it to me?"

"You're putting a strain on my chivalry," I said reluctantly.

I picked up the white bathrobe from the chair and walked to the edge of the pool. She swam in and rested her hands on the tiled edge.

"Just drop it right there," she said, "and turn around."

"I'm long-sighted, I wouldn't even see you," I said hopefully.

"You turn around or I stay right here!"

"All right," I said. "But you're killing the tourist in me."

I turned around and smoked my cigarette.

There was ten seconds' silence, then she said: "You can turn around now, I'm decent."

"You think that's an incentive?"

I turned around. She was belting the robe tight around her waist.

"Let's go into the house," she said. "I need a drink."

We skirted the edge of the pool, then crossed the white-flagged patio and went in through the open glass doors.

The living area was furnished modern style with a bar at one end. Kay Steinway walked around the serving side of the bar counter and looked at me. "What will it be?" she asked.

"Scotch," I said, "on the rocks, with a little soda."

I watched her as she poured two. She looked as good in real life as she did with a head twenty feet square on wide-screen.

She was a brunette with lustrous hair that came down to her shoulders. She had an elflike face with gray-green eyes that she must have traded from a small demon sometime. Her lower lip was very full and somehow had an expectant quality about it. The bathrobe molded a figure that was both generous and exuberant.

She handed me a glass and raised her own: "Here's to the Police Department," she said. "I was getting bored on my own tonight."

"You should go into the swimsuit business," I said. "You'd make a fortune just demonstrating!"

"I thought you were long-sighted?"

"I saw you dive in at the far end of the pool, remember?"

"Why Lieutenant," she purred. "A girl has no secrets from you at all."

"If I wasn't here on business," I said, "this would be a pleasure."

"You should combine the two," she said lazily. "Most places it's known as an expense account. Or don't you have one of those, Lieutenant?"

"I can spend what I like so long as it doesn't come to more than fifty cents a month," I admitted. "Do you know Georgia Brown?"

"I did once, vaguely," she said. "Isn't she going to be the new star of television come Saturday night?"

"Not any more. When did you last see her?"

"It must be three years ago now," she grimaced. "The day the coroner gave his decision on Lee Manning's suicide. She was in court. I didn't see her after that. I didn't know anybody had seen her since then, excepting Paula Reid."

"I saw her this morning," I said. "Somebody exploded a bomb in her apartment and blew her into small pieces."

She finished her drink and then topped the glass up with neat Scotch. She drank it down without a tremor disturbing the smoothness of her face. "That's tough," she said.

"She was going to tell the truth about why Manning committed suicide," I said. "She was going to prove her own innocence and she was going to name names."

Kay Steinway gurgled with laughter. "You kill me!"

"Did I say something funny?"

"That bit about Georgia and innocence. Georgia was about as innocent as a French actress asking a producer for a starring part."

"One of the names was yours," I said.

"That's crazy," she said evenly. "I knew Manning—who didn't? I was a nobody then. I'd had a speaking part, a one-liner. The band stopped jiving and the camera cut to a close-up of me. 'Solid!' I said and then they cut back to the band. They left the close-up on the cutting-room floor."

"Tell me some more about Georgia Brown," I said.

She poured herself a third drink, but without the urgency this time.

"Should I see my lawyer, Lieutenant?"

"I'm only looking for information. There were other names she was going to mention, I haven't talked to their owners yet. I just happened to pick yours first."

"Why?"

"My reasons were verified when I saw you dive into that pool," I said. "You could call it a hunch, coupled with the fact yours was the only feminine name on the list."

"Who are the others?"

"I have to keep some secrets."

"Why? I don't have any from you now. You're a slow drinker, Lieutenant ... Lieutenant? Do I have to keep on calling you that all the time I'm baring my soul to you. I've bared everything else already—can't we be friends?"

"Call me Al," I said.

"Al, short for what?"

"Just Al."

"That's stupid," she frowned at me. "Nobody gets christened Al."

"Never mind," I said firmly. "How about Georgia Brown?"

"She was a friend of Manning's," she said. "I don't suppose you ever knew Manning?"

"No."

"He was a first-rate louse, and believe me, in Hollywood it's hard to qualify, the competition's so keen!"

"So?"

"He liked girls, lots of girls, but they all had a few things in common—they were young and innocent, they had ambitions, and no contracts. His I-can-get-you-into-pictures routine was better than most, because he was in pictures and everybody knew it."

"It doesn't sound original."

"But it was effective. He'd have week-end parties with anything up to half a dozen young hopefuls out at his place—and I do mean young. He acted like he was a Turkish sultan or something, with his harem. I used to wonder how he remembered all their names. It would've been easier to just give them numbers."

"You were one of his party girls?" I asked.

She shook her head: "I was too old for him even then," she said. "When I first met him I was all of nineteen."

"He liked them really young."

"And innocent. I didn't qualify on either count."

"Sounds like a nice guy."

"He treated them rough, too," she said. "You could say he was one of the nicest perverts you could meet any place. I wouldn't say he was queer, either—just depraved."

"But with a setup like that, he committed suicide," I said incredulously. "All he needed was some vitamin tablets."

"It was a little more complicated than that," she said. "Norman Coates was his producer at the time and he was making independent films. The money came from Hilary Blain—you know, the financier?"

"I've heard of him," I said.

"Lee Manning picked the wrong girl finally. I guess it had to happen sooner or later. She was a kid from Arkansas or Tennessee or some place. Sixteen years old with all the qualifications necessary. She came out to one of his week-end parties. Maybe she had a weak heart or maybe he played a little too rough, but she died there."

I finished my first drink and she refilled my glass absently.

"It didn't look so bad at first, just unfortunate," she continued. "But then the police started digging and they found out just what type of party it had been; then they found out the girl's true age. They were going to hit Lee with half the statute book.

"That was one of the troubles with Coates' being an independent—he didn't have the sort of big organization that could hope to hush it up. It was a first-class scandal about due to hit the headlines. Then Lee grabbed the headlines for himself ... he always was a scene-stealer."

I offered her a cigarette, lit it for her and one for myself. "How did Georgia Brown fit into it?"

"Georgia introduced the girl to Lee. She introduced a lot of girls to him. There's a word for it, isn't there?"

"Procuress?"

"Something like that. It's not something they give Oscars for."

I nodded. "I can remember the headlines about Manning's suicide, and the hints in the scandal mags about the orgies and so on, but there wasn't anything definite. Nothing about a sixteen-year-old girl."

"After Lee was dead, they managed to hush it up," she said.

"How?"

"Well, Lee was dead anyway, so they couldn't bring a case against him. I think they sold it to the authorities on that and there was the angle that it wouldn't help the girl's family any to have her name dragged through the mud."

"Thanks," I said. "Any more?"

"Not that I can think of, Al. Why don't you stick around and relax a little?"

"I'd like to, but I have to keep on working, you know how it is."

She shook her head. "No, tell me."

"Some other time I'd enjoy it," I said sincerely.

I finished my drink and walked slowly toward the glass doors. She caught up with me on the white-flagged patio.

"You're sure you wouldn't like to stay a while longer, Al?"

"Not right now," I said. "But I'd like to come back soon."

"Come back tonight, why don't you?" she suggested. "I'm having a party. Some interesting people will be here. Paula Reid for one."

"She won't come now after what's happened," I said.

"She'll come," Kay said confidently. "I hate to say it myself but I'm Kay Steinway, remember? The biggest name in musicals since Ginger Rogers. Paula wouldn't dare refuse my invitation!"

"If I have time, I'd like to be there," I said, "and thanks."

"It'll be a very intimate party," she said. "I hope you make time to come, Al."

We walked toward the courtyard gate.

"How do you know so much about what happened that week end at Manning's?" I asked her.

"I was there," she said. "Georgia took me down with her, but Lee took one look at me and right away that was the end of it. I was too old and had too much experience for him. Besides, I'd left school!"

"Didn't the same apply to Georgia?" I asked. "What was she doing down there?"

"She was always there for his parties," Kay said coolly. "I guess she had a personal interest; after all, she got the girls for him. I guess she liked to study their performance. It was more fun than a day at Santa Anita for Georgia."

"She sounds like fun herself," I said.

"Like a Black Widow spider!"

I pushed the gate open. "Thanks again, Kay. I'll really try to make that party. I'd like to see you again soon."

"Even sooner than you think, maybe," she said casually. "I'm hot again. If I didn't have this pool, I'd go crazy in the summer."

She undid the belt of the robe and shrugged her shoulders free. The robe dropped to the flagstones and she turned toward me, her lower lip protruding a little. "How do you think I'd look in Cinerama, Al?"

I looked at the full, finely-sculptured breasts, the firm hips and long, slender legs, for a moment before she turned away.

"I hope you didn't burn when you were getting that all-over suntan," I said. "It would hurt."

She laughed with that husky gurgle for a moment, then turned and ran to the edge of the pool and launched herself in a racing dive.

I stood for a few seconds watching the splash, then stepped out of the courtyard, closing the door behind me.

I walked back to the Austin Healey with the clarion call of duty a derisive toot inside my head. The rocks moved over and made room for it.

CHAPTER FOUR

Norman Coates opened the door of his hotel room and the uncertain smile on his face vanished when he saw me.

"Yes?" he asked in a high-pitched voice.

I told him who I was, and that I wanted to talk to him.

"Perhaps you'd better come in," he said doubtfully. He stood there for a few seconds longer, then sighed deeply and led the way inside.

I followed him in, closing the door behind me. He wore a Paisley silk dressing gown, the color of a seasick Picasso dove of peace, and a lavender scarf tucked carefully around his neck.

"I've seen you before, Lieutenant," he said, a smile appearing and reappearing on his face like a nervous tic. "As I remember it was this morning?"

"And you didn't appreciate my talent, Mr. Coates," I said regretfully. "At house parties my impersonation of a bystander is a riot, straight out of Runyon, they say."

"I didn't stay," he said, fluttering his hands in front of him. "I thought the situation was becoming too absurd. I only wanted to contact Miss Reid to see if she could tell me where I could find Miss Brown. And that desk clerk ... Well, he upset me. You do understand, Lieutenant Wheeler, don't you?"

"What difference does it make," I said. "Why did you want to see Georgia Brown?"

"Well," his hand patted the wave deeper along the side of his head, "I understand she's going to rake up all that old stuff about Lee Manning on Paula Reid's program, and I'm hoping I can persuade her not to. It won't do anyone any good, you know. It's just like that Reid woman to think up something like this. I don't mind these interview programs on television but, really! This Reid woman is nothing but the end! Don't you agree, Lieutenant Wheeler?"

"I have good news for you, Mr. Coates," I said. "The program won't go on Saturday night."

"Really?" His face brightened a little. "You're sure, Lieutenant?"

"Quite sure—Georgia Brown is dead."

"Dead?" His face sagged as he repeated the word and two years' facials went down the drain. "I ... Excuse me, I must sit down."

He groped his way to a chair and eased himself into it carefully.

"Forgive me," he said, "it's the shock. Death always disturbs me, Lieutenant."

"It disturbed Georgia, too," I said. "She was blown to pieces inside her apartment. All we found was—”

“Please!” He shuddered and closed his eyes tight. “I can’t bear to think about it.”

“She was murdered,” I said. “My guess is she was murdered by someone who didn’t want her on that program, someone like you, maybe?”

He opened his eyes wide: “You can’t think that I ... why, it’s preposterous!”

“She was going to blow the works about Lee Manning’s suicide. Tell the story about his week-end parties and the sixteen-year-old kid with the maybe weak heart and how you managed to hush it up, wasn’t she?”

He dabbed his lips with a silk handkerchief. “I will admit that if she had spoken of those things it could have been embarrassing for me. Embarrassing, Lieutenant, but no more. I wanted to see her and appeal to her not to do it. I hoped I might reason with her. But kill her! The whole concept is ridiculous, Lieutenant. I couldn’t hurt a fly!”

“Somebody put that bomb in her apartment,” I said. “You had a good reason for killing her. Who had a better one?”

“How on earth should I know!” he said petulantly. “It’s your job to find the guilty person, Lieutenant, not mine.”

I looked at him with the poker face that everyone else says is just my normal blank expression. He shifted uneasily in his chair, glanced at me, then turned his eyes away quickly.

“I can’t think of anyone who would want to kill her,” he said finally.

“What about Hilary Blain?”

“Blain?” He shook his head. “He had no reason.”

“What about Fargo?”

“Who is Fargo?” he asked blankly.

“Kent Fargo,” I said. “Don’t tell me you haven’t heard of him? His name must have penetrated even where you live.”

“You mean the racketeer, Fargo?”

“I don’t mean Wells Fargo.”

“If he had any reason to murder Georgia I’m sure I know nothing about it.”

“Didn’t Fargo back your pictures starring Manning when you were working as an independent?”

“No, it was Hilary who backed me.” His hand brushed the side of his head again unconsciously. “Hilary was always ... well, terribly nice about money. I’m sure I could never have worked with a gangster!” He shuddered as he said the word.

“O. K.,” I said, “that’s your story and I’m stuck with it for now. You staying in Pine City long, Mr. Coates?”

“A few days.”

“Fine,” I said. “That means I don’t have to ask you to stay, doesn’t it?”

I took out a card and scribbled on it. "If you think of anything that could help us, Mr. Coates, I'd like you to call that number. If I'm not there, I've written my home number down. Anything at all, however trivial, I'd like you to call me."

He took the card. "Of course, Lieutenant. Certainly—anything you say."

I opened the door and stepped out into the corridor. The delicate scent of roses stayed with me till I reached the car.

Half an hour's drive got me to Hilary Blain's house. A butler opened the door and looked at me with polite inquiry in his eyes.

"I'm Lieutenant Wheeler," I told him. "From the County Sheriff's office. I want to see Mr. Blain."

"Good afternoon, Lieutenant," he said gravely. "Mr. Blain is at home. I shall inform him of your presence."

"I'd beware of the presence," I said, equally gravely, "for all you know, I might be a Greek."

"Indeed, sir," he said and left me standing on the doorstep.

He came back and took my hat while I wasn't looking. "Mr. Blain will see you in the library, sir. If you'll follow me?"

I followed him into the library and Hilary Blain got up from the chair behind his desk to greet me. He was a short, thin man with the last of his hair sitting on the crown of his head and a pair of gold-rimmed glasses sitting on his nose. He looked worried and the deep lines on his face pointed up that he'd been worried ever since he'd been born and had to rely on other people.

"Sit down, Lieutenant," he said abruptly, "what can I do for you?"

I sat down in a comfortable, leather-padded chair and lit a cigarette. He sat back carefully onto his own chair and looked at me with a pinched expression.

I couldn't think of an original gambit so I gave him the one about Georgia naming names and his being one of them, and about her being dead.

"I see, Lieutenant," he said.

He took off his glasses and polished them thoroughly with his pocket handkerchief, then replaced them on the bridge of his nose. The reflected light as he looked at me gave his face a peculiarly blank expression.

"Well, of course, I was connected with her at one time." He thought about that for a moment. "That is, we were associated for a time—it was purely business of course."

"You were backing Coates when he was making pictures starring Lee Manning," I said. "Georgia played in a few of them, too, didn't she?"

"Quite so," he said, "quite so. Though I fail to understand why she should mention my name in connection with her revelations about the Manning affair. I have nothing to hide."

"I've heard the story about the young girl who died," I said, "how it was hushed up after Manning suicided."

"Unfortunate!" he said sharply. "Most unfortunate. At the time if there had been any publicity given to the girl's death it would have been, well ..."

"Unfortunate?"

"Quite so! But now?" he shrugged his thin shoulders. "I no longer invest money in films made by Mr. Coates. In fact I no longer invest in films at all. So why I should worry about my name being mentioned in connection with— "

"I understand it wasn't actually your money, Mr. Blain," I said. "The way I hear it, you were only a dummy—the hard cash belonged to Kent Fargo."

He hesitated for a moment. "I neither deny nor affirm that statement, Lieutenant."

"Supposing, for the moment, it is true—*if* Georgia Brown had mentioned that in a television interview, wouldn't you have been embarrassed."

"I don't see why," he said abruptly.

"It could have embarrassed Fargo."

He whipped off his glasses and held them up to the light. With a small grunt of triumph he detected a minute smudge and polished it off vigorously,

"Why don't you ask Mr. Fargo about that?" he said cautiously.

"I will," I said. "Mr. Blain, I don't think we're being quite realistic about this. A woman has been murdered. Before she died she gave the names of the people she intended to denounce on Paula Reid's show. Your name was one of the four, Fargo's was another. It makes you both prime suspects, along with the other two. I'm looking for your help and you're not giving me any."

He glared at me for a few seconds. "Sincerely, Lieutenant," he said finally, "I can't help you. I wish I could. My own personal opinion is that Georgia Brown needed money badly, so she approached this woman interviewer with an invented story about being able to lift the lid on the scandal surrounding Manning's suicide. And her only reason for so doing was to make money from it.

"I think if the interview had taken place it would have been a complete anticlimax. There was only one person who had anything to fear if all the facts concerning Lee's death were made public!"

"Who's that?"

He grimaced. "It was Georgia Brown herself. I don't know how much you've learned of the circumstances, Lieutenant, but I gather it's a good deal from what you've said. You must surely know the role that Georgia Brown played!"

"I'd like to hear your version," I said politely.

"She was nothing better than a pimp!" he said. "She sought out the girls, the young girls that were Manning's weakness. She persuaded them that he could start them on the road to stardom, and inveigled them to his weekend parties. It was she who found the girl. She knew her true age, but it didn't stop Georgia."

"Georgia sounds like she was a homey girl," I said.

"Lieutenant," he said in a low-pitched voice, "Georgia Brown was an evil woman! A truly evil woman, and the world is well rid of her!"

He sat back in his chair and clasped both hands to his vest. "Now I suppose you'll arrest me?"

"I think you're voicing the majority opinion about Georgia Brown," I said. "I don't think that's a crime. Is there anything else you can tell me, Mr. Blain?"

"No," he said. "I've probably said too much already."

"Thanks, anyway," I told him.

I got onto my feet and walked toward the door.

"Lieutenant," he called.

"Mr. Blain?" I looked back at him.

"Whatever Georgia was, she wasn't a fool. I would say she picked out the four names she mentioned to Miss Reid very carefully, choosing the names that would have maximum publicity value—to increase her fee, if nothing else. If Georgia had known her comments about any one person might endanger her own life, she wouldn't have made them. She placed too high a value on her own skin to risk it knowingly."

"You mean—those four names mean absolutely nothing?"

"Absolutely nothing!" he repeated firmly.

I closed my eyes and counted up to four blondes.

"Why did I ever have to talk to you?" I moaned, and tottered out into the hallway.

The butler met me at the front door and bowed slightly.

"Your hat, sir."

"Thanks," I growled and snatched it away from him. I turned it over carefully in my hands. "I see the lining's still there."

"If I may say so, sir, a wonderfully preserved article of headgear," he said in his mellow voice. "Your father's, perhaps?"

CHAPTER FIVE

It was a nice bright night for a party. A three-quarter moon riding up into a cloudless sky, and it was warm without being uncomfortably hot. That was the way I felt when I knocked on Kay Steinway's door.

The door opened and the sound of music and people's voices came flooding out.

"Well," Kay said, "this isn't a surprise, but it's nice all the same."

"I just happened to be passing," I said, "it was only ten miles out of my way ..."

"Come on in," she said.

She wore a strapless gown of pink chiffon which was crushed—but not flat—over her bosom, down into a belt at her waist, then let fly. One deep breath and she'd catch a chill.

"I didn't know this was formal," I said, "or I wouldn't have dressed."

"Come and meet the other guests," she said. "See what a sanitary engineer has to face up to."

I followed her into the living room. There was a haze of blue smoke, a din of voices, a blur of faces—maybe a dozen people in all. Kay introduced me around. I didn't remember the names; it didn't matter, they didn't remember mine. Then there were faces I recognized.

"You taking time off, Lieutenant?" Paula Reid asked. "Or do you call this working?"

"Yes," I said, which seemed the easiest answer right then. I looked at her appreciatively. She wore a blue velvet gown with a neckline that plunged beyond the cleavage and could have only been supported by hope alone. Beside her, Janice Jorgens looked almost pure in a high-necked jersey sack.

"I'll get you a drink, Al," Kay said. "Scotch on the rocks?"

"With a little soda," I said.

I made a threesome, along with Paula and Janice, but not for long. Norman Coates joined us, a lurid-colored cocktail in his delicate hand.

"Nice to see you again, Lieutenant," he smiled at me.

Kay Steinway returned and handed me my drink. "Thanks," I said.

"Georgia's death must be quite a problem for you." Coates smiled at Paula. "I mean, what will you do for a show on Saturday night?"

"I'll manage," she said tersely. "You don't have to look so pleased about the whole thing, Norman!"

"Me—pleased?" He looked suitably sympathetic. "I'm very sorry for you, dear, I really am."

"I can imagine!" she said.

"I think it gives you a golden opportunity, darling," Kay purred to Paula. "Why don't you interview yourself?"

"Maybe I should interview you, darling," Paula smiled sweetly at her. "But my program's never been faded off the air yet, and I wouldn't want to spoil a record."

"I still like my original idea," Kay said. "That way you'd get more dirt than you've ever got. And that is the point of the program, darling, isn't it? To dig as much dirt as possible."

"Why don't we just go home?" Janice pleaded with Paula.

"Nonsense," Paula said tightly. "I'm just beginning to enjoy myself. Tell me, Lieutenant, have you asked Kay about Georgia Brown yet? She was very close to Lee Manning, I've heard. About as close as you can get even if you're married, which they weren't."

"We've talked," I said. "Kay told me she was too old for him."

"You don't have to convince me of that!" Paula laughed shortly.

"I was nineteen at the time," Kay said tightly. "If you'd been around he would have called you Mother!"

"Such a delightful sense of humor," Paula said. "She's the original anything-for-a-laugh girl. Have you heard her sing, Lieutenant?"

"Paula's the original blues girl, too," Kay smiled. "And don't believe those rumors about her hair being gray originally, Lieutenant. It was white."

"Why, you" Paula took a quick step toward her, but Janice caught her arm quickly and pulled her back.

"Remember your manners, darling," Kay said. "This isn't a television party, you know. Most of the people here work in films. They are somebody!" She walked away with that gentle roll to her hips that sailors admire so much they stay on shore.

Paula took a deep breath, which parted her enough from the blue velvet to show there were no secrets between her and anyone that happened to be looking. I happened to be looking.

Coates laughed nervously: "Nothing like the casual conversation between two stars in their own right for good clean fun!" he said brightly.

"One of these days I'll ..." Paula turned away. "Get me another drink, Janice."

"Don't you think you've had enough?" Janice asked nervously.

"I pay you too much to be a secretary," Paula snapped, "not a nursemaid!"

They both moved away toward the bar, leaving me with Coates. He took his pocket handkerchief out and dabbed his forehead with it. "It certainly gets warm when those two get together," he said.

"If not hot," I agreed. "Kay was telling me earlier about Manning."

"Lee?" he cleared his throat. "He was quite a ... character."

"A guy who knew what he liked," I said. "He must have run the most original finishing school in the country."

"A character," Coates nodded. "Not that I agreed with his ... amusements, you understand, Lieutenant."

I looked at him for a long moment: "I'll believe that," I said finally.

"Most unfortunate," he said. "But what could one do? I mean, at that time, he was a star, a great star, Lieutenant. He was box office."

"That meant he could get away with murder?"

"There was some doubt, you know," Coates said quickly. "I mean, the girl had a weak heart, that is, she could have had a weak heart. I mean ..."

"I get your message," I said. "Wasn't Fargo worried about it, after it happened?"

"I really don't know," he said. "If you'll excuse me, Lieutenant, I must really go and get myself another White Lady."

"Help yourself." I looked around the room. "You've got a wide choice."

"I mean another cocktail, of course," he said.

"Of course," I agreed, but he was already on his way to the bar.

I finished my drink and stood looking at the empty glass for a moment. I really didn't have too much time; I had to call on Kent Fargo before the evening was through. I went across to the bar and by the time I reached it Coates had disappeared. The only other person there was Paula Reid.

"Having yourself a time, Lieutenant?" she said.

"There seems to be a lot of interesting people here tonight," I said.

"Interesting?" she smiled thinly. "I suppose they are, particularly when you know them as well as I do."

She turned her back to the bar, surveying the rest of the people in the room. "There's an interesting character for you, Lieutenant. Over there, in the corner. You recognize him, of course?"

"Jackie Slade?" I said. "Sure, the blue jeans are a dead giveaway."

"The current teenage rebel," she said. "He's guaranteed to rebel against everything, except the money his studio pays him. The fading blonde beside him isn't his mother."

"No?"

"No, she taught him everything he knows, particularly about women. That's why she looks so haggard that even the beauty parlors pass her up now. I guess Jackie would like something more his own age, but she picked him up out of the gutter and owns fifty per cent of his contract. He's got more chance of becoming an actor than he has of getting rid of her. And he'll never be an actor!"

"Tough for Jackie," I said.

"He's young," she said, "but then he's a slob, too. You put them both together and all you get is a young slob. See Carol Hart over there?"

I looked at the willowy brunette with the urchin-cut and the large, soulful eyes. "She's worth looking at," I said admiringly.

"You have no chance, Lieutenant," she said. "She's shopping for a new husband right now. Anyone will do just so long as he has a million dollars, preferably plural. She's playing very hard to get at the moment— until the million comes along. Then she'll melt so fast they'll need a drip tray to catch her. I see she's drinking again."

"That's ususual?"

"She's been on the wagon while she's husband-shopping, but tonight looks as if it's too much for her. Four drinks and she strips at a party— I thought everybody knew that."

"I didn't," I said. "I wonder if she needs another drink yet?"

"Don't worry," she said. "It's as sure as death and taxes."

I found I'd finished the new drink so I poured myself a newer one. "You seem to be well informed," I said.

"I should be," she said expressionlessly. "I've been digging dirt—as Kay so charmingly put it—for the last two years. Show me a celebrity and I'll show you a stinker."

"Introduce me to Paula Reid," I said gently.

She smiled thinly: "I left myself open for that. Let me introduce you to someone else, Lieutenant. The short man over there, the one with the cigar and the bald head. That's Emile Brocales."

"The producer?"

"The most versatile producer of them all. Standing on his right is his current girl friend; on his left, his current boy friend."

"He has time to make pictures?"

"He has to make pictures. How else would he meet all his blackmail payments? You see the blonde with the impossible front?"

"You mean improbable," I corrected her.

"Impossible!" she said tersely. "Believe me, I know! I walked into her shower one morning just to check up. She graduated into pictures from a house in Mexico City. It took them a year to cure her of the habit."

"Dope?"

Paula shook her head. "Every time a man said goodbye, she'd insist on shaking hands with her palm up."

I lit myself a cigarette. "There must be some ordinary people in this business? Normal people, no better, no worse than average?"

"Here's Carol, right on schedule," she said.

The willowy brunette walked slowly into the center of the room, a dreamy look in her eyes. Someone started to whistle "All of Me," softly, and there was the sound of laughter around the room.

Carol didn't seem to hear it. She swayed slowly, her eyes closed and then peeled off her gown. She stripped down to her nylons and a pair of white-stitched blue pumps. She bent forward to take off the nylons and collapsed gracefully onto the floor. The hum of conversation renewed as everyone lost interest now the act was finished.

Carol lay where she was. A redhead in a hurry to speak to someone on the other side of the room stepped over her carefully on her way across.

"You were saying?" Paula asked.

"Isn't there anybody normal in this business?"

"Sure," she nodded. "There's me, for example—and you, Lieutenant."

"And Kay Steinway?"

Her lips stretched in that thin smile again. "Well now, I wouldn't really classify Kay as normal. She has too much vitality, I've always thought. It is a fact that she's the only girl who's had to chase a producer three times around the casting couch before she finally caught him. Kay lives for men, you know, Lieutenant. The doubt is, just how long her men manage to keep alive."

"It can happen to anybody," I said. "You keep on eating that breakfast cereal and before you know it ..."

"She always reminds me of the Black Widow spider," Paula said. "Isn't that the one that eats its mate after—"

"Don't spill any of that acid on my carpet, darling," a cold voice interrupted. "I happen to have paid rather a lot for it!"

Kay Steinway was standing directly behind Paula, a look of cold fury on her face.

"Hello, darling," Paula said easily. "I was just telling the Lieutenant about the men in your life and how you always seem to take the life out of your men." She looked at me and smiled. "Of course, it's not that Kay is so beautiful, just so accessible!"

Kay Steinway moved in between us. "I need a drink," she said tautly. "This one will do." She took the glass out of my hand and threw the contents into Paula's face. "You dirty-mouthed, lying old hag!" she said loudly. "You—"

I heard the trumpet sound Retreat, and retreated quickly across the room, then out into the fresh air. I walked out onto the flagstoned patio beside the pool. I saw a shapeless silhouette in front of me.

"Can I get you a drink, I hope not," I said.

Janice Jorgens turned around and looked at me slowly. "It's you, Lieutenant. No drink, thanks. I don't drink much at all, really."

"You sound as if you have the blues," I said. "That figures."

"That's strictly Paula's gimmick," she said.

"Anyway," I added, "she's still a very attractive young woman."

"I wouldn't be too sure about the young part," Janice's lips curled down at the edges. "Haven't you noticed those little scars under each ear?"

"Someone bit her?"

"Plastic surgery," she said.

"I remember the story about the dame who had her face lifted so many times she—"

"Maybe I will have that drink after all," Janice said quickly.

"Sure," I said.

"Do you drive that Austin Healey parked out front?" she asked.

"Sure, why?"

"I heard you arrive. It needs a tune, the carburetors are out of sync."

"How do you tell?" I asked in a hushed voice. "All know about it is there's a hole in the rear end where they put the gas."

"I've got a mechanical knack, I guess," she said listlessly. "And I like cars. You should get it tuned—it's a waste of an automobile otherwise."

"Thank you for those words of wisdom," I said. "In return I will go get you a drink."

I'd taken three steps toward the living room when it happened. The glass doors flew outwards violently and two figures burst out onto the flagstones, locked in a savage embrace.

It took me a couple of seconds to realize that Kay and Paula weren't embracing—they were fighting. They swayed and struggled their way past me toward the pool. Paula had one hand locked in Kay's hair, while Kay was trying desperately to pummel her opponent's face.

They reached the edge of the pool and Kay suddenly reversed her tactics. She grabbed hold of the top of the blue velvet gown and jerked her hands downwards in a ripping movement.

The gown and Paula parted company suddenly, leaving her naked to the waist. The sudden exposure of her white, pointed breasts, left her looking curiously defenseless. It didn't worry her opponent.

Kay caught hold of Paula's left arm and turned away, bending double from the waist, forcing the arm down across her shoulders. Paula shrieked wildly as she catapulted up over Kay's shoulder in a wild arc. A moment later she hit the pool with a resounding splash and sank out of sight.

"That's something you don't see very often," I said.

But Janice wasn't listening. With a thin wail of horror she was running toward the side of the pool, ready to fish her employer out when she surfaced.

I walked over and took Kay's arm and led her away gently from the side of the pool. Her gown had been ripped away right down one side, and her hair hung over her eyes.

"You need a drink," I said.

"That bitch!" she said passionately. "I'll teach her to—" She relaxed suddenly and leaned against me. "You're right, Al, I do need a drink, but not in there. Take me around the back of the house."

I walked her around the back of the house and she opened a side door that wasn't locked. I followed her into what was obviously her own room. She sank down onto the bed, her shoulders still heaving.

"Light me a cigarette," she said softly.

I lit two and gave her one. She dragged smoke down into her lungs, then exhaled slowly. "Thanks," she murmured. "There's some Scotch in that cabinet over there. Don't worry about the ice."

I found the Scotch and the glasses, and poured two drinks. I handed her one and she drained it instantly then gave the glass back to me.

"Give me another," she said. "I must look a sight!"

"You look wonderful," I said. "You couldn't look any other way if you tried."

She pushed her hair away from her eyes and looked up at me. "You really think so, Al?"

"Would I say it?"

"I guess not," she said. "You know, I feel good. That Reid witch had it coming to her! She's got everybody in the whole business so damned scared of her filthy program, they fall over her. Well, I showed her!"

"You certainly did," I agreed, and handed her the second drink.

She drank it a little more slowly, then tossed the empty glass onto the floor. It hit the thick rug and didn't break. She stood up slowly.

"I feel better," she said, "a whole lot better. In fact, I feel wonderful!"

"That's fine," I said and checked my watch. It was a little after nine-thirty. "I have to be going, I've still got some work to do."

"You don't have to go yet," she said. "Stay for a while."

"I really must go," I said.

"Nothing I can do to stop you?" she asked.

"Nothing, honey," I said. "It's been a wonderful party, never a dull moment."

She got onto her feet slowly and looked down at herself. "This gown cost me three hundred," she said. "First time I've worn it."

She undid the zipper and let the tattered remnants of the gown fall to the floor. Underneath she wore a strapless bra and a pair of white, form-hugging panties. She unhooked the bra and tossed it onto the bed. She stretched her arms lazily above her head and her rounded breasts lifted with the movement.

I took a step toward her and she laughed huskily. "I thought you were in a hurry to get some place, Al."

"I was," I said. "I still am. I just changed direction, that's all."

She peeled off the panties and kicked them across the room. The racket from the living room beat faintly around my ears.

"What about your party?" I said, and my voice was just as husky as hers.

"They'll never know I'm missing," she said. "Anyway, isn't this going to be a party?"

She stepped closer to me and suddenly swung her right fist so that it connected painfully with my solar plexus. She was panting slightly.

"Hit me!" she said in a muffled voice. "Hit me, why don't you!"

That fist in my stomach hurt. I pushed her clean off her feet so that she lay on her back across the bed.

She looked up at me and smiled. "That's better, Al. Now kiss me!"

"I should have known not to dress for your party," I said. "Should I switch off the light?"

"Why?" She sounded genuinely puzzled. "Are you modest or something?"

CHAPTER SIX

The offices of Fargo Enterprises were located on the twelfth floor of a midtown office block. Fargo lived in the penthouse above.

It was just after eleven-thirty when I rode the elevator to the penthouse. Maybe it was late to go calling, but not too late for calling on a racketeer, even if he was retired. I pressed the button and got chimes. I lit a cigarette and waited for the door to open. I nearly swallowed the cigarette when it did open.

A silver-blonde stood there, looking at me with nothing more than idle curiosity. Her eyebrows were thick and black and arched in perpetual surprise. Her mouth was open, which made her glamorous, or just hit you in the solar plexus, depending which way you looked at it.

She wore gold drop earrings, each a long-haired female nude in miniature. She also wore a gold bikini. From where I stood it looked like genuine 14-karat gold thread woven into the cloth.

She must have caught the glazed expression in my eyes. "It's hot," she said.

"You must be the original golden blonde," I said. "I never did go for that golden goose routine—no sex. Who gets excited about an egg?"

"What are you selling?" she asked suspiciously. "A mail-order college education?"

"I'd like to see Mr. Fargo," I said.

"He doesn't see anybody outside of office hours," she said. "Even then he doesn't see anybody, mostly."

I showed her my shield. "Lieutenant Wheeler is the name."

"A cop?" Her eyebrows got more surprised. "They get wackier every day."

She turned her head and called out, "Hey, Kent! There's a cop out here wants to see you. A lieutenant no less." She turned to face me again, shrugging her shoulders gently. "I've got to find out—maybe he won't talk to anybody except captains, you understand?"

"Bring him in!" a voice bellowed from somewhere inside. "You'll catch cold standing out there!"

The blonde smiled at me encouragingly. "Kent says it's O.K. for you to come on in. Don't let him scare you, he always bawls people out when his ulcer's kicking him around."

"He has an ulcer?"

"Why sure—he's an executive!"

I followed the carefree sway of the blonde's expensively clad hips into the entrance hall, and then into the living room.

There was a row of brightly lit fish tanks along one wall and even brighter tropical fish swimming around inside them. Fargo stood looking out of the massive plate-glass window at the panoramic view of the city.

He turned around and looked at me. "What do you want?" he asked wearily.

"Some questions," I said.

"O.K.," he said. "But make it quick, will you?" He looked at the blonde. "You better blow, baby, you're only a distraction around here."

"All right, sugar, anything you say." She blew him a kiss noisily, then waltzed out of the room, her anatomy going all ways at the one time.

"You like a drink?" Fargo asked me.

"Very much," I said. "Scotch, a little soda."

"Sure." He went over to the bar and switched on the panel lights on either side of it. I turned my head away as the dazzling brilliance of chromed metal hit me.

I watched him as he poured the drinks. He was short, with wide shoulders and long arms. He had crisp, black hair, crew-cut and flecked with gray at the temples. He had a thin nose and a tight mouth. His eyes, I saw as he walked back with the drinks, were a bright, pale blue.

"Thanks," I said as I took the drink.

He waved his hand toward a chair and sank into another beside it. I sat down and drank some of the Scotch; it was a very good Scotch.

"Questions," he said, "what about?"

"Georgia Brown."

"What about Georgia Brown?"

"She got herself murdered this morning." I told him the story briefly.

"Why tell me? I read about it in the evening papers."

I mentioned Manning's suicide, Georgia's appearance on Paula Reid's show, the threatening letters. He wasn't impressed.

"None of my business," he said and yawned loudly.

"The way I hear it, it is," I said carefully. "She was going to name names on that show, and your name was one of them."

"You're crazy," he said, "or somebody is. Why me?"

"That's what I thought you might tell me."

"It's always the same," he said. "Look, Lieutenant, I'm clean. I retired out of the rackets a few years back, I run a legitimate business now. You know that, every cop in town knows that. But soon as anything happens, somebody's got to toss my name around!"

"But you were mixed up with Manning at the time he killed himself," I said.

"Me?"

"You were backing his pictures through Hilary Blain."

He sat up straight in his chair: "Who told you that?" he asked softly.

"I heard it," I said.

"I'd like to know where," he said. "You want another drink, Lieutenant?"

"I'd prefer some answers. You've asked all the questions so far and that isn't the routine I had prepared."

I heard the outside door open and close. A moment later the living-room door opened and a character walked in.

"Kent!" he said. "I talked to Joe and he said Steve's been out of town for ... sorry, I didn't know you got company."

"This is Lieutenant Wheeler," Fargo said coldly. "This is Charlie Dunn, he works for me."

Dunn was a tall, thin young man with an expressionless face. "Good evening, Lieutenant," he said.

"Sure," I said.

"I go and come back, or I wait around?" Charlie asked.

"You wait around," Fargo said. "Toni's watching television—go and watch with her, but not too close!"

"My income bracket keeps me at a distance," Charlie said and went looking for the blonde. Why he needed television as well, I couldn't figure.

Fargo relaxed in his chair. "All right, so I was backing his pictures—that's legitimate."

"Sure," I said. "It's only Georgia Brown's murder that's illegitimate, so far."

"You want me to give you an alibi?"

"You've six guys who'll swear you never made a bomb in your whole life?" I asked him gently.

He glared at me for a moment then he grinned sourly: "O.K., so you don't want an alibi, what do you want?"

"Georgia was going to tell the truth about Manning's death," I said. "She—"

"What do you mean—the truth about Manning's death!" he said coldly. "He committed suicide, didn't he!"

"The circumstances that made him kill himself," I corrected myself. "The sixteen-year-old kid with the weak heart—I've heard the story. You were around at the time, maybe you could tell me who'd have a good reason for not wanting Georgia to speak her piece?"

He thought about it for a little while. "I guess there were quite a few people around at the time who wouldn't want it talked about," he said, "but murder!" He shook his head. "I don't see any of them going that far!"

"Nobody does," I said sadly, "that's the trouble. You don't, Coates doesn't, Kay Steinway doesn't, Blain doesn't. I wouldn't believe it myself—if Georgia Brown wasn't dead."

I was watching him as I tossed the names into midair. If he caught them, he gave no sign they meant anything in particular to him.

"Sorry I can't help you, Lieutenant," he said. "Was there anything else?"

I finished the drink and got onto my feet. "I don't think so. Thanks for your time, Mr. Fargo."

"Any time," he said expansively.

He walked with me to the front door.

"Georgia was a good-looking kid the last time I saw her," he said reflectively. "That would be about three years ago. She was a blonde with the best figure I'd ever ... I guess I'm morbid, Lieutenant, but how did she look?"

"Your guess is as good as mine," I said. "What they scraped off the wall wasn't photogenic."

He put a cigarette into his mouth and lit it. The fingers that held the match trembled slightly.

"You bastard!" he said softly.

That finished the interview on a conclusive note. I let myself out and went back to the Healey. I drove away from the curb at a leisurely pace and reflected that I did see life even if I wasn't going to live to an old age.

The lights were still burning in the Sheriff's office when I parked outside. I walked in past Annabelle Jackson's empty desk and regretted the Southern indolence that kept her from working twenty-four hours a day the way her boss did.

Lavers looked up from his desk and grunted as I came in.

"I bring you greetings," I said politely and sank into a chair.

"The only thing you ever bring me is grief," he said. "What did you find out, if anything?"

I gave him a condensed rundown on who I'd seen, what had happened. It didn't really sound like much—even to me—but then, of course, I hadn't told him the most exciting part.

"Fargo?" he said. "That's interesting. I'd like to tie something on his tail."

"It would be a crime to let that silver-blonde go to waste," I said. "What would she do for a living if Fargo wasn't there?"

"Are you kidding?" Lavers snorted.

"I guess I am."

He lit his pipe. "The news is still running hot over the wire services. This murder is going to be front-page news throughout the country in the morning."

"Yes, sir," I said.

"We need to crack it fast," he said. "I spoke to Inspector Martin. I told him I felt it was better if you had a free hand and he said you always do anyway! Captain Parker is handling it from their end. He gets anything, he passes it on to us. We get anything—" He stopped and looked at me for a moment. "Ah! what's the use of me talking! What are you going to do?"

"I thought I might take a run down to Laguna Beach first thing in the morning," I said.

"Laguna Beach!" His face reddened. "You think this is a good time to take a vacation?"

"Any time is a good time to take a vacation—but that's where Manning killed himself."

"Three years ago!" Lavers thundered. "You think you're going to turn up anything now that the police didn't when it happened?"

"I'd just like to get the feel of it," I said. "And that reminds me about the story about the star and the new French wife who couldn't speak any English. She—"

"Get out of here!" he said resignedly. "I don't need you—I've got an ulcer already!"

"Yes, sir," I said.

I went back to the car and drove myself home. It was close to one-thirty when I got inside the apartment. I put Julie London on the hi-fi machine and poured myself a drink. "Cry me a river," Julie pleaded breathlessly, and right then it was no trouble. Besides, anything Julie wanted was all right by me.

The phone rang and I grabbed it off the hook and held it at arm's length until Julie had finished. Then I put it to my ear and said: "This is the morgue here. What was your husband's name again?"

There was a short silence then a voice said dubiously: "Is that Lieutenant Wheeler?"

"It certainly is," I said brightly, because a feminine voice always has that effect on me.

"This is Janice Jorgens," she said. "I got your home number from the Homicide Bureau. I hope you don't mind me calling you?"

"I'm hoping it will be a pleasure," I said. "Are you lonely, bored with life? Has Romance passed you by? Just dial Wheeler for the whirl of a lifetime and—"

"Lieutenant, please!" she said coldly. "It's late and I'm tired, Paula is a nervous wreck after that shocking—"

"So if this is strictly business," I said equally coldly, "you have exactly ten seconds left to explain why the hell you called me in the middle of the night!"

"I'm sorry," she said. "I'm upset, I guess. I just wondered what progress you were making. I thought if you had anything definite on the murderer, the news might cheer Paula up a little."

"Nothing yet," I said, "but tomorrow is another day."

"You stun me, Lieutenant."

"I'm going down to Laguna Beach in the morning," I said. "Something big might break down there."

"Your leg?"

"I might just find the one piece of evidence I want," I lied with the ease of long habit. "The one thing I need to clinch the whole deal."

"It sounds exciting," her voice had thawed a little.

"Say!" I made it sound a brand-new idea. "If you're not doing anything vital tomorrow morning, why don't you come with me for the ride?"

"No thank you," she said firmly. "I have a fair idea of what a ride with you would involve, Lieutenant."

"But it wouldn't ... well, maybe it would, but—"

"Good night, Lieutenant," she said and hung up.

I put down the phone and picked up my drink. "I'm in the mood for love," Julie sang huskily.

"So am I, honey," I agreed. "But it's too late to go calling on Kay Steinway again."

"I'm glad there is you," Julie emphasized on a new track.

"And I'm glad there is you, too," I said. "And I'm also glad there are dolls like Kay and Paula. All three of you are beautiful, but the other two are obtainable!" I raised my glass in a silent toast.

And so to bed, as a character called Peeping Sam once said.

CHAPTER SEVEN

I was lucky when I reached the Laguna Beach police headquarters. The guy who'd handled the Manning case three years ago was on duty. His name was Lieutenant Monro, and he was short and gray-headed, with a face that had been chiseled out of rock.

"Sure, Lieutenant," he said, after I'd explained more or less why I was there. "Be happy to help you. But I don't know that I can."

"How exactly did he kill himself?" I asked.

"Threw himself over a cliff-edge," Monro said. "About a two-hundred foot sheer drop down onto the rocks—it was messy."

He thought about it for a moment. "What exactly is it you're looking for?"

"I don't know," I admitted. "The Georgia Brown killing ties in with the suicide somewhere."

"I'll take you out there, if it'll help," he said.

"I'd like that," I said, "thanks."

We drove out there in the Austin Healey. We left the car on the road, and walked across the brown grass to the cliff-edge. I looked down cautiously. It was exactly as Monro had said, a sheer drop for a long, long way. I watched the waves breaking over the jagged rocks below for a few moments, then turned away.

"He couldn't have picked a better spot."

"He sure couldn't," Monro agreed.

We got back into the car and drove about a quarter of a mile down the road. There was a split-level with the paint peeling and a general air of decay about it. Behind the house, the ground sloped gently down to the beach.

"That's where he lived," Monro explained. "You want to take a look?"

"I guess not," I said. "He left the house, he walked up to the top of the cliff and jumped over?"

"Yeah," Monro nodded. "They didn't miss him for a couple of hours— there was a party going on inside the house at the time."

"They?"

"Some of his friends were there. Maybe it wasn't exactly a party, but they'd been drinking pretty heavily. One of them saw Manning go out the back about midnight, but they thought he was just going for some air. It was around two o'clock before they started worrying about him not coming back."

"Sounds like it was a party."

"I guess it was. Manning had a reputation for throwing good parties,"

Monro said dryly.

"You remember who was there?"

"Only a few people," he said. "It wasn't very long after the girl—" he stopped abruptly.

"I know that story, too," I said. "The sixteen-year-old who had a bad heart—maybe."

He looked at me for a long moment, making up his mind: "You're well informed, Lieutenant."

"I guess I am at that, Lieutenant," I said. "Who was there at the party?"

He thought for a few moments. "It was a long time ago now. I remember that producer—the one who always gave me the creeps—he was there."

"Coates?"

"That's him, Coates. And the financial brain, Hilary Blain."

"How about Kent Fargo?"

"Sure, I remember now, he was there. And the dame you're worrying about—Georgia Brown."

"How about Kay Steinway?"

"You mean that overblown singer who can't sing?"

"Fullblown," I corrected him. "Was she there?"

"No," he said firmly. "Only the five of them, including Manning."

"Nobody else?"

"I'm sure, Lieutenant!" he said curtly.

I took a last look at the house and then started the car rolling again.

Monro lit a cigarette and relaxed a little in his seat. "Anything else, Lieutenant?"

"The girl," I said. "Tell me about her."

"It could be a sore point," he said cautiously. "Me, I'm just a cop—you know how it is."

"Sure," I said. "I know the whole thing was kept quiet after Manning jumped over the cliff. I'm not asking just for the sake of asking, Lieutenant."

"There's a bar on the next block," he said. "Why don't we stop off there?"

"I wondered what was worrying me," I said. "It's my thirst."

We stopped at the bar and sat in a booth. Monro drank rye and I drank Scotch.

"Her name was Geraldine Morgan," he said slowly. "She came from Louisville, in Kentucky. She looked a lot older than she was; we found out after it happened that she'd run away from home. A kid with a yen for the bright lights—she had ambitions. She wasn't original."

He drank some of his rye. "I got a daughter," he said. "She's nineteen now, and she's going to be a nurse. She was the same age as the Morgan kid when it happened. It can scare you, thinking about what can happen to a kid when she's got what it takes and no experience to back it!"

"I can imagine," I said.

"Her mother was dead," he went on, "her old man worked a night shift. There was an elder sister—around twenty, but she wasn't home often. The kid would come home from school most nights to an empty house. There wasn't much money around, the old man hit the booze, too. She got tired of it, so she quit."

He finished his drink. "So she comes to sunny California and she's going to work in pictures, but meantime she's broke. So she gets herself a job as a waitress, and that's where Manning found her."

Monro laughed mirthlessly. "It's a story so old nobody even wants to hear it. The big-time star, the young hopeful. In no time at all, Manning got her out at his Laguna Beach house every week end. She quit her job as a waitress on his say-so and then she's his housekeeper. She even wrote home to the sister, telling her all about it—or most of it.

"She really believed that Manning was going to give her a break, going to arrange a screen test for her, and if it was O.K. she'd have a part in his next film. She said if her family tried to do anything she'd kill herself. This was her big chance and she was going to take it."

"So they didn't do anything?"

He looked at me somberly. "They didn't have a chance. Four days later she was dead. I was on duty when the call came in. I went out there and found Manning in a robe and still stinking drunk. The kid was stretched out on the bed—he hadn't even thought to throw a cover over her. He didn't care about the kid—he just didn't want any publicity!"

"They tell me it was her heart," I said.

"Yeah," he nodded. "The doc said it was heart failure all right. But she had bruises all over her. Maybe the way Manning played it put an extra strain on her heart and it just quit. I asked the doc about it, when there wasn't anybody around to listen to his answer. 'You know why everybody dies,' he said, 'because their heart stops beating. That's why she died.' You know what I would have called it?"

"I guess so," I said. "Murder?"

"But me," he said, "I'm only a cop, not a politician. When it comes to an indictment, they don't ask me. Anyway, how can you indict a dead man?"

"You didn't like Manning," I said.

"I hated his guts," Monro said quietly. "And I didn't even know him until that night. You figure how the people who did know him must have hated his guts!"

"Was Georgia Brown his panderer?" I asked. "The way I hear it, she used to line up the girls for him—young and innocent, the way Geraldine Morgan was. Then she'd sit on the side and watch."

"I wouldn't know anything about that," he said. "All I know is what I saw that night."

"Lieutenant," I said, "you ever think what you might do if you had so much money it didn't matter any more—and people around you who'd pander to your each and every whim?"

"You figure he was maybe no worse than anybody else would be in his position," he said coldly. "But you didn't see the kid's body the way I did. Sixteen years of age! It could have been my own kid lying there!"

"Yeah," I said, "I see what you mean. But I'm still glad it was me that pressed that buzzer."

"Buzzer?"

"The one that blew Georgia Brown into little pieces," I said. "Shall we go, Lieutenant?"

It was afternoon when I got back to Pine City. I stopped outside the Bureau and found my way into Captain Parker's office.

"The big Wheeler himself!" Parker said jovially as I walked in. "I bet you got the whole case wrapped up, Al. Give me a break and tell me whodunit."

"I'll tell you how it's been," I said. "Yesterday I got some place, today I'm about back where I started. If somebody exploded that bomb again, we could start even."

"You disappoint me," he grinned. "You, the unorthodox cop, and the County Sheriff's white-haired boy. I can't wait to tell Lieutenant Hammond about this, he'll enjoy it."

"Break it down into words of one syllable before you tell it," I suggested, "otherwise he won't understand."

I sat on the edge of his desk and lit a cigarette. "What have you got?"

"Nothing much," he said. "That bomb fixed things all right. MacDonald says the bomb was a simple mechanism that anybody could make—a sort of homemade contraption. There's a report on it," he flicked a typewritten sheet on his desk.

"A blow-it-up yourself project?" I said. "Well, that helps a lot."

"I double-checked on Polnik's round of the other tenants and the janitor," Parker went on. "Nothing new, they all had the same story. Lavers tells me you've been chasing the Manning suicide angle down in Laguna Beach. Come up with anything exciting?"

"No," I said.

I gave him the broad outline of what Monro had told me, and added the gist of the interviews I'd had with the four people Georgia Brown had named.

"A nice guy, this Manning!" he said.

"It's a wonder he lived so long," I agreed. "But like Blain says, Georgia was even nicer."

"Yeah." Parker lost his grin. "This is starting to get under my skin, Al. We start off with a whole lot of facts and end up with nothing."

"You've got it," I agreed. "Well, I quit for the night—see you in Traffic."

"I wouldn't mind being called Sergeant again," Parker said earnestly. "It's just that you lose so much money, too!"

I shuddered. "I wouldn't like to be called Sergeant again, not with Hammond still a lieutenant."

I left the Bureau and drove back to the apartment. It was just on six when I got there. I felt I should do something energetic, something positive, live aggressively, but I didn't know where to start. If I had a next move, nobody had told me about it.

I put a Les Paul L-P onto the machine and let his multiple-recorded guitar work up and down my spine. It was better than a masseur but it didn't give me the mental inspiration I needed. Then the phone rang.

For sure it was Lavers and I was in no mood for Lavers. I picked up the phone and said: "We're sorry about that, sir, we can't understand just how he came to sit up. He was lying down all right when we put him into the hearse—"

"I want to speak to Lieutenant Wheeler!" a high-pitched voice said. "Tell him I must speak to him at once. It's ... terribly urgent!"

I closed my eyes and could see the wave in the blue-rinsed hair being patted carefully into place.

"This is Wheeler speaking," I said. "That's Mr. Coates?"

"Yes!" he said. "I'm so glad I found you. You told me to call you if anything happened."

"What's on your mind?"

"I need protection," he said breathlessly. "I must have protection, I demand it!" His voice held a rising inflection of fear. "My life has been threatened! They're coming here! You must come straightaway, Lieutenant Wheeler! At once! You understand."

"Take it easy," I said. "What's it all about? Who's been threatening your life—who's coming over there?"

"I can't tell you over the telephone," his voice dropped to a low whisper. "But you must come at once! I want police protection, you hear!"

"I'd need to be three blocks away before I didn't," I said. "Eardrums aren't replaceable."

There was a click in my ear as he hung up.

"You ham!" I said into the dead mouthpiece, then dropped the phone back onto the cradle.

I poured myself a drink and thought about it. I had nothing better to do, I might as well go over there and see what it was about. Maybe he was drunk or ... a million maybe's.... There was one easy way to find out. I finished the drink and went out of the apartment and down to the car.

It took me five minutes to find a parking space and then it was a block away from his hotel. I walked toward it, thinking the least Coates could do when I got there was to buy me a drink.

I walked through the foyer and rode an elevator up to his floor. I went down the corridor to his room and knocked on the door. Nothing happened. I knocked again and waited and still nothing happened.

I began to feel glad there was no buzzer so I wasn't tempted to push the button. One bomb in one lifetime is enough. Then I had a flash of brilliance and tried the handle—the door opened quite easily.

I stepped inside the room and fumbled for the light switch. My fingers found it and flicked it down. The room suddenly came to life. There was only one exception.

That was Norman Coates.

He lay sprawled across the bed, his eyes wide open but not seeing the overhead light. I walked slowly across to the bed and looked at him. He had been shot twice through the chest and the Paisley silk would never look the same again.

I walked across to the phone and got all orthodox as I lifted the receiver with a handkerchief. I dialed Homicide and asked if Parker had left. He hadn't. I wondered idly for a moment, while they connected me, what it would be like to have a conscience.

"Parker," he said heartily in my ear.

"Al Wheeler," I said. "I'm in Coates's hotel room. He's been shot." I gave the room number, the name of the hotel.

"When did it happen?"

I checked my watch. "It couldn't have happened more than half an hour ago. He rang me about six-fifteen."

"What did he want?"

"Police protection, *they* were threatening him, *they* were going to kill him—that's why I came over here." The only sound was a faint humming noise in my ear. "You still there?" I said.

"I was just wondering, Al, why didn't you give me a call right away. We could have had a couple of the boys down there in ten minutes."

"He sounded as if he was drunk," I said. "I didn't take him seriously."

"That's too bad, Al," he said heavily.

"I guess it is," I said coldly. "Send somebody out to take care of things, will you?"

"Right away. You'll wait there and take over?"

"I won't be here," I said.

"But—"

"Somebody murdered Georgia Brown to stop her talking,' I said quickly. "I guess they murdered Coates for the same reason. They could have a couple more murders on their mind. If I'm right and I move fast I might be able to stop one of them, anyway."

"Al!" he roared. "What in hell are you talking about? What do you think we got a Homicide detail for! You think you're a one-man—" I hung up on him while he was still talking.

I took a last quick look around the room. The drawers had been emptied, their contents still sprawled across the floor. The wardrobe was wide open; the two suits hanging there had been slashed almost to ribbons. The three suitcases were empty and torn apart. I wondered if the murderer had found what he was looking for.

I took one last glance at Coates. He looked back at me unseeingly. The blue-rinse wave was now permanently out of place.

CHAPTER EIGHT

I didn't bother with the front entrance this time. I went straight to the door of the courtyard and listened for a moment. There was a splashing noise coming from inside. I tried the door; it was still unlocked.

I walked into the courtyard, closing the door behind me and locking it. Then I headed toward the pool.

I was about three seconds too late. She was out of the pool, knotting the robe tight around her waist.

"If it isn't the long-sighted policeman!" she grinned. "I thought you might be back, Al."

"How have you been?" I said. "Lonely, I hope."

"Just swimming," she said. "Come in and I'll pour you a drink."

We went through the open glass doors and down to the bar.

"Scotch, as I remember, Al," she said.

"With a little soda," I nodded. "Tell me, do you ever wear any clothes underneath that robe?"

"I don't know that I should tell you," she said as she poured the drinks. She pursed her lips in pseudo thought.

"I might ... I'll make a deal. I'll tell you, if you tell me what Al is short for?"

"Who cares?" I said quickly. "It's a lot of weather we've been having, what with all day and last night and..."

She walked around the corner of the bar and stood in front of me, her lower lip drooping a fraction. "I'm beginning to think you're losing interest in me!" she pouted.

Her fingers loosened the belt and the robe began to slide open. The phone rang suddenly and she caught the robe in what the soap-opera boys would term the nick of time.

"Damn!" she said and walked over to the phone. I leaned against the bar and picked up my drink.

"Yes?" she said in a low voice. "Yes, this is the Kay Steinway. Who? ... Oh, how are you? You what? ... I didn't call you.... But ... I swear I didn't! I wouldn't do a crazy thing like that.... I don't know anything about ... You've got to listen to ... Hello?" She joggled the cradle for a few seconds, then gave up.

She walked back toward me slowly, a worried look on her face. "He hung up," she said dully.

"Who was it?"

"A wrong number, I guess," she said. "I need a drink!"

She picked up her drink. "Where were we?"

"Losing interest in you?"

"I remember," she brightened. "I was just going to give you the Steinway test. It's infallible! Watch!"

She pulled the front of her robe open dramatically. Underneath she wore a one-piece swimsuit, in knitted stripes of gold and black. It fitted her like a glove. Who looks at gloves?

"It's a swimsuit," I said, "used for swimming."

"You're cute, Al," she said. "But that's only the beginning."

She draped the robe across the bar and moved in close to me. She leaned against me, moving her shoulders rhythmically, and making a gentle purring noise. The noises increased in volume slightly and I looked down into her eyes. Now they were green with only the faintest flecks of gray showing in them. They had a soft, out-of-focus look.

"Like the man said," she purred huskily, "don't just stand there—do something!"

"I haven't finished my drink," I said gently.

She pulled herself away from me, her eyes narrowing. "Your resistance is high tonight, Al," she said lightly.

"But you haven't passed the final test yet."

She peeled off the swimsuit in one abrupt movement that took it down to her ankles. She stepped out of it daintily and stood there looking at me with her hands on her hips and her head thrown back. I had that 'I've-been-here-before' feeling.

Then I knew why. It was pin-up pose number two from the stag magazines that are no consolation through the long, lonely nights of adolescence.

"I think you're weakening, Lieutenant," she said softly.

I put one arm around her shoulders and the other around her knees, lifting her from the floor. She put her arms around my neck and purred with unqualified approval.

I carried her out through the open glass doors to the edge of the pool and then I let go suddenly. She hit the water tail first and disappeared in a fountain of water.

Five seconds later her head broke the surface and she looked at me with hatred smoldering in her eyes.

"I could have guessed you were a good swimmer," I said easily, "but that dive ... Man! That was really something."

She pulled herself out of the water onto the tiled edge, then got to her feet in one lithe movement. She walked toward me slowly, the fingers of each hand curling inwards slightly. "I'll kill you for that!" she said thickly.

"Don't think I won't hit a woman, because I will," I told her.

She turned away abruptly and walked back inside the house. I followed her into the living room and she took the robe from across the bar and slipped into it, knotting the belt tightly around her waist.

She moved around the bar and refilled her glass.

"The great lover," she said, "that's me!"

"You do need that drink!"

Kay emptied the glass in one smooth swallow and refilled it again. "You have it wrong, Al, I need a dozen drinks. Maybe more."

"Who was that on the phone? The wrong number that wasn't?"

"A creep. It's an unlisted number but I still get them. One of the hazards of displaying my charms on wide screen. They think there's enough to go round for everybody."

"Norman Coates was murdered tonight," I said. "Not more than an hour ago."

Her glass tilted sideways suddenly and good Scotch foamed a pool on the bartop.

"You're kidding!" she whispered.

"No," I said flatly. "I think he had a phone call before it happened. He rang me afterwards for protection but I got there too late. *They* were coming, he said, *they* were going to kill him."

Her hand brushed her throat. "I don't believe it. It's some kind of trick." She looked at something over my shoulder and her pupils widened into the same look I'd seen in Coates's eyes as he stared up at the ceiling of his hotel room.

"He's right, doll," a harsh voice said. "And you set up the whole deal with that lousy call."

The .38 in its holster, strapped around my waist under my coat, felt heavy—and useless. I turned around slowly, keeping my hands on top of the bar counter.

Kent Fargo stood there, a gun in his hand, and beside him was the thin young man, Charlie Dunn, who also had a gun in his hand.

"I phoned from just around the corner," Fargo said. "I figured you wouldn't expect me to call right away." He looked at me for a moment. "I see you got company."

"Kent," Kay said nervously, "I never called you. I don't know what you're talking about."

"Don't give me that," he said impatiently. "You picked me for the fall guy and I don't like it. You got maybe one chance. Where is it?"

"I tell you," she said, "I don't know!"

Fargo hunched his shoulders: "O.K., you want to play it the hard way, it's all right with me. You ever seen Charlie's fingers up close?"

Dunn extended the fingers of his left hand in front of him. His eyes glittered with excitement. The fingers were long and thin, almost delicate.

"Charlie's an artist," Fargo said. "Just the guy to knock a tune out of a Steinway! But sing the right notes, doll. You get off-key and they'll be playing your theme song on an organ!"

Dunn slipped his gun back to his pocket and walked leisurely toward Kay Steinway. She backed away until she came up against the wall behind the bar and couldn't go any farther.

"This is a free performance, Wheeler," Kent said, "but remember you're only the audience. Try to get into the act and I'll put you into the morgue instead."

"I should be a hero," I said, "with two months' insurance premiums not paid yet?"

"That's right," Fargo grinned, "be sensible and you got a chance of staying alive."

"You don't mind if I pour myself another drink? Screams make me feel nervous."

"Why not?" he said expansively.

Dunn reached the edge of the bar and looked at Kay. He licked his lips absently. "I'm remembering how you are now, honey," he said gently, "you won't look the same again."

Kay moaned softly, her eyes shining, polished by fear. "Why won't you believe me?" she whispered. "I'm telling you the truth."

"That's what Coates said," Fargo sneered contemptuously. "Look what happened to him—and he was telling the truth! You're luckier than Coates, you still got a chance."

Dunn moved around the other side of the bar and closed in on Kay. His back was toward me as I reached out for the Scotch bottle.

His fingers twisted into the lapels of her robe, ripping it open all the way down the front. He looked at her wonderingly for a moment: "And

Kent pays me for this!" he said. Then his fingers started to work and Kay screamed in sharp agony.

My fist closed around the neck of the bottle and I threw it in Fargo's direction, jerking myself backwards off the bar stool at the same time.

I rolled a couple of times as soon as I hit the floor, dragging the .38 out of its holster, hearing the blast of Fargo's gun at the same time.

A sliver of wood sliced my cheek as the slug plowed into the floor a foot away from my head. I came up onto my knees, rammed the heel of my right hand into my solar plexus to steady the gun, and fired.

Fargo dropped his gun and reeled backwards, his left hand clutching his shoulder. I heard another scream from Kay Steinway and jerked my head around toward her.

Dunn had slammed her back against the wall and was facing me, his gun in his hand. We fired simultaneously. Something slammed the top of my head, switching out all the lights. This time the dive to the floor was painless.

I opened my eyes and looked into the limp gray eyes that showed no trace of green.

"For a moment I thought you were dead," she said tremulously.

"So did I," I muttered. I managed to sit up, feeling the top of my head gingerly; my fingers came away sticky.

"I think the bullet just scraped the top of your head," Kay said. "I've been bathing it, it's not bleeding much now but the doctor should be here any minute."

"Should I see the other guy?" I asked her.

"Him!" she shuddered. "He's dead, I think. You shot him right between the eyes, Al! Did you mean to?"

"I wasn't really particular," I said. "I always figure you hit anything with a .38, you're lucky. What about Fargo?"

"He ran out," she said. "You hit him with that first shot and he started running then." Her lower lip curled slightly. "I didn't know he was yellow like that underneath."

"That's something nobody could accuse you of being, anyway," I said.

I got onto my feet. The room tilted for a moment, then decided to behave itself and steadied down.

"I rang the police," Kay said, "they're on their way."

"How long was I out cold?"

"About five minutes, I guess."

"Did the Scotch bottle break?"

"There's another. You want a drink?"

"Amen."

She stepped over to the bar and poured me a drink. She took good care not to go around the other side. I walked around and found out why.

Charlie Dunn was there, taking up the space. He'd slipped down onto his knees and his head leaned against the inside of the bar. I tugged the collar of his jacket gently and he fell backwards and lay on the floor, giving me a faintly surprised look. Kay was right; I had shot him between the eyes.

I went back the other side of the bar and picked up the drink Kay had poured me. I was two-thirds of the way through it when the boys arrived, headed by Sergeant Polnik. Behind him was Doc Murphy, who grabbed my ears and pulled my head down.

"Hah!" he said. "Like I thought—cast iron! The slug hit and bounced off."

"There's a corpse around the other side of the bar," I said, freeing myself of his painful grip. "Why don't you go insult him—he can't talk back."

Murphy started on his way and stopped suddenly, pointing at my glass. "Is that whisky?" He downed it in one gulp and nodded. "I thought it was."

"I'm glad you're O.K., Lieutenant," Polnik said. "The Captain is still over at the hotel with the Coates deal. He said he'd get over as soon as he could."

"Put out a general alarm for Kent Fargo," I told him. "For Coates's murder and the attempted murder of Kay Steinway."

Polnik gulped. "You sure, Lieutenant? I mean, that crease you got across your skull, maybe—"

"I'm as rational as you are," I said, "not that that's any recommendation. Do it!"

He moved across to the phone as Murphy's head appeared suddenly above the bar.

"That's the first time I've seen a mobile corpse," I told him.

"I'm not that stiff I couldn't use a drink," he leered and lunged for the open bottle.

I lit a cigarette and waited until Polnik had finished the phone call.

"I'm going over to Fargo's place," I said, "he may have gone back there. When Captain Parker arrives, tell him where I've gone. And tell him to leave a stake-out here in case Fargo decided to come back."

"Whatever you say, Lieutenant."

I walked toward the glass doors and Kay Steinway caught up with me as I reached them.

"I should say thank you, you saved my life," she said softly.

"Next time you call a cop," I said, "call anybody but me."

"Come back when you've got Fargo," she said, "then I'll be able to thank you properly ... if you don't throw me in the pool again."

Her eyes were changing from gray to green again. When she was finished with pictures she could always get a regular job as an off-beat traffic signal.

"My mother told me about girls like you," I said. "I used to lie awake nights worrying I wouldn't meet them."

CHAPTER NINE

I listened to the chimes and stood to one side of the door, the .38 in my hand.

Then the door opened and the silver-blonde stood there. It had cooled down a little. She had put on a turquoise sweater which contrasted sharply with the bottom half of the 14-karat bikini.

She looked at me and saw the gun. Her eyes widened a fraction. "What are you trying to do, scare me?"

"Is Fargo inside?"

"He's been out for the last three hours," she said. "Did you want to see him or something?"

"Or something," I said. "I'll wait."

She looked doubtful. "I don't know whether Kent will like that."

"I would," I said. I moved my hand casually so the gun was pointing at her defenseless midriff. "You're going to be a good girl, aren't you?"

She gulped. "It'll be a switch," she said nervelessly, "but who am I to argue with a cop when he's got a gun in his hand?"

She backed off smartly into the entrance hall and I followed her, closing the door behind me carefully. I checked through the place—the enormous living room, the dining room with the built-in color television, the automatic kitchen, the bathroom which could have inspired even Nero to fiddle his time away, the two bedrooms, and the room Fargo used as an office.

Fargo wasn't anywhere inside the penthouse.

I came back to the living room and found the silver-blonde at the bar.

"I told you he wasn't here," she said. "Do you want a drink or something?"

"I'll settle for a drink," I said. "And I'll wait for Kent."

"He won't like it," she said. "Would you like a martini?"

"Scotch, thanks," I said, "a touch of soda."

She poured the drinks, then looked at me over the rim of her glass. "What did he do?" she asked.

"Who—Fargo?"

"Don't kid me," she said. "You're trouble and I know it. He's done something. He was crazy-mad when he went out of here, and he took that Charlie with him!" She shivered. "That Charlie, he's not right in the head."

"He's O.K. now," I told her.

"How's that?"

"He's dead."

She choked on the gin that was only perfumed with vermouth. "Dead?"

"He got into an argument," I said. "Fargo's on the run, he's wanted for murder. Don't be on his side, honey, there's no percentage in it."

"Damn him," she said coldly, "now what am I going to do?"

"I don't know," I said. "I think you're out of my league, honey."

"Toni is the name," she said absently.

"You aren't a twin by any chance?"

"No—whatever made you think that?"

"I just wondered," I said. "If Fargo comes back here, you'll open the door to him and I'll be right behind you with a gun."

"He has his own key."

"We'll put the chain on the door so he'll have to ring," I said. "I could do that right now."

I went to the front door and hooked the chain into position. I came back and watched the tropical fish. They were smarter than people—they weren't going any place either, but they didn't hurry about it.

"That Fargo!" Toni said. "He said he was retired and I thought he meant it."

"Maybe he couldn't retire." I suggested. "Maybe something, or somebody, wouldn't let him."

"He was crazy down inside," she said. "Not vicious really, like Charlie, but crazy all the same. Imagine anybody carrying a torch that long!"

"What torch?"

"He never got over that cheap actress running out on him. Imagine! He nearly burst out crying after you'd gone last night—when you told him about it."

I turned away from the fish and looked at her. "You mean Georgia Brown?"

"Who else?" She was pouring herself another martini, not worrying about the vermouth this time.

"I didn't know he was that way about her."

"Half the time he wasn't sure himself," she said. "One time he'd be calling her all the names you could think of and another time he'd be moping around looking at her picture and everything, he wouldn't even see me! I used to tell him to make up his mind. One minute she was a lousy, double-crossing broad, and the next she was the only dame he'd ever really cared for. It made me sick!"

I picked up my drink and finished it. "I'm going to take a look around his office," I said.

"Help yourself," she shrugged her shoulders.

"You'd better come with me."

"What for?"

"I could get lonely—and you just might take that chain off the hook."

"Me?" she shook her head. "For Kent Fargo? You think I'm a girl Friday or something?"

"You can hold my hand," I said.

"All right," she picked up her glass in one hand and the gin bottle in the other. I let her go first. It was the second time I'd seen 14-karat gold hips in action—I hadn't overvalued them in the first viewing.

We got into Fargo's office and I sat down behind his desk. Toni slumped into a chair facing me, and crossed her long, nicely curved legs. She was going to be a distraction, for which I was grateful.

I started with the top drawer of the desk and worked my way down to the third, without finding anything really interesting. I opened the bottom drawer as the doorbell sounded.

Toni's glass hit the thick-piled rug, the gin leaving a widening stain.

"What if he's got a gun?" she said hoarsely.

"Don't worry, honey," I consoled her, "I'll be right behind you."

"So he'll have to shoot through me to get at you!" she moaned.

"Let's go answer the door," I said. "You wouldn't want him to wait so long he lost his temper, would you?"

She got up from the chair and walked in front of me on stiff, jerky legs. We reached the front door and I stood to one side of it and motioned with the .38 for her to open it.

Toni took the chain off the hook as the chimes sounded again impatiently. Then she closed both eyes tight and opened the door.

"I want to see Lieutenant ..." The voice that had started off crisply, tailed off into silence. "Are you real?" he croaked.

"Come on in, Polnik," I said, and put the gun away.

The Sergeant stepped inside and Toni closed the door again, hastily putting the chain back into place.

Polnik took another look at her, then he looked at me. "I'd like to put my old lady into an outfit like that," he said, "and have her walk around the block just once."

"So everybody could admire her?"

"Maybe she wouldn't come back," he said simply. "I got a message from the Captain, Lieutenant."

"O.K.," I said, "but right now, I'm busy. You stay here and keep an eye on Toni."

"This is Toni?" he pointed his thumb in the silver-blonde's direction.

"That's Toni," I agreed.

"Don't hurry, Lieutenant," he said. "Take all night if you got to."

I went back to Fargo's desk and the fourth drawer. I took the contents out and put them on the desktop in front of me. I lit a cigarette and opened the top folder. Maybe I'd hit the jackpot; I'd found something interesting at least.

The folder contained a bundle of newspaper clips concerning Lee Manning's suicide three years back. I read through them carefully. After the first one, they were mostly repetitive. I didn't read anything new.

As I finished the cigarette and was lighting another I heard a gentle cough and looked up. Polnik stood in the doorway, apologetically.

"Sorry to bother you, Lieutenant. I just remembered the Captain said it was urgent."

"What was?"

"He said he was going back to the Sheriff's office, and for you to go there right away. He said to tell you it was Lavers' idea and he figured you'd better go along with it."

"Thanks," I said.

He hesitated: "The blonde, Toni, she asks me if I want a drink."

"Do you?"

"Well," he licked his lips, "I figured I should talk to you first."

"It's all right by me," I said, "you can bring me one."

"Thanks, Lieutenant."

He came back a minute later with the drink and put it on the desk in front of me.

"You figure Fargo will come back here?" he asked.

"Not now," I said, "but we'd better stick around to make sure."

"You're right, Lieutenant!" he said happily. "Did you know Toni worked in a burlesque show once?"

"I would never have guessed," I said gravely.

"Yeah—she's been telling me about it."

"You'd better get back out there—you wouldn't want to miss any of it, would you?"

"You're right, Lieutenant!" he said vehemently. "You know something, Lieutenant? I like working with you! Who else would turn up a gorgeous doll like this one? I feel sort of lousy about you getting canned."

"Well, thanks," I said.

Then I looked up at him. "What?"

"That's what the Captain says," he stopped suddenly and looked unhappy. "There I go, shooting off my big mouth again."

"Just what did the Captain say?"

"He says if you did the right thing—you'll pardon the expression, Lieutenant—that Coates guy wouldn't have got knocked off. And then he says if you'd told him where you was going, he could have staked out the

Steinway broad's place and picked up Fargo with no trouble on his way in."

"The Captain might be right," I admitted. "Why don't you go ask Toni if she can do a reverse bump and grind at the same time?"

"Yeah," his eyes glistened. "I sure will, Lieutenant."

"If she can, I'd duck before she gives a demonstration," I added but Polnik was already out of the room. I went back to the last remaining clips.

I did strike something new a couple of minutes later. A write-up on the death of Geraldine Morgan, the sixteen-year-old with the maybe weak heart.

The story had been published a week before Manning's suicide. There was no reference to Manning, or the fact that she had died at his house. It was a one-column story on page five, probably written by a woman, playing the human interest angle.

She'd handled it well. The hopes and aspirations of the small-town kid who'd come to the Dream-Maker's City to make good. And Death had cheated her right at the beginning. The story quoted excerpts from the two letters she'd written home to her eldest sister, showing how wonderful Life had looked to her in Hollywood. The letters were what you'd expect from a starry-eyed, sixteenyear-old kid—an organized tour of the bright spots. One mentioned she had spent the week end at Laguna Beach but there was no reference to whom she had spent it with.

I finished reading the story and picked up the glass. My throat jerked spasmodically as I swallowed. It was my own fault, I realized—I should have named my drink. Polnik had brought me one of Toni's martinis— straight gin.

I turned over to the next clip and saw it was from the same day's paper as the story on Geraldine Morgan. It consisted simply of two smudged photographs, clipped from a page of pix of "People in the News."

The small head read: DEATH CUT SHORT HER DREAMS. The caption under the first photo read: "The dead girl, Geraldine Morgan, aged sixteen. See story, page five, column five," and the caption under the second photo read: "Mandy Morgan, elder sister of Geraldine."

I stared at the second photo for quite some time. The more I looked, the more familiar that face got. I folded the two clips and put them into my pocket. Then I walked out, into the living room.

Polnik sat comfortably in an armchair, a large glass of gin in one hand, an even larger cigar in the other. There was a look of pure bliss on his face.

In front of him, Toni wavered gently. "Well," she said thickly, "you see, this G-string, it had a kind of a fringe on it and I'd do a couple of grinds and—"

"I hate to break this up," I said, almost sincerely. Polnik looked at me, blinked a couple of times, then got onto his feet hastily. "Lieutenant?"

"I'm going," I said. "You'd better get a permanent stake-out set up here and wait till it arrives."

"Yes, sir, Lieutenant!" he said enthusiastically. "You going down to the Sheriff's office now?"

"I don't think so," I said.

"But what do I say if the Captain rings?" He sounded worried.

"Tell him ... maybe not."

I looked at the fish tanks. I'd had a feeling something was different from the moment I came back into the living room. I realized what it was—the tropical fish weren't swimming any more.

"What happened to the fish?" I asked.

Toni giggled loudly. "I put 'em to sleep," she said, and gestured toward the empty gin bottle standing on the bar. "They made me dizzy, whizzing around like that!" Her eyes were suddenly cold. "Fargo was crazy about them!" she added bleakly.

CHAPTER TEN

It was ten-thirty when I parked outside the Starlight Hotel. I went up to Janice Jorgens' suite and knocked on the door. She took a while to open it. When she did, she wasn't pleased to see me.

"Don't you ever give up!" she said in an exasperated voice. "What do I have to do—get myself police protection?"

"You've been holding out on me," I said reproachfully, "haven't you ... Mandy?"

She pulled the robe tighter around herself, her eyes suddenly dull. "I don't know what you're talking about," she said.

"Let me in and I'll explain," I said, not very brilliantly.

She turned away from the door and walked back inside the suite. I followed her. She stopped beside the desk and turned to face me.

"This must be your off-beat technique," she said. "You don't amuse me any more, Lieutenant."

I took out the newspaper clips and showed her the two photos. She looked at them for about fifteen seconds, then lifted her head slowly.

"Mandy Morgan—Janice Jorgens," I said. "The names are different, but not that different."

She turned away and walked over to the window, pushing it open wide as if, suddenly, there wasn't enough air in the room. She stood with her back to me, without saying anything.

"When did you change your name?" I said. "Right after your sister died?"

"I don't know what you're talking about," she said faintly.

"I can recognize you as Mandy Morgan from a lousy newspaper photograph, three years old," I said wearily.

"If you want to play dumb on it, all right. It won't be hard for us to find somebody in Louisville who will identify you, somebody like your old man, for instance."

"He's dead," she said in a sullen voice, "he died two years back. Hit and run; he was drunk of course."

"That's better," I said. "You are Mandy Morgan?"

"Yes," she turned away from the window and walked back toward the desk, "I'm Mandy Morgan."

"Why bother to change your name?"

"I was sick of everything," she said. "Sick of living in Louisville, sick of the old man being drunk all the time ... and then Geraldine was murdered! I wanted to make a new start; I didn't want anything that belonged to the past, not even my name. So I went to New York and became Janice Jorgens."

I sat down in the nearest chair and touched my forehead gingerly; it was still faintly sticky around the hairline.

"Tell me some more about it," I said.

She sat down behind the desk and lit a cigarette. "What is there to tell?"

"I'd like to hear it, even if it isn't exciting."

Her fingers touched the typewriter keys idly for a moment.

"I'd taken a secretarial course, and I had a job in an advertising agency for a time. They were the people who finally found a sponsor for Paula's program. I got to see quite a bit of her, one way and another. She was always in the office, or phoning in. When the series was definitely set, she offered me the job as her secretary. The money was better, it would be more interesting—I took it."

I looked at the clippings again. "Just how did a Los Angeles newspaper come to quote Geraldine's letters to you?"

"One of the police officers connected with the case came to Louisville and talked to me about it. I showed him the letters and he took them away with him. He must have told the paper, I suppose."

"You remember his name?"

She thought for a moment: "He was a Lieutenant, a nice man ... Monro, I think."

"He told you how your sister died?" I asked gently.

"He told me how she was murdered," she said flatly. "He told me about Lee Manning and his week-end parties at Laguna Beach. That was another reason for changing my name. It made me feel dirty, every time I thought about it."

"It caught up with Manning," I said. "He suicided a couple of weeks after your sister died."

"I know."

"But it didn't catch up with Georgia Brown."

"What do you mean?"

I got up and walked over to the desk. I stubbed the cigarette in the silver ash tray and looked down at her. "You know what Georgia Brown was, don't you?" I asked.

"She was a star," Janice said, without looking at me. "Everybody knows that."

"But everybody doesn't know the connection between Lee Manning and your sister. And everybody doesn't know just exactly what Georgia Brown was. She was worse than Manning in a lot of ways. She dealt cold-bloodedly in girls, girls like your sister, not even for cash —just for kicks. Monro knew it and if he told you about Manning, he told you about Georgia."

"You don't make any sense to me, Lieutenant," she said stiffly.

I would have liked a drink. "I was talking to Monro this morning," I said. "All I have to do now is to phone him. He'd remember whether he told you about Georgia Brown or not."

"All right!" she said tautly. "So he did tell me about Georgia Brown! What difference does that make?"

"There's a cop's handbook somewhere," I said, "and it gives certain fundamental rules. Things like looking for motive and opportunity in crime. Paula told me those names that Georgia Brown had mentioned to her, and that gave four people a strong motive for killing Georgia. So I started chasing around, because I had four hot suspects with a strong motive. I didn't think about opportunity."

"If you must give a lecture, do you have to pick me as an audience?" she asked tiredly.

"Right now I do," I said. "But it won't take very long. If I'd thought about opportunity earlier I could have saved myself a lot of trouble. I should have remembered that both you and Paula told me you were the only two who knew where Georgia Brown was."

"Are you trying to prove something?"

"I think I am proving it," I said. "I should have thought then that both of you had the opportunity to murder Georgia Brown. So next comes motive. What motive would Paula have? She was relying on Georgia's appearance on her show to boost her rating—the last thing Paula would want would be her non-appearance.

"But *you* had all the motive anybody could want. Georgia had been indirectly—or even directly—responsible for your sister's death."

Janice lit herself another cigarette: "You're out of your mind, Lieutenant!"

"You don't like men," I said. "You've got good reason not to like them, remembering what happened to your sister. You have a mechanical knack—I remember you mentioned my car needed tuning. The murderer had to be somebody Georgia trusted. Somebody she would let into that apartment without a question. Somebody who could stay there long enough to hook that homemade bomb into the buzzer circuit. I should have realized she would never have let any of those other four people inside the apartment for a second."

She pushed the chair back and got onto her feet and walked over to the window again. "It's a very interesting theory, Lieutenant, but you can't prove any of it."

"Not right now," I said, "but I will. Even if you made that bomb out of old tin cans, you still had to buy the explosive for it. Georgia first approached Paula in San Francisco, then you came here. You had to buy the explosive either in 'Frisco or Pine City. There aren't that many places you could buy it; we'll find out where you bought it. Add that to the motive and opportunity we can already prove and the State's got a good case."

The door opened suddenly and Paula Reid walked in. She wore a powder-blue negligee and her eyes were surprised when she saw me.

"I'm sorry," she said. "I didn't know you were here, Lieutenant. I hope I'm not intruding."

"Come right in," I said unnecessarily. "While you're here, I'd like to check a couple of points with you. How many people knew where Georgia Brown's hide-out was, did you say?"

"Just the two of us," she said, "Janice and myself, as far as I know, Lieutenant. Though obviously the murderer must have found out. How, I don't know."

She looked at me uncertainly, then across at Janice. "Is everything all right?"

"Just fine," Janice said. She smiled at me, tiredly. "I congratulate you on your technique, Lieutenant! You had me fooled. The only thing I thought you were really interested in was women."

"Fundamentally you're right," I agreed.

"Lieutenant Monro did tell me about Georgia Brown," she said. "After Manning killed himself I read about her sudden disappearance and I read all the stories in the magazines. Then it became stale news and I'd almost forgotten about her. But I could never forget Geraldine."

"Geraldine?" Paula said blankly. "Who was Geraldine?"

"Janice's sister," I said. "She died at Manning's Laguna Beach house a couple of weeks before he threw himself over that cliff ... it's a long story."

"Oh?" Paula said, even more blankly.

Janice ignored her. "Then Paula told me about Georgia approaching her and saying she wanted to tell the truth about what happened at the time of Manning's death. Paula explained to me Georgia had said she was innocent, and I knew then that she wasn't going to tell the truth. How could she, and reveal herself for what she was? She only wanted to get onto the program to smear other people!"

"So you killed her?"

"Not for that, for what she did to Geraldine, for what she must have done to a lot of other girls.... It was quite easy, really. I bought the explosive and packed it tight into a small canister and wired it up. The morning we arrived here, I called on Georgia. She knew I was Paula's secretary so she opened the door to me, then went back to her bath ..."

"That was when you hooked the bomb into the buzzer circuit?"

She nodded. "It only took a couple of minutes. Georgia was still in the bath when I left."

"Then you rang Lavers and asked for some protection for Georgia and Paula?"

"That's right," she said calmly. "I thought it would help divert any suspicion."

"So when you gave me the address, you knew that when I went out there and pressed that buzzer I was going to blow Georgia Brown into little pieces?"

"The thought did occur to me, Lieutenant."

"You!" Paula croaked suddenly. "You killed her!"

"I would have thought it was obvious by now, even to you!" Janice said coldly.

"I ... I can't believe it!" Paula said. She took one tottering step forward then fell suddenly to the floor.

Janice looked at her contemptuously: "She's a natural scene-stealer," she said. "Whatever the act, she's got to get into it."

"You'd better get dressed," I said. "I'll wait here."

"I don't think I'll bother," she said. "Good-bye, Lieutenant. I can't say it's been nice knowing you."

She stepped up onto the window-sill and then stepped straight out through the open window into space.

I reached the window in time to see her hit the awning over the hotel front. She hit and bounced off, then landed on the sidewalk. The screams of a couple of women close by reached me faintly. I walked back to the desk and made the necessary phone calls.

By the time I'd finished, Paula Reid had recovered from her faint. I helped her into a chair and she smiled wanly at me.

"It was the shock of hearing Janice admit she murdered Georgia," she said. "It was silly of me to faint, but..."

"Don't worry about it," I said. "I'll get us a drink, we both need one."

I moved over to the cupboard and got out a couple of glasses.

"Lieutenant ... where is she?"

"She went out the window," I said, pouring four fingers of Scotch into each glass.

"You mean she ... jumped?"

"Walked, actually. But the result was the same."

"How dreadful!" she breathed. "She's been with me ever since the show started, Lieutenant. I ... I still can't believe ... Oh!"

I turned and looked at her inquiringly.

"I'd almost forgotten," she said. "She gave me something yesterday, she asked me to keep it for her ... I suppose I should hand it over to you now?"

"What was it?"

"I don't know. I mean, it was a sealed envelope and she said it was valuable and she was frightened of losing it, so I offered to put it in my strongbox."

"I'd better have it," I said.

"I'll get it." She got up from her chair and went out the door.

I drank the four fingers of Scotch neat, then refilled the glass. I'd added ice to both drinks by the time she came back and handed me a heavily sealed envelope.

She took the drink from me gratefully and sank down into the chair again. "I still can't believe it," she muttered, "Janice!"

I ripped the seal open and shook the contents of the envelope into the palm of my hand. It was a negative, about an inch by an inch and a half in size. I held it up to the light and looked at it. There were three figures carrying something, but that was all I could make out; the negative was too small to see any more detail. I replaced it in the envelope and put it in my pocket.

I looked up and saw the curiosity quivering in Paula's eyes. "Something interesting, Lieutenant?" she asked in what was meant to be a casual voice.

"I don't know yet," I said. "But I'll find out."

CHAPTER ELEVEN

I walked into the Bureau at eleven forty-five. I bumped into Polnik on his way out, just inside the door.

"Lieutenant!" he said hoarsely. "Where you been?"

"Out," I said. "Did something happen?"

"They waited for you in Lavers' office till eleven," he said. "Then they came back here. They're in Parker's office now. They're about ready to put out a general alarm for you!"

"Maybe I'd better say hello, then," I said.

He shuddered: "I think you're going to need to say more than that, Lieutenant; a whole lot more!"

I went into the lab and found Kaplan there. He grinned at me over the top of his steel-rimmed glasses.

"The guy who makes with the bangs!" he said. "I hear Murphy did his quickest autopsy ever! He only had half a torso and a pair of legs to work with!"

"Why don't you try for a job with Art Linkletter?" I asked him. "You could tell bedtime stories to the kids."

I gave him the negative. "Do me a favor, Kap. Make a blow-up of this right away for me, and bring it up to Parker's office as soon as it's through—don't worry much about it being wet."

"O.K.," he said. "I'll make a deal—you lend me that Austin Healey of yours one night next week, and I'll do it. I got me a new broad and she's crazy for hot-rods. Maybe she's crazy for guys who take her out in hot-rods?"

"Maybe she's just crazy." I suggested. "O.K., it's a deal, you blackmailer, but make it fast, will you?"

"Coming right up!" he said.

I went out of the lab and along to Parker's office. I opened the door and put my head inside. "Surprise!" I said brightly. "Where is your wandering boy tonight? Fear no more, for I am here. Bring out the fatted calf and—"

"Come inside and close that door, Wheeler!" Lavers said thickly. "I wouldn't want any junior officers to hear this!"

I stepped into the office and closed the door behind me gently. Parker looked through me stonily. Lavers, massacred a good cigar into shreds between his teeth.

"You," he said finally, "are finished! This is the last time, Wheeler, that you ever—"

"Would you like me to dictate Janice Jorgens' confession now, Sheriff?" I asked him finally. "Or will I wait till you've finished whatever it is you're going to say?"

His mouth worked for a few moments: "Janice Jorgens' con— What the hell are you talking about!"

"She made a complete confession, before she jumped out of her hotel window," I said. "I thought you knew?"

"How would I—" He made a gigantic effort. "All right, Wheeler, let's hear it!"

"She made a confession to you, then killed herself?" Parker asked coldly.

"That's right," I agreed.

"Just you? Nobody else heard it?" The sneer was in his voice if not his face.

"Paula Reid was there, too," I said. "She heard it—or enough of it to testify."

"Uh," he sounded almost disappointed.

Lavers clapped a hand to his face and squeezed the jowls cruelly. "All right," he said finally, "tell me!"

I told him the story as it had happened. I took the clips out of my pocket and both he and Parker stared at them, disbelievingly. I lit a cigarette when I'd finished.

Lavers and Parker looked at each other for a long moment, then they both scowled at me.

"It still leaves a hell of a lot unexplained," Lavers grunted. "Why did Fargo kill Coates, and then threaten to kill the Steinway girl?"

"Not forgetting of course," Parker added gently, "that if Wheeler had handled things properly, Coates probably wouldn't have been killed and we would have picked up Fargo before he got inside the Steinway girl's house!"

"I'm not forgetting those things for one moment," Lavers growled, "and neither is Inspector Martin."

"Have you picked up Fargo yet?" I asked.

"No," Parker said morosely. "And it's not going to be easy, either. He knows too many people in this town. There'd be dozens of them glad to give him a hide-out."

There was a knock on the door and Kaplan walked in.

"Here it is, Al," he said and put a dripping wet eight-by-six print on Parker's desk in front of me. "O.K.?"

"Thanks, Kap," I said.

"Think nothing of it," he said. "Just have the heap tuned before I take it out, will you?" He went out of the office, closing the door behind him.

I looked closely at the print.

"What's that?" Lavers asked.

"Janice Jorgens gave Paula Reid a sealed envelope yesterday," I said, "and asked her to mind it for her, so Paula gave it to me. There was a negative inside—this is the print from it."

They crowded in on either side of me to look at it. It wasn't a very good picture, but it was good enough. It showed three people holding a body. Coates and Hilary Blain had an arm each while Kent Fargo held the legs.

"What does it mean?" Lavers said. "Some sort of horseplay?"

"Some sort of murder, Sheriff," I said. "You recognize the guy they're holding? That's Lee Manning."

"Manning?" he peered closer at the print. "So it is—Manning!"

"I recognize the spot where this shot was taken," I said. "It's the top of the cliff above Manning's Laguna Beach house."

"But that's where he ..." Parker stopped abruptly.

"You're so right, Captain," I agreed. "We've got a new switch. He didn't jump, he wasn't pushed, he was thrown."

Lavers straightened his back painfully. "That means the three of them are equally guilty of Manning's murder."

"That was the thing that worried me," I said. "It was so convenient, Manning's suicide I mean. With Geraldine Morgan's death, the lid was ready to blow right off. The scandal would have ruined all of them—Manning himself and, along with him, Fargo, Blain, Coates and Georgia Brown. But then Manning generously tossed himself over a cliff so they could all live happily ever after."

"I'd like to know who took this picture," Lavers said slowly.

"Georgia herself," I said. "Who else? How would Janice Jorgens have gotten hold of it otherwise? She must have found it in that apartment when she took her bomb and went calling. This photo is what Fargo was looking for, and the reason why he killed Coates."

"Why would he think Coates had it?"

"Somebody must have told him so. Janice Jorgens could have called him and said Coates had the negative. But she obviously wouldn't say who she was—" It hit me suddenly. "She must have said she was Kay Steinway. Coates was producing her films now. Fargo would know that there was a tie-up between them."

"Why would Janice Jorgens say she was Kay Steinway?" Parker asked skeptically.

"Kay and Paula Reid had a fight at her place the other night," I said. "I don't think Janice liked Kay. It might be her way of hitting Kay. After Fargo killed Coates and couldn't find the negative, he thought he'd been double-crossed by Kay, so he phoned her. I was there when she got the call. The first thing Fargo said when he came into the room was that she'd set up the whole lousy deal with that phone call."

"Fargo is a little, shall we say, headstrong?" Parker said gently.

"We all know what Fargo is," I said. "And he always had a soft spot for Georgia Brown. He'd figured whoever had that negative had killed Georgia to get it. He killed Coates and found it wasn't him; so then he thought it must be Kay Steinway, because he believed Kay had given him the false lead to Coates."

"Makes sense," Lavers admitted gruffly.

"That Janice," I said. "What a cozy little character she was!" I smiled politely at Parker. "I hope you don't feel quite so bad about Coates's death now, Captain? After all, it only saved the State an expense."

Parker glared at me: "I'm beginning to realize why Hammond feels the way he does about you!" he said slowly.

Lavers' lips twitched for a moment. "We still aren't finished with this, anyway. Blain's got to be brought in and booked for Manning's murder." He tapped the print with his knuckle, "We've got all the proof we need right here."

"I'd like to ask a favor, sir," I said. "Could I take Polnik with me and bring him in?"

"Don't worry, Al," Parker said. "You'll get your picture in the papers, anyway."

"All right, Wheeler," the Sheriff said. "But if you lose him on the way, I'll ..."

"Thank you, sir," I said. "You don't mind if I take this with me?" I lifted the photo from the desk. "The lab is holding the negative, so it doesn't much matter what happens to a print."

"Don't take too long about it," Lavers glanced at his watch. "We've still got time to make the morning papers, but I want Blain safely on his way back here before I give the story to the reporters."

"I'll hurry," I said.

I went out of the office and found Polnik. "Big deal," I told him. "You're coming with me."

He blinked. "Are you still a lieutenant, Lieutenant?"

"I was the last time I looked," I said. "There are times, Polnik, when I feel you don't have faith in me."

"It's not that, Lieutenant," he said earnestly. "It's just that I get a feeling sometimes that it's too good to last. One day you'll just disappear," he snapped his fingers, "like that! and take all those beautiful dames with you!"

"So long as I don't leave them behind," I said. "You had me worried for a moment there."

We drove out to Blain's home in a prowl car. It was one-thirty when we reached the house and parked on the driveway. Polnik came with me up the front steps.

"What do we do now, Lieutenant?" He looked at the house hopefully. "Some dame lives here, huh? Some society dame with nothing to do all day, and all night to brood about it, huh, Lieutenant?"

"You know something, Sergeant," I said as I pressed the bell, "when you get home, I think your old lady's going to be surprised."

I kept on pressing and finally a light came on in the hallway. A few seconds after that the door opened and the butler stood there, blinking at me. He was wearing a faded green flannel dressing gown; the moths had dined from the edges.

I looked at it slowly. "An interesting relic," I said. "Your grandfather's perhaps?"

He took a deep breath, then exhaled slowly. "Mr. Blain has retired for the night ... sir. Hours ago!"

"Then tell him we're putting him back into active service," I said. "We'll wait in the library."

"The library yet!" Polnik said in a hushed voice.

The butler gave up. He moved to one side to let us pass, then closed the front door. I watched him plod slowly up the stairs, then I led the way into the library, switching on the lights when we got there.

I lit a cigarette and sat in a chair while Polnik looked around.

"Lieutenant," he said, "what do people buy books for?"

"To read, I guess."

"Don't they have television?"

"I'll ask him," I said.

He shook his head wonderingly. "I'd like to be rich, I wouldn't waste my dough on junk like this."

"You wouldn't?"

"No, sir!" He sucked his teeth for a moment. "Those pants that Toni was wearing—they was genuine 9-karat gold, huh?"

"Fourteen," I said.

"Yeah," he nodded slowly. "And this guy buys books with his dough!"

The door opened and Blain walked in. He was fully dressed, and he didn't look happy.

"Really, Lieutenant!" he said coldly. "I hope you can justify this intrusion into my household at this time of night!"

"I think so," I said. "I won't take much of your time, Mr. Blain. I just wondered if you could identify any of the people in this photograph?"

I put the print down on his desk and he came over and peered at it. He straightened up slowly, took off his glasses and began to polish them vigorously.

"You'll have to come with us, Mr. Blain," I said.

"On what charge?"

"Murder."

"I demand to see my lawyer!"

"You can call him to meet you down at the Bureau, if you want," I said.

His fingers shook as he replaced the glasses on the bridge on his nose. His hand reached out toward the phone, wavered for a moment, then dropped to his side.

"It was Fargo's idea," he whispered. "He talked us into it, he made us do it!"

"Why don't you tell me about it?" I said. "Coates is dead, Georgia Brown is dead, and Fargo is on the run, wanted for another murder. There's really only you left, Mr. Blain. You could make it easier for yourself."

He walked around his desk stiffly and lowered himself into the chair behind it. "I'd like a drink," he said.

"Sergeant," I said to Polnik, "pour Mr. Blain a drink." I corrected myself hastily. "Pour all of us a drink."

"Sure thing, Lieutenant!" Polnik followed his nose to the liquor cabinet.

Blain sat staring dully at the desk top in front of him.

"Manning invited the four of us down to his place for the week end," he said in a low voice. "I went because I had nothing else to do and I was worried like the rest of them. The death of that young girl was going to cause a scandal that would ruin all of us."

"I know all about the girl and the scandal," I said. "It's the murder I want to hear about." I leaned over and tapped the photo with my index finger to emphasize the point.

"That was the Saturday night," he said. "We were just sitting around, drinking, without saying much. There didn't seem to be anything to say. We knew the coroner's court would be held the following Wednesday, and that would be the end of everything."

Polnik put a drink down in front of Blain and then handed me one. I noted the level in his own glass was an inch higher than in either of the other two. Blain drank some of the Scotch, then put the glass back onto the desk.

"Lee went over to the bar and Fargo poured him a drink," he went on. "They talked for a time while Manning finished his drink, then he suddenly collapsed to the floor. Fargo told us he had drugged the drink and Manning would be unconscious for at least another three hours. Then he made his proposition."

"To murder Manning?"

"He said it was our only hope. With Manning out of the way, there would be a chance we could kill the story about the young girl's death. Fargo argued that there would be nobody left to blame if Manning were dead and the story would be hushed up for the sake of the girl and her family. It made sense."

"So you all agreed to help murder Manning?"

He winced. "Not all of us, Lieutenant. Georgia was enthusiastic immediately, but Coates and I weren't. Yet there seemed no other way out."

"Why did so many of you have to get into the act?"

"That was Fargo's idea," he said. "Fargo maintained we all had an equal stake and if we shared the guilt it would stop any one of us ever telling the police how Manning had really died."

"Symbolic act—or something?"

Blain nodded. "Something like that. Finally Coates and I agreed, so that was what happened."

"And Georgia Brown?"

"She was Fargo's strangest supporter, as I said before, Lieutenant. But she sprained her ankle getting out of the car. It was very convincing," he laughed mirthlessly, "she certainly fooled both Coates and myself. She lay on the grass, apparently sobbing with pain, while the three of us men carried Manning to the edge and threw him over."

"So it was Georgia Brown who took the picture?" I said. "Didn't the flash tell you what was happening?"

"She didn't use flashlight photography," he said. "She used another process—infrared, I believe they call it."

"You mean she just happened to have that sort of equipment with her?"

Blain finished his drink and looked up. "If you don't mind, I'd like another drink?"

"Polnik," I said, and held out my own empty glass just in case he overlooked it.

"You aren't making sense," I said to Blain. "You told me that Fargo suddenly sprung this idea on you out of the blue, and—at the most an hour later—you took Manning up to the cliff and threw him over. Yet in that time Georgia suddenly acquired a camera with infrared plates!"

He shook his head tiredly. "We only found out about the camera later, Lieutenant. That was when the blackmail started."

I grabbed the new drink out of Polnik's hand. "I really needed this," I told him.

"You see," Blain laughed, this time with almost genuine humor, "it was what you would call a put-up job, Lieutenant. Fargo and Georgia planned it between them. She had the camera already hidden in the car. Fargo had to actually help us throw Manning over, to stop us becoming suspicious of him. But why should we have been suspicious of Georgia's ankle?"

"So afterwards they blackmailed you—and Coates?"

"For three years we have been paying," he agreed. "I have been bled white over that period!"

"Then why did Georgia disappear immediately after the coroner's court?"

"She couldn't have been honest with anyone," Blain said. "It wasn't in her. She cheated on Fargo. She held the negative and she ran out on him, still holding it. Don't you see, Lieutenant? Fargo was in that picture himself. She forced him to collect the blackmail money for her, and more than that, to pay up as well!"

Polnik had a look of open admiration on his face "What a setup!" he said. "You have to hand it to that Georgia Brown dame!"

"Even if she did get herself blown to bits," I agreed.

Blain finished his second drink and got onto his feet. "I don't think there's anything else, Lieutenant. I'm ready to go now."

We went out of the library and down the hallway to the front door. The butler opened it for us and I let the other two go first. I stood and watched while Polnik put Blain in the back seat of the car and got in beside him. There was a gentle cough from behind me.

"Excuse me, sir," the butler said, "but when can I expect the master to return?"

"Not in your lifetime," I said truthfully and walked out to the car.

Polnik took care of the formalities when we got back to the Bureau. Lavers was still in Parker's office when I went in. He was looking almost happy. I told him Blain's story about the Manning murder.

He grunted when I'd finished. "I had Miss Reid down here," he said. "She just left. She made a statement which corroborates your story about Janice Jorgens' confession to Georgia Brown's murder. It's all wrapped up now. You can come down sometime tomorrow morning and dictate a formal statement. All we have to do now is find Fargo and everybody will be happy, including me."

"Yes, sir," I said. "You mind if I leave now? It's been a long day and a long night and now it's starting to be a long day again."

"Twenty-four hours' work and it kills you!" he said contemptuously.

"One thing about being a Sheriff," I said. "You don't ever have to ride herd with the posse."

"Get out of here before I challenge you to a draw, partner!" Lavers said jovially.

"You feeling all right, Sheriff?" I asked him anxiously. "You just made a joke."

I reached the door and stopped.

"Go on, Wheeler!" Lavers said irritably. "You made your exit line!"

"There's just one thing I don't get," I said. "Georgia Brown had a perfect blackmail setup—it was making her a fortune. Yet she came to Paula Reid and volunteered to appear on her show and tell the truth about Manning's death. Why would she want to throw away everything like that?"

"Maybe she was crazy!" Lavers snarled. "Who cares why she did it! The case is finished, Wheeler. You *do* need a rest!"

I went out to the Austin Healey and drove back home to my apartment. I saw the dawn break but the dull thud inside my head was migraine.

I wearily turned the key in the lock, pushed open the door and walked inside the apartment. The lights were on in the living room. I tripped over a suitcase which wasn't mine and fell headlong.

Then I lifted my head slowly and surveyed the half dozen other suitcases littering the floor, which also weren't mine. Then I climbed back onto my feet and saw the mink spread across the couch.

I felt my jaw sag as I watched the silver-blonde's head rise slowly above the mink.

"You're late!" she said coldly.

I glared at her.

"The janitor let me in," she said defensively. "He said what difference did one more make."

"What in hell did you come here for?"

"I was frightened of the reporters," she said. "And I was frightened that Kent might be mad at me. I couldn't think of any other place that would be safe."

"What makes you think you're safe with me? That's an insult to my reputation."

"I don't mean that sort of safe," she said casually, "I mean real safe."

The migraine neatly sliced off the top of my head, filled it with red-hot rivets and replaced it with a sharp slap.

"Never mind," I croaked. "Can you cook?"

Her eyes widened with disbelief. "You mean food and stuff like that?"

"Can you make coffee?" I pleaded.

"I could mix you a martini," she said brightly.

I shuddered. "I've tasted your martinis. Try the coffee, it's not really hard."

"If you say so."

She got up onto her feet and took off the mink. Underneath she was still wearing the turquoise sweater and gold bikini pants. She was the answer to a stockbroker's prayer and she came gilt-edged. All I hoped was she made a success of the coffee.

I went into the bedroom and collected a robe and a pair of pajamas. Then I went into the bathroom and stripped off my clothes and stood under the hot shower for about ten minutes. Cold needle-sprays are for men with those sharp, pointed heads. I toweled myself dry, put on the pajamas and the robe, and went out into the living room again.

Toni had the coffee made and on the table. I lifted the cup and sipped it cautiously. "That's not bad," I admitted grudgingly.

"If I could stay here just for the night," she said. "I'm booked on a plane to Vegas in the morning—nine-thirty. I wouldn't be any trouble."

"O. K.," I said, "but I sleep in the bed!"

Her perpetually surprised eyebrows looked even more so.

"Sure," she said. "I'm a reasonable girl, Lieutenant. I didn't expect you to sleep on the floor."

Maybe it was the coffee, but right then the migraine vanished.

CHAPTER TWELVE

"Honey," I said drowsily, "we must have something—I can hear bells ringing."

Then another layer of sleep peeled away and I realized it was the phone I was hearing. I got out of bed, staggered into the living room and picked up the receiver.

"Lady," I said, "we got three hundred acres and seventy thousand permanent residents at Peaceful Pastures. If we put your husband in the wrong plot, I'm sorry. You want we should dig him up again?"

There was a silvery tinkle of laughter in my ear. "Lieutenant," a soft, feminine voice said, "you're awful!"

"I feel it, I look it, I admit it," I said. "Who is this?"

"I hoped you'd recognize my voice." She sounded vaguely disappointed. "This is Paula Reid speaking. I wonder if I could see you today. It's really very important."

"I guess so," I said. "I have to make a statement down at the Bureau this morning. How about this afternoon?"

"That would be wonderful," she said enthusiastically. "This place is chaos at the moment—could we make it somewhere else?"

"Why not my apartment," I said, and thought that would stop her kidding around.

"That sounds fine," she said brightly. "What time would suit you, Lieutenant?"

"Around four?"

"I'll see you then," she said softly into my once shell-like pink ear. "Bye now." There was the faintest click as she hung up.

"I have something she wants?" I asked myself out loud, feeling the stubble around my chin. I dropped the receiver back onto the rest and headed toward the bedroom.

I guess I should have looked where I was going. The next moment I was flat on my face. I picked myself up painfully and counted them; there were seven suitcases scattered over the floor just the way they had been the previous night.

The bathroom door creaked slightly and then Toni walked into the room. She wore what everybody is wearing this year in the Turkish baths—a towel. It was a short towel and she was a tall girl.

"Hi!" she gave me a dazzling smile.

"That thing you hear spinning is my mind, not a roulette wheel," I said coldly. I glanced at my watch, which read eleven o'clock. "I thought you were supposed to be in Las Vegas by now."

"I missed my plane," she said. "But there's another one. I made some coffee—it's in the kitchen."

"I have an appointment here at four this afternoon," I said.

"My!" her eyebrows tweaked. "We are a busy man, aren't we!"

"Do something for me," I said. "Get a plane before then, will you?"

"Of course I will," she said. "You don't think I want to stay here, do you?"

"I'd say no if I were sure you were sane," I said doubtfully.

"Are you going to take a shower?" she asked.

"I always take a shower," I said, wounded.

"Right now, I mean?"

"Yeah."

"You might as well take this with you then," she said casually.

She unwrapped the towel and tossed it to me, "Catch!"

I caught it and just stood there for a moment. She had the smallest waist I'd ever seen on a girl. Or maybe that was only by comparison. Maybe I should say she had the biggest ... I closed my eyes. "I think I should have some coffee first," I said weakly and went into the kitchen.

Half an hour later I was on my way out of the apartment. Toni was playing "Frankie" on the hi-fi. She wore a white linen skirt with a blood-red silk shirt above it. I stopped at the door and looked back at her.

"Were you ever in New Orleans?"

She shook her head slowly. "No, why?"

"I just wondered. Naming that streetcar was coincidence then?"

Her marble forehead puckered. "You know, Al, an awful lot of times you just don't make sense!"

"Agreed," I said. "You have any bright ideas where Fargo might be holed out?"

"Poor Kent!" she said. "He must be a worried man. Fargo Enterprises won't be the same without him. He's a very keen executive, you know."

"It was my own fault," I said, "I asked. Don't be here at four o'clock."

"Al?"

"What now?"

"Is this what they call a lovers' farewell?"

"Not exactly," I said. "That has roses around it."

I went down to the Bureau and dictated a statement about Janice Jorgens—Mandy Morgan. I waited for it to be typed, then signed it. I heard that Fargo was still loose. I left the Bureau around noon and drove over to the County Sheriff's office.

Annabelle Jackson lifted her head and looked at me over the top of her typewriter. "Well," she said to nobody in particular, "look who's here. The bleary-eyed bloodhound. Come to pick up your bone, Lieutenant, or wag your tail while the Sheriff pats your head?"

"I just walked in," I said to nobody in particular, "I didn't say nothin'."

"Having himself such a time," she said. "What with television stars and Hollywood stars and gangsters' girl friends in solid gold bikinis."

"How come you can sit upright with your ear so close to the ground?" I asked breathlessly.

"The Sheriff is in his office, Lieutenant," she said coldly. "And if you trip and break your neck on the way in, I promise not to scream—just laugh."

"Maybe they put the mint into vases and the magnolia blossoms into glasses this year," I said as I walked past her desk, "that's why the juleps are tasting so sour?"

I knocked on Lavers' door, opened it and walked into his office.

"Glad you dropped in, Wheeler," he said. "Sit down, have a cigar."

"This sounds awful close to the kiss of death," I said suspiciously as I sat down. "You know I never smoke cigars."

"You think I'd offer you one if you did?" he said.

I felt a little easier—this was the Lavers I knew.

"Have you read the morning paper?" he asked.

"I haven't been out of bed long enough," I said.

"The whole thing went very well, very well indeed," he said complacently. "The credit shared nice and evenly between this office and Homicide."

"Congratulations, Sheriff," I said politely.

"There is a mention of Lieutenant Wheeler, temporarily attached to the Sheriff's office, having helped in the investigation," he said. "At least, there was in the first edition...."

"I'm glad they took it out," I said. "I get any more press clips I'll have to rent another apartment to live in. There just isn't room for both of us."

"When they pick up Fargo, it'll be all over," he said. "Maybe he's in Florida by now."

"Maybe," I said. "Can I go back to Homicide? I like the life there, they have nice complicated cases like a wife stabs her husband then phones in and tells you where to collect both of them."

"I used my influence on your behalf," Lavers said benignly. "You have a free week end. You don't report back to this office until Monday."

"Thanks," I said, stunned.

"Anyway," he sort of leered at me, "I guess you'll need some time between now and tomorrow night to practice."

"Practice?" I repeated blankly.

"Maybe not," he said, "there's quite a lot of ham in you already."

"If it's not a rude question," I said, "what are you talking about?"

"You mean you don't know?"

"I'm trying hard to understand," I said, "but I only speak English."

He slumped back into his chair and began to laugh. Then he guffawed, he couldn't stop. He thumped his fist down on the desktop and the calendar was suddenly airborne.

"I won't spoil it for you!" he stuttered helplessly. "I wouldn't dream of spoiling it for you, Wheeler! Have a nice, quiet week end."

"The only thing that appeals to me about this is you'll probably have a coronary any second now," I said stiffly. I got up from the chair and walked out of his office, the sound of his laughter following me all the way.

I stopped beside Annabelle Jackson's desk on my way out.

"Did you say something funny in there, Lieutenant?" she asked coldly. "Or maybe he just looked at you?"

"What have I done to deserve this treatment?" I asked helplessly. "Did I set fire to you and not remember?"

"You don't have to stop and talk to me, Lieutenant," she said. "I'm not a fan!" Her typewriter rattled furiously. I shrugged my shoulders resignedly and walked out.

I bought myself a lunch I couldn't afford and reflected that today was Friday and I was free all the way through to Monday.

I got back to the apartment just after three. I let myself in cautiously and sighed happily when I saw there wasn't one suitcase on the living-room floor. I checked each room just to make sure, but I didn't find a silver-blonde in any one of them.

It was my first date with a blues girl—even if she was only coming to ask my advice about getting a new secretary cheap—so I thought I should make some preparations.

I cleaned up the place, put a selection of records at the ready on the machine, chipped some ice and polished some glasses—well two, anyway.

The buzzer went at four o'clock precisely and the Wheeler apartment went to battle stations with the ease of long-practiced routine.

I opened the door and she smiled warmly at me. "Hello, Lieutenant, it was nice of you to ask me over here."

"Come on in," I said, and held the door open wide. She walked past me into the living room. I closed the front door and followed her.

"I like your apartment," she said, "it has an intimate atmosphere."

"That's the aim," I said modestly.

"Do you mind if I call you Al?" she said. "I feel we know each other much too well to persist with the formalities, don't you?"

"I certainly do, Paula," I agreed. "Won't you sit down?" I maneuvered her so she had no choice but the nearest couch.

"Thank you," she said, sat down and crossed her legs.

I looked at them with respect. She wore a sapphire-colored dress in crinkled silk chiffon which swirled around her shoulders, then plunged recklessly in a gouge-neckline.

"I'll get us a drink," I said. "Your usual?"

"How do you know my usual drink?"

"It has to be gin and tonic," I said, "the color harmonizes."

"I take that as a compliment, Al," she said slowly.

I poured the drinks while she got up and had a look at the hi-fi setup. By the time I got back with the drinks, she was back on the couch again.

"You like music?" she asked.

"Sure," I said. "Would you like some now?"

"I'd love some," she said.

I went over to the window and pulled down the shade.

"All that sunlight," I explained, "it's bad for the eyes."

I crossed to the machine and flicked the switch.

"Music for you, Paula," I said.

"My usual music?" she queried.

"Of course," I said, "what else but the blues?"

I sat down beside her on the couch. I was glad she was wearing crinkled chiffon because it wouldn't look any different when she stood up again.

Tommy Ladnier high-stepped his cornet into "Traveling Blues," and the five speakers put the notes all ways at the one time, which is the way it should be.

"Al," Paula said earnestly, "I came to ask you a favor, a very great favor."

I looked at her and took a deep breath. "I'm sure we can make a deal, honey," I said.

"You know my show for tomorrow night was ruined when Georgia Brown was murdered?"

"Sure," I said sympathetically.

"Well, Kay Steinway agreed to come on the show as my main guest. Much as I dislike her she's really news now since Fargo tried to kill her. But I feel it isn't quite enough. I need somebody else to really tie the story into shape."

I thought for a few seconds then gave up. "I'm sorry, honey," I said sincerely, "I can't think of anyone who would—"

"I can!" she said excitedly.

"Who?"

"You!"

I closed my eyes for a moment and thought I should have seen the slow curve coming before the fast break hit me. I heard again the sound of Lavers' raucous guffaw in my ears. Now it began to make sense.

I opened my mouth to tell her she was crazy if she thought I'd appear before her cameras and risk around five million people making rude comments about my ancestry. Then I closed my mouth again quickly before I said a word.

I suddenly remembered she was going to pay Georgia a fee of five thousand dollars for her appearance. I spent the fee in five seconds' rapid mental calculation. The Healey paid off, a hi-fi in every room of the apartment, with remote control. I could still have enough left over to afford a vacation this year.

"Will you, Al?" she asked urgently.

"Why, sure honey," I put my arm around her and patted her shoulder gently. "How could I refuse you anything?"

"You're wonderful!" she said simply. "I knew you'd do it. If I tell you a secret, will you promise not to get mad at me?"

"I promise."

"Well, I thought I'd better clear any barriers before I asked you. And it's quite all right with Inspector Martin and the County Sheriff if you appear on the show."

"Fine," I said without any great enthusiasm.

"And they said naturally you couldn't accept any fee, so I'm paying a thousand dollars into the police fund you have for widows and orphans."

"You're what!" I shouted.

"Al!" she said reproachfully. "You promised you wouldn't get mad."

"But I don't have any widows or orphans."

She laughed gently. "You always see the funny side of things, don't you, Al?"

"That's me," I said bitterly. "Laugh, clown, laugh!"

She turned toward me, her eyes glittering. "You don't know what this means to me! I don't know how to thank you."

"The old-fashioned way is still the best," I said.

"I guess you're right, Al," she said softly. "Why didn't I think of that?"

She got up from the couch just as the second record dropped and Peggy Lee came in with the first line of "Blues in the Night." It was bad timing.

Paula pulled the blue chiffon over her head, then looked down at me. "Do you think a woman is two-faced, Al?"

"If her face is as beautiful as yours, it's an asset," I told her.

"Not only virile but gallant!" she grinned mockingly. "Why don't we stop kidding one another? This is your price and I'm looking forward to paying it."

I watched fascinated as the fragile heap on the carpet grew. The slip that followed the dress was a pale blue. So were the bra and the panties that followed it. Her garter belt, what there was of it, was a deeper shade, almost royal blue. I wondered if it made me a knight.

Then she lay down on the couch, her hands stretched up over her head, idly plumping a cushion out of shape. Her hair and her nails were blue, but the rest of her was a breathtaking whiteness. Her hands reached out, twining themselves around my neck, pulling me down toward her with a sudden fierceness.

"You're so right, Al!" she whispered eagerly. "The old-fashioned ways are always the best."

Around six o'clock I poured us both a drink. I carried glasses back toward the couch and she sat up lazily.

"You know something, Al?" she said. "There's something under that cushion. It has a sort of metallic feel to it."

"Yeah?" I said absently.

I sat down beside her, the two glasses still in my hands. She reached under the cushion, pulled something out and held them in front of her. I closed my eyes as she studied the pair of bikini pants.

"Well!" her laugh was two octaves flat. "It looks like somebody forgot something, doesn't it? And that looks like a genuine gold-thread, too!"

"Fourteen karat," I said in a hollow voice.

She got onto her feet quickly. She got dressed quicker than a stripper when the cops pile into the joint.

"Thanks again, Al," she said as she pulled the blue chiffon into place. "Could you get out to the studio around four tomorrow afternoon? We'll have a sort of rehearsal just to get you used to the cameras and the lights. I never work to a script so you don't have to worry about learning anything."

She was already halfway to the door. "I can't tell you what this means to me! I'll be eternally grateful ... don't bother to get up, I know my way out. See you tomorrow at four then ..." The door closed behind her quietly.

"Toni!" I said disgustedly. "You are nothing but a tramp. I hope you catch cold!"

CHAPTER THIRTEEN

I got down to the Bureau a little before ten the next morning and went along to Doc Murphy's office. He raised his eyebrows as I came in.

"Ah, Wheeler!" he said. "They tell me you're playing the lead in an adult Western tonight. I told them not to be stupid, how could you ever qualify?"

"So many comics going to waste," I said. "Anyway, it's the horses that are adult. You can always get another actor, but a good horse takes years to train."

"I shouldn't rib you," he said. "You're my pal. You're the boy who's going to do away with autopsies entirely. No more bodies, just bits!"

"Did you ever think of running a funeral parlor?" I asked him. "You'd be a riot there."

"Don't need to," he said cheerfully. "My brother runs one. I'm his best salesman!"

"Supplier would be the word," I corrected him.

He cackled like something out of *Macbeth*.

"I was wondering," I said, "about that body. Was any formal identification made?"

"Are you crazy?"

"Well, did anybody try and make a comparative identification then?"

"If you know anybody who was on such intimate terms with Georgia Brown's left tibia and right fibula that they could identify them," Murphy said, "bring them along. I'd like to meet them."

"I just wondered," I said.

"You should go far, Wheeler," he said coldly. "You're just stupid enough to be made an inspector or a county sheriff one of these days!"

"Come the day and there'll be a new doctor around here," I said as I headed toward the door. "Make the most of things, Murphy, it's later than you think."

I left his office and went over to Missing Persons, to Captain Parsons' office. He was three years from retirement and he'd been carefully nudged into Missing Persons because Inspector Martin thought that any precinct captain who still had a spittoon around his office was outdated.

Parsons scratched his bald head and grinned at me as I came into his office. "If it isn't the white-headed boy himself! What are you doing—slumming?"

"I'm looking for a blonde," I told him.

"Aren't we all?" he said passionately. "The youngest female I've got in this office is forty-five, and her idea of fun is to have mustard on a hot dog once in a while."

"Tough," I said. "Do you have any missing blondes on your books, Captain?"

"I got any kind of female or male you want," he said. "This is a city of missing persons! What did you have in mind, specifically?"

"I don't have much," I said. "She would be a blonde, probably in her late twenties or early thirties. She would have been missing for a couple of weeks, maybe a little less than that."

"I'll get the wheels of industry churning," Parsons said cheerfully and picked up his phone.

Ten minutes later we looked at the list. We had started off with six names and had them reduced to two.

"This one," Parsons jabbed his pencil point against the name. "Ella Scott. She was reported missing by her mother. The mother thinks she might have gone to San Diego with a sailor. She says Ella's always going away with sailors but she never stayed away this long before, so maybe this time she went farther."

"All the way to San Diego?"

"You could be right," he grinned.

I lit a cigarette and he grunted and pushed the bridge of his glasses farther up his nose.

"That leaves Rita Tango," Parsons said.

"Rita who?"

"That's what she calls herself anyway. Reported missing by the owner of the rooming house where she lives. Been gone for three days before she was reported missing. That was ten days ago—she hasn't turned up yet. Age twenty-nine, height ... you want the detail on the personal description?"

"I don't think so," I said. "I might run over there and talk to the owner. What's his name?"

"O'Shea," he said, "and it's a Mrs."

"Thanks, Captain," I told him.

"If you ask me," he grinned, "you're going about getting yourself a blonde the hard way!"

"I have a feeling you could be right," I agreed.

Mrs. O'Shea was out when I got to the rooming house. A freckle-faced kid around thirteen who was lounging on the stoop told me she'd be out all day. She'd gone to see her brother and she wouldn't be back before six, she never was. I said it didn't matter.

The kid stuck his hands into the pockets of his jeans and looked me over slowly: "Who are you anyway?" he asked.

"My name's Wheeler," I said.

"You one of them skip-tracers or something?" he asked.

"Sort of," I said. "I'm not really looking for Mrs. O'Shea, I'm looking for Rita Tango."

"You're out of luck, mister," he said, "she's skipped again."

I lit myself a cigarette. "I guess I am, if that's the case," I said. "Did you know her?"

"Sure. Used to see her around all the time, she didn't work much."

"What did she do when she was working?"

"She was in pictures, she said." He shrugged his shoulders contemptuously. "I never saw her in any. Big deal!"

"Did she have an agent, do you know?" I asked.

"Sure, she used to go in about once a week to see him. I asked her about it once. I said how come this guy wasn't even in Hollywood if he was such a big agent, and she said it was only a branch office out here."

"You wouldn't remember the name of the branch office?"

His eyes were suddenly shrewd. "Just how much does she owe that finance company of yours, mister?"

"Ten bucks," I said.

"Ah! You wouldn't be wasting your time chasing her for a lousy ten bucks!"

"You're too smart for me, I guess," I said. "How much is it worth?"

He took a deep breath. "Five bucks?" he said hesitantly.

"It's a deal," I said.

I stood beside him on the stoop and stared down at him coldly, then I opened my coat a little so he could see the gun. His eyes widened as he looked.

"You ever heard of Kent Fargo, kid?" I said softly out of the side of my mouth.

"Yeah, s-s-sure," he gulped.

"Fargo's looking for her, kid," I said. "You make sure you're giving me the right dope, huh, kid? You look a little young to wind up dead."

"I'm giving you the right dope, honest, mister!" he said. "The guy's name is Chuck Finley, he's got an office over on Mortlake Street some place."

"O.K.," I said.

He gulped again. "You don't need to worry about no five bucks, mister, I was just kidding!"

I took a five out of my wallet and gave it to him. "We made a deal, kid," I said, then walked back to the Healey.

It was two-thirty when I walked into Finley's office. There was a dyed blond receptionist who looked like she had died a couple of years back but nobody had done anything about it.

"Name?" she said.

"Wheeler, I—"

"Save it!" she said. "He ain't doing anything—go right on in."

I opened the door of Finley's private office and walked in. He was sitting behind a desk littered with photos and the remains of his lunch. He was fat and bald and repulsive.

"My name's Wheeler," I said, "I'm a—"

He held up a hand. "Don't tell me, brother, I'll tell you." He looked me over carefully then shook his head. "No," he said, "I have to tell you, brother, you just don't have it!"

"I saw a doctor," I said, "he fixed it."

"You don't have the looks to get to first base on a big deal," he said. "Character playing?" He shook his head again. "I can see it from here, you just don't have the character for it! Extras, they can get them in Hollywood without paying the bus fare from Pine City. You can pay the receptionist on your way out, sorry."

"Pay?"

"Five bucks for a consultation," he said. "You wanted to know whether you could get into pictures, didn't you? That's what you come here for, wasn't it? It takes my time, my expert knowledge—it cost me a lot of dough to be an expert."

"An expert what?"

"What do you—" his eyes narrowed. "Just who are you anyway?"

I showed him my shield, and his face suddenly looked thinner.

"I'm running a legitimate business here, Lieutenant. I'm sorry I shot my mouth off when you came in, I—"

"Shut up!" I said.

"Was I talking?" he said nervously.

"You've got a girl on your books here named Rita Tango. I want to talk about her."

"Anything you say, Lieutenant."

He got up from his desk and pulled open the top drawer of the filing cabinet.

"Rita Tango," he said, thumbing through the files. "They're all Rita, since Hayworth! They don't have her talent, that's the difference!" He pulled out a file, dropped it onto his desk and slumped back into the chair.

"Tell me about her." I said.

"She's registered with me," he said. "A bit-player. I get her parts here and there."

"You got a photo of her?" I said.

"Sorry, Lieutenant, I don't."

I took the file off his desk; he made a half-hearted grab for it, but I put the flat of my hand against his face and pushed him back into his chair.

I opened the file. There was only a sheet of paper that had her name, address and phone number on it and half a dozen photos.

"She takes a good photo," I said dropping the file back onto the desk. "How does she look with clothes?"

He gestured vaguely with his hands. "You know how it is, Lieutenant. They do anything to get in pictures. I guess she figured that if any producer sees one of those shots, maybe he's a little more interested in her and she gets the part."

"When did you last see her?"

"About ten days back," he said. "Two weeks, I'm not sure."

"Who gave her the job?"

He jumped. "Job? I don't know what—"

"She's dead," I said evenly. "You weren't in on that as well?"

He tucked his fingers inside the edge of his crumpled collar and pulled on it. "Dead?" he repeated hoarsely.

"Who gave her the job?"

"I got a phone call," he said. "A week-end party, maybe longer. I figured there was going to be some big names at the party and they wanted to make sure there wasn't any trouble. Rita was the girl for it, she just has a room in town, no folks, no strings... Dead, you say?"

"Who made the phone call?"

"A dame."

"So she was a female, what was her name?"

"I'll get crucified for this," he said.

"You might," I said, "if you don't give me the name."

"O.K., O.K.! It was Kay Steinway."

"You'd done business with her before?"

He shook his head. "But she said Kent Fargo had told her to ring me, that was good enough reference."

"How did she pay off? Did she come in here, or did you go to her?"

"She put fifty bucks in the mail," he said. "Cash."

"All right," I said, and picked up his phone. I rang Johnson, the boss of the Vice Detail, and gave him the name and the address.

"Something exciting, Al?" he asked.

"You want to get into pictures?" I said. "Why not be an intimate entertainer instead? We have clients who'll pay fifty bucks for an evening— and the liquor is free."

"One of those!" he said. "I love those characters. I'll have a couple of guys over there in about ten minutes. Thanks."

"My pleasure," I said and hung up.

I walked over to the window and watched until I saw the car stop outside and the two men get out and cross the sidewalk to the front entrance.

"Your last clients are on their way up," I said to Finley. I picked up the file from his desk. "You won't need this any more."

I walked out of the office closing the door behind me.

"Mr. Wheeler!" the receptionist said. "I got your receipt made out already. That's five dollars."

I shook my head sadly. "Honey," I said, "you aren't worth it."

CHAPTER FOURTEEN

"You feeling all right, Al?" Paula asked, glancing at her watch. "There's only fifty minutes to go now. You aren't nervous or anything?"

"Just thirsty," I said.

"We can take care of that," she said. "I'll have Lonny Hughes look after you while I'm changing. You sure you've got it O.K.?"

I looked at the battery of arc lights, the cameras, the trail of cables across the studio floor. "I think so, honey," I said.

"It won't be so tough," she said soothingly. "Just the three of us, Kay, you and myself, sitting around a table and talking. You remember the signs?"

"Sure," I said. "Speed up, slow down, two minutes to go.... I remember them all right."

"That's fine," she said. "Then I'll have Lonny look after you while I go and put on something feminine." She glanced down at the dark blue slacks she had on. "I wear these while I'm working, because the crew say I wear the pants around this show, anyway."

"That's very amusing," I said politely.

"Sure," she grinned. "I'll save it for my memoirs. Hey Lonny!" she yelled suddenly.

The character with the crew-cut gray hair who looked as if he should have been on Wall Street instead of television, came over to us.

"Look after Al while I get changed, honey," Paula said to him. "And I think he's thirsty."

"Sure," Hughes said. "I can take care of that right away. Follow me, Lieutenant!"

We finished up in someone's private office. Hughes opened up the built-in icebox and started making the drinks.

"What will you have, Lieutenant?"

"Scotch on the rocks," I said automatically, "with a little soda."

"A man after my own heart," he smiled.

He handed me the glass a few seconds later. "Here's to tonight's show," he said. "It should be a smash! You know, you're a lucky man, Lieutenant. You're getting the kindest treatment anybody ever got on this show!"

"How's that?" I asked him.

His grin broadened. "Well, every other time we're putting over a controversial subject—that means somebody who's got something to hide—Paula has a whole trunkful of gimmicks to make them come across."

"I don't get it," I said.

"She's a smart girl, that Paula!" he said. "That 'blue' gimmick has gone over big, you know. Everything blue —even to a blues musical theme." He shook his head and grinned. "But I was talking about getting people to open up, wasn't I?"

"I think so," I said cautiously.

"Paula always talks to them before the show," he said. "She always asks them if there's one particular topic they don't want to discuss, because if they tell her about it, she won't mention it on the show."

Hughes chuckled appreciatively. "You can guess what the first question is she asks them!"

"There's nothing like ethics, is there?" I said.

"You know how it is in this business," he said. "Dog eat dog. It'll be cat eat cat with Kay Steinway on tonight!" He sobered down a little. "Imagine Kay being mixed up with all these murders! That guy Fargo trying to knock her off!"

"You know Kay Steinway?" I asked him.

"Sure," he said, "I had her on the floor at the Excelsior."

"Nobody cared?" I asked politely.

He grinned. "Technical term, Lieutenant. Studio floor, I was a director with Excelsior at the time. That was the name of Norman Coates's outfit."

"I see," I said.

"Sure," he said. "When I think about how it was then! Manning was right on top—they must have made a fortune out of his pictures. After he died, the box office was even better. People take a morbid interest in seeing a star who's dead."

"Maybe Fargo thought of that," I said.

"I wouldn't be surprised," he said. "The only thing I'm sorry about is that Morgan kid, the elder sister, I mean. ... Hell! Janice! It's easier to call her that after knowing her by that name the last two years. I'm sorry she walked out of that window. If you'd known Georgia Brown, Lieutenant, you'd agree with me that Janice should have got a medal for killing her!"

"Is that a fact?"

"She used to line up the kids for Manning," he said. "And just for the kicks she'd get out of watching him go into action with them. Somehow it wouldn't have been so bad if she'd done it for money!"

"Yeah," I said.

"Another drink, Lieutenant?"

"I don't think so, thanks."

He checked his watch. "I guess we'd better get you over to make-up."

"Make-up?"

"Sure. Don't worry," he grinned. "We won't give you a false mustache or anything. Just a little pancake to take out the creases."

"Creases?"

"You're beginning to sound like a star already, Lieutenant!"

The time went fast. Ten minutes before the show was due to start Hughes brought me up to the table, where the other two were already seated.

Paula looked like a million dollars in a low-cut sharkskin gown. The sparkling sapphires around her throat gave emphasis to the clear, deep blue of the gown.

Kay Steinway wore a number, gunmetal in color, which looked deceptively simple at first glance and very elegant and very expensive at the second glance. It was cut a good two inches lower in the neckline than Paula's, and that ensured the second glance.

I sat down on the vacant chair between the two of them and Kay smiled at me slowly.

"I haven't seen you around lately, Al," she said huskily. "You must have been busy."

"He's been busy all right," Paula said easily. "I pleaded with him to appear on the show tonight," she laughed throatily, "the villain!"

"Villain?" Kay queried.

"Straight out of the old-time melodrama," Paula said. "I had to make a deal with him. An old-fashioned deal, very old-fashioned, as a matter of fact." She laughed again. "He's really quite a guy, this Al Wheeler, isn't he?"

"Quite a guy!" Kay said coldly.

"Take my advice, darling," Paula said confidentially, "once you get into his apartment, he just won't take no for an answer!"

"Al," Kay said brightly, "do you still have that apartment? It seems such a waste, I mean, you've been practically living at my place!"

"I'm sure you're exaggerating, darling," Paula said. "I know Al has better taste!"

"And I know he isn't blind," Kay said. "He can see right through you!"

"Well, I must admit he could have when I was in his apartment," Paula said. "I wasn't wearing very much at the time...."

Hughes came over to the table. "Five minutes to go, folks," he said. "Everything O.K.?"

"Just fine," Kay said from between her teeth. "We're just one big happy family, Lonny." She gestured gracefully with one hand in Paula's direction. "Have you met Mother?"

Hughes beat a hasty retreat, and I wished I could have gone with him.

A brooding silence set in and it lasted until the show opened. The second before the cameras became live, the two girls broke into brilliant smiles.

It wasn't so bad once the show started. I could concentrate on Paula and almost forget the cameras and the brilliant lights. She handled it superbly. This was an on-the-spot show from Pine City, she told her audience. The city that had been stunned in the last seventy-two hours by two brutal murders, a suicide, the revelation that Lee Manning had been murdered three years before, and that even now a killer, Kent Fargo, was still loose within the city limits.

It was all good stuff. She built it up beautifully, then introduced Kay. She questioned Kay about the night Fargo and Dunn had arrived at her house.

Kay was equal to the occasion. She described the scene and you could see the fear shining out of her eyes as she faced Dunn again. She built me up into something more than a hero, using me carefully as a foil for her own part in the affair.

I glanced at my watch once and suddenly realized that twenty minutes of the show had gone already. There was a break for the commercial, and then Paula turned to me.

I told my story as quickly as I could. When I'd brought it up to the point where Blain had been arrested and told his story about the blackmail photograph, Paula smiled her thanks at me.

"It's a terrible story, Lieutenant," she said. "But a fascinating one. Is there any further comment you would like to make?"

"A couple of things happened today," I said. "You might like to hear about them."

"Of course, Lieutenant," Paula said. "Please tell us."

I went quickly over what had happened from when I talked to Murphy to the time Chuck Finley's business came to an abrupt halt.

Paula looked at me with a puzzled look in her eyes for a moment after I'd finished.

"I'm sorry, Lieutenant," she said, "but I'm not quite sure I get the full implication of what you have just told us. Would you please explain further?"

"It's basically simple," I said. "The missing girl, Rita Tango, is the blonde who was blown to pieces in that apartment. *Not* Georgia Brown. The real Georgia Brown hired her as a decoy. She probably planned to murder the girl herself, but Janice Jorgens beat her to it."

"Wait a minute, Lieutenant!" Kay said tautly. "You said that man—Finley was it?—told you *I* called him and hired the girl? That's a lie!"

"Is it?" I said. "The one thing that worried me after hearing Blain's story was why Georgia Brown would want to throw away the perfect blackmailing setup she had. There could only be one reason—if she'd made enough money, not only out of the blackmail but maybe out of something else as well, she could want to retire. But if she stopped the blackmail there was always the danger that Fargo might catch up with her.”

“I see what you mean, Lieutenant!” Paula said breathlessly. “If Georgia Brown died, then nobody would keep on looking for her. So she hired the Tango girl to impersonate herself, planning to murder her!”

“That’s exactly right,” I said.

“What you are really saying, Lieutenant,” Paula faltered for a moment, “is that ... Kay Steinway is really Georgia Brown!”

“I am not!” Kay screamed wildly.

“That’s the way it looks,” I agreed, ignoring Kay’s outburst. “Fargo said it was Kay Steinway who called him and lied about Coates having the negative. Finley said it was Kay Steinway who called him and booked the Tango girl—”

“Lies!” Kay dissolved into a flood of tears. “All lies!”

“And if you remember,” I went on talking to Paula, “as you told me in the first place, Georgia Brown was going to name names on your show, and she mentioned four. Fargo, Blain, Coates ... and Kay Steinway.”

“I do remember, Lieutenant!” Paula said excitedly. “Those were the four names she ...” Her voice died away.

There was a sudden, deathly silence. Kay stopped crying and raised her head, her tear-filled eyes open wide.

“That’s right,” I said. “But it wasn’t Georgia Brown who gave you those names—it was Rita Tango. And that’s impossible—*she* couldn’t have known any of those people. The only person who could have named those four people was the real Georgia Brown herself.”

Paula shook her head faintly. “I’m ... confused,” she said. “The excitement, it’s been too much.”

“You were really very clever,” I said. “You changed not only your appearance but your personality. You had your looks altered by plastic surgery. You built a whole new personality around this television show, with the accent on the color blue. Everything about you was blue—who would wonder why you had your hair dyed the same color? It fitted with the rest of the gimmick.”

“You must be crazy!” she said.

“You were a good enough actress to imitate Kay Steinway’s voice when you phoned Finley to hire Rita Tango,” I went on. “And again when you rang Fargo and told him Coates had the negative. But Janice Jorgens pulled a fast one on you by killing Rita Tango. She thought she was avenging the death of her sister.”

Paula bit down hard on her lower lip.

“After Janice walked out of that window,” I said, “you played it real cool. You told me the story about Janice giving you a sealed envelope to hold for her, and said you’d get it for me. You walked into your own suite, sealed the negative in an envelope and brought it back to me."

"I won't listen," she said tautly. "I won't—"

"Didn't you notice the way I handled it?" I asked her gently. "How careful I was to hold it by the edges? We checked the prints before we made the photograph from it. There was only one set of fingerprints on that negative, Paula—yours!"

She slumped back into her chair and looked at me. Her eyes were suddenly tired. "All right," she said sullenly, "I'm Georgia Brown."

CHAPTER FIFTEEN

"You ham!" Lavers said bitterly. "That story about checking her prints on that negative. It's not true, is it?"

"No," I admitted. "But it seemed like a good clincher at the time. It was something I should have done, but I didn't."

"Supposing she still denied it?" he said. "What would you have done then?"

"How could she?" I grinned. "Like I said, Rita Tango couldn't have given her those four names, only the real Georgia Brown could have known them. She couldn't talk her way out of that."

"I'm glad she didn't try anyway," Lavers grunted. "I guess we'd better get her downtown and into a cell."

"Sometimes I'm not quite as bright as I should be," I said modestly. "I'm just remembering something a blonde told me. I don't think she's as dumb as she makes out."

"What are you raving about now!"

"Let me play a hunch, Sheriff," I pleaded with him. "Let me take Paula up to Fargo's penthouse for an hour, no more. It won't make any difference to things as they are now."

"If you're suggesting I'd let this woman have a last fling with you, Wheeler!" Lavers face was apoplectic.

"I want to use her as bait," I said. "If she wants a last fling, she can fling herself out of the window the way Janice Jorgens did. I want to play a hunch and use her as bait for Fargo."

Lavers sneered contemptuously: "You don't think he'd be dumb enough to come anywhere near that penthouse of his! We've had a stake-out around that building since the night he killed Coates!"

"I said it's a hunch, Sheriff," I said patiently. "If I'm wrong, what have you lost—an hour. Nothing more." He hesitated for a moment. "All right. Sometimes I think I'm as crazy as you are. One hour—no more, no less!"

"Thank you, Mr. Shylock," I said. "Shall we go?"

The Sheriff sat in the front of the car beside the driver. Paula Reid sat between me and Polnik in the back. She didn't say a word the whole way.

We stopped outside the building and Lavers looked at me.

"All right, Wheeler, this is your affair. You have one hour exactly. The Sergeant and I will wait for you here in the car."

"Thank you, sir," I said.

I took Paula's arm and propelled her across the sidewalk to the front door of the office block. One of the guys on permanent stake-out there came over and opened the front door for us. He gave me the key to the penthouse and then we went inside.

We rode the elevator to the top floor. I unlocked the front door of the penthouse, opened it and stood to one side to let Paula in first.

She walked in and I followed her, switching on the lights and closing the door behind me.

"Let's get this over with," she said shortly. "What's the idea of bringing me in here?"

"A hunch," I said. "Maybe it's no-good. We'll find out."

"It's a pity that bomb didn't take you with it!" she said savagely.

"Make yourself comfortable," I said. "We're going to be here for an hour, anyway."

I walked through the other rooms slowly. The penthouse looked just the same as it had the last time I'd been here. I came back into the living room and saw Paula had opened up the bar and poured herself a drink.

"You can pour me one too," I said.

"You can go to hell!" she said. She took her glass with her and walked over to an armchair, then sat down.

I went over to the bar and got behind it. "If I have to pour my own drinks, I'm going to be barman and give my feet a break," I said.

She pointedly ignored the remark and looked out of the plate-glass window at the view. I took the .38 out of its holster and put it on the small shelf underneath the bar counter. Then I poured myself a drink.

The time seemed to drag by slowly. I finished the drink and poured myself another.

"You want another drink?" I asked her.

"You can go to hell!" she said.

"You said that."

She looked out of the window again. I sipped the second drink and looked at the dead fish floating on top of the water in the tanks. Maybe they were symbolic. Then I blinked. One of the tanks was moving of its own accord.

It moved quickly, swinging through an angle of ninety degrees, and a whole section of the wall behind the tank went with it.

And a moment later Fargo stepped into the room.

"Don't move, copper," he said. "I'd as soon let you have it first, anyway!"

I looked at the gun in his hand and shook my head. "I'm a statue," I said. "Just keep the dogs away from me."

Paula sat staring at him, her hands gripping the arms of the chair so that the knuckles showed white.

"Hello, Georgia," Fargo said softly. "You look different all right. I would never have picked you!"

"Where does the hole in the wall lead to?" I asked him. "Your offices downstairs?"

"I had the stairway built in when I bought the place," he said. "I thought it could come in useful sometime. There's a peephole cut in the wall there just behind the tanks."

"That's where you've been all the time? In your offices downstairs?"

"Sure," he said. "I've been coming up here when I felt like a drink. If you coppers were only half smart you would have noticed Fargo Enterprises closed down for business the day after you shot me in Kay Steinway's place. The only guy who goes in and out is the office manager, and he's a friend of mine!"

"Where did I get you?" I asked interestedly.

"In the shoulder," he said. "It was a lousy shot. I got it fixed the same night by a doctor. I got a lot of influence in this town!"

"I guess you have," I said. "You caught Paula's show on television tonight?"

"I watched it up here," he said, then added abruptly. "We've stalled enough!"

He half turned toward Paula and she shrank back into the chair.

"You got it coming, baby," he said slowly. "For three years you made a monkey out of me! Then you really fixed me good. You told me it was Coates, and I'd taken care of him before I looked for that negative. I would have taken care of the Steinway babe if it hadn't been for the flatfoot over there! And it was all your idea!"

"Kent!" she said in a low voice. "Kent! You know you were the only guy I ever really—"

"Sure," he laughed. "You were crazy about me! Well, I'm crazy about you, baby, and this proves it!"

He pressed the trigger and the gun exploded into sound that re-echoed around the walls of the room. Paula's body arched forward in agony, then fell back into the chair. Fargo kept on pressing the trigger until the gun was empty.

The room was suddenly quiet. Paula was slumped against the ripped and bloodstained upholstery of the chair.

Fargo looked up at me and grinned, almost sheepishly.

"That's something I always used to tell Charlie," he said. "Never lose your temper, because you're liable to do something stupid!" He looked down at the empty gun in his hand. "I guess I did something stupid!"

"I guess you did," I agreed.

He tossed the gun onto the carpet and started to walk toward me slowly. "Well, that's it. You can take me in, copper!"

"Not this trip, Fargo," I told him.

I lifted the .38 clear of the counter and shot him carefully, twice in the chest. The impact of the slugs hitting him spun him around and he dropped across the chair on top of Paula's body.

I just had time to finish my drink before they arrived.

Lavers came to a stop in the middle of the room, staring down at the two bodies in the chair. Behind him were Polnik and the rest of them.

"What in hell happened!" Lavers gurgled.

I pointed to the opening in the wall behind him. "He came in through there—he's been hiding out in his own offices on the next floor all the time. One moment there was just the two of us up here, and the next second, Fargo was here."

"What then?"

"It happened so quickly," I said. "Fargo had a gun in his hand. As soon as he saw her, he started pumping slugs into her. She was dead before I had a chance to get my own gun. As soon as I got my gun out, I shot him, of course."

"That was all?"

"I thought it was enough," I said.

"If it happened so fast, how the hell do you know that stairway leads to his offices!"

"We're on the top floor of the building now," I said. "Where else would it lead—Mars?"

"All right!" Lavers growled.

He bent down and picked up Fargo's gun and examined it.

"His gun's empty!"

"Is it?" I said carefully. "You mean, that he couldn't have shot me even if he wanted to, Sheriff?"

"I should have known better than let you play one of your so-called hunches!" Lavers said.

"Anyway," I shrugged my shoulders, "it saves the State an expense."

Lavers looked at me for a few seconds, his eyes thoughtful: "You keep on saying that, Wheeler. Now I come to think of it, it makes an interesting sequence...." He ticked them off on his fingers: "The blonde gets blown to pieces because you press a button. Coates gets murdered because you don't get over to his hotel quick enough. You shot Fargo's man and killed him. You exposed Janice Jorgens as the blonde's killer and she suicided. You exposed Paula Reid as the real Georgia Brown and she gets murdered by Fargo!"

He glared at me. "Maybe we should call you Death-Watch Wheeler!"

"I'll try and stay out of your woodwork, Sheriff," I assured him.

He looked around the room again. "There's something here that stinks!" he said.

"The goldfish," I said. "They've been dead a couple of days."

"Maybe I should get smart," he said tiredly. "All right. I'll settle for the goldfish!"

"Can I go home now?" I asked him. "This is my free week end, remember?"

It was just after midnight when I finally did get home. I opened the front door of the apartment and saw the lights were on. I heard music. I took a step forward and fell flat on my face.

I climbed back onto my feet slowly and counted them. There were exactly seven suitcases scattered around the floor.

Toni was curled up on the couch, watching me with mild interest showing in her eyes. "You always do that," she said. "Maybe it's a conditioned reflex?"

"How many planes have you missed now?" I snarled.

"I lost count," she smiled. "I heard about you being on television tonight and I couldn't miss that, could I?"

"The janitor let you in again?"

"We're old friends now," she said. "I showed him my burlesque pictures."

"I need a drink again," I said, and went about getting one.

"Did you find Fargo?" she asked.

"Yeah," I said. "It took me over twenty-four hours to get that crack of yours about him being so anxious about his office. You knew about that secret stairway?"

"I knew," she said. "What happened to Fargo?"

"I took Paula Reid up there with me," I said. "Fargo came in through that stairway and shot her."

"And what happened to Fargo?"

"He got shot, too."

"You shot him?"

"I shot him," I agreed.

"That figures," she said evenly.

I turned around and stared at her, the two glasses in my hands. "What do you mean—that figures?"

"You have a hero complex, Al," she said. "Didn't you know?"

"I never admit it," I said.

I handed her a drink and sat down beside her on the couch. "For a girl who was Fargo's plaything up to a couple of nights ago, you've got awfully smart all of a sudden."

"I majored in psychology," she said. "You know what it got me?"

"Tell me?"

"An office full of psychopaths," she said seriously. "So right then I decided to take advantage of the gifts bestowed upon me by Mother Nature."

She got up from the couch and stretched luxuriously. She was wearing the top half of a pair of shortie pajamas in apricot nylon.

"You have to admit that Mother Nature's been generous to me," she said contentedly. "And whoever heard of a female psychologist wearing mink?"

"You never seem to wear anything much," I said. "Why did you really come back here?"

"I left my bikini bottom behind," she said. "I thought I'd look silly in Las Vegas swimming in the hotel pool in just a bra."

"Silly isn't exactly the word," I said.

She sat on my lap and made herself comfortable. "There's a plane at nine in the morning," she said. "I could catch it."

"It so happens I have a free week end," I told her. "So long as there aren't any interruptions."

The phone rang shrilly. Toni got up off my lap and walked across to the table. She lifted the receiver and said crisply: "This is Mr. Wheeler's personal secretary. I'm afraid it's no use calling him this week end, he's very busy. If you want the name of another good mortician, take a look in the directory." Then she hung up.

"You're getting to be quite an asset around here," I said admiringly.

She flicked off the light switch on her way back to the couch.

"Finish that drink, Al. You can't hold a glass and a girl at the same time!"

THE END

ALAN GEOFFREY YATES BIBLIOGRAPHY
(1923-1985)

As Carter Brown/Peter Carter Brown

Series:

Al Wheeler (no U.S. edition unless otherwise stated through to Chorine Makes a Killing)

The Wench is Wicked (1955)
Blonde Verdict (1956; revised for the U.S. as The Brazen, 1960)
Delilah Was Deadly (1956)
No Harp for My Angel (1956)
Booty for a Babe (1956)
Eve, It's Extortion (1957; revised as Walk Softly Witch!, 1959, and further revised for the U.S. as The Victim, 1959)
No Law Against Angels (1957; revised for the U.S. as The Body, 1958; 1st U.S. Wheeler)
Doll for the Big House (1957; revised for the U.S. as The Bombshell, 1960)
Chorine Makes a Killing (1957)
The Unorthodox Corpse (1957; revised for the U.S., 1961)
Death on the Downbeat (1958; revised for the U.S. as The Corpse, 1958)
The Blonde (1958; reprinted in the U.S., 1958)
The Lover (1958)
The Mistress (1959)
The Passionate (1959)
The Wanton (1959)
The Dame (1959)

The Desired (1959)
The Temptress (1960)
Lament for a Lousy Lover (1960) [includes Mavis Seidlitz]
The Stripper (1961)
The Tigress (1961; reprinted in the UK as Wildcat, 1962)
The Exotic (1961)
Angel! (1962)
The Hellcat (1962)
The Lady Is Transparent (1962)
The Dumdum Murder (1962)
Girl in a Shroud (1963)
The Sinners (1963; reprinted in U.S. as The Girl Who Was Possessed, 1963)
The Lady Is Not Available (1963; reprinted in U.S. as The Lady Is Available, 1963)
The Dance of Death (1964)
The Vixen (1964; reprinted in the U.S. as The Velvet Vixen, 1964)
A Corpse for Christmas (1965)
The Hammer of Thor (1965)
Target for Their Dark Desire (1966)
The Plush-Lined Coffin (1967)
Until Temptation Do Us Part (1967)
The Deep Cold Green (1968)
The Up-Tight Blonde (1969)
Burden of Guilt (1970)
The Creative Murders (1971)
W.H.O.R.E. (1971)
The Clown (1972)
The Aseptic Murders (1972)
The Born Loser (1973)
Night Wheeler (1974)
Wheeler Fortune (1974)

Wheeler, Dealer! (1975)
The Dream Merchant (1976)
Busted Wheeler (1979)
The Spanking Girls (1979)
Model for Murder (1980)
The Wicked Widow (1981)
Stab in the Dark (1984;
  Australia only)

Larry Baker

Charlie Sent Me (1965; revised
  from Swan Song for a Siren,
  1955)
No Blonde Is an Island (1965)
So What Killed the Vampire?
  (1966)
Had I But Groaned (1968;
  reprinted in the UK as The
  Witches, 1969)
True Son of the Beast (1970)
The Iron Maiden (1975)

Barney Blain (no U.S. editions)

Madam, You're Mayhem (1957)
Ice Cold in Ermine (1958)

Danny Boyd

Tempt a Tigress (1958; no U.S.)
So Deadly, Sinner! (1959;
  reprinted in the U.S. as Walk
  Softly, Witch, 1959, 1st U.S.
  Boyd; different version of the
  Wheeler title)
Suddenly by Violence (1959)
Terror Comes Creeping (1959)
The Wayward Wahine (1960;
  published in Australia as The
  Wayward, 1962)
The Dream Is Deadly (1960)

Graves, I Dig (1960; revised from
  Cutie Wins a Corpse (1957)
The Myopic Mermaid (1961,
  revised from A Siren Sounds
  Off, 1958)
The Ever-Loving Blues (1961;
  revised from Death of a Doll,
  1956)
The Seductress (1961; published
  in the U.S. as The Sad-Eyed
  Seductress, 1961)
The Savage Salome (1961;
  revised from Murder is My
  Mistress, 1954)
The Ice-Cold Nude (1962)
Lover Don't Come Back (1962)
Nymph to the Slaughter (1963)
Passionate Pagan (1963)
Silken Nightmare (1963)
Catch Me a Phoenix! (1965)
The Sometime Wife (1965)
The Black Lace Hangover (1966)
House of Sorcery (1967)
The Mini-Murders (1968)
Murder Is the Message (1969)
Only the Very Rich (1969)
The Coffin Bird (1970)
The Sex Clinic (1971)
Angry Amazons (1972) [includes
  Randy Roberts]
Manhattan Cowboy (1973)
So Move the Body (1973)
The Early Boyd (1975)
The Savage Sisters (1976)
The Pipes Are Calling (1976)
The Rip Off (1979)
The Strawberry-Blonde Jungle
  (1979)
Death to a Downbeat (1980)
Kiss Michelle Goodbye (1981)
The Real Boyd (1984; Australia
  only)

Paul Donavan

Donavan (1974)
Donovan's Day (1975)
Chinese Donavan (1976)
Donavan's Delight (1979)

Max Dumas (no U.S. editions)

Goddess Gone Bad (1958)
Luck Was No Lady (1958)
Deadly Miss (1958)

Mike Farrel

The Million Dollar Babe (1961;
   revised from Cutie Cashed His
   Chips, 1955)
The Scarlet Flush (1963; revised
   from Ten Grand Tallulah and
   Temptation, 1957)

Rick Holman

Zelda (1961; 1st U.S. Holman)
Murder in the Harem Club,
   1962; reprinted in the U.S. as
   Murder in the Key Club, 1962)
The Murderer Among Us (1962)
Blonde on the Rocks (1963)
The Jade-Eyed Jinx (1963;
   reprinted in the U.S. as The
   Jade-Eyed Jungle, 1964)
The Ballad of Loving Jenny
   (1963; reprinted in the U.S. as
   The White Bikini, 1963)
The Wind-Up Doll (1963)
The Never-Was Girl (1964)
Murder Is a Package Deal (1964)
Who Killed Doctor Sex? (1964)
Nude—with a View (1965)
The Girl from Outer Space
   (1965)

Blonde on a Broomstick (1966)
Play Now… Kill Later (1966)
No Tears from the Widow (1966)
The Deadly Kitten (1967)
Long Time No Leola (1967)
Die Anytime, After Tuesday!
   (1969)
The Flagellator (1969)
The Streaked-Blond Slave (1969)
A Good Year for Dwarfs? (1970)
The Hang-up Kid (1970)
Where Did Charity Go? (1970)
The Coven (1971)
The Invisible Flamini (1971)
The Pornbroker (1972)
The Master (1973)
Phreak-Out! (1973)
Negative in Blue (1974)
The Star-Crossed Lover (1974)
Ride the Roller Coaster (1975)
Remember Maybelle? (1976)
See It Again, Sam (1979)
The Phantom Lady (1980)
The Swingers (1980)

Andy Kane

The Hong Kong Caper (1962;
   revised from Blonde, Bad and
   Beautiful, 1957)
The Guilt-edged Cage (1963;
   revised from That's Piracy, My
   Pet, 1957; published in
   Australia as Bird in a Guilt-
   Edged Cage)

Ivor MacCallum (no U.S.
   editions)

Sweetheart You Slay Me (1952)
Blackmail Beauty (1953)

Randy Roberts

Murder in the Family Way (1971)
The Seven Sirens (1972)
Murder on High (1973)
Sex Trap (1975)

Mavis Seidlitz

Honey, Here's Your Hearse (1955; no U.S.)
The Killer is Kissable (1955; no U.S.)
A Bullet For My Baby (1955; no U.S.)
Good Morning, Mavis! (1957; no U.S.)
Murder Wears a Mantilla (1957; revised for U.S. as same title, 1962)
The Loving and the Dead (1959; 1st U.S. Seidlitz)
None But the Lethal Heart (1959; reprinted as The Fabulous, 1961)
Tomorrow Is Murder (1960)
Lament for a Lousy Lover (1960) [includes Al Wheeler]
The Bump and Grind Murders (1964)
Seidlitz and the Super Spy (1967; published in the UK as The Super-Spy, 1968)
Murder Is So Nostalgic (1972)
And the Undead Sing (1974)

Unrelated Novels/Novelettes (all non-U.S. unless otherwise noted)

Death Date for Dolores (1951)
Designed to Deceive (1951)
Duchess Double X (1951)
Forever Forbidden (1951)
The Lady Is Murder (1951; reprinted as Lady is a Killer with Murder by Miss Take, 1958)
Three Men, One Love (1951)
Uncertain Heart (1951)
Your Alibi Is Showing (1951)
Alias a Lady (1952)
Blackmail for a Brunette (1952)
Blondes Prefer Bullets (1952)
Hands Off the Lady (1952)
Kiss Life Goodbye (1952)
Larceny Was Lovely (1952)
Meet Miss Mayhem (1952)
Murder Sweet Murder (1952)
She Wore No Shroud (1952)
Sssh! She's a Killer (1952)
Chill on Chili/Butterfly Nett (1953)
Cyanide Sweetheart (1953)
Dead Dolls Don't Cry (1953)
Dimples Died De-Luxe (1953)
Judgement of a Jane (1953)
Kidnapper Wears Curves (1953)
The Lady Wore Nylon (1953)
The Lady's Alive (1953)
Lethal in Love (1953; reprinted as The Minx is Murder, 1956)
Madame You're Morgue-Bound (1953)
Meet a Body (1953)
The Mermaid Murmurs Murder (1953)

Model for Murder (1953; different from 1980 Al Wheeler title)

Moonshine Momma (1953)

Murder is a Broad (1953)

Penthouse Pass-Out (1953; reprinted as Hot Seat for a Honey, 1956)

Rope for a Redhead (1953; revised as Model of No Virtue, 1956)

Slightly Dead (1953)

Stripper You're Stuck (1953)

Widow is Willing (1953)

The Black Widow Weeps (1954)

Felon Angel (1954)

Floozies Out of Focus (1954)

The Frame is Beautiful (1954)

Fraulein is Feline (1954; reprinted with Moonshine Momma & Slaughter in Satin, 1955)

Good-Knife Sweetheart (1954)

Honky Tonk Homicide (1954; reprinted with Chill on Chili & Butterfly Nett, 1955)

Homicide Harem (1954; reprinted with Good-Knife Sweetheart & Poison Ivy, 1955; with Felon Angel, 1965)

The Lady is Chased (1954; reprinted as Trouble is a Dame, 1957)

A Morgue Amour (1954)

Murder—Paris Fashion (1954)

Murder! She Says (1954)

Nemesis Wore Nylons (1954)

Pagan Perilous (1954)

Perfumed Poison (1954)

Poison Ivy (1954)

Shady Lady (1954)

Sinsation Sadie (1954)

Slaughter in Satin (1954)

Strip Without Tease (1954; reprinted as Stripper, You've Sinned, 1959)

Trouble is a Dame (1954)

Wreath for Rebecca (1954)

Venus Unarmed (1954)

Yogi Shrouds Yolande (1954; reprinted with Poison Ivy, 1965)

Curtains for a Chorine (1955)

Curves for a Coroner (1955)

Cutie Cashed His Chips (1955; revised for U.S. as The Million Dollar Babe, 1961, as Farrel series)

Homicide Hoyden (1955)

Kiss and Kill (1955; reprinted with Cyanide Sweetie, 1958)

Kiss Me Deadly (1955; reprinted as Lipstick Larceny, 1958)

Lead Astray (1955)

Lipstick Larceny (1955)

Maid for Murder (1955)

Miss Called Murder (1955)

Shamus, Your Slip Is Showing (1955; reprinted with A Morgue Amour, 1957)

Shroud for My Sugar (1955)

Sob-Sister Cries Murder (1955)

The Two Timing Blonde (1955)

Baby, You're Guilt-Edged (1956; reprinted with Pagan Perilous, 1959)

Bid the Babe Bye-Bye (1956)

Blonde, Beautiful, and – Blam! (1956)

The Bribe Was Beautiful (1956)

Caress Before Killing (1956)

Darling You're Doomed (1956)

Donna Died Laughing (1956)

The Eve of His Dying (1956)

Hi-Jack for Jill (1956)

The Hoodlum Was a Honey (1956)

The Lady Has No Convictions
(1956; reprinted with Slightly
Dead, 1959)
Meet Murder, My Angel (1956)
Murder By Miss-Demeanour
(1956)
My Darling Is Deadpan (1956)
No Halo For Hedy (1956)
Strictly for Felony (1956)
Sweetheart, This is Homicide
(1956)
Bella Donna Was Poison (1957)
Cutie Wins a Corpse (1957;
revised for U.S. as Graves, I
Dig!, 1960, as Boyd series)
Last Note for a Lovely (1957)
Lethal in Love (1957; different
than 1953 title)
Sinner, You Slay Me (1957)
Ten Grand Tallulah and
Temptation (1957; revised as
The Scarlet Flush, 1963, Farrel
series)
That's Piracy, My Pet (1957;
revised as Bird in a Guilt-
Edged Cage, 1963, as Kane
series)
Wreath for a Redhead (1957)
The Charmer Chased (1958)
Cutie Takes the Count (1958)
Deadly Miss (1958)
Hi-Fi Fadeout (1958)
High Fashion in Homicide (1958)
No Body She Knows (1958; with
Slaughter in Satin, 1960)
No Future Fair Lady (1958)
Sinfully Yours (1958)
A Siren Signs Off (1958; with
Moonshine Momma; revised for
U.S. as The Myopic Mermaid,
1961, as Boyd series)
So Lovely She Lies (1958)
Widow Bewitched (1958)

The Blonde Avalanche (1984)

As Tod Conway (western
stories)

As Caroline Farr

The Intruder (1962)
House of Tombs (1966)
Mansion of Evil (1966)
Villa of Shadows (1966)
Web of Horror (1966; reprinted
in the U.S. as A Castle in Spain,
1978)
Granite Folly (1967)
The Secret of the Chateau (1967)
Witch's Hammer (1967)
So Near and Yet... (1968)
House of Destiny (1969)
The Castle on the Lake (1970)
The Secret of Castle Ferrara
(1970)
Terror on Duncan Island (1971)
The Towers of Fear (1972)
A Castle in Canada (1972)
House of Dark Illusions (1973)
House of Secrets (1973)
Dark Mansion (1974)
Mansion Malevolent (1974)
The House on the Cliffs (1974)
Dark Citadel (1975)
Mansion of Peril (1975)
Castle of Terror (1975)
The Scream in the Storm (1975)
Chateau of Wolves (1976)
Mansion of Menace (1976)
Brecon Castle (1976)
The House of Landsdown (1977)
House of Treachery (1977)
Ravensnest (1977)
The House at Lansdowne (1977)
Sinister House (1978)
House of Valhalla (1978)

Heiress Of Fear (1978)
Room Of Secrets (1979)
Island of Evil (1979)
A Castle on the Rhine (1979)
The Castle on the Loch (1979)
The Secret at Ravenswood (1980)

As Raymond Glenning
(stories)

Ghosts Don't Kill (1951)
Seven for Murder (1951)

As Sinclair Mackellar

Prompt for Murder (1981)

As Dennis Sinclair

Temple Dogs Guard My Fate
  (1968)
Third Force (1976)
The Friends of Lucifer (1977)
Blood Brothers (1977)

As Paul Valdez (stories & novelettes)

Hypnotic Death (1949)
The Fatal Focus (1950)
Outcasts of Planet J (1950)
Jetbees from Planet J (1951)
Escape to Paradise (1951)
Fugitives from the Flame World
  (1951)
Kidnapped in Chaos (1951)
Killer by Night (1951)
Suicide Satellite (1951)
The Time Thief (1951)
Flight Into Horror (1951)
Murder Gives Notice (1951)
The Corpse Sat Up (1951)
The Maniac Murders (1951)

Satan's Sabbath (1951)
You Can't Keep Murder Out
  (1951)
Kill Him Gently (1951)
Feline Frame-Up (1951)
Celluloid Suicide? (1951)
The Murder I Don't Remember
  (1952)
Kidnapped in Space (1952)
There's No Future in Murder
  (1952)
The Crook Who Wasn't There
  (1952)
Maniac Murders (1952)
The Mad Meteor (1952)
Operation Satellite (1952)

As A. G. Yates

The Cold Dark Hours (1958)

As Alan Yates

Novel:

Coriolanus, the Chariot (1978)

Stories & Novelettes:

Client for Murder (*Leisure
  Detective #7*, 195?)
The Corpse on the Carpet
  (*Leisure Detective #8*, 195?)
Farewell, My Lady of Shalott!
  (*Action Detective Magazine #6*,
  1952)
Hush-a-Buy Homicide (*Leisure
  Detective #9*, 195?)
Margie (*Action Detective
  Magazine #5*, 1952)
Merger with Death (*Leisure
  Detective #12*, 195?)

Murder in the Family (*Leisure Detective #11*, 195?)
Murder Needs Education (*Action Detective Magazine #2*, 1952)
Murder! She Says (*Detective Monthly #2*, 195?)
My Love Lies Murdered (*Action Detective Magazine #7*, 1952)
Nemesis for a Nude! (*Leisure Detective #10*, 195?)

Genie from Jupiter (*Thrills Incorporated #14*, 1951)
Goddess of Space (*Thrills Incorporated #20*, 1952)

No Pixies on Pluto (*Thrills Incorporated #22*, 1952)
Planet of the Lost (*Thrills Incorporated #17*, 1951)
A Space Ship Is Missing (*Thrills Incorporated #16*, 1951)
Spacemen Spoofed (*Thrills Incorporated #23*, 1952)

Autobiography

Ready when you are, C.B.!: The autobiography of Alan Yates alias Carter Brown (1983)

THE UNORTHODOX CORPSE

In which Lt. Al Wheeler must figure out—
♦ who stuck in the knife in the back of one of the
students at an all-girls school during a magic show
♦ whether The Great Mephisto is really victim
number two or is just faking his own death
♦ what the victims have in common when another
student is found with a knife in her back, too.

DEATH ON THE DOWNBEAT

In which Lt. Al Wheeler must solve—
♦ a murder in a jazz club that happens on the stage
in front of everyone, but without a killer, or a
weapon
♦ the reason behind this crazy killing of the
hophead son of a local newspaper tycoon
♦ the mystery of Midnight O'Hara, sultry singer
and owner of the nightclub, who may not be as
innocent as she seems.

THE BLONDE

In which Lt. Al Wheeler must discover—
♦ who blew up Georgia Brown before she could
reveal the secrets of the 3-year-old filmland suicide
of Lee Manning
♦ the four names Georgia was going to reveal on
the Paula Reid show and what do they have to do
with Manning's death
♦ the secret the four have in common that is now
causing their sudden and untimely deaths